NOT AGAIN THE FALLOUT

A novel by Maria T. Henriksen

Book two of the Not Again series

Copyright © 2022 by Maria T. Henriksen

Print 978-1-7333904-2-2

All scripture is King James Version (KJV).

Printed in the USA.

Cover & Formatting by

Fury Cover Design

Dedications

To my husband Dave for providing me with sustenance as I worked tirelessly on this sequel. Thanks to your thoughtfulness, I was able to stay focused and be more productive.

To my dear friend, Lori Chasko who was with me every step of the way. There is no doubt your prayers got me through many tough challenges.

Last but not least, to my friend, Peggy Patterson who supported me in the midst of her own major trials.

This novel would not exist without those closest to me. I'm blessed to have such devoted people in my life.

*I can do all things through Christ
which strengtheneth me.*
Philippians 4:13

A Note from the Author

Dear Readers,

This is a story involving sexual assault and the aftermath, as well as other mature topics. My desire is that each reader draws closer to God from the healing process that takes place within these pages. I hope that I have treated the weighty subjects with the sensitivity they deserve.

Many blessings,

Maria

Not Again

The Fallout

The Not Again Series Book Two

Turning Trauma into Triumph

Maria T. Henriksen

Prologue

The morning sunlight poured through my bedroom window as I sat in front of the mirror with great anticipation of the day ahead. I stared at my reflection, studying my features. I saw a 17-year-old young woman with long, curly, mahogany brown hair, a tan face kissed by the summer sun, a mix of brown and green eyes with flecks of yellow framed by long thick dark eyelashes, and a smile that had been bursting to make an appearance.

My smile disappeared recalling how the Martin boy down the street robbed me of my innocence one midsummer day before we began our freshman year of high school. Not allowing the memory to take me down a haunting path, pleasant memories of my first boyfriend and first love took its place. Avery and I were together from our freshman year through the summer before our junior year. Little did Avery know how much he helped me get through the toughest time of my life as I refused to tell anyone what happened at the Martin's house four years ago.

After the first day of school our junior year, Avery broke up with me unexpectedly over the phone with no explanation. He changed schools without telling anyone and made it clear that he didn't want any contact with anyone from his old life, which included his lifelong best friend, Joey. Both Joey and I shared in the abrupt abandonment of Avery, and several months later our close friendship blossomed into a high school romance. Joey was the perfect boyfriend, but he wasn't Avery.

As I shifted in my seat in front of the mirror, I was reminded how once again the summer I envisioned was not meant to be. About ten weeks ago, during senior week after graduation, I had another breakup that was unexpected although amicable. My reaction to the mere mention of marriage broke Joey's heart. Once he saw the look on my face as he brought up our future together, he knew he had to end it.

Spending my summer before college without Joey wasn't at all how I imagined my life. My breakup with Joey wasn't nearly as bad as my breakup with my first love. It wasn't that I didn't love Joey, because I did, at least as much as my heart would allow. Joey wasn't blind to the fact that a big part of my heart still belonged to Avery, no matter how much I fought to move on from him. Although Avery left me decimated, I treasured the sweet moments we shared and prayed that someday I could get over him.

Luckily for me, the summer flew by with me working at the clothing store in the mall and spending time with friends, especially Morgan Ricci, my smart, athletic, redheaded friend who had the spirit of an angel. She continued the Bible study she hosted the summer before, complete with my favorites, pepperoni pizza and chocolate milkshakes. Usually those in attendance were my sweet friend, Katie, Katie's spirited best friend, Amy, and Abby who I was starting to get to know better from our Bible studies, but I still didn't know why she struggled with her weight. I'd like to think we all enjoyed the fellowship and digging into the Word as much as we enjoyed the pizza and milkshakes.

Really, the milkshakes had nothing to do with the fact that Mr. Ricci was my favorite parent of all my friends. He remembered me by name, even when he didn't remember our other friends by name. Mr. Ricci went as far as to give me my very own nickname, Radio. *Who am I kidding? I would spend every day at Morgan's house if her dad made milkshakes! Wild horses couldn't keep me away!*

On occasion, I went to church with Morgan's family. They attended a local Presbyterian church, which offered a Sunday school class for our age group called, "College and Career" where Morgan and I were the youngest members of the group having recently graduated from high school.

One Sunday in College and Career the topic was "What Would Jesus Do?" This made us consider what we would do in any given situation, to put ourselves in Jesus' sandals and act accordingly. Over a period of time, these Jesus sanctioned actions began to demonstrate a lifestyle that is acceptable to God and noticeable to others. The Riccis were the epitome of this lifestyle by spreading the gospel through their hospitality, hosting Bible studies.

"And they continued stedfastly in the apostles' doctrine and fellowship, and in breaking of bread, and in prayers" (Acts 2:42).

Prayer

Dear Heavenly Father,

I lift up each reader to you as they take a journey through the next chapter in Christina's life. Allow the pages speak to them and may they feel uplifted by the scripture and inspirational messages. Let each reader see how you are faithful and will never forsake us. May each reader draw closer to you. I pray that if anyone needs to be healed in any way that the restoration will begin to take place while reading *Not Again The Fallout.* I ask all these things in Your Son's precious name.

Amen.

Maria

Chapter 1

I T WAS TIME TO SAY GOOD-BYE to my mom before I went off to college. Hugging her was like embracing a China doll, hard and cold. "Bye, Mom," I said with reservation.

"Good-bye, Christina. Be careful." My mother pulled away from me as if I were toxic.

I nodded and turned my full attention to my younger brother who was entering his sophomore year in high school, and said, "Bye, Jared."

"Later." He turned and glued himself to his video game. *Guess he won't be missing me.*

Half-jokingly I said, "Don't do anything I wouldn't do.'

"What's the fun in that?" Jared responded without looking up.

My dad helped me load the car with everything deemed necessary to live on campus, courtesy of the list provided by the college in preparing for campus life. We headed out with my dad's favorite tunes of the oldies playing on the radio. The first song was, "All I Have To Do Is Dream." I was dreaming of a time when love was lasting, promises were kept, and "forever" wasn't just a dream.

Leaving the humdrum town of Pennsford behind felt exhilarating. It was time for me to spread my wings and discover new and exciting adventures as I stepped into a life of limitless possibilities. I welcomed my freshman year with open arms while leaving the safety and security of home behind. With much eagerness and enthusiasm, I was on my way to Sylvania Ridge University, a medium sized private school tucked away in small-town Pennsylvania.

When we pulled up to Williams Hall, the all-girls dormitory where I was to live until sometime in May, the song, "Twist and Shout" came on the radio. This reminded me of the movie, *Animal House,* and I wondered if the fraternities would be anything like they were in the movie. Would there be wild parties with people in togas and an endless flow of alcohol available in every room and even out on the lawn?

Reality struck when I grabbed a few bags and headed to the third floor. *What, no elevator? I've got bags to carry up three flights of stairs.* I reached the top of the stairwell and turned right. *Ah, here it is!* The door was ajar, so I walked in. A petite blonde with teased bangs wearing cut-off shorts as short as she was turned around.

"Hi, I'm Betty Lou Parkes. You must be Christina De Rosa. Nice to meet ya! Looks like we're going to be roommates," she said in the perkiest voice I've ever heard. I didn't know someone that small could talk so fast.

"Hi, Betty Lou." When my dad walked into the room, I introduced them. "Dad, this is my roommate, Betty Lou."

"Nice to meet you, Betty Lou." My dad was the best, always outgoing and friendly to people.

"Nice meeting you too, Mr. De Rosa." Betty Lou turned away from my dad and looked in my direction. Glancing over to the bed she was standing next to, I noticed that it was piled high with her belongings. "This is my bed." She pointed to a closet. "And that's my closet."

After nodding in consent, my dad and I lugged all my stuff up every step and said our goodbyes.

"Pooch, your roommate seems nice." Dad whispered to me.

"Yeah, she does."

"All right. Take care of yourself and call us once in a while, okay?" He gave me a hopeful look.

"Okay, Dad." I stole my emotions so I wouldn't break down and cry in front of him.

"I love you, Pooch." His eyes were misty.

"I love you too, Dad." We hugged each other as a final good-bye, and my independence officially commenced once my father walked away, his footsteps seeming a bit heavier.

Back in my room, I worked at sorting my things and putting them where I wanted them. As I finished putting clothes in drawers, Betty Lou said, "Hey, my brother and his friends are going out tonight to a party. Wanna come with us? He's a junior, and he said to invite my roommate, so what do ya say?"

"Ah, sure. Sounds like fun." Since school didn't start for a few days, I wasn't worried about a late night out.

"Okay. Cool. I'll let him know. We should see if our neighbors wanna come too." Betty Lou bounced her way out of the room. I could still hear her bubbling voice from across the hall.

A couple minutes later, Betty Lou bounded into our room with two girls. "Christina, this is Nancy." A tall slender girl with ironed-straight jet-black hair that fell on her shoulders waved. I wondered if she was fortunate enough to have mocha-colored skin year-round.

My attention refocused when Betty Lou continued, gesturing toward the girl next to Nancy who was a few inches shorter, "And this is Jill."

"Hey," Jill said with an abrupt wave. Her light wavy long hair and porcelain skin contrasted with her roommate's, but her looks did not fail in comparison as she was equally stunning.

Betty Lou, clearly in her element as ringleader, chimed in again, "So, we're all going out with my brother and his friends tonight. I can't wait. It's going to be so much fun!"

We went our separate ways to get ready for the party. Dressing for both comfort and style, I put on my Sergio Valente jeans, a stylish oversized purple shirt, rose blush and purple eyeshadow and short black boots.

When the four of us gathered to leave, my nostrils and eyes twinged from the pungent smell of Betty Lou's sweet perfume. The second thing I noticed was Betty Lou's hair pulled over to the side in a high ponytail with a pink scrunchie. She wore an oversized pink shirt that hung to the left leaving her left shoulder exposed, a jean mini skirt, chunky hoop earrings and bracelets, and had on lots of makeup, including thick eyeliner and blue mascara. *Farm girl meets Cyndi Lauper.*

We met Betty Lou's brother in the lobby of our dorm a few minutes later. A super good-looking guy took the lead. "Girls, this is Jeff and Caleb. Guys, meet the girls. Oh, yeah and I'm Matt."

My jaw dropped and I may have been drooling when I gazed upon big brother's dark wavy hair, sultry brown eyes, amazing tan, and the most adorable dimples. Matt was hot! He reminded me of an older Joey, wearing Levi's and a nice collared green shirt. His overall clean-cut appearance was totally my type. *Don't even think about it, Christina, not your perky roommate's brother.*

"Hey Caleb. Hey, Jeff," Betty Lou began, batting her eyelashes, "I figured you two would be joining us." *Betty Lou knows Matt's friends.* She gestured toward me, "This is my roommate Christina." Then she motioned to Nancy, followed by Jill. "This is Nancy and Jill. They're roommates across the hall from us."

I followed Jeff's eyes to Nancy's pierced belly button. She was wearing a cropped blue, pink, yellow, and white horizontal striped top paired with white shorts that showed off her gorgeous, bronzed legs. She wore her straight hair down and parted to the side, her makeup natural, understated.

Jeff then settled on Jill who let her natural beauty shine through and adorned a pretty yellow loose blouse that went well with her long flowing golden locks, jeans, and brown fringe moccasins.

"Sweet!" Caleb exclaimed as he checked us over, after which we all exchanged pleasantries.

The guys led the way to my first college party. After walking for about 15 minutes and passing college students along our trek, we arrived at a large, dilapidated house with large sections of chipped paint on the exterior. From the driveway, I could hear music thumping inside the walls. We were greeted by a guy standing outside collecting money. "That'll be two dollars each, ladies."

"What's the charge for?" I asked, completely caught off guard by his statement. There was no mention of paying money to go to a party.

"Beer. All you can drink beer with this cup," he said as he held up the big red plastic cup.

I questioned, "But what if you don't drink?" I held my stance… I didn't like beer, nor did I drink.

The money collector gave me the once over. "Hey, look, I'll let you slide, but Shhh." He held up his finger to his lips. "Don't tell anyone." He winked and let me slide on through. *How did everyone else know to bring money?*

Once inside I was able to identify the music as Bon Jovi's, "You Give Love a Bad Name." While singing along in my head, Matt and his friends high fived a bunch of guys. I sensed that there was something each of these guys had in common, but I couldn't put my finger on it yet.

Without warning, Jeff dropped a drink in my hand and ran off. "Here, hold this. I'll be right back."

There were college students scattered throughout the house. Everyone held a red plastic cup filled with beer from the tap, including me now. A new song cued up. It was "I Can't Wait" by Nu Shooz. The music was loud but appropriate for a party.

Most of the guys were dressed in t-shirts and jeans or shorts.

As for the girls, it was a mixed assortment of mainly jeans, but some shorts, and a few leggings and miniskirts. The girls that wore the miniskirts tended to wear a lot of makeup and jewelry for their multiple piercings.

While I was taking in my surroundings, Caleb started talking to me. He was average height, easy on the eyes, athletic build, and he wore his shirt popped up at the collar paired with jeans. Based on appearance alone, I could see why Caleb and Matt were friends. "Christina, right?"

"Ah, yeah. Caleb, right?" I remembered his name because Betty Lou kept repeating it on the way over. Perhaps it was her way to let us know she knew other students at Sylvania Ridge besides her brother and us.

"So, why don't you drink?" He gestured to the full cup I was holding, knowing it wasn't mine.

"I, ah, I don't like the taste of beer," I replied, tucking hair behind my ears.

My dad let me try a sip of beer when I was 11, and it tasted disgusting, but that's not the only reason why I don't drink. I didn't feel like shouting the main reason, which was not wanting to take the chance of becoming an alcoholic. I learned in health class how anyone can become a victim of the disease.

Our lengthy conversation was strained over the music that was playing "Danger Zone" from the *Top Gun* soundtrack, when a soccer ball came flying in my direction. Since I didn't react quickly enough, the ball hit me and knocked the drink out of my hand, spraying the guy who had his back to me.

He turned around and began screaming at me. "What do you think you're doing spilling your drink all over me?" He called me all kinds of names. I resisted the urge to burst into tears. Caleb jumped in and grabbed the guy's shirt and told him to back off. Matt came running over to break up Caleb and the screamer. I wanted to crawl under a rock, even though it wasn't my fault.

After Matt broke up a potential fight, he turned to me and asked, "You okay?" I nodded.

Matt hollered to anyone in hearing distance, "What idiot kicked the soccer ball?"

A random person yelled, "It was Smitty."

"Be right back." Matt said and took off to another room.

"You sure you're okay? That guy really laid into you," Caleb said with caring eyes.

"Yeah, I'm fine," I replied above normal speaking volume, as well as nodded so there wasn't any misunderstanding. *That's the last time I'm holding someone's drink.*

Matt came back with a guy on his heels. "Apologize to the young lady," he said to the guy.

With a sheepish look on his face, the culprit said to me, "Hey, uh, I'm sorry. I hope you're okay." He did manage to look somewhat repentant, yet my inner sarcasm got the better of me. *Someone went ballistic on me, but yeah, never been better.*

"Yeah, I'm fine. Thanks." I lied again.

"I hope you'll forgive me." He took my hand. *Why are they making such a big deal out of this?*

"Totally." I withdrew my hand from his and turned away from his rancid breath.

Matt started yelling toward the screamer who stood nearby. "Yo, you!" Screamer pointed to himself in a who, me? manner. "Yeah, you!! Matt reiterated. "Come here!"

Screamer strode over. Matt was in his face. "Apologize to the young lady. You should know that wasn't her fault. You don't go screaming at people for an accident." *What's with the young lady bit?* It sounded ridiculous.

"Hey, I'm sorry. No hard feelings?" Screamer shifted from one foot to the other.

"Nah, I'm cool." *Apparently, I'm cool. Must be why I'm shaking.* I tried to shrug it off.

Screamer left our circle, and Matt explained, "Look, I'm really sorry. We have these parties here, and we want people to feel welcomed and have a good time. I can't have these bozos messing things up for everyone."

Matt joined Caleb and me, and the three of us chatted for a while. They told me how they had been roommates since their freshman year and have been best friends ever since. Countless partiers popped in and out of our circle to greet the two friends. I met too many people to be able to remember each of their names, and half of the time I couldn't even hear them. I simply nodded and smiled to the point that my cheeks started to hurt.

One girl with teased curly shoulder-length brown hair wearing bright, heavy make-up and gold jewelry wrapped her arms around Matt and whispered in his ear.

It was then I realized the girls I came with were nowhere in sight. *That's odd. Usually, girls stick together.*

I heard a scream, not a terrified or angry scream, but a playful scream, followed by laughter and shouting, more like chanting. Matt abruptly fled our little group leaving glamor girl resembling a character from the television series, *Dallas,* looking dejected.

The song changed to "Walk This Way" by Run-D.M.C. when Caleb grabbed my hand and pushed through the crowd toward the merriment. Upon our arrival, we saw Betty Lou standing on the kitchen table dancing. The guys were chanting, "Dance, dance, dance…" I cringed at the sight of her wild behavior. She was dancing like a stripper in a seedy club you see on TV.

"That's Matt's sister!" Caleb said.

Matt cuffed his hands around his mouth. "Yo, Betty Lou, get down from there!" The dancing and chanting continued. "Caleb, help me get her down."

"Catch me!" yelled the wanna be dancer. At the insistence of big bro, Betty Lou stopped dancing and fell into Caleb's arms. Caleb dropped her like a hot potato. Perhaps he didn't want to experience the wrath of big brother.

After Betty Lou's fits of laughter, she pounded on her brother's chest. "You are such a party pooper!"

Matt responded, "It's time to go home, Betty Lou."

"But I just got here! I can't go home! Classes start in a couple days!" She started to tear up, and a pout puckered her full lips.

"I don't mean home, home. I mean back to your dorm room," Matt explained.

"Oh!" She giggled. After partying for hours, having to hold up Betty Lou all the way home was exhausting. The entire night was enough drama to last a lifetime.

Chapter 2

T he four of us girls went to breakfast the next morning. While we were sitting at a square table eating, Betty Lou said with a huge smile on her face, "So, there's a party tonight at a frat house. Who's coming?"

"I'm in." said Jill without hesitation.

Nancy followed with a definitive, "Me too."

"What about you, Christina? You coming?" asked my roommate.

"Uh, maybe. I'm not sure." *I don't want a repeat of last night.*

Betty Lou gave me a puzzled look. "What are you unsure of?"

"She's probably afraid of being yelled at again. Right, Christina?" Jill said.

Betty Lou replied, "Oh right! Well, I doubt that guy will be there tonight. So, what do ya say?"

I shrugged my shoulders. "I guess so." I poked at my eggs, not positive I wanted to go.

The bubbly blonde clapped her hands. "Great! This is going to be so much fun!"

"Who's going to be there?" asked Nancy.

"A bunch of fraternity brothers." Betty Lou giggled at the thought.

"Will your brother and his friends be there?" asked Jill with a hopeful tone.

"I don't know. I found out about the party from one of the guys I met last night. Why?" She absentmindedly pushed a strand of stray hair out of her eyes.

With a shrug of her shoulders, Jill answered, "No reason." She took another bite of her bagel smeared with cream cheese.

"Okay, are you crushing on my brother and his friends?" Betty Lou demanded with her hand on her hip.

"No, I was wondering if we will know anyone there," she pulled through with a plausible response.

"Oh, okay. My friends are always crushing on my brother, but he never once gives them a second thought." That made me feel despondent, but I didn't examine why.

The girls and I were ready to party. At first, I wasn't excited about going to another party after being screamed at the night before, and then I thought about it. *What were the chances of someone yelling at me again?*

I decided to wear a fun striped blue and white oversized shirt with a pair of my pleated Jordache edgy rock-style acid washed jeans and pulled the outfit all together with a wide white belt.

Betty Lou led the way. She seemed to know the lay of the land. *She must have visited her brother in college when she was still in high school.* The rest of us had no clue where we were going.

After walking for about ten minutes, we approached an old house with four big white pillars and Greek initials on a banner hanging below the dormers.

Before I knew it, I was downstairs in a musty, sticky basement. It was dark with strings of multi-colored lights that enabled us to see just past our hands.

The room filled up fast. Before long, we were squashed like sardines. Loud music pumped through the sound system. "Get Down On it" by Kool and The Gang started to play. I couldn't help but move to the beat. Every so often when someone walked by their drinks would spill. Thus, the sticky floor. The wobbling started back up again.

A gangly looking guy who towered over us appeared before my new friend group. "Hello! You girls having a good time?" he asked us.

Betty Lou was quick to answer. "Yeah, great party!"

"Good. Good. I'm Neil. I'll be your host for the night," he said with a sappy grin.

"I'm Betty Lou and this is my roommate, Christina. That's Jill." She pointed to her. "And that's Nancy," my roommate said as she gestured toward the bronzed beauty.

Neil's head moved up and down and his eyes formed deep crow's feet from the upward motion of his lips. "Awesome!"

"Jack and Diane" started to play on the loud sound system. I loved this song. It was so small town. Perfect for the town that housed Sylvania Ridge University.

"Are you freshmen?" Neil asked us as a whole.

Betty Lou answered for all of us, "Yes, we're all freshmen. What about you?"

"I'm a sophomore." We all nodded and smiled like being a sophomore was some great feat.

We were talking to Neil when his friend with a curly shoulder length mullet haircut came by. "Yo, Neil! What's up? Who are your friends?"

Neil gave the introductions. Warren was on the shorter side with bulging muscles and seemed to be taken by Betty Lou. They engaged in their own conversation while Jill, Nancy, Neil, and I continued our strained chat over the loud music.

John Cougar Mellencamp belted out "R.O.C.K. In the U.S.A.," and we all spelled out the letters with him. We continued to make the most of the party by dancing and swaying to the music. A million songs came and went like "If You Leave" by Orchestral Manoeuvres in the Dark which took me back to the movie theater watching Molly Ringwald in *Pretty in Pink*. When "Stuck With You" by Huey Lewis and The News dispersed from the speakers, people started to clear out. Although the music stopped, I swayed back and forth from an overwhelming feeling of being dead on my feet. I looked around and noticed that we were among the few still stuck to the icky floor.

Jill told Betty Lou that she wanted to go home. Betty Lou looked at her watch and exclaimed, "Oh my gosh! We can't go back to the dorms now. By the time we get there, it will be closed."

"What do you mean closed?" Jill asked, her brow furrowed.

"The dorms close every day from three to six in the morning. We won't be able to get in because they lock all the doors." Instead of being horrified, Betty Lou giggled about our predicament.

Whhhaaattt? We're stuck here for the next three hours! No wonder no one else is here. How did I let this happen? I had no idea it was so late. That explains why I'm so tired.

I felt like I could keel over any second as the fatigue hit me hard and fast.

"What are we supposed to do? Hang out here?" Jill questioned as she looked around the sparsely furnished room.

Betty Lou answered, "We have no choice but to stay here." Another giggle escaped from her mouth as if she didn't have a care in the world.

"Everyone needs to clear out of here right now!" yelled a fraternity brother.

Great! Now, we're getting kicked out. I searched the room for a familiar face. *What happened to Neil and Warren? They were just here a minute ago.*

A minute later Neil approached us. "Hey, we have to clear outta here. They're cleaning up. Follow me."

They clean? You sure could have fooled me!

We followed Neil up the stairs. It was dark. *Didn't anyone put lights on?* I didn't want to cause any trouble, so I remained quiet. All I wanted to do was sleep.

There was a group of us, the four of us girls and a handful of guys. I sat on a chair on the perimeter of the room, while the rest of them huddled in a circle. From what I gathered they were playing Poker. I dozed off and awoke when I heard a lot of commotion. It turns out they were playing Strip Poker. I scanned the room. No indecency yet. Part of me wanted to stop the strip show, but I didn't. It caused too much effort for my fatigued body to even talk, much less break up the party. *Dear God, don't let this get too far. Please God...*

The bobbing of my head woke me from a slumber. I could see that the party was breaking up. People were dispersing. I didn't know what time it was. Everything seemed to happen in slow motion and rapidly at the same time. Sleep was calling my name.

It was Nancy. "Christina, hey. Wake up." I thought I was awake. "Betty Lou left us. She went with Warren." *Okay.* "I don't know where she is. We need to find her." She sounded anxious, and I could hear the pleading in her voice.

"What time is it?" I asked.

Jill checked her watch. "It's five fifteen."

I mentally calculated when we could leave considering travel time to get back to our dorm. *We have nowhere to go for another half hour.*

"Let's split up and look for Betty Lou," Nancy suggested. *Then what?* I thought.

"No, we need to stick together," I countered.

"Right, no one walks off on their own," Jill confirmed.

The three of us tiptoed throughout the house, careful not to make any loud noises. It was dark and quiet. We opened bedroom doors to find that the beds were empty. *Where is everyone?*

As the three of us approached a room, Jill put a finger over her mouth. She leaned in toward the closed door. Nancy and I followed her lead with our ears pressed against the door.

"Yeah, Warren is one lucky dude," someone behind the closed door said.

"So that freshman has no idea that two other guys are in the room with her?" another snickered also able to claim anonymity.

"Nope and she never will. Unless…" There was a meaningful pause.

"Yeah?" We heard another respond.

"Unless they decide to, you know." Laughter erupted from behind the door.

Nancy put her hand over her mouth as I watched her eyes bulge. Jill put her finger back on her mouth. My stomach was in knots hearing their perverse discussion. I wanted to scream, but I knew that wouldn't be prudent. Taking deep breaths, I was able to control my disgust, my anger.

"Where are they? Warren's room?" One of the guys behind the closed door asked.

"Yup. That's always where the action is."

I motioned to the girls to step away from the door. The three of us huddled together. "Let's see if we can find Warren's room," I whispered. Both Jill and Nancy nodded.

Something caught my eye. I noticed a red handkerchief tied around a door handle. I looked above and saw a sign on the door that said, "Warren's Room." This time I put my finger on my mouth. I didn't want to barge in. Instead, I knocked on the door. "Betty Lou, are you in there? We must leave now. It's urgent, and we're not leaving without you." Jill gave me the thumbs up. No response, so I knocked again. "Betty Lou, we have an emer—"

The door swung open. There was a crazed look on Betty Lou's face. "What's going on? What's the emergency?"

I motioned for Betty Lou to follow me. "Come on. We'll tell you on the way. We have to leave now!" I stated, clenching my fist.

"Just tell me now." She stalled in the open door.

"Shhh! Just wait," I whispered. I grabbed her hand and pulled her with me.

Jill, Nancy, and I bolted out of the frat house, yanking Betty Lou behind. The brisk weather was a rude awakening to my dragging system.

As soon as we got outside, Betty Lou said, "Okay, we're outside. Would you mind telling me what's going on?"

"Not yet. We need to get away from here before…" I couldn't finish the sentence.

"Before what?" Betty Lou demanded, her eyes narrowed.

"Before I lose it!" I felt the veins throbbing in my neck and wanted to shake some sense into that little flaxen head of hers.

"What are you talking about?" Betty Lou stomped her feet.

"We will tell you when we get away from here. Now come on!" I pulled on her hand again.

When we made it to a clearing, Jill stopped, gasping for breath. "I, I have asthma. I have to stop. Can't breathe." We gathered around Jill as she pulled out her inhaler.

"Okay, Jill. Let's all sit down," Nancy suggested. After a few seconds passed, Nancy continued, "Are you okay now?"

Jill nodded with a reassuring look, although still gasping for air. She put her finger up to give her a minute.

"Maybe we should give her some space," I suggested. Betty Lou, Nancy, and I inched away from Jill to give her breathing room.

She squeezed the inhaler a few times. "Okay. I can breathe now. Good thing I brought my inhaler," she said as the pearlescent color returned to her pale skin.

That was the first time I ever witnessed someone struggling to breathe and hoped it was my last.

"Yeah, what would happen if you didn't have your inhaler?" Betty Lou asked.

Jill shook her head, and her eyes were glassed over. "I don't want to find out."

"Well, I'm glad you're better now," I said, hoping that was the end of our excitement for the night.

"Now that that's over. What is going on? Why did we have to leave in such a hurry?" Betty Lou questioned. Jill, Nancy, and I looked at each other. "Well?" She gave us each a stony stare.

"We overheard a couple guys talking and…" Nancy stopped.

"And what?" Betty Lou demanded, her eyes growing wider.

"They said that two other guys were in the bedroom with you and Warren," Nancy continued.

"What!? There weren't any other guys in the room with us," she said, her eyebrows knitted together.

"They were hiding," Jill stated as if it were an effort to talk.

"What do you mean hiding?" Betty Lou scrunched up her face.

"Betty Lou, they were watching you and Warren and…" I couldn't finish my sentence. That one horrid afternoon at the Martin's house returned to the forefront of my memory, rendering me speechless.

Betty Lou barked, "And what? As if this isn't bad enough."

This isn't about me. You need to tell her. "It sounded like…" I attempted to finish my previous statement but couldn't get the words out.

"Like what? Come on, spit it out!" Betty Lou was beyond impatient.

Nancy put her hand on my leg and said to Betty Lou, "It sounded like they were planning on joining you two."

Betty Lou exploded, "WHAT!?" She sprang to her feet. The rest of us got up too. "Those low life dirty rotten pigs!" *I couldn't have said it better myself.* "The nerve of them!" She stomped off in the direction of the frat house.

"Wait! Where are you going?" Jill asked Betty Lou.

"To give them a piece of my mind!" Betty Lou spat, her face burned a fire-engine red, her eyes were bulging out of their sockets.

"Oh, no you don't," I said with authority.

"Why not?" She rounded on me, and I stepped back, not wanting to get caught in her line of fire.

"Because it's not safe for you to confront them," I answered.

"Then come with me," Betty Lou suggested.

"No, there are only four of us girls and at least five frat brothers. We don't stand a chance against them." I reasoned.

"She's right," Nancy agreed, nodding her head.

"Yeah, let's go back to our dorm and get some sleep. I'm exhausted," Jill suggested as she struggled to keep her head up.

Knowing that Jill recently experienced a scary moment not being able to breathe, we all decided to head back to the dorm at a normal walking pace. No more running for us. Sleep would have to wait a few more minutes.

Chapter 3

I was never so thankful to be able to sleep. I slept until eleven-thirty and felt quite sluggish. The four of us went to brunch shortly after. Betty Lou was as chipper as ever.

Jill struggled to keep her head up. "Betty Lou, how is it that you're so lively? I can hardly walk."

Betty Lou tossed her head back. "Oh, well, I'm used to getting up real early to milk the cows after going out late, so this is nothing."

Ah. That explains it. Perky Farm girl. I hope I start feeling better. I don't want to feel like this my first day of class.

I ate faster than usual because I was so hungry. I started to feel better once I got some food in my stomach.

"I don't know about you guys, but I'm starving!" Betty Lou said. *Where does she put all that food in her tiny frame?*

Nancy replied, "Me too. My stomach won't stop growling."

Jill growled, unable to form words.

"I have such a headache," I moaned.

"Me too," Nancy responded.

"I feel like death," Jill informed us before she plopped her head on the table.

"So, who wants to go out tonight? I found out about another party," Betty Lou said as she looked at us with great anticipation.

"You have got to be kidding me." Nancy said.

Jill interjected, turning her head on the table, "Uh-uh. No way."

Betty Lou turned to me and asked, "How about you, Christina? Wanna go out tonight?"

"Uh, I think I'll pass." *Is she kidding? I won't be able to function if I go out tonight. I'm hoping I can get through the day.*

After brunch, we walked back to our dorm rooms. Jill waved us off stating she was going to hit the sack. I knew better than to take a nap like Jill did. That would have only made me groggy and would have messed up my sleep schedule.

Betty Lou, Nancy, and I decided instead to go on a scavenger hunt that our dorm was hosting. The intention of the hunt was to explore the town. No driving was permitted. With the list in hand, the three of us walked to town. First item on the list was hair products. Nancy spotted a hair salon a block away like it was a beacon. "There's a hair salon," she shouted with excitement.

Ding!

A chime went off when we opened the door to the salon. The foul stench of the chemicals used to process permanents wreaked havoc with my nostrils and burned my eyes.

"Hi, we're here for a scavenger hunt," Nancy announced.

"Oh, yes, here you go." The woman behind the white counter gave us each a bag of samples of shampoo and conditioner. We each thanked her and went to the next item on the list.

As we walked from one store to the next, we saw other girls from our hall. Cold air hit my face when I opened the door to the beverage store. They gave us each a magnet shaped like a soda can that said Sylvania Ridge Beverages. What were girls living in a dorm room supposed to do with a magnet? Then I remembered that some rooms had a magnetic message board hanging on the outside of their door. Betty Lou and I didn't have anything on ours.

Our last stop was McDonald's. A town is not complete without a Mickey D's. A group of girls raced by us. Betty Lou yelled, "Hurry up! Let's get what we need and run back!"

The scent of French fries teased my taste buds even before we opened the door to the famous fast-food establishment.

"Scavenger hunt?" A geeky looking guy in a brown polyester uniform asked as soon as we entered.

"Yes!" I yelled back, finding a boost of energy that must have come from Betty Lou's pep talk.

"Here you go!" He handed us a white bag displaying the golden arches.

Betty Lou whisked the bag out of the hands of the man in brown, thanked him, and waved us out of the golden arch building.

Nancy asked, "What's in the bag?"

Without skipping a beat, Betty Lou opened the bag, and a waft of chicken nuggets enveloped our nostrils. All I could think about was eating the bite size chicken imposters. "I could go for one of those McNuggets® now," Nancy said while salivating.

Betty Lou sped up. "No time for eating. Chop, chop," she commanded.

Chop, chop? She sounds like a girl scout leader.

"Give me the bag!" shouted Nancy with great intensity.

"You saw how that other group was ahead of us. We can't stop now," insisted Betty Lou.

"Betty Lou, you better give me that bag or else!" Nancy demanded, running after her.

"Or else what?" Betty Lou taunted.

"Or I will tackle you!" Nancy threatened.

"You wouldn't dare!" Betty Lou replied.

"You're going down!" Nancy warned as she sprinted after Betty Lou and lunged toward the bossy blonde.

Betty Lou threw the bag at her and kept running. "There! Satisfied?"

After taking a bite of one of the golden nuggets, Nancy said, "Now this is the best part of the scavenger hunt. Want some, Christina?"

I was hungry and the smell of the fake fried chicken was too tempting to resist. "Yeah, thanks." She held the bag open, and I grabbed a crispy critter and popped it in my mouth. Phony food never tasted so good.

"Let's go, girls. Stop lollygagging!" Betty Lou urged us on.

I saluted Bette Lou, "Okay, Sarge!"

We ran back to our dormitory and headed straight to the lobby. The other group of girls beat us for first place. Sandra, the graduate assistant in charge of our dormitory, was checking over the items the group before us collected against the master list. "You missed this one," Sandra said.

"Oh man! So close!" One of the girls exclaimed.

"You still have a chance of winning. It depends on if any other groups get all the items on the list."

Betty Lou sprinted toward Sandra and handed her our bag. "Here you go! Everything's there!" she said with confidence.

After checking off each item one by one with the help of little Miss Sarge, the grad student asked, "What was in the McDonald's bag?"

"Chicken nuggets," Betty Lou fired back.

"Where are they?" Sandra asked.

"Uh, we ate them," I replied, swallowing my guilt.

Sandra said with a sad face, "I hate to break it to you, but you disqualified yourselves."

"What?!" Betty Lou shrilled, clenching her fists. I think they heard her back at McDonald's.

"Yeah, you were supposed to bring back the contents in the bag." Sandra shrugged, like she could have cared less.

"It doesn't say that on the paper," Betty Lou was quick to answer.

"This is a scavenger hunt. What did you expect?" Sandra barked back.

"Humph!" Betty Lou stomped her foot and stormed off. "You two ruined it! This is all your fault! If you didn't eat the nuggets, we would have won!"

Nancy and I looked at each other and smirked.

When we got back to the hallway of our dorm rooms, Nancy waved me toward her room. Jill was standing in the doorway of their room and asked, "What's wrong with Betty Lou?"

I followed Nancy in her room and answered Jill, "Betty Lou is ticked off that we lost the scavenger hunt because we ate the chicken nuggets."

"What?" Jill asked, perplexed.

"Yeah. She morphed into this crazed person because she wanted to win. Then she got upset when we lost because we ate the McNuggets®, which by the way, were delicious and worth every bite," I added with a snarky grin.

"That's it? You ate the nuggets, so you lost, and now Betty Lou is mad?" Jill asked, leaving her jaw hanging to the floor.

"Pretty much," I replied, smacking my lips together.

In disbelief, Jill said, "Man, I'm glad I didn't go. Too much drama." She walked over to her bed and sat down.

"Yeah, you guys mind if I stay here a while?" I asked.

Nancy answered, "No, it's cool. Stay as long as you like. I wouldn't want to be in the same room with her right now either." We all giggled at that thought.

We were talking when we heard a knock on the door. Nancy stood up to answer it. I could hear garbled voices, and a brunette of average height who had a short wedge haircut and freckles walked in the room.

Nancy gestured toward the new girl, "Hey, this is Linda. She lives next door."

Another girl whose brown hair was streaked with blonde highlights and teased a mile high stood behind Linda. Nancy introduced Aqua Net girl, "This is Cassie. Linda and Cassie are roommates."

"Cassie," Nancy motioned to Jill, "this is my roommate, Jill, and Christina lives across the hall."

Roommates get top billing around here with introductions.

Jill asked our neighbors, "So where are you two from?"

Cassie began, "I'm from New Jersey, a beach town called Seaside Heights, not too far from New York City."

"I'm from a small town in Pennsylvania just north of here," Linda said.

After about an hour of getting to know each other, there was another knock on the door. This time Jill yelled, "Come in!"

Betty Lou framed the doorway. "Hey, I was wondering when you guys were going to dinner."

Nancy replied, "I'm always ready to eat."

While our neighbors left to get their meal cards, Betty Lou turned to Nancy and me, "Look, I'm sorry for the way I acted earlier. I can be a little competitive and not having enough sleep last night pushed me over the edge. Can you forgive me?" She had enough sense to appear regretful.

I made a mental note to myself that a competitive spirit plus sleep deprivation equals a crazed Betty Lou. "Sure. Why not?"

Luke 6:37 crept in my mind, "Judge not, and ye shall not be judged: condemn not, and ye shall not be condemned: forgive, and ye shall be forgiven:"

Nancy followed my response by saying, "Forgiven. Now, let's get something to eat."

Chapter 4

Our classes started the next day. Betty Lou and I went to lunch together. She spotted her brother who was with one of his friends, Caleb.

Betty Lou greeted them with a broad smile, "Hi, Matt. Hi, Caleb." She waved to each of them.

The guys sat down at our table, and we exchanged greetings. "How are your classes so far?" Matt asked.

Betty Lou was quick to respond, "Good. I only had one class so far."

Matt turned his attention to me, "How about you, Christina?"

"So far so good. I already had two classes." Once I heard my reply, it didn't seem like much.

After discussing our first impressions of our teachers and classes, we talked about our schedules.

Betty Lou asked, "I have a night class tonight, is that normal?"

"Oh yeah, I have one tomorrow night," I followed.

Caleb said, "Yeah, your classes can be all mixed up, especially as freshmen. You get to pick your classes for the next semester."

"Good to know," I said, liking the fact that I will have some control over my schedule.

I watched the lunch line double in size from when we arrived, relieved that we didn't have to wait as long to get our meal.

Betty Lou stood up. "Speaking of classes, I have to head back to the dorm to get my stuff for my next class." She turned her head in my direction, "You coming with me, Christina?"

"I'm coming." I stood up to leave and walked out with my roommate as we all said our good-byes to each other.

Betty Lou wasted no time once she reached our room as she swapped out her books and walked out.

Several minutes later, I heard, "Man on the floor!" *It's so weird how we have to announce when a guy is on the floor.* It did make sense, because any girl could be walking to and from the bathroom to take a shower and not be properly attired for male company.

There was a knock on my door. Expecting to see one of my neighbors, I was surprised to see Matthew's figure in front of me.

"You just missed her," I said.

"I have some time before my next class, so I thought we could hang out." He smiled slyly.

It wasn't like I was planning on doing any homework from the two morning classes I had, so I motioned for Matt to come in. "Oh, all right. Come in."

I plopped on my bed while Matt grabbed Betty Lou's chair, turned it around and sat down so his legs straddled the back of the chair. He hunched forward as he hugged the chair and appeared eager to talk.

This is weird. Why is Matt here? Doesn't he have a million places he could be besides here with me?

Matthew began without hesitation, "I thought we could get to know each other better. You know, since you're my sister's roommate and all."

Not buying Matt's spiel but going along with his statement, I replied, "What would you like to know?"

"Do you have any brothers and sisters?" He asked.

I criss-crossed my legs, "I have a younger brother who is a sophomore in high school." I realized then that I didn't miss him much.

"Do you two get along?" He idly tapped his fingers on the back of the chair.

"Uh, not really. We certainly don't hang out. We would never be seen together socially unless it was a family affair." I wondered where these questions were going.

"What's his name?" Matt continued to tap on the chair.

"Jared. He's a soccer player like you." *Should I have said that?*

With a surprised look on his face, he asked, "How did you know I play soccer?"

"I'm guessing that we were at the soccer house our first night here when I met you, based on the flying soccer ball that came barreling at me."

He bowed his head, then gave me a look of being ashamed. "Oh, yeah. Sorry about that. It won't happen again."

"I survived," I shrugged.

"We're probably having another party this weekend if you wanna come." Hopeful light shone in his eyes.

The thought of going to another one of those parties was not appealing in the least bit.

"We'll see," I said dryly as I didn't want to commit, nor did I want to completely decline. I wanted to keep my options open, but I wasn't feeling it at the moment.

He shot me an encouraging smile. "I promise no more soccer balls will hit you."

"You say that, but you can't really guarantee that," I replied coyly.

Matt flashed me a dimpled-grin, "Sure, I can. I will make certain of it."

Brushing a strand of hair out of my eyes, I said, "You don't need a boring freshman like me at your party."

"Who says you're boring?" He asked with a glint in his eyes.

"Well, you won't find me dancing on tables," I laughed.

"Yeah that." Matt shook his head. "Sometimes I don't know what to do with Betty Lou. That's all the more reason for you to go, especially if Betty Lou goes. She gets out of hand sometimes."

Recalling how Betty Lou was acting like a sergeant on the war path during the scavenger hunt had me laughing, yet I was curious to hear more stories. "Do tell," I encouraged as I batted my eyes.

"I don't know if I should tell you. Betty Lou would be mortified."

"Of course, you should tell me." I smiled in a mischievous way. "It's for her sake as well as mine. I need to know what to expect to protect us both." That sounded plausible, but I wasn't planning on being Betty Lou's keeper.

"Well, since you put it like that. Betty Lou gets super bossy when she's tired." He winked at me like we were partners in crime.

I stared at him, sarcasm lacing my voice. "You don't say."

"So, you've seen her bossy side?" His eyebrows arched as he smirked.

I shot him a look. "You could say that," I said with a playful hint.

"Uh oh. What did she do this time?" he asked as to suggest she was a repeat offender.

"She went a little crazy when our dorm had a scavenger hunt in town," I revealed.

He sat up straighter in the chair. "Crazy how?" His left eyebrow went askew, evidently I peaked his attention.

"She was screaming at us to hurry up, and went ballistic when we lost, because we ate the chicken nuggets." I tried not to laugh, because now it just seemed so silly of her.

"You lost?! Well, that will do it right there. Betty Lou hates losing," he stated, shaking his head.

"Get out! I would have never guessed," I said bleeding sarcasm.

"But if you like winning, she's a good one to have on your side."

I looked him straight in the eyes. "I'm not super competitive."

"Something tells me you do all right for yourself," he fished.

I shrugged. "I can't complain."

We talked for a while, and the conversation became easier between us. He looked at the time and said, "I better head out. I have class in 15 minutes across campus."

"I have class too, but it's on this side of campus."

"Lucky. We can walk part way together." He smiled, and I melted.

"Ooh. I have my own personal escort," I joked.

Smirking, he said, "Don't get too excited. I'm not walking you door-to-door."

My face flushed with embarrassment, even though I knew he wasn't walking me to my classroom. That would be absurd.

"What do we have here, are we blushing?" Matt teased.

We? "I don't see anyone blushing," I replied as if innocent.

"Would you like me to walk you to your class?" He asked as if he were offering.

"No, no. Of course not." *Oh, my goodness, I'm getting flustered.*

"I'll come by tomorrow to walk you to class," he promised.

"My class is at nine thirty. I'll wait with baited breath." I said, trying to sound clever.

"I can meet you at the lobby. I have a class then too. Let's say nine-fifteen."

Is he serious? I was only kidding, but I don't want to hurt his feelings. "Okay. Let me guess. Your class is on the other side of campus?" I presumed.

"Nope. I figure I can steal a few extra minutes of seeing you." Matt winked, and I almost blushed again.

Wha-? He didn't just say that. "It will be your lucky day then," I replied, not even sure if what I said made any sense.

"Definitely," he said with another wink.

Is he kidding? I thought Matt never dated Betty Lou's friends.

As we approached my building, he stopped and said, "This is you. Good luck with the rest of your classes. See ya tomorrow."

"Thanks. You too." I gave him a small wave.

Matt picked up his pace and headed toward his next class while I proceeded to go to mine.

"Man on the floor!" The yelling continued until I heard a knock on my door.

When I opened it, I saw Matt standing in front of me. I didn't want to assume he was here for me or for Betty Lou, so I said, "Hey, what are you doing in this neck of the woods at this time of night?"

He leaned against the door frame like he was Joe Cool. "I came by to see you. I hope it's okay."

"Uh, yeah. Come in. What's going on?" *Really, Matt, why are you here in my dorm room twice in one day?*

"I came by to see my favorite freshman." He winked at me AGAIN.

"Betty Lou isn't here. She has a night class," I stated, ignoring the obvious.

"I mean you, but speaking of Betty Lou, have you told her I stopped by earlier today?" I detected a hint of worry in his voice.

"No. I haven't even seen her since lunch. Why?"

Matt grabbed Betty Lou's chair and sat down. "Here's the deal. I like you, and I was hoping we could go out." He sat back with his chest puffed out and clasped his arms behind his body.

That was blunt.

He gave me an expectant look, "So what do you say? Are you interested in going out with me?"

I considered his offer for a minute, twirling a strand of hair around my finger. "Betty Lou said you don't date her friends."

He flashed me a charming smile. "Yeah, well, I want to date you, if you're game."

What? That was unexpected.

I felt like I was missing something, like there was more to this story.

Matt massaged his eyebrows. "I want to keep it between us though. I don't want Betty Lou to know. At least not right away."

"How come?" I wasn't against the idea of dating this hottie, but why the secrecy?

"She gets weird about things, and I don't want her to get in the middle of our relationship."

Heh? "Sorry. I'm not following you. Why would she be in the middle of our relationship if we did start going out?" I asked, my eyes narrowed.

"Remember, she likes to control things." Matt had the decency to look sheepish.

I responded with a lilt, "How could I forget?"

Chapter 5

*M*att and I hung out for the next few days. He was fun to be around, and I didn't see much harm in it since we weren't romantically involved. I didn't feel the need to tell my roommate, especially since my relationship with her brother was strictly platonic.

One evening we were sitting around talking about his life growing up on a dairy farm, and how they drank milk straight from the cows without it being pasteurized or homogenized.

"And you don't get sick from your milk not being processed?" I asked.

"No, we're used to it, so it doesn't bother us," he answered with a slightly closed-lipped smile.

There was a lull in the conversation when Matt stood up from sitting on Betty Lou's chair and headed toward my bed. He sat down and I could sense his sudden intensity. His head gazed downward as if in contemplative thought. Three seconds later our eyes met. "It's been great getting to know you these past few days," Matt began. I felt his hand settle on my thigh. "I was hoping we could take things to the next level," he continued.

As much as I was attracted to Matt, I wasn't sure about getting involved with him. I felt like I needed more time to at least get to know him better. I wasn't quite there yet.

Matt leaned in, and I jerked back in response. I promised myself no boys before I started college, and this didn't feel right.

"I'm sorry," I said. For some reason I felt like I owed him an apology. "I'm not quite there yet… I need more time to get to know you."

I thought about how I knew Avery for years before we started dating, and he was my long-time crush since fourth grade. As for Joey, the two of us hung out for months after Avery and I broke up before I even considered going out with him, and I adored Joey and knew him to be a great guy.

With a look of rejection and disappointment in his voice, Matt said, "Oh, yeah, I get it. It's cool." He stood up and said, "I better get going anyway. I have a ton of homework."

I'm sure it was Matt's pressing schoolwork that pulled him away and not the rejection he felt. I wondered when he was doing his homework, since we were spending so much time together. I figured his course load had to be more challenging than my general education classes.

"Yeah, I should probably do some homework too," I said in agreement, glad to end the awkwardness.

With a slight lift of his chin, Matt said, "Catch ya tomorrow." It was a statement, not a question, so I took it to mean he'd be stopping by again.

The next day Matt came by. We both stood by the door when he said with a smoldering look on his face, "Hey, are we cool?"

"Yeah, we're good," I said, as I motioned for him to enter. We chatted until we walked to our next class.

The next few days were more of the same. We got along great, and it was fun getting to know someone on a deeper level. I still didn't tell Betty Lou that her brother and I were spending time together. We didn't see much of each other because our schedules didn't match up, although we ate some meals together.

"I have to go to the bathroom," I said. "I'll be right back." On my way out, Matt stood up and walked up to me.

"Christina," he began as he caressed my hands. "We've been spending a lot of time together, and it's been great. Well, for me at least." He hesitated. "I was hoping…" Another pause transpired. He looked me in the eyes and continued, "Are you there yet? I mean are you ready to take the next step with me?" he asked in the sweetest manner.

My heart blushed. Apparently, my face did too. Matt cupped my face and leaned in to kiss me. This time I didn't pull away. The kiss was gentle. He kissed me again. It was longer with more intensity. A millisecond later, I found myself embracing him as we broke through the friendship zone. "Definitely worth waiting for," Matt said with a satisfied smile.

At a loss for words, we came together again and kissed with a little more passion. Lost in the moment, we began to settle in together. A loud scream separated us. "Oh, no you don't!"

Startled, we both let go of each other and looked toward the source of the screaming. Betty Lou stood there, all five foot two inches, with one hand on her hip and the other wagging a finger at us. "What do you think you're doing?"

I didn't know if she was directing this to both of us, to Matt or to me. What I did know is that if humans could produce smoke coming out of their ears, I would have seen it billowing from hers.

Matt pushed me behind him and held his arms out to protect me. Betty Lou's face was crimson as she started to poke Matt. *Why is she freaking out like this?*

"Betty Lou, calm down," Matt said in a placating manner. "It's all right. Breathe."

What the heck? She is crazy!

"I come home early from class, and this is what I see?" She yelled. "How long has this been going on? Huh? How long have you been hiding this from me?" She yelled as she started hitting Matt.

No wonder he jumped in front of me.

"You....," she started to come after me with her arms stretched out. Matt held her at bay.

"Betty Lou, calm down. It's okay. Take a deep breath. There you go. Again. Breathe." His words seemed to be working this time, for some unknown reason, but I didn't trust my crazed roommate.

"Here, Betty Lou, have a seat," Matt motioned to her chair. She approached the wooden structure in slow motion. I rolled my eyes. *What next?* "Keep taking deep breaths, Betty Lou," Matt's soothing voice seemed to placate her.

He whispered to me, "You may want to find another place to sleep tonight."

"What?" I said incredulously.

"I'll stay here with Betty Lou. See if you can crash with your friends," he advised, flexing his jaw.

I promptly left my room and knocked on Linda and Cassie's door. *I can't believe I have to do this.* Cassie opened the door. "Hey, I was wondering if I could sleep here tonight."

"Why? What's going on?" Cassie asked.

"I can't explain right now. Let me get my stuff, and I'll be right back, okay?"

"Yeah, okay," Cassie shrugged.

Where am I supposed to sleep in their room? On the floor? This isn't fair to me. Now I really have to pee. After I went to the bathroom, I opened the door to my dorm room and peered in. *Unbelievable! I'm scared to enter my own room.*

Betty Lou was lying on her bed with Matt by her side. I waved Matt over. When he walked over, I whispered to him, "I don't think this is fair. Why do I have to leave? I didn't do anything wrong. It's my room too."

"Well, I can't bring her back to my place. I live with a bunch of guys. Do you want to sleep at my place?" That made no sense. *Why is it okay for me to stay at Matt's but not Betty Lou?*

I felt my forehead pulsate. "No. I want to sleep in my own bed. Why can't I do that?" This was getting crazier by the second.

"Because I don't know what Betty Lou will do if I leave you two alone." Matt explained.

"Are you serious?" The situation was incredulous. *This can't be happening*

Matt scratched his head. "Unfortunately, yes, I am. I didn't think she would react this badly though." I looked over at my psycho roommate. She was bunched up in a ball.

"Matt, this isn't cool. I need to get my rest. I don't want to sleep on the floor in someone's room, and I don't want to go to your place. Got any other suggestions?" I was not happy about my current situation at all.

"Wait a minute." He lightly snapped his fingers. "Your RA should have an extra bed in her room. Why don't you ask if you can sleep in there?" And just like that, he thought he had found the perfect solution.

"I barely know my RA."

"Well, you're about to get to know her better." He acted confident that I would be bunking with my RA.

"How long until Betty Lou snaps out of it?" I needed to know how long this lunacy would last.

He shrugged. "I don't know. A couple days maybe."

I suppressed a scream with an exasperating whisper, "A couple days! No way! I can't live like this for a couple days." *Unbelievable. Totally unbelievable.*

Matt got a fearful look in his eyes. "Well, it's better than the alternative."

"What alternative?" When a petrified look overtook his face, I got concerned. "Matt, what alternative?" I tugged on his shirt. Betty Lou stirred, and tension filled up the room. I grabbed onto Matt's arm.

He looked at me for a moment, then relented. "Look, I'll get Betty Lou to take her medicine."

"What kind of medicine?" I asked, almost afraid to know the answer.

He whispered, "Anti-psychotic medicine."

This keeps getting better and better. I think I like the idea of staying in someone else's room instead. "Oh. Why didn't you tell me before? How could you put me in this predicament?" I said as I slapped his arm.

Betty Lou leaped out of bed and lunged toward me. "Get your hands off my brother!"

Matt braced her and said, "Christina, you better leave NOW!"

In a fury, I grabbed my container of toiletries, my towel, and my pajamas and ran out of the room while Matt held off Betty Lou.

I heard Matt recite, "It's okay, Betty Lou. Don't worry. It's all going to be okay."

I flew down the hallway and knocked on the door to Linda and Cassie's room. When Linda answered the door, I darted in and locked the door.

"Are you okay? What is going on?" Linda looked at me like I was the lunatic.

I held up my finger for them to give me a minute to compose myself. I caught my breath and said, "It's Betty Lou. She went ballistic on me."

Cassie gasped, "What do you mean Bette Lou went ballistic on you?" Deep lines appeared on her forehead.

"I think she tried to kill me." I said that in a matter-of-fact way, so I wouldn't sound dramatic.

Linda's eyes popped out of their sockets. "What? Just now in your room?"

"Yeah, her brother is there with her now." *Hopefully, he is restraining her, so I won't get killed today.*

"Why? What happened?" Linda pressed, her eyes remained wide open.

I blurted, "She walked in on Matt and me kissing."

"You and Matt are an item? I knew it!" Cassie exclaimed, slapping her thigh.

I tried to make it sound like it wasn't a big deal, "We kissed for the first time when she walked in the room. Nothing was going on between us before that." I held up my hand like I pledged to tell the truth in court, "Honest."

Cassie's forehead creased. "I don't get it. Why is she so upset?"

I rolled my eyes, "I have no idea, and I don't really care. Matt said it wasn't safe for me to be alone with her."

Linda questioned, "So, what are you going to do?"

I shook my head in disbelief. "I don't know."

Linda put her hand on my arm, "You can stay here as long as you need to."

"Thanks, but I need a permanent solution. There is no way I can live with Betty Lou after she came after me not once but twice." This college roommate thing was looking rather sketchy.

"You gotta tell us the whole story," Cassie said.

After giving them the blow-by-blow, I said, "I'm going to wash up. Anyone else need to use the bathroom? Please. Matt can't protect me in the bathroom."

Cassie volunteered, "Yeah, I'll go."

I came back from the bathroom to find a sleeping bag on the floor. "A sleeping bag? Why did you bring a sleeping bag to college?"

Linda replied, "I was a Girl Scout. You can never be too prepared."

"Well, thank God for Girl Scouts." I laughed. At least I didn't lose my sense of humor in the middle of all the craziness.

The following morning, I got up early and packed up the sleeping bag. Linda and Cassie were still asleep. I unlocked the door to my dorm room and peaked in. Matt was sitting on my bed. Betty Lou was asleep on hers.

Matt whispered, "I hope you don't mind, but I slept on your bed."

At least one of us was comfortable in my bed.

"It's fine. I need to grab a few things before I head out," I returned at a low volume.

Matt's arm reached out to me. "Listen, I called my parents after Betty Lou fell asleep last night. They're coming to pick her up today.

She doesn't know yet. Don't say anything." He talked quietly, so he wouldn't wake up the nutcase.

I'm fine if I never see her again. "Okay. What about you? Don't you have class?"

"Yeah, but I can't leave her alone." He ran a hand through his bedhead. "Get what you need, including your backpack and books, okay?"

I nodded and Matt grabbed my arm, "Hey, I'm really sorry."

I returned with a shrug and proceeded to gather my belongings.

I didn't know when I could return to my room. At least Linda and Cassie were letting me hang in their room. I was spent from not being able to sleep well on the hard floor.

I decided to go to breakfast. I ate my scrambled eggs and bacon in solitude. Breakfast was not at the top of the list for the rest of the campus. Too bad for them because the crispy bacon made my taste buds dance. My neglected body began to return to normal after filling it up with protein.

I headed to the library after class to go over what I learned earlier and to get a jump-start on my reading. I couldn't help but wonder what was going on with Betty Lou. After a couple hours, I went straight to my next class, then I headed back to my room not knowing what to expect.

I pulled on the handle to see if the door was locked. Despite it being locked, I braced myself. The door opened to a room that was half-empty. All of Betty Lou's belongings were gone. Not even a note was left. Although relieved my psycho roommate was gone, my heart began to race. *What does this mean? Will I get a new roommate? Do I have to pay extra for a single now?*

I dropped my backpack and sank in my bed. *This is good, right?*

I took a short walk down the hall. "She's gone," I said to Linda and Cassie as I stood in their doorway.

"Yeah, we saw her moving out. Her parents arrived a little after you left this morning," Linda said.

"Did she say anything to either of you?" I asked them.

Linda replied, "I think she said goodbye to Nancy and Jill."

I'm sure they blame me for her leaving.

"She didn't say goodbye to either of you?" I questioned.

"No, we had class, so we couldn't stick around," Linda said.

It was as if a lightbulb went off in Cassie's head when she asked, "Does this mean you get the room all to yourself?"

My eyes narrowed, "I don't know. All I know is that she's gone, and all her stuff is gone."

"What's going on with you and Matt?" asked Linda.

I shrugged my shoulders. "I haven't seen him since this morning when I went to grab my stuff for class."

Cassie stated, "As cute as Matt is, I wouldn't want Betty Lou as a sister-in-law."

Linda agreed with an eye roll, "Me neither. Too much drama for me."

No way do I want Betty Lou as a sister-in-law.

"So, what are you gonna do, Christina? Do you still want to go out with Matt?" Cassie asked.

"For all I know I may never see Matt again." I said in a deadpan tone.

"Is that what you want?" Linda looked at me with caring in her eyes.

"I don't know. I can't think about that now." *I don't want to think about it.*

The next day my half-empty room greeted me after lunch. *I could get used to living alone.*

The knock on the door startled me. On the other side of the door stood the catalyst of my new living arrangement. "Hey, Matt." I opened the door wide enough for him to walk in my room.

"Hey, how are you?" he managed to ask with concern in his voice.

"Fine," I replied in a matter-of-fact tone.

"I'm sorry I didn't get here sooner. Things were a little crazy yesterday, as you know." He shifted from one leg to the other.

"You could say that," I said with sarcasm.

"I was hoping we could talk, or is it too soon?" He had that hopeful puppy dog look in his eyes.

Too soon?

"Yeah, we can talk." I figured, why not? What did I have to lose?

Matt grabbed the extra chair in the room, Betty Lou's old chair. "I'm sure you figured out that Betty Lou left. For good that is. I mean she's not coming back this semester anyway." He paused and cast his eyes downward, "Honestly, I don't know if she'll ever be able to go away to college."

As much as I felt bad for Betty Lou, I didn't forget she came after me. So many thoughts hit me at once. *What is wrong with her? Why did Matt pursue a relationship with me knowing his sister is nuts?*

"Ah," he said, raking his hair. "I'm really sorry about all this. You probably want to know what's wrong with Betty Lou."

"That's a start." I stated with an edge of annoyance.

"Well, first of all, she's not my real sister. That came out wrong." With a guilty expression on his face, Matt hesitated for a second, yet redeemed himself by saying, "What I mean is she was adopted."

"Now, it's starting to make sense," I said, rubbing my chin.

"Yeah, you see, she was abused as a toddler, like it really screwed her up. My parents knew that, but felt like they could help her somehow, so they fostered her first, and eventually adopted her."

Hearing about Betty Lou's tragic life as a little girl made me feel guilty for thinking the worst about her. *But she tried to attack me. Why?*

Matt's eyes shined as he recounted life with his adopted little sister. "Betty Lou was the cutest little sister. She acted like I could do no wrong. I didn't know she was abused. I was too young to know that. All I knew was that she was like a puppy for me to play with. At least that's how my parents described it. She laughed all the time when we played together. Her laughter filled the room."

Matt looked up and away as his mouth quirked upward. "For the most part we got along great, better than most siblings, and we still do, but every now and then something would happen that would trigger an outburst from Betty Lou."

Matt's fingers combed his hair as he sighed heavily. "One day, Betty Lou watched my girlfriend and I break up. We didn't know anyone was around, and it was a rather bad break up. I was 15 at the time, and my girlfriend was 17."

Upon recalling the good old days with his girlfriend, Matt grinned, "I thought I was so cool for going out with a really pretty girl who was two years older than me. She was our babysitter from when we were younger and was like a sister to Betty Lou."

"How old were you when she babysat you?" I asked.

"I was 13 and Betty Lou was 11. Justine was 15. She babysat us for a year before we started going out. We hooked up before that. I snuck down while Betty Lou was in bed to… you know," Matt bobbed his head.

"No, I don't know. Care to elaborate?" I didn't want to make any assumptions.

"We just fooled around at first," He stopped to thread his fingers through his hair.

He slept with his babysitter! How could I be so stupid? I can't believe I put myself in this predicament. He totally played me.

"We didn't start sleeping together until I was 14." His confession did not make me feel any better.

"Oh well, that changes everything," I said with a major eye roll.

"Hey, I never said I was a saint," he protested.

"No, but you conveniently left that part out." I pointed my finger at him.

"Look, I'm super attracted to you, and I think you're a nice girl…"

I cut him off before he could finish. "What I want to know is how does Betty Lou fit into all this?"

Shaking his head, Matt continued with his story. "Yeah, right. You see, Betty Lou caught us breaking up, and it wasn't pretty. We were screaming at each other in the old barn. We didn't think anyone was around. I thought Betty Lou was at her therapist's. She's seen a therapist since she was four years old when my parents took her in."

Absent-mindedly, Matt rubbed the nape of his neck. "I found out later that Betty Lou was raped as a toddler. Her mother was paid by men to let them defile her. She was so young that she didn't have any memories, but she still had the feelings, and some events triggered outbursts."

The bile sat at the top of my throat ready to escape. I swallowed hard and fought back tears, tears for a girl who tried to kill me. *Poor Betty Lou.*

Understanding the look on my face, Matt said, "I know this is a lot to process. I'm getting there."

He sucked in a deep breath. "Like I said, our breakup wasn't pretty. More like it was explosive. Justine was… Let's just say she was beautiful but very insecure."

Matt moistened his lips before continuing," We were screaming at each other. Justine began hitting me, like punching hard. She was hysterical. I didn't fight back because you don't hit girls. She bent down to pick up a shovel when Betty Lou came out of nowhere and jumped on her back. I had to pry Betty Lou off Justine while they were screaming at each other. Justine didn't want to hurt Betty Lou, but Betty Lou looked like she could have killed Justine to protect me."

After inhaling deeply, Matt said, "My guess is that Betty Lou overheard Justine call her a psycho when we were arguing. Justine witnessed Betty Lou freak out a few times by that point."

With a shake of his head, Matt said, "Anyway, after I got Betty Lou off of Justine, Betty Lou picked up the shovel and took a swipe at Justine. Betty Lou managed to whack Justine across her legs. Justine went down fast and wailed from the pain. She screamed for Betty Lou to get away from her. Betty Lou collapsed like a stack of cards after she walloped Justine. Then she got up and charged after Justine again. I had to restrain Betty Lou and calm her down."

Matt closed his eyes and winced, "She hit Justine so hard, shattering her leg. We paid for all her medical expenses in hopes that Justine's parents wouldn't sue us. Her parents milked us for everything, but thankfully they didn't sue."

Matt's mouth became as straight as an arrow, "Betty Lou started seeing a psychiatrist who put her on anti-psychotic meds, and she seemed to be doing much better until... well, until yesterday."

"What about the scavenger hunt? Don't you count that?" I wasn't about to let that one go.

Matt scratched his head. "Yeah, a... no. I wouldn't necessarily count that. She didn't physically go after anyone, although I do suppose that was symptomatic."

He knew all this time that Betty Lou was a psycho, and he still put me in danger. I started yelling, "You knew about Betty Lou's mental state, and you didn't warn me! You didn't think to clue me in? You're just as bad as her, if not worse!" I threw my trembling arm toward the door and felt my nostrils flare, "Get out of my room and don't EVER come here again! In fact, don't even look at me again! Do you hear me? Get out!"

"Wait, Christina, hear me out!" Matt said with urgency. "I'm in love with you!"

What?! "You don't know what love is! You don't put someone's life at risk if you love them." I caught my breath as I tried to make sense of this mess.

"I know. I'm sorry. I really am. We can make this work. You and me." His eyes pleaded with mine.

"You are demented if you think I would go out with you," I stated, feeling the veins in my neck throbbing.

Then it hit me. Matt was delusional, or he was lying. Either way he could hurt me. *Smooth it over. God, help me get out of this.*

Matt stood up. "Look, I'm really sorry. I'll make it up to you. I will do anything for you. You have my word."

Although I felt suffocated, I knew I had to think clearly. My mind felt like it was going in slow motion, and I needed it to speed up to give me a viable solution. *Lord, give me the words.*

"Matt, I get it. I feel the same way, but…" It was a lie that needed to be said, and I knew I had to sound convincing, especially after I screamed at him.

"But, we have to think about Betty Lou and her feelings. It wouldn't be fair to her if we continued our relationship. Every time she looked at me, she would feel guilty or ashamed. That could cause her to have a relapse. We couldn't do that to her. She's in a fragile state as it is, and it's not even her fault. We have to be strong for her and fight our feelings for each other."

The bile returned and was begging for its release. I swallowed my pride and in self-preservation said, "Don't you see? We are a tragedy." I sounded like I was acting in a Shakespeare play. "We have to sacrifice our love for each other to spare Betty Lou." I laid it on thick, and Matt's eyes softened as he gave me an abashed look.

Matt hung his head, then looked up, and said, "You're right. We have to end it for Betty Lou's sake. I'm sorry, Christina, but it's best if we go our separate ways."

Not realizing I was holding my breath, I exhaled. It was possible that I held my breath since Betty Lou flipped out. "Take care, Matt." *Please stay out of my life.*

"Bye, Christina. I'm sorry it didn't work out between us."

"Me too," I feigned my sorrow. *Just leave!*

He finally walked out the door and out of my life. That had to be the shortest and strangest relationship in history. I needed to go for a run to process the ordeal from the past twenty-four hours.

Deciding to go for a run was a great idea. I was able to explore the town and take in the beauty of the landscape with its sprawling green hills and amazing sunsets. My ponytail swung back and forth as I ran. It reminded me that I was alive and able to take things in stride. Even though Betty Lou had attempted to kill me, I didn't have any ill feelings towards her. I felt sorry for her and wished her well. *Lord, please give Betty Lou the healing she needs.*

Running gave me the opportunity to put the Parkes behind me, both Betty Lou and her brother. *I dodged a bullet with each of them but wasn't going to hold a grudge.*

I thought of the verse Mark 11:25, *"And when you stand praying, if you hold anything against anyone, forgive them so that your father in heaven may forgive you your sins."*

As I moved onward with my run, I was looking forward to the next chapter in my life, and I was confident that good things were on the horizon.

I looked to the following verse to give me hope for a brighter future, "For I know the thoughts that I think toward you, saith the Lord, thoughts of peace, and not of evil, to give you an expected end" (Jeremiah 29:11).

Chapter 6

A couple weeks went by, and school was in full swing. I enjoyed my general education classes, not finding them too difficult. The challenging part was deciding on a major. I had no idea what I wanted to do after graduation, so I remained undeclared.

Jill and Nancy continued to party. After the episode with the sneaky fraternity brothers, I decided that scene wasn't for me.

Linda and Cassie told me about a Christian group they attended on campus, and I decided to tag along.

Christian Fellowship met on Thursday nights for their scheduled meetings. It was a wonderful time of worship when faith-filled students gathered in the main union building. The musically inclined students played their instruments on stage while the rest of us sang the songs displayed on the overhead projector. The music, rocky and upbeat, was like jamming at a rock concert! A great change from what I was used to at Sunday school. *Bye-bye, boring! Hello fun!*

A hilarious guest speaker addressed a relevant topic using scripture to tie it all together and peppered it with jokes. Topics like how to be secure and single. Apparently, everyone who wasn't attached was looking. It was a great time to scope out prospects. I meant to say, to interact with other believers. *Oh, he's cute! So is he! Oh my gosh, he's looking at me! Stop checking those guys out! Okay, okay! Geesh! Focus upward, Christina. You promised to work on you. No boyfriends! Look at what happened with Matt.*

I also joined one of the single-sexed Bible studies called "cell groups" that met once a week and focused on a topic or book of the Bible. As a result, I was able to stay the course with my faith and socialize with others trying to do the same. They were all girls, so no distractions there. I was reminded of the verse, "For where two or three are gathered together in my name, there am I in the midst of them" (Matthew 18:20).

The main group was rather large and boasted the highest-grade point average of any social group on campus. With lots of people to choose from, I forged great friendships with people like me who were studious enough to get good grades, but fun loving enough to enjoy our new-found freedom.

We dined together for lunch and dinner, hung out on a regular basis as well as making meaningful contributions in the community, Christian Fellowship in action. We basically ran the race together.

For example, many of us volunteered our services to raise money for a crisis pregnancy center along with restoring the building it housed. We were given pizza for our efforts. If they threw in milkshakes I would have lived there. All in the name of the Lord. Serving, not the pizza. *Now I want a milkshake.*

The concept of the Christian Fellowship campus organization was based on the following verse, "And let us consider one another to provoke unto love and to good works: Not forsaking the assembling of ourselves together, as the manner of some is; but exhorting one another: and so much the more, as ye see the day approaching" (Hebrews 10:24-25).

Chapter 7

I also did something unexpected and ran for one of the freshman student government positions as a senator. I won! *Yay! Victory Dance!* With little campaigning, I managed to become a senator. I was no Bob Dole, Republican leader of the Senate House, but I embraced my new political career. *Look out, world, I could be the first United States woman president. Or not.*

As I strode across campus, I felt like a celebrity. My classmates told me that they voted for me, even though I had no clue who they were. Others congratulated me even before I knew I won.

For some reason, I didn't mind this type of attention. Maybe because it was for the greater good? It wasn't just about me, but how I could improve the university. Or maybe, just maybe, I was discovering a new and improved Christina, one who doesn't shy away from attention.

Nonetheless, I welcomed the responsibility of being on the senate and formed unexpected friendships during my tenure. I became friends with a short, brown-haired guy named Jacob Perry, also known as Jake, who was a sophomore senator.

We ran into each other at the senate board room to which we had access 24 hours a day via a special key each of us was given. I liked studying there instead of going to the boring old library where I managed to fall asleep and woke up with drool on my arm. EVERY. SINGLE. TIME. *Gross! I know, right?! How embarrassing!* And the board room was way better than being cooped up in my single-sex dormitory with a bunch of boy crazy girls who watched TV all the time.

Jake was quite the lady's man, but at first, he didn't let on to that fact. He was very personable, funny, confident, intelligent, and attractive. Another cute boy in my path. *Lord, are you trying to tell me something? Chill, Christina! Guys are off limits!*

For the most part, I sat and listened to Jake talk about his escapades. He was always picking up girls at parties. Jake's pick-up lines alone were entertaining. "So, those beautiful lips of yours, are they just meant for drinking beer or are you willing to share them?" I would have loved to have seen him in action; a fly on the wall so to speak.

I knew Jake wasn't for me, but I found his stories irresistible. *No more boyfriends, Christina!* Yes, I had to constantly remind myself of my no dating rule.

Somehow, I managed to get my homework done despite the constant chatter. *Cute, funny boys are the best distractions! Down, girl! You promised yourself not to get involved with someone!* I couldn't help myself.

I didn't date the rest of my freshman year, despite the frequent offers. I refused to allow myself to become vulnerable again or dependent on a guy. One girl attacking me was one girl too many.

I realized I was still shaken up by my breakup with Joey and felt that I couldn't be with someone until I was completely over Avery, no matter how long that took. It wouldn't be fair to deceive yet another guy into thinking that my heart belonged to only them. I knew I hurt Joey terribly, and for that I felt horrible as I truly loved him. The problem was my love for Avery seemed to be taking up permanent residence in my heart, not allowing room for anyone else, including a guy as special and dear to me as Joey.

I also felt like I had to make it on my own without depending on a boyfriend to make me happy. After delving even deeper I had to reconcile my inappropriate behavior with my former boyfriends, more specifically to come to terms that getting almost naked before marriage is not pleasing to God. This was extremely challenging, because I had to face the uncomfortable feelings of shame and guilt and promise myself and God that I would refrain from such behavior prior to marriage. I knew I had to trust in the Lord for that indescribable peace, joy, and security, but I didn't realize how much at the time.

I received encouragement when I read the verse, "Now the God of hope fill you with all joy and peace in believing, that ye may abound in hope, through the power of the Holy Ghost" (Romans 15:13).

Chapter 8

My sophomore year, a few girls from Christian fellowship and I got an apartment across campus and wound up living next to Jake. We discovered we were neighbors on moving day, my first day back. Amid the chaos that day, I met Jake's roommates as well as their parents.

His roommate Ryan, a tall, very handsome guy, seemed beyond annoyed when his mom said that I would be the perfect girl for him. "Oh, Ryan, dear, she's perfect for you. Look how pretty she is, and she's so sweet. You two would make the perfect couple! Imagine how beautiful your children would be."

With that comment, "Ryan Dear" slammed his bedroom door. *Geez, I'm not that bad!*

Eventually, Ryan did ask me out, but I turned him down flat. One day when I was alone in my apartment, Ryan walked by and asked if I wanted company. I didn't want to be rude, so I said, "Sure, come on in."

He sat on the couch and patted it next to him. I ignored his gesture, but that didn't stop him. He said wiggling his thick dark eyebrows, "Hey, how about you and me right here, right now?" I gracefully declined.

He persisted. "Yo, if it's privacy you want, my frat brothers can lend us a bedroom."

Again, I refused his distasteful offer, and he sneered at me. The cords in his neck became rigid, and his jaw clenched.

I jumped to my feet and looked out the huge windows that framed the door to our entranceway willing my roommates to come home. It was rare for anyone to be alone in our apartment at any given time.

After unsuccessfully wooing me, he stormed out of the room, saying, "You'll regret this!"

As expected, I was petrified because of the unspeakable act that Creepoid—the nickname I gave my despicable classmate and hometown neighbor still felt right, even several years later—committed against me. Once again, my nightmares returned in full force, and I began having trouble sleeping again.

After that, the real life torment began.

One day I came home to my apartment after class to find a nasty poem on my make-up mirror ironically written with my favorite L'Oréal lipstick called Le Fleur, meaning flower in French. The poem stated, "Roses are red, violets are blue, you are a bitch and I hate you!"

Needless to say, I was freaked out by the message and demanded to know who let someone in our bedroom, and who touched my personal things.

"Oh, Ryan went in our room," my roommate Cassie informed me without any further explanation.

There was no reason for him to be in our bedroom since we had a spacious common room in between the two bedrooms. I was not only furious but frightened. I felt violated, even though I knew what it was like to be ultimately violated.

When I went to bed later that evening, I discovered that my sheets were short-changed. *How dare he rearrange my bed sheets like that!* It only got worse from there.

The following week, one of the guys in the apartment next door asked me if I had a Bible they could borrow. After I went into my room to retrieve the Bible, I discovered that Rex, the one who asked for the Bible, had left.

I walked over to his apartment to give him the Bible when Ryan grabbed hold of me and dragged me to the other side of the room and handcuffed me to the bathroom door of his bedroom. I pretended not to care, even when the pizza guy came to the door and saw me handcuffed sitting on a chair with the bedroom door wide open exposing me and my plight.

I convinced myself that if I showed Ryan how frightened I was, he would continue to harass me. As I sat handcuffed to the door, I prayed in silence to my Heavenly Father.

Dear Lord,

Please get me out of these handcuffs. Give me the strength and courage to get through this captivity without appearing rattled. Help me to take this in stride, Lord. Have Ryan get bored and unlock the cuffs to let me go. Please God, I feel helpless and scared. Please give me peace.

I repeated one of my favorite verses, "Cast thy burden upon the LORD, and he shall sustain thee: he shall never suffer the righteous to be moved" (Psalm 55:22).

Finally, Jake came home and demanded that Ryan unlock the handcuffs. "Let her go, Ryan! You're nuts for cuffing her like that." Because Ryan idolized Jake, he freed me as Jake was the only one to whom my captor would listen.

One evening while I was in bed, I heard something through the walls. Someone chanted in a deep, throaty voice, "Christina, Christina…" repeatedly as if it were a scene from a scary B movie, although it wasn't scary. It was annoying, and I needed to sleep.

The next day I mentioned it to my roommates who refused to admit to hearing anything even though they were in the room with me throughout the entire evening.

Ryan mocked me, claiming that it was all my imagination. My roommates seemed to be enjoying Ryan's so-called prank, thus revealing their naiveté.

Since Jake wasn't at his apartment, I went to the senate boardroom to ask him to tell Ryan to stop the nonsense, but Jake was nowhere to be found. The lights were off in the boardroom. I didn't have a key anymore to further explore since I didn't run for the unpaid Senate position. I decided instead to get paid for tutoring through student services.

The haunting continued for the next few nights. By that time, my roommates were fed up, because the noise kept them awake at night too. They told Ryan to cut it out, but he flat out denied having anything to do with the irritating prank.

Ryan acted a little crazy when he claimed he didn't make the noises. He appeared very aggravated, like a wild animal defending his territory. His reaction deeply troubled me to the core.

I prayed constantly for the terrorizing to stop. The Lord helped me through much worse times, and He would help me again.

I knew better this time than to tell Satan to bring it, the way my dear friend Miss Brenda who worked at the old folk's home suggested years ago when I was struggling with the accusing word 'nark' painted on my high school locker.

That was bad advice. One should never invite the devil to do his dirty work.

The following Wednesday night, I went dancing at the campus dance club when Bob and Tony, the prankster's roommates, asked me to help them out with a photography project.

"Will Ryan be there?" I asked.

"No, he's hanging out with his fraternity brothers at their frat house," Bob said. *Ryan should go live with them. Then we would all have peace and quiet!*

Tony begged in the cutest boyish manner, "Oh, come on, Christina, please! It'll be fun!" I agreed after much pleading on their part.

They took pictures of me, a novice, playing quarters. Much to my surprise, it turned out to be fun just like they said. I flicked the quarter in the shot glass with ease. I realized this was a game for drunks, but I was amazed at myself for being able to repeatedly get the quarter in the tiny beverage container.

Bob and Tony were sweet and apologized on behalf of Ryan for tormenting me. They said they did it for fun in the beginning but then admitted Ryan got out of hand. They told him to stop, but frat boy continued to terrorize me.

That night, Tony got on one knee and asked, "Will you marry me?" He thrust his arms from his chest mimicking his heart pumping out of his chest and offered me the pull tab of the soda can as the engagement ring.

He said I was the girl of his dreams and couldn't understand why Ryan had become so hateful towards me. They apparently didn't know about my rejecting Ryan, and I decided not to tell them. *What good would it do?* I considered it might perpetuate how Ryan felt and prolong his antics.

Not once did I mention the ineffable act to anyone, but I did mention to my roommates that I was having nightmares after my room was defiled. Perhaps that's how Ryan came up with the idea to perform "Nightmare on Campus" through the walls.

I shuddered thinking of Ryan's creepy performance as I lay in his roommate's bed. Exhausted after a long night of dancing and playing quarters, I lacked the energy to walk back to my apartment next door. The pull of Bob's bed and the late hour caused me to give in to the lure of sleep. Bob thoughtfully covered me with a soft blanket, and he and Tony talked quietly nearby while I rested.

When Ryan came in and saw me lying on Bob's bed, he made the most repulsive suggestion in the most serious of tones and intensity, "Yo, guys, this is our chance! We can all take turns with Christina while she's passed out! I'll go first, okay?"

"Dude, you are disgusting! Get the hell out of here!" an appalled Bob replied.

Tony piped in, "Ryan, leave her alone! She's a nice girl. You really are sick, man! Get lost!" Seconds later, the door slammed.

You tell him, boys! My heroes!

The rejected one's words cut right through me. I froze. I didn't want to give any indication that I was awake, although my heart hammered out of my chest. Creepoid's enraged face was plastered in my memory. I cursed the day the Martins moved down the street from my house. The Martin boy destroyed my life, and visions of that summer day continued to terrorize me.

Please God, take these dreadful thoughts away!

It was a good thing that I memorized a ton of Bible verses five years ago to deal with my ongoing nightmares from that unspeakable act against me at the Martin's. The following verse came to mind, "Let your conversation be without covetousness; and be content with such things as ye have: for he hath said, I will never leave thee, nor forsake thee. So that we may boldly say, The Lord is my helper, and I will not fear what man shall do unto me" (Hebrews 13:5-6).

With the reminder that God was there with me, protecting me, keeping me safe, I felt at peace again.

After several minutes, when I thought the coast was clear, I got up and left. Bob and Tony didn't say a word, and Ryan was nowhere in sight.

Much to my relief my bedroom returned to normal from its brief time as the House of Horrors. The haunting through the walls ceased, and there were no more awful rhymes on my mirror or short-changed sheets on my bed.

I prayed that the nightmare was over, but that was only the beginning. It was the calm before the storm.

A few weeks had passed since I hung out with Bob and Tony and overheard Ryan say that he wanted to—*gulp*—gang rape me.

I was so grateful to both Bob and Tony for sparing me and wished I could thank them accordingly, but I didn't want them to know that I overheard the distressing conversation with their emotionally disturbed roommate. Some things were left better unsaid.

"The fear of man bringeth a snare: but whoso putteth his trust in the LORD shall be safe" (Proverbs 29:25).

Chapter 9

One cold, dark Tuesday evening, on my way home from tutoring a freshman in English composition, someone grabbed me from behind.

"Scream and I cut your throat. Got it?" the frightening voice threatened. I nodded. At first my body stiffened, and I swallowed a scream. Every cell in my body trembled.

It took me a moment to realize to whom the voice belonged which only heightened my fear. Ryan grabbed a tight hold of me. His arm pressed underneath my chest squeezing my rib cage, his other arm twisted around my neck like a noose. "Now, do as I say or else!" he commanded.

I tried to break loose knowing if he took me to a secluded spot, I would be doomed for sure, but I couldn't free myself. Ryan's grip on me was insanely fierce.

My heart pounded like a jackhammer on speed. I prayed someone would see us, even though we were at a remote spot, the back stairwell on the far end of the apartment complex. The posterior of the apartment complex backed up to a wooded area, only a few yards away.

I searched for a plan, but my mind went dark like a black hole. Ryan pulled me into the woods. I couldn't see a thing, for it was a starless night and the trees prevented any light from shining through.

My neck jerked back and forth as I choked on a scarf being tied by my abductor. From the stiff texture of the scarf, I could tell that it was brand new. The taste and smell of the ink from the dye caused me to gag.

"Please God save me!" I screamed within.

Ryan tied my arms behind my back with another stiff scarf. He pushed me, and I jostled forward from his forceful shove. I gasped on the handkerchief and sucked in its nauseating ink.

"Move it!" he shouted, keeping an exceedingly tight grip on me.

I cried internally, *Lord, help me! I need you!*

After a few minutes, we came to an open field in the middle of the woods. It wasn't a vast space, just several feet in diameter.

Ryan threw me on the ground and straddled me. The ground was hard and cold and unwelcoming. I felt rocks, grass, and tree roots beneath my shaken body. They were cold to the touch by my bound hands, yet my hands began to sweat.

"You asked for this! Move and you die! Vengeance is mine!" Veins throbbed in his temples, his eyes bulged out of their sockets.

With jagged movements, I pleaded through the scarf, but there was only a garbled response on my end as every fiber of my being fought to break free. Pain shot through my shoulders and down my arms. The weight of our bodies was enough to crush my imprisoned hands.

I could see the fury in Ryan's dark, soulless eyes. His chiseled features were contorted with nothing but hate and revenge. Trepidation sank to the pit of my stomach.

All I could do was pray. *NO! Don't! Oh my God! I can't believe this is happening! NOT AGAIN!!! Please God, help me!* My entire life flashed before my eyes. *I am not going to survive this time. Please God, save me! Please God! Oh, Please! Dear God, spare me! Oh God...*

NOOOOOOOOOOOOOOO! Someone please help me!

My mind instantly transported me back to the Martin's on that wicked summer day before my freshman year of high school. I pictured Creepoid lying on top of me. The horror returned. I screamed for my classmate to get off me, not realizing where I was or with whom.

Cold sweat trickling down my back snapped me back to reality. My desperate cries fell on deaf ears. *Oh no! Not Again!* I was left feeling completely shattered once again.

An instant later, a surge of adrenaline coursed through my body, giving me the strength to fight back, yet Ryan still had me completely pinned down. Fear and desperation consumed me. I furiously attempted to move my body, but I remained motionless despite my efforts.

Above me, Ryan made swift, jarring movements. At first, I saw glimpses of shiny, mirrored reflections until I watched Ryan hold a butcher knife above his head that was pointed at me above my chest. He glowered at me, baring his teeth, ready to devour his prey.

My entire body constricted without permission. Breathing eluded me. Tremors wracked my body.

I thought I heard something, someone. My imagination must have been playing tricks on me.

A few seconds later, I distinctly heard some rustling, followed by what sounded like voices. At first, I couldn't make out what was being said. The voices sounded faint, muddled, distant. Then they became louder, clearer, closer, more distinct. A flash of light appeared, disappeared, then suddenly reappeared.

"Ryan! Yo, Ryan, we know you're in here. Don't do anything stupid."

At that moment, Ryan bolted. The weight of his body was no longer present. I heard the rustle of leaves as he scurried away.

The tension in my body eased slightly, but I didn't know what was happening to be sure I was safe from harm. I leaned forward and looked around. I tried to get up, to make my escape. The binding of my hands behind my back prevented me from being able to stand up. Just then, someone approached and threw something over me.

"Bob, go get some help! Call nine one one! Hurry!" As my rescuer barked commands, he untied the scarf that stifled my cries. I choked on air. "Christina, it's me, Jake. You're going to be okay."

The Lord spoke to me through scripture, "He will fulfill the desire of them that fear him: he also will hear their cry, and will save them" (Psalm 145:19).

Everything went black.

Chapter 10

I woke up in a hospital bed. A middle-aged woman came to my side and introduced herself as a patient advocate for violent crimes. She asked me how I was doing and if I remembered what happened. It was a chore to move my head up and down, but speaking was worse.

She told me that the police wished to speak with me and that she would be present the entire time. There was an older nurse in the room as well. *Thank you, Lord, for protecting me!*

After I gave my police statement, the nurse stated, "The three young men that saved your life are waiting to find out about your condition. They are very concerned about you and have been here the whole time. Is it okay that I inform them of your condition?" I nodded, giving the caring nurse the cue to leave the room.

When she returned, she told me that one of the young men who saved my life wanted to see me. "He told me to tell you that his name is Jake, and he seems very worried. Would you like to see him?" I gestured affirmatively.

After a few moments, Jake entered the room. He had the deepest look of concern on his face.

"Hey, how are you feeling?" he asked with immense warmth and compassion in his eyes.

"Alright, considering," I said sheepishly, my voice a little coarse.

"Bob and Tony are waiting out there too. Bob ran to get paramedics, while Tony stayed back with me."

My eyes darted back and forth as I pulled my blankets up to my neck. I must have looked mortified since my study buddy told me not to worry. "Don't worry. I covered you up with my jacket. We didn't see anything. I promise." They suspected what happened and already gave their statements to the police.

"How did you know?" I asked.

Jake gave me the abbreviated version. When Jake came back to his apartment that night, he asked where Ryan was. When his roommates said he mumbled something about "sweet vengeance," he grabbed his car keys and ran to see if I was home safe in my apartment.

When he confirmed I wasn't in my apartment, he told Bob and Tony to follow his lead. Jake figured Ryan would return to that particular location in the woods where they found me.

Weeks ago, Bob and Tony showed Ryan Jake's secret romantic place he took his dates during the day—a quaint and secluded spot where Jake took many a girl on a picnic lunch sprawled out on a blanket.

Later, while the roommates were joking about Jake's date spot in the woods, Ryan's eyes dashed with the look of fury and whispered, "sweet vengeance," under his breath.

At the time Jake didn't know what he meant by that, but he quickly put it together. Jake brought his car keys, because they contained a little flashlight on the key chain, thus explaining the flashes of light I saw.

When I asked him why he thought I was in danger, he told me Ryan had been acting strange lately and made some disturbing comments to Jake and his roommates about me, babbling something about "Vengeance is mine."

Jake told Bob and Tony to look out for me when he wasn't around, but they didn't realize he meant indefinitely, even after Ryan seemed to cool things down. In other words, Ryan stopped blatantly terrorizing me, so they assumed he was through with his antics.

Shortly after Jake finished telling me about rescuing me, the nurse told him to leave. By then I was told that the police would provide 24-hour protection for me and that I was to stay overnight in the hospital for observation.

Jake told me he was going to keep vigil out in the lobby until I received a clean bill of health. He and his roomies bought me a small bouquet of pink roses that brightened my dingy room and kept me company. It was comforting to know that someone cared enough to demonstrate sincere concern for me in the aftermath of the turmoil. *Thank you, Lord, for Jake, Tony, and Bob! They are truly godsends!*

I gave permission for the medical staff to contact my parents as I didn't have the heart to tell them what happened. My parents insisted on driving the two and a half hours in the wee hours of the night to see me.

When my parents arrived, they spoke to the patient advocate first. My mom rushed by my side and smoothed back my hair with a shaky hand. Her bloodshot eyes welled up with tears, but she managed to hold them back. There were dark circles under her eyes and the lines on her forehead ran deep. "Christina, oh, my Christina! My God, look at you. Are you okay? Are you hurt?"

I assured her as best as I could, "I'm fine, Mom. Really." She started to cry upon hearing my weak tired voice and turned away from me.

"Pooch, you're going to be alright," my dad said as if it were more of a question than an affirmation.

The medical exam confirmed that I had in fact been raped, but they did not have the resources to determine proof of the assailant.

The next day the police told me that they had some information for me pertaining to my case. They made sure that the advocate and my parents were present when I received the news that they found Ryan's body below the railway trestle bridge. "We think it was a suicide," the police concluded.

I shuddered, envisioning him jumping from the bridge. I felt some sense of relief that the nightmare was over, but I knew from experience that a different type of terror was destined to replace it. I just didn't know how the post trauma would manifest itself this time.

I had no intention of telling anyone what happened that terrifying day at the Martins five and a half years prior. My most current rape was enough for them to handle at once.

This time I faced death in the eyes and survived. I continued to thank God for saving me.

The following verse held special meaning for me from that moment on, "For the Lord your God is he that goeth with you, to fight for you against your enemies, to save you" (Deuteronomy 20:4).

Chapter 11

The doctor suggested I leave school to start the healing process. As it was close enough to the end of the fall semester, my teachers agreed to give me my standing grade without taking any finals, for which I was extremely grateful. There was no way I could have sat through any finals or completed any assignments. My brain was a complete fog, and it was excruciating to think.

Upon arriving home, I was greeted by my brother, Jared. "Hey, what's going on? Mom and Dad won't tell me anything, only that they had to go to see you in the hospital in the middle of the night. Are you okay? What happened?"

Before I had a chance to say anything, my mom said, "Jared, help us unload the car."

"Why do I have to? It's her stuff!" Jared complained.

My dad barked orders, "Jared, do as your mother said!" It was rare that my father yelled, but when he did, you knew he meant business. Jared knew better than to argue with him.

"Christina, go lie down. You need to rest," my mother said in her sweetest voice that was practically foreign to me.

Since I didn't have the strength to unload, I did as suggested and headed upstairs.

On my way to my bedroom, I heard Jared whine, "Will someone tell me what is going on?"

One by one, my parents and Jared came into my room to drop off my stuff while I lay in bed under the covers with my back turned to the door. I heard my dad say, "Well, Pooch, this is the last of it. Let us know if you need anything."

What do I need? Nothing came to mind.

I confined myself to my bedroom once I arrived home. The moments I spent alone caused me to go to deep dark places, and I was alone most of the time. I revisited both rapes over and over. The loop of those horrific episodes replayed in my mind. I fell to my knees and begged the Lord to stop the torment. I didn't care that anyone could hear me, since they already knew about my most recent rape. I just wanted the pain to stop.

Dear Lord, please stop this torture. I can't take this anymore. Push these memories from my mind and replace them with your goodness.

Nightmares jolted me out of bed several times a week, I lost weight from not being able to eat, and I jumped at every turn. It took me years to cope with the former rape, and I found myself starting from scratch. Not again!

I stayed in my room most of the time because I didn't want to bring anyone down with my doldrums. I could only read a few verses at a time. Meditating on verses was all I could manage. My memory was shot though. I didn't have memory problems before. I struggled to retain new verses, so I stuck with the tried-and-true ones.

As a result, I repeated the following familiar verses, "Be careful for nothing; but in every thing by prayer and supplication with thanksgiving let your requests be made known unto God. And the peace of God, which passeth all understanding, shall keep your hearts and minds through Christ Jesus" (Philippians 4:6-7).

Prayer sustained me through my private, most vulnerable moments. I considered cutting but managed to refrain by the grace of God.

One day when I was heading from the bathroom, Jared approached me. His concern for me was written all over his face. His eyebrows were slightly raised while his forehead tightened. With his head slightly cocked, he said, "Hey, Mom and Dad still won't tell me what happened to you. You've been home for a week, and I'm still in the dark. What happened, Christina? Why were you in the hospital?"

The pain was too raw, too fresh for me to discuss, and to share it with my baby brother was more than awkward. "I can't talk about it," I said, breaking eye contact with him.

"Why not? I promise I won't say anything to anyone. You can tell me," Jared assured me as I caught a glimpse of his pursed lips.

"I can't. I just can't," I said with a scratchy voice from continually sobbing.

"Everyone is so gloomy around here. It's worse than when Avery broke up with you."

Jared's words stung in more ways than one. I didn't realize how gloomy it was. I only knew how gloomy I felt, and the mention of Avery only made me sadder. "You wouldn't understand," I said, shaking my head.

"Try me," Jared suggested.

I walked a few paces to my bedroom, too drained to even bother closing the door behind me. "I just want to be left alone." I sat on my bed as Jared followed me in my room and took a seat at my vanity.

He didn't waste any time pursuing his quest for information about what happened to me. "You've been alone for a week now. Things around here are not any better. I'm part of this family too. Don't I deserve to know what's going on?" Jared persisted.

"Jared, stop." I said, folding my arms.

He turned the chair around to face me, leaned forward, and demanded, "I'm not leaving until you tell me why you're home now and not in school and why you were in the hospital."

"Don't do this," I pleaded. I wanted nothing more than to be left alone. Was that too much to ask?

Wanting to know why his household was so melancholy, he held his hands out in frustration. "Don't do what? It's not like I don't care. You're my sister. What affects you affects me too. Just because I don't go to church doesn't mean I'm a bad person." I could hear the pleading, concern, and confusion in his voice.

"I never said that," I retorted in my defense.

"No, but you've tried to talk me into being a Christian a few times."

"I didn't try to talk you into it. It has to be a decision you make freely," I stated my case.

"Whatever. Just tell me what happened. I do care." His cheeks remained taut for a moment.

Jared wasn't giving up. *Okay, Lord, should I tell him? He is my brother after all, and I feel bad for all the gloominess in this house.* "All right. I came home because—because…" *God help me say the words.*

"You know Mom and Dad visited me in the hospital, right?"

"Why were you in the hospital?" he asked again.

"Because a guy from school attacked me." Blurting out the specifics was too painful.

"Did he hurt you?" He asked with a mixture of fear and concern in his voice.

In the worst way possible. I nodded, my eyes welled up.

"How did he hurt you? He didn't—" Jared inched his head forward. His eyes became misty.

Another nod barely escaped me.

"But you got away?" Jared asked perplexed, his voice quivered.

"He ran away when he heard voices calling his name."

"Did the police catch him?" He probed.

"Not exactly. They found him dead. Apparent suicide."

Jared hung his head, and his eyes were teary. "I'm so sorry."

I shrugged as it was too difficult for me to get the words out. The questioning continued by my concerned and curious brother, "Who was calling his name?"

"His roommates. One of his roommates figured out what he was up to, and three of them went searching for us."

"Oh man. They're heroes." They were heroes. Hearing my brother say that struck a chord with me, and I began to choke up.

I started sobbing thinking about what would have happened if Jake didn't figure out what his roommate was up to. Never was I ever so thankful for anyone other than Jesus. Jake, Bob, and Tony saved my life. They really were heroes. They spared me a gruesome fate as I pictured Ryan holding the knife above me. It was like I was face-to-face with him, fearing for my life, terrified that I was about to die a violent and painful death. The feelings I fought to forget returned with a vengeance. No longer could I suppress them.

With tears streaming down my face, I cried, "He, he held a knife to my throat." I gasped for air in between sobs and blurted out, "He was going to kill me, Jared!" The floodgates were released as my cries were boisterous and raging.

Jared leaped from the chair and put his arms around me. "I'm so sorry that happened to you."

I continued to sob and could tell that he was upset based on his sniffling that turned into tears he wiped away when we broke apart.

Jared and I forged a closeness from a reason that no other brother and sister should ever have to bond over. *Only God can create something so special out of something so despicable.*

Romans 12:21 says, "Be not overcome of evil, but overcome evil with good."

Another week had passed since I came home from college when Morgan called. I never bothered to answer the phone anymore. I was sitting on my bed when I heard a knock on the door. My mom asked through the closed door, "Christina, Morgan's on the phone. Do you want to talk to her?"

I sat in silence, not having enough energy to decide what to do. The door opened. "I think it might be good to talk to your friends." My mom knew Morgan and I were best friends since elementary school.

"Fine," I replied, breaking the silence barrier.

I reached over to my phone and picked up the receiver.

"Hey. Give my mom a sec to hang up the phone."

"Okay," replied Morgan.

After we heard a thunk, Morgan began, "I wasn't sure if you'd be home yet. Glad I caught you. You wanna get a couple people together and go out for dinner tomorrow night? I promised my parents I would stay home tonight."

I guess Morgan doesn't know. I wonder if anyone knows. "No, I think I'll pass."

"What do you mean you'll pass? You don't usually pass on things unless something is wrong. What's going on?" Morgan asked.

Morgan knew me well, but I wasn't about to divulge what happened over the phone. I wasn't ready to discuss it anyway. "I have a lot going on right now that I can't discuss. I'm not up for going out in public."

"Why? What's the matter?"

"I won't discuss it over the phone," I said.

"It sounds serious. Do you want to talk about it later in person? I can come to you." Morgan pressed.

"Uh, no. That's okay. You said your parents are making you stay home."

"I can tell this is serious. My parents will understand," Morgan stated.

"No, don't worry about it. I'll be fine." I couldn't say the words without choking up a teeny bit, because I didn't know if I'd be fine. I couldn't lie anymore. There was no reason to lie anymore.

"You don't sound fine. I'll talk to my parents and call you back. Okay?"

What choice do I have? I don't have any energy to fight this. "Okay." I relented.

Ten minutes after agreeing that Morgan would come over, I heard the doorbell ring and waited for her to come upstairs. I left my door open for her to walk in. A tall pretty redhead with cat-like green eyes appeared in my doorway. "Hey, Christina."

"Hi, come in and close the door." I motioned for her to sit on my bed. "Have a seat."

"So, what's going on?" My best friend asked.

I sat at the head of my bed with my back against the headboard. "Morgan, I, eh…" The words refused to come out. Morgan waited without moving a muscle. I started again, "I have something that's very hard for me to tell you."

Her voice was soft, "Okay. Take your time."

I took a deep breath. "There was a reason why I left school early…" I struggled to get the words out. "Um, this is so hard for me to say," I started to choke up. "I'm sorry. I just haven't told anyone yet." *Other than Jared.* "It's a… it's…" *Just say it.* "I was raped, and he almost killed me with a knife."

Morgan's jaw dropped, and her face became snow white as she lunged toward me with a hug. "Oh my gosh! Are you okay? Are you hurt?" She grasped my arms and said, "I'm so sorry. What can I do? Do you need anything?"

"I'm fine, physically that is. It's just a lot to process. There's nothing anyone can do. Please don't say anything to anyone. I don't want people talking about me. I will let people know in my own time."

With a quick reply, Morgan said, "I promise I won't say anything to anyone."

"Actually, you can tell your mom and dad, so they can pray for me, but no one else. Okay?"

"Okay." Morgan promised.

"You probably want details." I dreaded talking about it. I had a tough enough time telling Jared what happened.

Morgan said as she grazed my arm, "Only if you want to tell me."

"I should probably get used to telling my story." Morgan was the perfect person to start with.

After telling Morgan the sordid details, she sat in silence on my bed and shook her head.

"What?" I asked her.

Morgan shifted her body from one side to the other. "So, what now? Are you going to counseling?" Since Morgan and I had been acquainted with a couple of girls who went through counseling for different things, the concept of counseling wasn't foreign to us.

"Yeah, I think so. I haven't started anything yet though." I wasn't sure if I was ready for that.

"Do you know if you're going back to school?" Morgan asked.

"I don't know yet. I'm thinking no at this point." *What is the reason to go back to school? So I can face more heartbreak and violence?*

"That's understandable." Morgan sat with a pensive look on her face.

"I feel like I need to get on with my life, but I feel so heavy. Everything takes a lot of energy." I felt drained all the time.

"Yeah, I can get that," Morgan said, piercing her lips together.

A thought crossed my mind, and I didn't hesitate to follow through with it, "Maybe you can help me. Can you get Katie and Amy together? I can tell them about this together. They are still close, right?" I figured I could share my story with the ones closest to me first.

"Yeah, pretty sure they are. When do you want to get together?" Morgan responded with a hopeful look in her eyes.

"Whenever. I know I have to get this over with to start the healing process." *Although I'm dreading it.*

Morgan raised one eyebrow at me. "You sure you haven't been to counseling?"

"Positive. Why?" I asked, curiously.

"You sound like you had some counseling."

You're noticing all the years of hard work I put into trying to get over my first rape. Telling Morgan about the first villainous act was not an option. The shrug of my shoulders and grimace prompted her to move on with the conversation.

"All right. I'll contact Katie and Amy. Where do you want to meet? Can I suggest my house? This way you can get out of your house. I can have my dad make his famous milkshakes," she suggested. Morgan's dad made the best milkshakes. My mouth started to water.

"As long as mine is chocolate, I'm in." Her dad always made chocolate shakes, so I'm sure that wouldn't be an issue.

"I wouldn't have it any other way," Morgan said, spoken like a true chocoholic. She took my hand in hers and looked me in the eyes. "I'm really sorry. Let me know if there is anything else I can do to help you. How 'bout we pray now?"

I nodded and closed my eyes.

Morgan bowed her head, closed her eyes, and began praying aloud, "Father God, I ask that you lift up Christina. Wrap her in Your healing arms and give her the strength and courage to get her through this traumatic time in her life. May she call out to You in her time of need and feel Your presence like a warm embrace. May she be fully restored and even stronger through it all. Thank you for our friendship and keep her safe. I faithfully ask these things in Jesus's holy name. Amen."

Humbled by her words, I responded, "Amen. Thanks."

The next night I drove over to Morgan's house. As requested, I walked around back to enter through the backdoor. Morgan answered the door. "Hello, are you ready for this?"

"As ready as I'll ever be," I answered.

"All right. We'll wait for Katie and Amy to arrive."

Moments later, they appeared at the back door like I did. I could hear Amy's booming voice. "Hi! Long time no see! How ya doing?"

To that Morgan replied, "Good. Come in. Hi, Katie. How are you?"

"Good. Thanks. How are you?" Katie responded.

"I'm fine," Morgan said.

"Hi, Christina!" Amy and Katie said at the same time as they walked into the family room.

I waved. "Hi."

"Let's all go downstairs." We followed Morgan down into her finished basement. We sat down in the lounge area.

"So, what's everybody been up to?" Amy started.

I shot Morgan a look and she said, "Well, I just got home yesterday."

"Yeah, me too," Amy replied.

Katie added, "Well, you all know I've been commuting and working to save money."

"Yeah, how's that going? Is it hard to work and go to school at the same time?" I asked.

"It's not too bad. The upside is that I don't have any student loans to pay," Katie said, elevating her chin.

"Hey, that's great," I responded with as much enthusiasm as possible.

Amy jumped in, "While I'm already up to my eyeballs in debt."

Katie clarified on Amy's behalf, "You mean your parents are up to their eyeballs in debt."

"Yeah that." Amy laughed as she waved her hand. "Not everyone can get sports and academic scholarships like Morgan."

"Hey, I worked very hard for that. Thank you very much," Morgan said with a smile.

Katie turned to me and asked, "Didn't you get a scholarship too, Christina?"

I confirmed, "Uh, yeah, a small one."

"Every bit counts," Amy declared.

I nodded. My energy was fading fast. I glanced over at Morgan to let her know it was now or never. She motioned for me to say something.

I began, "Even though I received a small scholarship for each year, I may not go back to Sylvania Ridge."

"Why not?" Amy asked.

"Morgan asked you guys over, so I could tell you both something at the same time, and it's difficult for me to talk about it." I began to shake deep inside.

"We're listening," Amy said.

"I...uh..." *Just say it. You were able to tell Morgan and Jared. Breathe.* I sucked in a deep breath. "I ended my semester on a really bad note. It was so bad that I left early without taking any finals. My teachers were very understanding under the circumstances."

"What circumstances?" Amy asked.

"That I was raped." *There, I said it.*

"Oh my gosh!" They said in unison, followed by their jaws dropping and staring into space. Katie and Amy were still in sync with each other.

"I'm so sorry!" Katie said after she picked up her jaw.

"Yeah, that's terrible, even worse than I thought you were going to say. I thought you failed out or something. This is way worse. Did they catch the guy? Is he in jail?" Amy would have continued if Morgan didn't cue her to stop talking.

"To answer your question, Amy, no he's not in jail. He's dead."

"Oh, my goodness, you killed him!" With a look of horror, Amy threw her hands up to cover her mouth.

I almost laughed at Amy's response. Almost. "No, I didn't kill him. He committed suicide."

"Oh," Amy said. Then a nano second later, she realized the severity of it, and said, "Ohhh." Her eyes bulged.

I was finishing up with my story when Morgan's dad called us up for the shakes.

"By the way, no one else knows except my family, Morgan's parents, and now you guys. Please don't say anything to anyone. This has been traumatic enough without me being the topic of conversation. Okay?" I said, feeling the need to make my wishes known.

"Um hum, yeah, no. I won't say anything," Amy fumbled over her words. *Guess she'll be telling people. Everyone will know in no time.*

At least I trusted Katie when she said, "You have my word." *Not much good that will do when Amy will blab it all over.* I think I knew deep down Amy couldn't keep it a secret.

As we indulged in the delicious extra thick, extra chocolatey shakes compliments of Mr. Ricci, the conversation turned to more pleasant topics. Morgan told us about her new boyfriend, Derek. "We met through Inner Varsity."

"Inner what?" Amy asked for clarification.

"Inner Varsity. It's a Christian group on campus. I wasn't too involved last year because it was too much with me playing field hockey and learning the ropes of college."

Katie added, "Yeah, I know what you mean. Working and going to school takes its toll too. It's a lot to manage."

Amy leaned forward and asked, "So, what's your boyfriend like? Is he tall, dark and handsome?"

"Well, yes actually, and as far as looks are concerned, you'll have to see for yourself when he visits."

"Ooh, show and tell. Can't wait!" Amy squealed as she clapped her hands. "When's he coming?"

"Hopefully, next week sometime, pending parental approval. He lives in Virginia."

Virginia? "Is he staying here?" I asked.

Morgan held her breath, then released it when she said, "That's what I'm hoping for. Okay. I've been meaning to tell you…" She made eye contact with each of us. "I should probably tell you that he's black."

"Oh, so he *is* really tall, dark and handsome. How handsome is he?" I couldn't resist.

Katie exclaimed, "Christina!"

"What? I just want to know if he's cute. That's all," I smirked.

"Well, I think he is. He's actually mixed. His mom is white, and his dad is black." Morgan explained.

"So, I'm not the only one with secrets," I teased.

"It's not a secret. It's just that I don't go around stating the color of people's skin normally, but I thought you should know," Morgan spoke, motioning with her palms up.

"As long as you like him, Morgan, that's all that matters," Katie said.

"And your parents are okay with this?" Amy asked out of curiosity.

"They say they are, but they are concerned for me because interracial relationships can be challenging. Well, any relationship can be, but they think that being in a mixed relationship can cause extra problems."

I blurted, "They're right, you know. There's a lot of prejudice in this world, but it shouldn't matter what the color of their skin is. This is the 80s. People need to get with the times and accept people for who they are on the inside, not what they look like on the outside."

"Nicely stated, Christina," Katie praised.

"It's true, you know," I said, making eye contact with everyone.

"Well, unfortunately, many people don't agree with you," Morgan confirmed. "We get weird looks at school when we're together. It's not too bad in Inner Varsity, but outside of it, the stares are jarring."

At least you don't have people attacking you.

I had to ask, "Does anyone say anything?"

"Like to our faces?" She asked.

"Yeah," I replied because I wanted to know how brazen people were.

"No, but we do get looks like we should feel ashamed, especially when we're off campus together." Morgan looked sad, and I felt bad for her.

"Try not to let it bother you, although I'm sure it's not easy," I said.

"Well, my parents would kill me!" Katie declared. We all looked at her. Katie squirmed in her seat and shrugged, "I'm just saying."

Morgan waved her hands, "See what I mean?"

"I'm not suggesting you break up with him or anything," Katie said. "I mean, you're already going out with him. I just know my parents would flip. That's all," she ended with her mouth twisted.

With a crinkled nose, Amy stated, "Yeah, I don't think my parents would take too kindly to it either, come to think of it."

"What about your parents, Christina? What would they do?" Katie asked.

I thought about it for a second as I rubbed my chin. "Hum, I don't know. I don't think they would be too surprised though."

"Why wouldn't they be surprised?" Amy asked.

"I have always been more open-minded with these kinds of things. I think they might be concerned about the difficulties that may arise, like what Morgan said, but they would ultimately let me live my life the way I see fit. I think our parents have our best interests at heart, but they don't always know what's best for us. Only God knows what's best for us, and it's up to us to figure that out for ourselves."

To lighten the mood, Morgan laughed, "Well, on that note, who wants some popcorn?"

The evening was a success. I got to share my story and Morgan shared hers.

Before going to bed, I mulled over the following verse, "I will run the way of thy commandments, when thou shalt enlarge my heart" (Psalm 119:32).

On the verge of sleep, it became evident to me through all my struggles that God enlarges our hearts when He bestows wisdom upon us. *It's up to us to do God's will knowing He will grant His grace upon us.*

Chapter 12

A week went by since we gathered at Morgan's, and she was looking forward to introducing us to her boyfriend that she met at college. Since Katie had to work, it was just the four of us, Amy, Morgan, Derek, and me.

Morgan answered the door with a broad smile on her face. "Hey, Christina, come on in. Amy's not here yet." She motioned toward a tall, well-built guy. "Let me introduce you to Derek. Christina, this is Derek. Derek, this is my best friend, Christina."

"Hey, great to meet you. I finally get to meet the famous Christina,"

The famous part threw me off. I looked over at Morgan and turned back to Derek. "Well, I don't know what Morgan told you, but I'm not famous."

Did Morgan tell Derek about what happened to me? I took deep breaths in an attempt to hide my anxiety.

"Famous in that you're highly spoken of. Morgan told me what a good friend you are to her." He reassured me.

I smiled in return and said, "I'm the lucky one. Morgan is the best."

Morgan blushed and turned to me, "Alrighty then. Can I get you something to drink?"

"No, I'm good. Thanks," I answered.

After hearing a knock on the door, Morgan rushed over to answer it. Amy walked in, saw Derek and said, "You must be Derek. I'm Amy." She lunged at him and wrapped her arms around his thick waist. Derek stumbled back from Amy's unexpected force. She released her hug and said, "Any friend of Morgan's is a friend of mine."

"It's good to know Morgan has such good friends." He said with reservation.

"If you hurt her, I'll have to kill you," Amy said in jest.

Morgan shot me a look that didn't go unnoticed by Derek or Amy. Amy's hand flew to her mouth as she gasped.

All of a sudden, I felt nauseous, and the room began to spin. Derek grabbed hold of me before I hit the floor.

"Put her on the couch." Morgan commanded in a worried voice.

Derek scooped me up like I was a football and gingerly placed me on the couch.

It all happened so fast. Amy exclaimed, "Oh, my gosh, this is all my fault."

My body wouldn't move as I stared into space.

With a concerned tone in his voice, Derek asked, "Do we need to call an ambulance?"

"No, no. Give her some room. I'll get some water." Morgan ran into the kitchen and returned with a glass of water. "Here, Christina, drink this." Without hesitation, I took the glass from Morgan and took a sip. "How's that? Do you feel better?"

I managed a slight nod. Morgan sighed heavily.

"What happened? "What's going on?" Derek asked.

My mouth couldn't formulate any words. I sat there frozen, unable to move or speak.

I heard Morgan's voice again, "Christina, are you okay now?"

Again, I moved my head slightly up and down. There was a long pause before I said, "I'm fine."

"She doesn't look fine," Derek whispered.

"I'll be okay. Just give me a minute." I took another sip of the water.

Morgan knelt beside me. "Can I get you something else? A chocolate milkshake maybe?"

Yeah. A chocolate milkshake sounds great. Life is better with shakes. Nothing came out of my mouth for a moment. "I just need a few minutes."

"Okay. Let me know if you need anything. I'll be right here," Morgan said. She got up and sat on the couch next to me, but far enough away to give me breathing room. "Amy, Derek, why don't you sit down?"

On Morgan's command, Amy and Derek found their seats. I peeked over in their direction, curious to see how they reacted, yet I still couldn't speak.

Amy's freaking out. Is she biting her nails? Derek has no clue what's happening. His creamy cocoa colored skin turned to white chocolate. *I need to say something.* I couldn't formulate what to say. A few moments transpired, I sat up and said, "I'm okay now."

"Oh, thank God!" Amy said with relief and released her hand from the hold her mouth had on it.

I found my words again. "I'm sorry. I didn't mean to scare you."

Morgan tilted her head, "It's okay. We understand."

Derek admitted, "I'm glad you understand, because I don't."

Morgan shot Derek a look.

"It's okay. Let me explain," I said.

Morgan shook her head and leaned forward, "No, you don't have to explain. Really you don't."

"It's fine," I assured her.

I turned to Derek, "Derek, when I was at school before break…" *How do I tell my best friend's boyfriend I was…?* "I was…" My pulse started to race. I felt my body start to tremble. *Just say it.* "My next-door neighbor attacked me and held a knife to my throat…"

"I'm so sorry. I had no idea." He bowed his head after his eyes dashed to Morgan.

My best friend held up her hand, "I promised her I wouldn't tell anyone."

My mouth curved slightly upward as I glanced toward Morgan in appreciation for her keeping her word.

Considering my recent breakdown, I suggested, "Maybe it's better if people do know."

"Whatever you want is fine with me. If you don't want me to say anything, I won't," Morgan replied.

Amy piggy backed on what Morgan said, "That goes for me too." This time Amy sounded more convincing.

"I guess you should use your best judgment. I don't want to be a topic of conversation for sheer entertainment. Living with this nightmare is bad enough." I nervously brushed my hair behind my ears.

"We get it," Amy relayed.

"Yeah, we want to help you any way we can," Morgan said.

I looked at Derek and said, "I'm sorry about all this, Derek."

"Hey, don't worry about it. I'm glad you're okay now," he said, leaning over with his elbows on his thighs.

Morgan's dad made us milkshakes after coming home from dining out with Mrs. Ricci. Derek found my love for milkshakes amusing. "I never saw anyone so passionate about milkshakes," he stated.

"Oh, this is typical for Christina. Watching her drink a shake is better than the shake itself," Amy interjected.

I put my index finger over my mouth. "Shhh! Don't say that in front of the shake. Shakes have feelings too, you know," I joked.

Morgan's dad popped his head in the room. "So, how are those milkshakes?"

"Delicious as always, Mr. Ricci. You haven't lost your touch," I answered.

"I aim to please." With that, he departed, leaving us to enjoy his masterful culinary creation.

"So, Derek, do you play any sports?" The question was burning in my mind ever since I laid eyes on his muscular physique.

"Ah, I used to. I got injured playing football my first season in college."

"Aww, that's too bad," I replied.

"What did you injure?" Amy asked.

"My knee. I had to have surgery. It hasn't been the same ever since."

"So, you can't play anymore?" Amy asked.

He shrugged. "No, not on the collegiate level."

Amy volleyed another question, "Do you miss playing?"

Derek sat up straighter. "Not as much as I thought I would. I had so much free time on my hands this fall that I decided to join Inner Varsity. That's how Morgan and I met, and I couldn't be happier."

Amy gushed while Morgan turned bright red. "Aww, that's so sweet," responded Amy in her typical spirited manner.

Derek smiled. "Yeah, she turned things around for me. I was bummed out since I couldn't play anymore," he admitted.

"What do you do to stay in shape?" I couldn't resist asking.

"Christina!" Amy admonished me since Katie wasn't here.

Morgan cracked up as she rubbed her face up and down with her hands.

"What? I'm curious. He has to do something to look like that," I said, putting my hand on my bicep.

Derek rubbed his lips together. "Actually, I do. I lift weights."

"See, I told ya," I stuck my tongue out at Amy.

"Lovely," Morgan said sarcastically while we both giggled.

"And you use that tongue to sip milkshakes. Shame on you!" Amy joked.

"Yes, I do and will continue to," I stuck my tongue out at her again.

"You girls are…" Derek paused as we waited for him to finish. "Not what I expected," he said, shaking his head.

"Well, what's the fun in that?" I asked in a joking manner.

"I wouldn't have it any other way," Derek said with a wide smile as he glanced over to Morgan who was rubbing her face again as she chuckled.

The night ended upbeat in stark contrast to how it began. It was nice getting to know Derek and to see the fondness he had for Morgan.

Chapter 13

I noticed how much better I felt telling people about my rape, so I made an appointment to seek professional help. I started seeing a therapist named Dr. Frazer. The woman with caramel-colored shoulder length wavy hair labeled my outbursts. "You are experiencing panic attacks. Your symptoms can include your heart racing, uncontrollable sweating, trembling, and you may have difficulty breathing."

I cut in, "All those things happen to me."

"You have what's known as post-traumatic stress disorder or PTSD for short. It's common for people who have experienced a traumatic event like yourself to develop PTSD," she explained.

"Will I have PTSD forever?" I asked.

"Not necessarily. You can do some cognitive behavioral therapy if you want to. Keep in mind though, that it takes about ten to twelve sessions, and they should be done in a specific time frame, not spread out. If you decide to go back to school, I wouldn't recommend starting them now. You could try meditation and other relaxation techniques first." Dr. Frazer laid out my options.

"I started meditating again, but it's not helping," I said as I wrung my hands in my lap.

"Perhaps I can recommend a therapist at school for you?" She offered.

I don't want therapy to interfere with my schoolwork. "No, that's okay. Maybe it will go away. That's possible, right?" I asked with hopefulness for the first time in weeks.

"Yes, it's possible but unlikely without proper treatment." She was anything but blunt, that's for sure. *Not exactly the reaffirming words I had hoped for.*

I went to therapy a couple more times. During one of those sessions, Dr. Frazer guided me through the use of visual therapy where my mind created a safe place that made me feel calm and relaxed. Her voice was so soothing and calming as I went through the guided imagery exercise, but in the end I continued to have nightmares and episodes. I did manage to minimize my attacks by breathing slower. I learned to count to five while inhaling and then count to five again upon exhaling.

At first, I wasn't going to return to school after winter break, but I felt a certain resolve after discussing it with my therapist.

"Ultimately, it's up to you, Christina. No one will blame you for not going back to school. What you went through was very traumatic. Try not to be so hard on yourself. Give yourself some grace."

Grace.

I decided to face the embarrassment of being the girl who got raped and was almost killed by the guy who eventually committed suicide. Not exactly every girl's dream.

The head of the tutoring department with whom I had become good friends, told me about a counseling program that I could go through and for which I could possibly get credit. We worked it out that in the beginning of the semester, I would write about my experience and share my story with local churches, schools, and organizations. This would count as a public speaking class as well as provide some emotional therapeutic healing in the process.

The psychology department informed me that if I wrote a separate journal about my public speaking experience and how it helped me heal, I could earn another three credits.

Through this experience, I was able to earn a total of six credits, which was two fifths of my semester credits. This was not a typical way for college students to earn credits, but the exception was made for me, and I accepted it with tremendous gratitude.

I was able to fill in the other three classes with basic requirements, keeping me on track for graduation. At this point I was still undeclared in my major. It was more of a challenge for me to figure out what to major in than it was to speak in public. *What crazy person finds it easier to speak in public than to pick a major? Me, that's who. Pinball machine crazy, here I am again!*

The serious nature of the content of my speeches proved critical in my ability and willingness to perform effectively in public. When I spoke to the churches, I incorporated a Christian component to make my experience especially relevant to believers. I talked about calling on the Lord in my most desperate time of need and how the Lord granted my prayers of rescue.

I frequently quoted Psalm 46:1, "God is our refuge and strength, an ever-present help in trouble." It was by the grace of God that Jake was intuitive enough to realize what his demented roommate was up to and then to follow through with his suspicions.

Chapter 14

ake's secret date spot became a crime scene for which he harbored the worst guilt. Jake struggled with his inner demons, blaming himself for my rape. "It's all my fault, Christina! I'm so sorry!" he repeated in distress.

He claimed that if he didn't brag about where he took his dates, Ryan would never have had a convenient, secluded place to rape me. Jake never intended Ryan to know about his secret spot, but nonetheless, Ryan found out through their envious roommates.

I persisted, "Jake, it's not your fault. I don't blame you for what happened. If it weren't for you, I would probably be dead." We all knew those words to be true.

Not wanting Jake to harbor guilt, I shared the gospel with him as I had numerous times before, but this time it took. Jake had become a believer. *Another person will enter the kingdom of heaven as Jake's name is written on the book of life! Praise God!*

Jake changed his ways too. No more picking up girls and dismissing them shortly thereafter. He declared that he was committed to being in a serious relationship and vowed to respect women.

My relationship with Jake remained platonic. My three neighbors, Jake, Bob, and Tony continued to look out for me. I felt blessed to have a group of guys care so deeply for my well-being.

I found out that Bob and Tony both grew up in Christian homes and found their way back to the straight and narrow as their eyes were opened again to God's goodness.

The hard part was never knowing if I would run into Ryan's frat brothers. During my first week back, I was walking along the cement pathway from my last class of the day on my way back to my apartment on campus, when two guys recognized me. One of them said, "Hey, isn't that the girl who killed Ryan?"

My feet couldn't move fast enough without running. "Yeah, that's her. Hey, you!" They started to chase after me, and I bolted into the Union Building hoping I could outrun them. I dashed behind the information center/candy store and squatted down with my finger over my lips.

Joanne McHugh, a woman with short gray hair who managed the store, knew me from my freshman days as a senator and nodded. She was the staff member who supervised the Student Handbook committee that I led as a Freshman senator. *Thank you God for having me work with Joanne on publishing the student handbook for this year's edition.*

When I first met Joanne as the information clerk, she scared me with her usual curt responses and sour puss facial expressions, which was not ideal for a welcoming position, nor did it seem fitting for a clerk doling out candy. It wasn't until we worked together that she shared her faith with me, and we bonded through our Christian beliefs.

The guys came in and one of them yelled to the stern candy lady, "Did you see a girl come running in here?" She nodded again. "Where did she go?"

"She ran upstairs," she replied without giving me away.

As soon as they took off upstairs, I thanked Joanne, strapped my backpack to my shoulders, and ran as fast as I could to my apartment. I didn't dare look back but kept a quick pace. *Lord, please let me get to my apartment safely.* From a few yards away I saw my roommate Linda open the door, and I screamed, "Don't shut the door!" The door automatically locked when you closed it, and I didn't want to dig for my key. Without any explanation to Linda, I ran into our bedroom, threw my backpack on the floor, dove on my bed, and cried my eyes out. Once I calmed down, I told Linda what happened.

"That's awful! I can't believe how deranged they are to accuse you of killing him. Maybe you should go to the police. Just in case. You know, so they at least have a record of it. I'll go with you," she suggested like any criminal justice major would.

I decided that it was a good idea to notify the police. The evening I was in the hospital when I made my statement to the police, they said that I should have reported Ryan harassing me.

Another time I was standing in line at the cafeteria during lunch with Jake when I recognized the guys who chased after me. Jake looked at me and said, "You look like you saw a ghost. What's wrong?"

I sucked in a deep long breath as I counted to five and then exhaled another five seconds. Jake knew about my episodes, so he patiently awaited my response.

"They're the guys that chased after me," I said as discreetly as possible.

"Are you going to be okay? We can sit down if you need to."

I shook my head because I didn't want them to have any more power over me. The breathing helped that time.

The guys started screaming and pointing at me, "Yo, that's the girl that killed Ryan!" People began looking around while I ducked my head. Since I realized I was being obvious, I tried to act nonchalant.

With his hands, Jake gently drew my head upward and said in a soft tone, "Focus on me, Christina. Just look at me. Breathe slowly. That's it. You're doing great." Jake had a way of calming me. If anyone else was there, I would have freaked out.

I heard someone else say, "Are you friends with that scumbag that raped and held a knife to that girl?"

"You don't know what you're talking about!" yelled one of the frat boys.

"Look, man, knock it off and leave the girl alone, or you have all of us to contend with. Got it!?"

Then I heard other voices shout, "Leave her alone!" "Yeah, leave her alone!"

I whispered to Jake, "Who are those guys that defended me?"

After trying to get a better look at them, Jake shook his head and said, "I have no idea." I took a peek and saw that it was Matt, Caleb, and Jeff. *Well, I'll be darned.* "Who are they, Christina?"

"Guys I met last year."

"How well do you know them?"

"I haven't spoken to them since the beginning of the school year last year."

"Lucky for you, you made some kind of an impression on them." I nodded. *Lucky for me. Maybe I won't have nightmares tonight thanks to them and Jake.*

There was another incident. I went grocery shopping at the local supermarket with my roommate Cassie, since she only had a meal plan for lunch. She was pushing her grocery cart outside when it got snagged on something. She lunged forward with the cart and bumped a guy. "I'm so sorry. My cart hit a bump. I didn't mean to hit you," she said.

He said, "Next time be more careful." He turned to me and started screaming, "You're the girl who killed Ryan!"

He came after me and Cassie grabbed the Mace on her keychain and sprayed him.

"Ahhhhhh!" he yelled bloody murder.

Cassie yelled at my accuser, "That'll teach you not to mess with someone who lives near New York City."

A security guard came out and whisked the guy away as witnesses stated he came after me.

I shared every bit of my experience and my relationships with the church groups and in my journal. In it of itself, I saw and reaped the therapeutic advantages of disclosing everything concerning that dark, menacing night in the woods, the episodes leading up to it and the aftermath, including how I was harassed by the fraternity brothers and experienced ongoing nightmares and panic attacks.

When I meditated on the following verse, I imagined a hedge of protection surrounding me to get me through the constant turmoil I suffered, "We are troubled on every side, yet not distressed; we are perplexed, but not in despair; Persecuted, but not forsaken; cast down, but not destroyed" (2 Corinthians 4:8-9).

Chapter 15

I finished my spring semester sophomore year at Sylvania Ridge and furthered my speaking engagements at local churches in my hometown during summer break, wanting to offer hope for those who were in despair.

I often quoted Jeremiah 17:14, "Heal me, O Lord, and I shall be healed; save me, and I shall be saved: for thou art my praise."

My healing was emotional in part, and I constantly reminded myself that Christ delivered me through a violent and traumatic time, and that thanks to Him I have eternal life for which I must voice my praise.

Thank you, God, for keeping me safe and for providing me with tools to help me heal. Give me the strength and guidance to help others who struggle with pain, whether it be physical, emotional, mental, or spiritual.

A few days after I came home for the summer, I walked into the local Catholic church, St. Jude's, to give one of my talks. I described my account of how I was raped and was moments away from a violent death at the hand of my next-door neighbor in the woods of my college campus.

Afterwards a petite woman with short dark hair approached me. As she drew closer, I realized she was my neighbor from around the corner, Mrs. Carlisle. My cousin Jessie was best friends with her daughter.

Mrs. Carlisle smiled and asked, "Hi, Christina. How are you?"

"Hi, Mrs. Carlisle. I'm well. Thanks. How are you doing?" Even though Mrs. Carlisle and I seldom spoke before, I felt like I knew her through her daughter Sherrie. Sherrie and Jessie spent a lot of time together, and we all lived in the same neighborhood. I could see the resemblance between mother and daughter. They both had thick, dark curly brown hair with a light complexion.

"Well, it's good to see you, although I wish it weren't under these circumstances. I knew you would be speaking, so I made a point to be here." I waited because it appeared as if she had something on her mind to share. "You are very brave to talk about your experience." She shook her head and closed her eyes. I could tell she was struggling with something. "You know my daughter, Sherrie, right?"

"Yes, of course. She and Jessie are best friends," I acknowledged.

My neighbor's lips formed a thin line across her face. "Yes, well, perhaps you heard then." She paused for a brief second and with glassy eyes, she stated, "Sherrie was raped by Paul Martin."

I felt the blood drain from my face. "Oh my… I had no idea. I'm so sorry." I struggled to get the words out. I wanted to run and scream, but it wasn't about me. It was about Sherrie. *Breathe. One, two, three, four, five. Exhale. One, two, three, four, five.*

"Well, Sherrie stopped eating after it happened a couple years ago. She's still anorexic, but we're keeping a close eye on her. Anyway, we didn't know the cause of it until she was near death, and she finally told her therapist. The therapist strongly advised she tell us. I'm so thankful she did, because it seems like it was the first step in her making any progress."

"I'm terribly sorry. I knew nothing about this," I somehow managed to hold back my tears, anger, and disgust.

"Anyway, I wanted Sherrie to come today to listen to you speak, but she wouldn't come. I wish she did. You are very inspiring. I wish Sherrie had your faith." Mrs. Carlisle paused and turned away to stave off her tears.

"Thank you." I didn't know what else to say. My mind was a series of fleeting thoughts. *This is my fault. If I had told someone that Paul raped me, he wouldn't have raped Sherrie.* My emotions were an unfortunate mix of negative feelings. Anger, guilt, sorrow, hate, and regret held me captive.

Mrs. Carlisle placed her hand on my arm. "Oh, dear, I didn't mean to upset you. Honestly, I'm not sure why—Do you think it would be too much trouble to talk to Sherrie?" She rubbed her hands together. "You know, help her heal?" She pleaded with me, her eyes welled up with tears.

"Uh, sure. I'd be happy to help her in any way," I assured her with an affirmative head bob. *It's the least I could do since this is my fault.*

"Oh, good, good. Perhaps I can call you sometime to stop in when I think it would be a good time for you to talk with her," she said hopefully.

"That would be fine. No problem at all. Call anytime," I replied, meaning every word.

I couldn't get home fast enough. After getting on my running gear, I flew out the door as I needed to run off the guilt I felt for causing Sherrie's rape. The early afternoon sun was very persistent, so I decided to take a scenic route along the river trail where it provided coverage from the sun. Pacing myself was key in order to provide enough energy to return home. *Slow and steady wins the race, but I'm not racing. Far from it. What am I doing? Distracting myself. Burning off all this negative energy. Just keep going. Keep running.* There were tons of people on the trail, cyclists, runners, walkers, dog walkers. *No wonder I don't run here. There's no place to scream privately. I need to scream!*

It's all my fault. I should have told someone. Anyone. It never occurred to me that he would rape someone else. I thought it was personal. He blamed me for his mother's breakdown. How could he do that to Sherrie? She was only twelve. My God. I was only thirteen. What if he raped someone else? NOOOOOO! My hands folded over my head as I found myself in an overgrown path. Slowing to a dead stop, I looked up at the towering trees surrounding me and searched for answers. *How many lives did Paul ruin?* Tears poured down my cheeks. My shaken body nearly collapsed save for my hands resting on my thighs. *Sherrie. Oh God. How long has Jessie known? He could have raped Jessie instead.* A dry heave escaped my body. *Paul Martin is a monster. He should be behind bars. Why wasn't he? Lord, what can I do to make this right? Let me help Sherrie somehow. Please God...*

Every moment was torture knowing I was the reason Sherrie was raped. My heart felt like a tree fell on it. I prayed for Sherrie every chance I got. Her cute little face was painted in my memory, except I pictured her in anguish, the way I was after Paul raped me. I considered begging for her forgiveness, but what good would that do? *What's done is done.* It didn't make sense to tell anyone at this point. My secret was safe after all these years, so why not keep it that way? They knew about Sherrie's rape. My rape wouldn't matter. It would look like I was a magnet for rapists. *It's bad enough that people knew about the rape at college. I would look like a total freak if everyone knew about rape number one as well. They would think that I asked for it—like Paul said. I never asked for it. I didn't deserve to be raped. Sherrie didn't deserve to be raped either. No one does.*

The nightmares returned with vehemence. *I was jogging toward The Blue Lagoon swim club when I heard screaming. I followed the screaming along the brook adjacent to the swim club. As I got closer to the distressing sounds, I could see a boy straddled on top of someone. A quick shift of his body allowed me to see the other body's face. It was Jessie, my sweet little cousin, and he had a knife to her throat the same way frat boy had to me.*

Jolted by the sight of my cousin being assaulted, I woke up in a beaded sweat with my heart racing. I attempted to pray myself back to sleep per usual, but my mind refused to settle. My usual techniques to lull myself back to sleep were failing me. Without any effort, familiar and calming songs played in my head. The lyrics to "Awesome God" by Rich Mullins filled between my ears. The chorus is what I imagine angels sounding like in heaven. Envisioning being surrounded and protected by angels, I dozed off into a deep and peaceful slumber.

Chapter 16

A few days passed when I received a phone call from Mrs. Carlisle. I went right over to her house around the corner. I prayed along the way that I could help Sherrie. *Dear Lord, help me say the right words to Sherrie. Allow me to be a good witness to her. Let me help her in any way I can.*

Mrs. Carlisle came to the door a second after I rang the doorbell. She appeared frazzled from the moment she answered the door. "Oh, Christina, thank goodness you're here. Sherrie just had a meltdown. Do you mind talking to her? She's upstairs in her bedroom, second door on the right."

I nodded and climbed the staircase, not knowing what to expect. Knock, knock. "Sherrie, it's Christina. I came to talk to you or listen. Whatever you want." I waited a moment and considered walking away when the door opened.

"Hey, come in," Sherrie motioned with her head for me to enter her bedroom.

"Thanks."

Sherrie plopped down on her bed with a sigh and folded her arms. "I know my mom called you. She thinks you're some kind of spiritual guru or something."

"Well, I don't know anything about that, but I'm here if you need a sounding board. I'm a good listener," I said in a sweet and reassuring tone.

I hadn't seen Sherrie in years. Taller and paler with long curly dark hair, she was all but skin and bones. Her frail and ghostly appearance gave me the chills. *I did this to her. Dear Lord, give me the words...*

"So, you know what it's like—to be—you know..." She bobbed her head for me to fill in the unspoken words, the words she refused to say, the same words I couldn't say for years. Those unspoken words bonded us. They brought us together but destroyed us at the same time.

I sat down at the edge of Sherrie's bed. "Yeah, I know," I said at a low volume.

The white curtains were drawn, blocking all the natural light. Her room was exceptionally tidy. Nothing was out of place, including all her colorful stuffed animals displayed on a white bench. Posters of teen idols like Corey Haim from the *Lost Boys* hung on her walls. Shivers ran through me thinking of vampires and their darkness, even though I knew it was fantasy. I made a point not to watch those type of movies. I couldn't risk the sinister themes seeping in my subconscious.

Out of nowhere, Sherrie asked, "How do you do it?"

I turned to give Sherrie my full attention. "Do what?" I asked.

"Live."

My heart stopped beating that instant. *Lord, give me the words.* Expelling the long breath I didn't even realize I held, I replied, "Jesus." My response came out without thinking.

"What do you mean, Jesus?" Sherrie asked as she tucked back a curl that popped out of place.

"Sherrie, I came to know Jesus when I was about your age. People told me about Him. They told me that Jesus died on the cross for our sins." My words seemed to come forth without thinking.

Sherrie sighed heavily. "I know the story," she stated with resignation in her voice.

"Well, do you believe it? Did you accept Jesus in your heart?" I questioned with an intentional tenderness as I spoke.

Sherrie gave a dismissive wave of her hand. "I guess not, because I don't have what you have."

"Do you want what I have?" I asked her. *Please God, let me help Sherrie.* I never sensed such despair in a person before. Her plea for help was silent but desperate, almost palpable.

Sherrie began to cry and said through her sobs, "I w-want what you have. I want to be h-happy. I-I want to live a-a normal life. I feel like I-I'm in a fog all the time. I'm s-sick of living l-like this." She wiped away her tears with the back of her hand.

"I promise you it gets better with Jesus. You have to have faith. Your problems don't magically disappear, but with the help of Christ, you will get through this," I encouraged her with the sort of conviction one develops through experience.

With a look of despondency, Sherrie pleaded, "C-can you help me g-get there?"

"Do you want to ask Jesus into your heart?" I asked without breaking eye contact.

With a few swipes of her hand, Sherrie wiped the sloppy mess off her cheeks, took a deep breath, and replied, "Yes, can you tell me how?"

My heart smiled, and I nodded. "Okay, then repeat after me." I placed my hand on Sherrie's pale arm and bowed my head. "Heavenly Father, I know that I am a sinner, and I want your forgiveness."

Sherrie repeated, "I know that I am a sinner, and I want your forgiveness."

I continued, "I believe your son Jesus died on the cross for my sins and then rose from the dead."

Sherrie echoed my words. "I believe your son Jesus died on the cross for my sins and then rose from the dead."

The words flowed out of me with ease. "Help me not to sin again. I invite you into my heart and to do your will as I accept you as my Lord and Savior."

"Help me not to sin again..." She gasped.

I repeated, "I invite you into my heart."

"I invite you into my heart," she parroted.

I went on, "And to do your will as I accept you as my Lord and Savior."

"And to do your will as I accept you as my Lord and Savior," she repeated.

I squeezed Sherrie's arm to let her know I was finished. She looked up at me with her big brown eyes. "Is that it?"

"That's it," I said with delight.

A smile broke through Sherrie's once distressed exterior. She tilted her head and laughed. "I kinda feel different."

"You do? How?" I asked, even though I already noticed a difference in her.

"I feel… like a bowling ball was lifted off me." She smiled as her face glowed.

"Yeah, that's about right." I reassured her.

With another smile Sherrie said, "Thanks."

"You're welcome." I related to Sherrie's metaphor and felt the same way after witnessing her transformation.

"I feel like I should tell my mom, since she's been so worried about me and all."

"That's a good idea," I said to encourage her.

Sherrie leaped off her bed, opened the door, and yelled, "Mom!" I could hear her mom running up the stairs.

"What is it, Sherrie? Are you okay?" Mrs. Carlisle asked in a panic.

"Yeah, Mom. Never better." She glanced my way, then turned back to her mother with a reassuring smile.

With relief and hope in her voice, Mrs. Carlisle responded, "Really?" as she lovingly cupped her daughter's face.

"Really, Mom." They hugged each other, and I could sense the love and joy from across the room.

Sherrie's mom's face lit up. Her eyes began to well up. "Can you tell me what brought on this sudden change?"

"Jesus," Sherrie answered. Mrs. Carlisle's glassy eyes released their tears. These were welcomed tears, tears I imagined that replaced the many tears that were spilled out of the sorrow, pain, confusion, doubt, and fear she experienced out of the love and empathy she had for her daughter.

At that moment, I felt like bursting with pride, but pride had no room there. It was all Jesus. Sherrie would continue to need therapy, but now she had a solid rock to cling to. She would be fine.

God's love was so powerful that I could feel the warmth of His Son radiating in the Carlisle home as mother and daughter embraced, rejoicing in newfound peace and joy. "And we have known and believed the love that God hath to us. God is love; and he that dwelleth in love dwelleth in God, and God in him" (1 John 4:16).

Chapter 17

No matter what I did I couldn't rid myself of the guilt I felt for Sherrie's rape. I felt responsible. At least she was saved now. *God works wonders.*

Avery's church, Pennsford Methodist, invited me to speak. I never spoke to an entire congregation during a regular service. I tended to speak at women's Bible studies or groups of women teenage years and older. This time I spoke to a woman's group.

I walked to my gray Honda Civic after my speaking engagement. Avery was in the forefront of my mind because of going to his church that we once attended together, the church where I became saved, where my life became anew.

My charm bracelet, another reminder of my once sweet boyfriend, was clanging and glistening in the sun on this warm summer day. I felt compelled to wear the thoughtful gift that Avery gave me for my fourteenth birthday during our first year together. I stopped wearing it after we broke up because the memory of Avery was too painful to bear.

I was afraid I would burst into tears every time I looked at it. These days it didn't matter if I cried. Rather it was expected, so I put it on.

More charms had been added to it since that birthday and Christmas. In addition to the C for Christina, the rose for De Rosa, the cross from Christmas, the heart for Valentine's Day, and the lock and key from our last summer together, Avery gave me a charm that said "Italian Princess". It came with a crown and a four-leaf clover with double implication, my maternal Irish heritage and good luck. *Well, so much for good luck!* Maybe it meant, "Good luck dealing with everything after I rip your heart out."

I watched the charms sparkle in the sunlight as I strolled along the parking lot. I smiled a toothless grin and sighed with relief. I no longer cried when I looked at it, a sure sign that I was stronger. My thoughts were diverted as I approached my car.

"Christina," a vaguely familiar voice called. I turned around to find Avery Evans standing before me. He wore aviator sunglasses which concealed much of his face, but his voice gave him away. It was an octave or two lower but recognizable. "Christina, do you have a minute?"

My mind was aflutter. My stomach sank to the ground. *A minute? Did I have a minute? After all these years, did I have a minute?* Part of me wanted to tell him to go somewhere, but I knew that wasn't the right thing to do. After all, I was in a church parking lot, after giving a talk about going to God amid the midst of challenges. I felt my heart quicken, my breathing labored.

"I suppose so," I managed to spit out with the sun beaming down on my face.

I scanned Avery from head to toe and couldn't help but think how attractive he was. I hadn't seen him up close in years.

He had filled out and was broader for sure. His fair hair was a couple of shades darker, and he wore prominent sideburns. Once again, my thoughts were interrupted by Avery's deeper voice.

"Well, I was kind of hoping you had more than a minute." He stood there about six foot two and determination exuded from him.

I craned my neck towards him. Looking at him was almost like being blinded by the sun. It was tempting to look at, but permanent damage was imminent if you stared too long. Like getting your heart broken.

"What did you have in mind exactly?" I asked, giving a sideways glance.

"Can we go for a cup of coffee?"

I couldn't help but take his question literally. "I don't drink coffee," I replied. *Don't look directly at him! Avert your eyes!*

"Do you still drink milkshakes?" he grinned, showing off his pearly whites.

An unintentional smile drew across my face. His quirky question made me feel a little more at ease. "Yes, I do. I still drink milkshakes." *I run 15 miles a week to accommodate my milkshake habit.*

"Some things never change." He took off his sunglasses. He gazed at me with those gorgeous Caribbean Sea blue eyes that shimmered in the early afternoon sun.

"Don't look at me like that," I blurted without meaning to speak aloud. *Those eyes. I can't resist those bottomless pools of blue.*

I went weak in the knees. *How dare you bewitch me with those enchanting eyes?* I tried to compose myself. *What is wrong with me?*

"I'm sorry. I didn't mean… It's just that I heard you were speaking here, and I wanted to… I was hoping to…" I looked at him with a blank stare on my face. "You look beautiful."

Where did that come from? He had the nerve after all these years to waltz up to me and tell me I look beautiful, as if we should pick up where we left off before he shattered my heart into a million pieces. I was stunned. Speechless.

I replied, "Thanks, I should get going." I turned away from the enticing windows to his soul to get into my Honda, to make a clean break.

"Christina, wait!" Avery called with urgency. Taking my time, I turned around. "Please!" He captured my attention again like the sun had when I wanted to get a tan; even though I risked getting burnt, I still took the chance to acquire that deep golden hue. "I came here to tell you why I did what I did."

"You mean, why you dumped me?" I retorted.

"Why I let you go!" I hadn't thought about it like that. Avery looked and sounded sincere, almost desperate. Desperate and determined. *What is going on here?*

My heart pounded out of my chest. Of course, I was curious to know what happened, but what difference did it make now?

I examined him more closely. What stood before me was not a 16-year-old boy, but a young man. Avery still flaunted boyish good looks, and he aged exceptionally well.

"Okay, so tell me," I said, wondering what he could possibly say to justify his actions from almost four years ago when he broke up with me with no explanation.

"How about over a milkshake?" He suggested with a hopeful look. *Again, with the milkshake.* I knew what he was doing. He wanted me to be relaxed, and I was never more relaxed and happy than I was when I was slumped over a milkshake. *Life is better with a milkshake.*

"You can tell me now," I replied, attempting to resist the temptations dangling before me.

"Please, the shake is on me," Avery pleaded as his ocean blues danced in the sunlight. *Look away!*

How could I resist both—Avery's gorgeous blue eyes and a chocolate milkshake? I looked around the parking lot to see a few church goers walking to their cars. My head was spinning like a toy top.

With a huge sigh, I surrendered. "Okay. Fine." *Now what?*

While indulging in a thick chocolate milkshake and juicy cheeseburger at the diner, a former familiar meal and setting for Avery and me, Avery divulged all. The look of determination returned to his face, so I braced myself for what was to come.

Avery began by telling me it all started with the youth group. At first it was fantastic. It was a fun, safe, innocent, social gathering for Christian youths.

Then one day a boy named Walt from another school showed Avery an adult magazine with naked photographs of women. At first Avery stared at the pictures, not knowing what to do or say. It didn't take long before he became controlled by the pages inside.

Avery started hanging out with Walt more, and more and they began watching adult films on television at Walt's house. He even showed Avery how to hook up his cable to receive the same type of shows. Avery was all set up in his soundproof basement to watch X-rated shows on his television without his parents knowing.

The year was 1984. Avery had turned 16 that year in January, our sophomore year. It was sometime in May and baseball season was over, so Avery had time on his hands.

Avery sat there day after day, hour after hour hypnotized by the images he saw on the screen. "I couldn't stay away. I found myself completely engrossed," he admitted after taking a big slurp of milkshake.

I took a bite of my sumptuous burger. The hot melted American cheese hit the spot as it made its way to my awaiting stomach. I listened without interrupting, while recounting our relationship during the time of the seduction. Avery claimed he needed time to catch up on schoolwork, since baseball had previously taken up much of his time. In between bites of his cheeseburger, Avery said, "I know I told you that I had to study and stuff, but in actuality my grades went down, because I was constantly watching porn." This became a ritual over the next month and throughout the summer. We were going out that entire time! *How could you?!*

My chest started to constrict, hearing Avery describe the beginning of his destruction, and I had no idea any of that was happening at the time. I found myself wondering where the story was headed, knowing where it ultimately led him, us.

He continued with his narrative as I chomped on seasoned French fries. Back then Avery reminded himself of his pledge to remain a virgin until marriage, how it was an effort to remain chaste.

One typical day in the summer, Avery thought he was alone in the house. His mother walked down the stairs to find Avery in a compromised position. Aghast, Mrs. Evans screamed, "Avery, what are you doing? What are you watching? Turn that off right now! Right now, Avery! How could you do something so despicable while watching that filth?!"

I tried not to show any reaction as the tale unfolded, so as not to interrupt Avery's flow. I found my eating a fattening meal comforting while my first love explained his reasons for ripping my heart out.

Shame fell over Avery when his mother discovered him for what she considered defiling himself as he watched pornography. The corners of Avery's mouth took a dive before he said, "Seeing my mom react like that caused me to reevaluate my life." Avery clarified that it wasn't the act he was doing that caused him shame while he was watching the X-rated program, as much as it was being controlled by the porn. However, his mother's reaction gave him pause to take a look at his attitude and behavior, and he eventually came to realize that he had a major problem with pornography.

That was the beginning of the end for Avery watching pornography. He would sneak in some magazines, but his parents kept a diligent watch over him. While wiping ketchup off his mouth, he hung his head, shaking it like he wanted to shake away a shameful memory. "Yeah, I got busted when my mom found my porn stash under my mattress. She flipped out all over again." His head dropped like a lead weight pushed it down.

Hearing the story made me quiver with disgust. My stomach felt queasy with disdain. Perhaps the greasy burger and fries didn't agree with my stomach after all.

At that point, I asked Avery if it was necessary for me to hear all the gory details. He insisted it was. It was important for him to explain everything to me. I listened to every painful facet of how my then 16-year-old boyfriend was addicted to porn while shoveling fry after fry down my throat.

As it turned out, Avery had addictive tendencies and feared he would eventually become a sex addict. Knowing this, Avery broke it off with me to keep me pure, to protect me. Little did he know that I was already tainted.

He explained his actions further for my benefit as well as his. "I just couldn't involve you in this vicious cycle, so I had to break it off with you." He glanced downward and wrung his hands together, meeting me with his eyes. "I felt so ashamed. I couldn't bear to tell you what happened. I couldn't even look you in the eye, which is why I copped out and enrolled in Pennsford Christian." His lips drew a thin line. "I know what you're thinking."

My eyes bulged at his assumption. "You do?" I asked. I didn't even know what I was thinking. So many thoughts darted through my mind, fleeting and jumbled as they were.

Turning his hands palm up, Avery proceeded with his explanation. "Yeah, like what's the big deal? It's only porn. Like I could just snap," he snapped his fingers for effect, "out of it and have my life back, but that's just it." He shook his head. "I couldn't go back to the way things were." He raked his hair with his fingertips. "I wimped out. I changed schools because I couldn't face you or my friends. I was a coward."

His head hung low for a split second and then raised it to where we remained eye level to each other. "I convinced myself that I would grow in the Lord if I went to Pennsford Christian Academy." He shifted in his seat yet kept his full focus on me. "It was my way of restitution. I did my best to start a new life."

I was beginning to understand and remained quiet to prevent any distractions.

I watched Avery's eyes roll back as I chewed my cheeseburger. He took another sip of his milkshake and said, "I even told Joey to take a hike. He figured out for the most part what happened." He bobbed his head back and forth as well as sideways and grimaced. "I gotta give Joey a lot of credit. He was a lot swifter than I initially gave him credit for, but you probably already knew that."

There was a sadness in his eyes upon saying, "I know you two went out. I saw you a few times at his house. I also heard about it through the grapevine. Erin kept me updated at church and youth group, so I know you and Joey went to Prom and the Senior Ball together. Then something happened. You two broke up, but I never found out why." Avery stopped talking and became motionless.

I dipped my fry in ketchup, not feeling the need to tell Avery why Joey and I broke up just yet, if at all. I thought about how Avery not only hurt me but also Joey.

Avery munched on his cheeseburger as he stroked his furrowed brow. His forehead wrinkled enough to hold a straw in it. He swallowed hard and said, "I heard you went to Sylvania Ridge and then I heard about..." He hesitated again, practically choking on his words. His lips pierced. "I'm so sorry, Christina."

I didn't know if Avery meant my rape or the devastating effect he had on me when we broke up. I saw the deep suffering across his face. His cheeks tightened, his hands quivered. Tears welled up in his eyes.

Avery wiped his hands on a napkin and sat up straight. "I'm sorry about everything. I'm sorry for watching all that porn. I'm sorry for lying to you. I'm sorry for not coming clean sooner. I'm sorry someone else hurt you in such a despicable way. I hope you can find it in your heart to forgive me." I watched as the tears fell down his contrite face. He tilted his head downward and took a moment to compose himself, wiping away the tears of remorse.

Watching my former love sob before me messed with my composure. Unable to maintain my emotional distance, I choked up as he yanked on my heart strings. Knowing the risk, I let him in. Again. No longer could I contain my emotions. I felt the wetness of the tears stream down my cheeks. It felt good to release the dam.

Avery's once familiar gaze was upon me, only this time there was a distinct look of shame and regret. His blue eyes turned a brighter hue while the whites of his eyes turned red from crying.

After witnessing Avery bare his soul, I could no longer remain reserved. On impulse, I reached out to hold Avery's trembling hands. Through squinted eyes, Avery seemed to notice the charm bracelet but made no mention of it.

Instead, his voice quavered. "Please forgive me, Christina. I am in counseling now for my pornography addiction, and part of my therapy is to explain what I have done to those I have hurt and seek their forgiveness. I have asked God to forgive me, and now I'm asking you."

I was dumbfounded. I didn't know what to say or how to react, but I knew for Avery's sake I had to give him my undivided attention. I was still hurt, even after all this time, and especially since hearing his reason for shattering my heart in pieces. However, I loved him deeply. Still. After all those years. Even after I heard his story of his porn addiction.

I recalled how the Bible teaches us to forgive others as God forgives us.

"Forbearing one another and forgiving one another, if any man have a quarrel against any: even as Christ forgave you, so also do ye" (Colossians 3:13).

I squeezed Avery's hands and looked directly into his soul. "Avery, I forgive you," I gasped in between sobs, then wiped away my tears.

Chapter 18

*A*n urgent need to run surged through my body at daybreak. I bolted out of bed, laced up my running shoes, and pulled my hair up in a ponytail with a black scrunchie. *Avery.* I couldn't get him out of my mind. Visions of his handsome visage kept me company all night. The more I tried to erase him from my mind, the more persistent his presence became. I even dreamed about him.

Avery was riding a beautiful white horse as he called my name with urgency, "Christina, grab onto me!" I held out my hand and just like that I was whisked onto the galloping creature. I leaned forward and wrapped my arms around Avery's waist and nestled into him, holding on for dear life. I watched as the green landscape quickly passed before my eyes in the open field as we headed for trees along the horizon. The boisterous sound of our transportation was somehow comforting as we raced to the tree line.

The mere memory of this caused my pace to quicken. My heart rate increased as well, and beads of sweat fell from my forehead and stung my eyes.

We entered the thick dark forest with a canter. I leaned back and took in the beauty of the majestic, wooded surroundings. We arrived at a clearing and were greeted by a pond that glinted from the sparkling rays of sunlight. Avery dismounted the horse and held out his hand for me to take hold. I fell into his arms, our lips landing within an inch apart from each other. We remained motionless, entertaining the possibilities and willing for the moment to never cease. A tingling sensation fell over me as I realized that I was literally swept away.

I gasped for air and suddenly stopped dead in my tracks. Leaning forward to catch my breath, I couldn't shake the feeling of being in love.

I've had worse dreams, but I needed to get over him. Why did he have to come into the picture again?

I opened my eyes and stood up to discover Avery standing in front of me. *Is my mind playing tricks on me?* In disbelief, I blinked several times to confirm what stood before me, and it became evident that every part of my crevices was oozing sweat.

"What are you doing here?" I asked in disbelief that the object of my dream materialized before me in the flesh.

"I saw you running." He lifted his shoulders in explanation.

"You saw me running?" I asked incredulously.

"Yeah, when I was mowing the lawn."

After taking in my surroundings, I realized I was about a block away from Avery's house. *I never went this way alone on a jog before.*

"Why don't we grab some breakfast at my house? I'm sure my parents would love to see you." He suggested as if he were offering me a piece of candy.

What?! "Uh, no. I don't think so." I smelled rancid.

"Why not? You used to come over all the time."

"That was when we were dating. We're not dating." I explained.

He put on a huge, beguiling smile. "Come on. I'll say we ran into each other," he said in jest.

"Funny."

"You run super-fast. I could barely catch up to you." His admission stunned me.

"You followed me?" I asked, somewhat creeped out at the notion of being followed. I didn't know if Avery was mowing a nearby neighbor's lawn or his own. I didn't even hear him running behind me nor did I realize I ran in his neighborhood.

"Well, kinda. I guess. I'm glad you stopped. You were like lightning." He laughed.

Huh. Like lightning. I wonder how fast I was going. "Listen, I have to get going," I stated as I didn't want to continue the conversation. *I had no place to be, but that sounded plausible.*

"Hey, let's get together again, okay?" He implored.

"Avery, I just saw you yesterday. What's going on?" I was getting a little impatient.

"I really miss you," He said with the most passion and sincerity one could in so many words.

My heart stopped for a fleeting moment. He was always direct. *I miss you too, if you only knew how much. I'm even dreaming about you. I can't do this again. Not again. Not with you. Not now.*

"Say something, anything," he pleaded with not only his words, but also with his beautiful blue eyes that danced in the sunlight.

"I... I need to go." *Before I crumble right before you.*

"Say you'll go out with me, and I'll let you go," he offered.

"You'll go out with me." I smirked.

"Funny."

"You're not the only one with jokes." I couldn't resist chiding him. We always did have playful banter.

As he took hold of my sweaty hand, I felt the electricity surge through me. There was no denying the chemistry was still there. We said each other's names at the same time. "Avery."

"Christina." I inhaled as I heard him say, "You go first."

I released my hand from his hold. "Let's not do this," I replied, shaking my head.

"Do what?" As if he didn't know.

"It was nice catching up yesterday. You got to clear the air, but..." I searched for my words.

"But what?" He asked, tilting his head.

"I can't do this." I motioned back and forth between us with my index finger. "Us. There is no us anymore." *You broke my heart. It shattered into a million pieces.*

There was more begging. This time with his entire being. "Let there be an us." He leaned in, placed his hands over my ears and as he held my head in his hands, he kissed me in the middle of the street.

Oh my...! Fireworks exploded in broad daylight. I felt a hundred pounds lighter.

"Wow! That was just like the first time we kissed at Paul Martin's house," he said with delight.

A flashback of what Creepoid did to me raced to the forefront of my memory, erasing any trace of the wonderful kiss I just experienced. "I, I gotta go," I blurted and took off running.

I needed to be alone, to lose the memory. *Maybe if I run fast enough this memory will get left behind.* I ran hard and dug deep as if my life depended on it because it did. I had to leave the memory behind. *It's been years. Why does it still hurt so much? Why can't I move on? Why doesn't my most recent rape hurt more? He held a knife to me and would have killed me if it wasn't for Jake finding me. This makes no sense. Ahhhhhh!*

My legs moved faster and faster as my arms pumped in a matching rhythm. My breathing was becoming labored, yet I felt compelled to keep running. I reached the opening of the woods and dashed past the trees like I was on a mission. My entire body was on fire. Sweat was pouring from every orifice in my body. I had to stop.

"NOOOOOOOO!" I shouted in the dark enclosed woods with all my might, followed by heavy panting. Every inch of me throbbed, including my toenails.

I stood erect. "I can't live like this!" I declared to no one, nearly breathless. *This has gone on far too long!* "Ahhhhhh!"

I was too anxious to walk, so I compromised with a light jog. My feet landed on bumpy twigs and branches, hard rocks, and crunchy dead leaves as I meandered my way through the dark windy path. Bright beams of light greeted me as I jogged on to the open street. It was a straight clip home, just one block away. *See, I'm not running from anything. I'm running home.*

"And not only so, but we glory in tribulations also: knowing that tribulation worketh patience; And patience, experience; and experience, hope:" (Romans 5:3-4).

The Lord placed that verse on my heart. *There's always hope with the Lord by my side. He will bring me through this. He did it before, and He'll do it again.*

I collapsed on my bed after a refreshing shower. My early morning run was intense, and I needed to recuperate. I also needed a good distraction. *Music. That's it. I'll listen to music. Christian music should do the trick.* My first choice was "El Shaddai" by Amy Grant.

I love this song. It's so beautiful. El Shaddai always soothed my soul, so I played it a couple times in a row.

The next song "Because of Who You Are" sung by the talented stylings of Sandi Patty began to work its wonders on my fragile heart. *I wish I could sing like her.*

"Oh, Lord You're Beautiful" by Keith Green penetrated every fiber of my being and gave me a good reason to shed a tear. The lyrics spoke to me on a deeper level. Music was such a good release. It was always an excuse to cry, but I didn't want to wallow anymore.

A smile fought its way into my heart when I heard the secular tune, "Next Time I Fall in Love" by the duet, Peter Cetera and Amy Grant on my mixed tape. I couldn't help but think of Avery, the kiss… *What an amazing kiss that was!* I could almost feel his lips on mine.

Somehow Avery had penetrated the barriers I had formed. I let him in, and it felt incredible. For a fleeting moment I experienced the type of elation I hadn't experienced in years, not since I had dated Avery. No one could ever measure up to the way Avery made me feel, not even Joey, although he was a close second.

Steven Curtis Chapman came on next with "Dying to Live" as a catchy uplifting tune. The music caused my emotions to go from feeling blessed to be a child of God to having fond memories of a treasured love. As much as I tried, memories of Avery crept in. Was I ever going to be able to put him in the past and keep him there?

Two hours of listening to music went by fast. The song, "Friends" by Michael W. Smith reminded me of Morgan.

Fresh air beckoned me, so I grabbed the book Morgan gave me, called *This Present Darkness* by Frank E. Peretti and headed to the back patio. Since Morgan raved about it, I trusted it to be a good read. The trees dividing the property along our neighbor's yard provided shade. *Morgan was right. This book is fascinating. Now all I need is a Cabana boy to supply fruity drinks.*

Fully engrossed in the spirit world in the pages before me, I was startled when I heard my name.

"Christina, your mom said you were back here," Avery said as he walked toward me.

"What are you doing here?" *Three times in two days after years of not seeing you. Enough is enough.*

"I wanted to make sure you were okay. You ran off suddenly." *Suddenly and intentionally. Get the hint. But, yeah. Don't remind me. I spent all day trying to forget.* I didn't know what to say to him. All I wanted was to be left alone with my book. I watched as he sat down next to me. Words would not escape my mouth.

"Whatcha reading?" He asked.

I held up my book. "*This Present Darkness* by Frank Peretti."

"Any good?"

Seriously? You came all this way to ask me about my book? "Yes, it's good, really good." *Which is why I want to get back to reading it.* I felt my heart leap. The mixed emotions were toying with me. On one hand, the old warm, fuzzy feelings of love were present. *How is it that you have an effect on me after all these years?* On the other hand, I didn't want to experience the feelings of hurt, the awful pain of a breakup. *I can't risk those crushing feelings again. Please go.*

"Can we talk about earlier today? I didn't mean to upset you. Do you really hate me that much?" he asked like his heart was wounded.

Hate you? I don't hate you. I could never hate you. Far from it. "I don't hate you," I said.

"Then why run off like that?" He asked, abashed.

"I don't want to start anything new with you. That's all." *There. That should work. The lies are coming back too easily. I hate this. I hate living like this. When will it ever end?*

He frowned like I stole his Teddy bear. "Christina, tell me what's going on. I thought you enjoyed the kiss until you ran away." I sensed confusion in his voice.

Why can't you just leave me alone? I took a closer look at him. *Oh my... You look so good in that blue Izod. It brings out the blue in your eyes.*

Avery leaned forward, and I became captivated by his handsome face as if it were a beautiful museum display. "Look, I can't stop thinking about you. What can I do to make things better? Christina, please talk to me," he implored with his words as well as his mesmerizing eyes.

Huh. "I'm sorry. What?" I got caught up in staring at him. *How embarrassing.*

"Are you okay?" Avery asked as he squinted.

"Uh, yeah. Fine. I'm fine." I started to fan myself. "It's getting hot." *Boy, is it ever?*

"Yeah, it is hot. How about we go see a movie? *The Seventh Sign* is still playing, or we can get a bite to eat? My treat," he offered with a hopeful grin.

My lips flatlined before I released a sigh, rejecting his suggestion. "Avery, I don't think that's a good idea."

"Why not?" He challenged.

"I just don't," I said, shaking my head from right to left.

Avery inched closer as the legs of the chair scraped against the concrete patio. Chills ran through my body. I wanted to leave, to run away again, but my feet were planted in cement preventing me from fleeing. I couldn't move my body. I couldn't speak. I was at his mercy. My mind went blank as I stared at this gorgeous creature who once stole my heart. *Dear God. Don't break my heart again.*

The intensity between us grew as he moved closer to me. My heart was beating faster and faster, yet the moment felt like an eternity. Avery leaned forward. I closed my eyes with anticipation. The gentle touch of his lips on mine was even better than I imagined. It always was with Avery. I felt like I was home. Well, I was home, but I felt... alive again.

"Good. You're not running. I wouldn't be able to catch you anyway," he said as his mouth curled upward.

Lighthearted laughter escaped me before panic took over. "You would let me get away again?" I asked.

Avery held his gaze on me as he considered my question. His eyes glazed over like the possibility of losing me would be unbearable. "No, never again."

Good answer. Now what? I feel like a puddle of mush. I searched for something clever to say. "How can you guarantee that?"

He leaned in closer and held my hands. "Christina, I can't live without you. After seeing you yesterday and earlier this morning, I know we belong together."

You sound so convincing. I want to believe you, but I don't want to get hurt again. Not again. I tried to keep my emotions under control, but I found myself feeling weepy, vulnerable. From Avery's reaction I could tell I couldn't conceal my fears.

"Christina, I promise you, whatever it takes to win your heart back, I will do it," he said.

You never lost my heart. It always belonged to you. "How can I trust that you won't hurt me again?" I asked as a tear rolled down my cheek.

As Avery held my hand in his, I saw the sincerest expression in his eyes. "If I hurt you, I hurt myself. I'm tired of being in so much pain. I'm sorry for the way I left things off. Please forgive me."

Forgive you. I thought I did. Didn't I? "I told you already that I forgave you. That's not it. Not really."

"Then what is it? I want to make this right," he pleaded as his eyes darted from side to side.

What is it? "It's over between us. It's been over between us. I can't go through all that again," I began to share my fears.

"Go through what again exactly?" Avery asked. His squinted eyes searched for answers as they focused on me.

"Another break up with you," I replied, my voice revealing my vulnerability.

"Who says we'll break up?" he said with a hopeful tone.

"It's inevitable," I said, shrugging my shoulders.

"No, it's not. Don't say that. We owe it to ourselves to try again," Avery pleaded with his eyes.

"No, we don't," I argued, shaking my head, feeling anxious.

A look of awe appeared on Avery's face. It was as if he found the meaning of life and wanted nothing more than to share his profound discovery as he inched closer. "Christina, I haven't stopped loving you. I have loved you this entire time. I can't get you out of my mind. Believe me, I tried. We are destined to be together. I know you know that. Don't you feel it? Tell me you feel it too," he said with urgency.

"I feel… I feel…" My voice trailed. Trepidation kept me from bearing my soul.

Avery's eyes locked on mine, he licked his lips, and I felt his breath on me. "I love you, Christina, with all my heart. I can't let you go. Ever."

I could feel my heart slowly knitting itself back together after hearing his profession of love, but was it enough?

"I never stopped loving you, Avery. As God as my witness, I tried, but YOU BROKE MY HEART." I pounded on his chest. "It's taken me years to put the pieces back together. I don't have the strength to go through that again. I just can't." I started to sob.

Avery drew me closer and embraced me. I felt the warmth of his love as the sun beat down on us. Even though I felt comforted in his arms, I was afraid to make that leap into a relationship with him again. He stroked my hair and repeated, "I'm so sorry I hurt you. I'm so sorry."

His words rang true to me, but I was broken. I needed to move forward but didn't know how. Nothing I did helped heal the pain from that summer day at the Martin's. Avery was a reminder of that. He brought up all those dreadful memories. If I let him in, I would be admitting defeat. At least that's how it felt.

His words persisted with deep regret, "I'm so sorry I hurt you."

I couldn't let him take all the burden. "It's not just you," I blurted.

"What do you mean?" Avery asked.

"I was hurt really bad by someone else."

His voice was laced with genuine concern. "Who hurt you? Was it that guy from college?" I nodded. He began a rapid fire of his thoughts. "This is all my fault. If we were together, that may never have happened. I'm so sorry. Is that why you ran away this morning? You can tell me anything, Christina. I just want to help." I could hear all the guilt, regret, sorrow, confusion, and caring in his voice, so I considered his words.

If it were only that easy. It is that easy. When I told people what Ryan did, I felt somewhat freed. Maybe... I pulled away from Avery and with all the courage I could muster, I said, "No, that's not why I ran away. I... I have a confession to make." I paused to gather my thoughts. "This is so hard for me to say, and I don't know why." I gulped a huge amount of air and started to shake.

With love and patience in his voice, Avery stated, "It's okay, Christina. Take your time. Whatever it is, I'm here for you."

My eyes kept blinking. I tried to keep them open as I licked my lips. *Okay, already. Just say it.* "I was raped before college." *There I said it. Well, almost.*

"When? Do I know him?" Avery's face turned a little red.

"Uh, yes, you do. It was the summer before our freshman year of high school. I never told anyone before."

Avery shook his head, his eyes became wide, he swallowed a breath of air like it was cyanide, then his eyes began to twitch. "Who was it?"

I inhaled deeply and swallowed the saliva that formed at the top of my throat. "Paul Martin." For the first time it happened, I was able to say his name out loud.

Avery jumped up from his seat and threw up his arms. "I'll kill him!" he exclaimed.

"Wait! No, he moved away," I said trying to calm down an irate Avery. "Sit down. There's more." I waited for Avery to take a seat. I tried to compose myself, but memories of that cursed day gained control. Giving in to my raw emotions, I fumbled through hysterical tears, "He ra-aped someone else an-nd it's all m-my fault." I wiped the salty moisture off my cheeks and sniffled.

"Come here." Avery drew me into him. "Shhh! It's not your fault. It's not your fault," he repeated as he smoothed my hair. I wept into him.

I found solace in Avery's arms until I remembered what Paul threatened me. *"I will kill you and your little boyfriend."* I gasped for air and started heaving. I broke away from Avery to regain control of myself. I pictured Paul's feral look which shook me to my core.

Avery held onto my arms, and said, "You're shaking like a leaf. It's okay, Christina. He's not here. He can't hurt you anymore."

I lunged forward into Avery's arms. "Don't let him kill us," I cried.

"He won't kill us. I won't let him. I promise," Avery assured me. Overwrought with emotions, I sobbed on Avery's chest. He held me tighter. The safety and security I felt all those years ago with Avery came rushing back as a welcomed reprieve. "It's okay. It will be okay. I promise. Everything's okay. He can't hurt you anymore," he said as he caressed my hair.

I hung on every word Avery said until they started to sink in. After several minutes, I began to settle down. *Inhale. One, two, three, four, five. Exhale. One, two, three, four, five.* My breathing slowed down to a normal pace. I sat up and wiped my nose realizing at that time I used his shirt as a giant tissue. My crinkled nose gave away my disgust.

"What?" Avery asked.

"I slobbered all over you." I said in repugnance.

He pointed to a dry spot on his shirt. "Here, you missed a spot."

I looked up through my eyelashes, "Is this your way of getting me back in your arms?"

"Whatever works." He smirked.

My stomach growled. "Did you hear that?" I said through a faint smile.

"Yeah, your stomach and my stomach agree we should get something to eat. What do ya think?" Avery's eyebrows danced.

How could I say no after what I put him through? "Sure. Let's go," I relented.

After we ordered lunch, Avery put his hand over mine. We locked eyes as he squeezed my hand. "I want you to know that I am here for you. No matter what. Whatever you need, I will be there for you," he stated with a love and commitment that I didn't even realize I craved until I heard the words.

As I looked across the booth, I couldn't help but think that Avery was speaking from his heart. "I think you've proven that," I said as I returned my appreciation with a squeeze of his hand.

Avery leaned in. I could tell he had something on his mind. I wasn't surprised when he said, "Can we talk about what happened? I don't want to upset you, but you left me with a lot of questions. You don't have to talk about it if you don't want to."

The hard part was already over. He knew my deep dark secret. "It's okay. We can talk," I replied.

"Why didn't you tell me before? About you know…," he said, tilting his head slightly and shifting his eyes upward in the same direction.

"He threatened to kill us both if I said anything," I responded in a matter-of-fact manner. It didn't sound stupid hearing it out loud for the first time, and it felt good at long last to let it out after all those years of keeping that dreadful day to myself.

"So, you kept it in all this time, even after he moved," he said with a puzzled look.

I could tell that Avery didn't understand why I kept my secret for so long, so I did my best to explain. "I was so scared for so long. I promised myself I wouldn't tell anyone. I was ashamed."

"Ashamed? Ashamed of what?" he asked.

I drew in a deep breath knowing this would be hard to explain, and it would be best if he understood. "I felt guilty, ashamed, dirty, unworthy. It's normal for victims of sexual assault to feel like that. He made the point of mentioning how you and I were kissing at his house the night of the beauty pageant. Paul," I shuddered at the sound of his name, "made me feel cheap and said that no one would believe that I wasn't a willing participant, since I made a public display of myself kissing you."

"Oh, come on!" He exclaimed, exasperated.

I motioned with my hands for Avery to keep it down. He leaned forward and whispered in anger, "That creep had the nerve to say that after what he did to you!" Avery slammed his fist on the table, causing the utensils to clang against the tabletop.

My eyes darted back and forth suggesting he control himself. "Avery, please. This is hard enough for me as it is."

He had enough prudence to look remorseful. "You're right. I'm sorry. Go on." He leaned back in the booth and waved me on to continue.

"What else do you want to know?" *I can't believe I'm offering to talk about it.* An hour ago, I was taking my secret to the grave.

"When did it happen exactly?" Avery asked.

"The day after you and I played video games for the first time at your house." That moment was forever etched in my brain, corroding the good, the decent, and the pure from the instant of its inception.

It took a second for the lightbulb to go off in Avery's mind. He captured the day when his eyes gazed upward. "We were supposed to hang out again that day, but I had a doctor's appointment."

"Yeah, I can't believe you remember that," I said, impressed with Avery's recollection.

"How could I forget? Everything was fine..." He turned his head a bit, his eyes widened as he played back the memories of our summer before freshman year, six years prior. "That's why you wouldn't take my calls. You had Katie break it off for you." He scratched his head. "Oh man, I get it now." I nodded allowing him a moment to take it all in. "But then why did you eventually go out with me again? Not that I'm complaining."

Feeling like Avery deserved to know the truth, I answered, "You were very persistent and made me feel safe. I trusted you." *Like I do now.*

Deep regret penetrated Avery's face. "Oh man, then I blew it. I'm so sorry." He grabbed my hands again.

It hurt to see how that one moment continued to pollute people's lives, not just mine. I wanted to end the ugliness. "We've been through this before. You don't have to keep apologizing." I said, wanting desperately to move forward, to put a stop to the torment.

"I know, but I feel terrible. I had no idea. You were probably still struggling with this when…"

"You broke up with me," I said, filling in the blank for Avery.

"When I let you go," he said with a slight quiver in his voice.

"Ave, it was a high school romance." I shrugged, trying to lighten the burden that displayed on his face.

"Is that how you saw our relationship?" He asked. I could tell I wounded him with that remark.

"Ave." My eyes pleaded with his. I didn't know how to mend our broken hearts. Talking about it was new territory for us, but it seemed to be putting us on the right path.

"Christina, you hung the moon as far as I was concerned." The love and admiration he felt for me was apparent in both his voice and eyes.

"Then why did you break—let me go?" I fired back.

"I did it to punish myself! I didn't deserve you!" It was clear that Avery meant what he said as his eyes welled up with regret.

"Oh, Avery. We really made a mess of things, didn't we?" A piece of my heart broke for him. All those years he was suffering too. If we had only talked it out…

The waitress placed our lunch in front of us. The aroma of our cheesesteaks made my mouth water. "Now, here we go, two cheesesteaks with fried onions and ketchup and two chocolate milkshakes. Can I get you two anything else?" she asked as she tossed a separate glance at each of us.

"No, thank you," We answered in sync.

"All right. Enjoy," she said and walked away in a hurry.

I became aware of the song, "The Greatest Love of All," that was barely audible yet recognizable as it was sung by the beautiful and talented Whitney Houston.

I was about to dig into my lunch, when Avery said, "Wait. Let's pray." We both bowed our heads and closed our eyes. "Lord, please bless this food to our bodies, and let our conversation be pleasing to you. Amen."

"Amen," I stated under my breath.

We each took a bite of our cheesesteaks. Per usual, I couldn't resist making yummy sounds. "Um, this is so good. You can't get food like this at Sylvania Ridge," I said as I licked off a bit of ketchup with a side swipe of my tongue.

"You were incredibly brave to return to school," Avery stated before taking another bite of his cheesesteak.

"Oh, yeah. I considered not going back at first."

I watched him take a sip of his milkshake. "Was it hard going back?" He asked as he swallowed.

"Not as hard as I thought it would be and harder in some ways."

"Meaning?" Avery asked me to elaborate.

I held up my finger for Avery to give me a moment to chew my food. "Well, I didn't have as many flashbacks as I thought I would for some reason. But, I did have guys yell at me for killing their fraternity brother."

He exclaimed, "Whoa! They blamed you for that after what he did to you?" He shook his head with incredulity.

I nodded. "Yeah, I know. Crazy right? They were delusional."

"I'm glad you realized that. Must have been hard," he empathized.

"It was, but I tried not to show it. I didn't want to give them the satisfaction, although there were times I bawled my eyes out."

A sorrowful look came across Avery's face. "I'm so—That took a lot of courage to stand up to them." Avery caught himself before he apologized again. He's catching on. I nodded as words were not necessary.

After a short while, Avery broached the subject again. "So, what do you think? We'll give it another go!? You and me?" he said as he waggled his eyebrows.

Could you be any more endearing? "I think I can be persuaded," I teased as I took a bite of my cheesesteak.

"So, what's it going to take on my part to convince you to go out with me?" he grinned with anticipation.

I swallowed my last bite. "Well, let me see, what's your influence on world peace?" *Perhaps the absurdity of my question will make him realize the absurdity of his.*

"I know I would be at peace if you would say yes." *Clever.*

"Oh, Ave. I don't know. Are you ready for a relationship? I mean I haven't even considered your issues." *I'm not so sure how I feel about you being a porn addict or whatever you call it.*

Avery wiped his hands on a napkin and looked me dead in the eyes. "I have nothing to hide. I told you everything and plan on keeping the lines of communication open between us," he said, not breaking eye contact.

His comment reminded me of my counseling sessions. "You definitely had therapy, haven't you?" I said, already knowing the answer.

"You can tell, huh?" He asked, sipping his shake.

"Yeah. It sounds familiar." Those sessions were more worthwhile than I thought.

Avery smirked. "We make quite the pair."

I let out a chuckle. "We do, don't we?" I agreed on so many levels, but I didn't want to encourage Avery too much.

"So, it's settled then? You're my girl again?" Avery said in the most endearing way.

Only Avery would say it like that. I literally blushed. *He's so corny.* "Sure, why not?" I said nonchalantly.

"Don't sound too excited," Avery said, using a sarcastic tone.

Eek. I wounded him again. "All right, you. Come here." I bent my index finger toward me, and we both leaned in and kissed. Our lips separated leaving my forehead to rest on his. I breathed in a deep sigh of satisfaction and smiled through my question, "Is that proof enough of my excitement?"

"It'll do. For now," he said in a tongue and cheek manner. I playfully slapped his arm to show my disapproval of his lack of enthusiasm. "Hey, what was that for?"

"Don't push your luck." I smirked.

He held up his hand. "You have my word," he promised.

"Good. Now that we have that cleared up…" I listened to Robert Palmer sing "Addicted to Love" while I sipped my chocolate milkshake. *Life is better with milkshakes.*

Chapter 19

A new day greeted me with a feeling of dread that I couldn't shake. Although I was happy about getting back together with Avery, something else was gnawing at me. After telling Avery about my first rape, I felt the greatest sense of relief. I knew I had to tell people what happened. *How do you tell people that you've been raped not once but twice?* I already felt like a freak at times, and this would make it ten times worse. *There are stranger things in life, aren't there?* It became a matter of how, when, and who I would tell.

My mom was sitting at her usual spot at the kitchen table with her cup of tea in hand. Jared still had a few weeks of school left, so that meant we were alone. *Do I tell her now? What a way to start the day.* "Mom, I have something to tell you."

She looked at me as I sat down across from her. I swallowed traces of saliva that lingered at the back of my mouth. "Remember when you came to visit me in the hospital?"

"Yes," she said and nodded.

"Well, that meant a lot to me." There was no response, not even movement from my mother.

Boy, she doesn't make this easy. It's like talking to the ice queen.

I paused and then stated, "Well, that wasn't the first time."

"The first time what?" My mother asked.

"That wasn't the first time I was raped." At that moment, I was looking at a faint resemblance of my mother as her face lost all its color.

My mother's eyes squinted as she inched forward. Her face contorted like she was watching a horror show. After what seemed like a gigantic pause, her mouth opened, "You're telling me that you were—were raped before—by the same person?"

"No, I was raped in high school." Somehow my statement rolled off my tongue.

My mother gasped. "High school?!" I nodded. "My God, Christina, why didn't you tell me this before?"

"Because he threatened to kill me if I did."

My mother tilted her head slightly, and asked with a shaky voice, "Who—who threatened you?"

For the longest time I couldn't say *his* name, but that meant he won that battle. *No longer.* With a firm grasp of my words, I replied, "Paul Martin." The simple uttering of his name left me with chills.

I watched my mother's eyes fill up with tears. She pursed her lips, shook her head as if in shock and said, "Oh my G—." She paused as she closed her eyes. "When—when did this happen?" She asked with as much composure as she could manage. It was odd seeing my mom struggle like that, and I felt bad that I was the one causing her to feel upset.

"A couple days after the pageant," I answered with ease and waited for my mother to process this news.

She shook her head and inhaled. "Have you told anyone besides me?"

"Yes, Avery. I told him yesterday. You two are the only ones who know." I scooped back locks of curls behind my ears.

"Are you two back together?" She asked with a tilt of her head.

"Yes." *And you're the first to know.*

My mother nodded and took another deep breath. "Why are you just telling us now?"

I inhaled as I stretched my arms out before me. Releasing my breath, I said, "Because I realized how much better my healing has been after telling people about what happened in college. That was even more terrifying because he held a knife to me." My lip quivered, and I started to choke up as images of him straddling over me with a shiny knife took up residence in my mind. "Mom, he was going to kill me." Tears fell down my cheeks, and I couldn't wipe away the soggy mess fast enough.

At this point, my mother was sobbing. That was the first time I ever watched her shed a tear. Her crying made me sob all the more. She leaped out of her chair and wrapped her arms around me as I was still seated. I stood up and folded my arms around her waist. "I'm so sorry. I'm so sorry. I had no idea. Christina, my dear sweet, Christina." My mother cradled me as she stroked my hair. We both cried an ugly cry, but it was cleansing for the soul.

While still in my mother's embrace, she admitted with regret, "All this time I had no idea you were going through such a horrible time. I thought it was typical teenage stuff, so I left you alone." She gasped. "You were all alone too. I should have known better." We both continued to sob, letting it all out. It felt good to release the burden I held for nearly six years.

After a few minutes of unbridled crying, I regained composure. Letting go of my embrace, I gently pulled away and said, "Mom, I know now that I should have said something. I should have told someone, anyone, but I was scared." A very brief moment passed. There was a hint of shakiness in my voice when I said, "I thought he would kill me and anyone I told, so I didn't take the chance."

"I'm so sorry, Christina. I failed you as a mother. I should have known. That's my job as a mom." Her voice quavered.

I jumped in because I couldn't bear to witness my mom beat herself up for something that wasn't her responsibility. "No, mom, don't do that. It's not your fault. I hid it from you and my friends. That's why I spent time at the old folks' home."

With a glint in my mom's eyes, she cupped her hand on my cheek and said, "You are so brave. Look at you. I always knew you were strong, but this just confirms it. You got through this on your own. I'm so proud of you, Christina."

"Mom, I had help along the way. Without people even knowing it, they helped." I hesitated, wondering if I should say what actually helped me or who helped me. "I couldn't have done it without my faith. My belief in Christ is what really pulled me through."

"Well then, thank God for Jesus," she smirked.

Hope filled my being, and I became excited. "Mom, do you believe that?" I wanted to know if my mom was a Christian. The mere thought of that was thrilling.

"Believe what?" She had no idea what I was talking about.

I couldn't ask her fast enough. "Mom, are you a believer? Are you a Christian?" I needed to know, so I spelled it out for her.

"I'm not vocal about my beliefs, but I suppose you could say I'm a Christian," she said offhandedly.

Were my ears deceiving me? "So, you believe Jesus is the son of God, and He died on the cross for our sins?" The eagerness I felt to hear her answer was evident.

My mother's lips curled upward, not a familiar look for her, and she replied, "Yes, I suppose I do."

What does that mean? I suppose I do. "Mom, either you do, or you don't. Which is it?" I was both exasperated and hopeful at the same time.

The smile on her face grew larger. "I do believe Jesus is our Savior."

"Why don't you go to church? Why didn't you share your beliefs with me?" Part of me wanted to jump up and down because my mom was saved. The other part wanted to know why she didn't worship collectively and why she wasn't vocal about her faith.

My mom grimaced and performed a slight eye roll. "Oh, Christina, religion was forced down my throat. It's a miracle I came away believing the way I do," she said, waving me off.

"Mom, I get it. Well, kind of, but that's no excuse for not attending church. We are called to gather together to worship the Lord," I replied steely.

After smacking her lips, my mother gave me a sideways glance and said, "Christina, I worship God privately in my own way, and if it's good enough for me, it should be good enough for you."

"It doesn't matter what I think, Mom. What matters is what God thinks."

"When did you get so smart?" My mom brushed a strand of hair behind my ears. She sounded impressed.

Relieved that my mom didn't reprimand me for calling her out, I returned with a slight smile. "Mom, I go to church. I'm in Bible studies. I literally talk about Jesus in my talks at churches. That's how I grow and learn. That's why it's important for you to go to church. Iron sharpens iron. Proverbs 27:17."

With a stern look, my mother volleyed, "Now, you're quoting the Bible?"

"Mom, I quote the Bible all the time during my talks in churches. It's how I stay grounded. I would be a train wreck if it weren't for my faith. I probably wouldn't be here if I wasn't a believer."

"What do you mean by that?" I detected a tinge of shakiness in her voice.

"I used to cut myself." My mother's eye twitched. "Right after I was raped, I grabbed the razor. I cut for several weeks."

Unable to control her reaction, my mother winced. "And you stopped once you became a Christian?"

"No, it wasn't that simple. God put people in my life that cared about me and showed me love, like Avery and Miss Brenda from the old folks' home. They pointed me in the direction of Christ, and that love of Christ prevented me from picking up the razor again."

The beginning of a grin appeared when she said, "There is power in your words, Christina. I can see why you're so popular with those talks. I'm glad that helps you."

Do I sense a little pride from you? "I have another talk this Saturday if you want to join me," I suggested.

"Let me think about it." She pursed her lips.

I never felt closer to my mother. Being able to tell her about my rape after all those years was liberating. Another chain was broken. The wheels of healing were turning. I knew then who to tell next, and I had a new mission… Getting my mother to church.

I invited Avery into my house. It had been a few hours since the conversation with my mom. I figured she would want to see Avery after all these years. We didn't discuss my relationship with Avery, so I knew I was taking a chance. I walked in the kitchen with Avery trailing behind to where my mother was sitting at her usual spot at the kitchen table.

Avery greeted my mom with a short wave. "Hi, Mrs. De Rosa. How are you doing?"

My mom gave Avery a once over as if she'd never seen him before. "Hello, Avery. It's good to see you… I think."

Uh oh.

Avery turned to me in a plea for help. *Nope, you're on your own.* I shrugged. I needed to see how he would handle himself. After all, I didn't blame my mom for having reservations about him. She knew he broke my heart after witnessing my depression for months after he let me go, turning my world upside down. Avery was one person that I put my trust in. It took months before I could put my trust in someone else, at least in a romantic capacity.

Avery bobbed his head and pierced his lips. "I guess I deserve that." He looked over at me and continued, "I don't know what Christina told you, but my intentions are good."

My mom inspected him with piercing eyes, "And what are your intentions?" She lilted.

Avery stood up straight and inhaled deeply. "Well, I want to start fresh with your daughter. You know, to start over. I never stopped loving her."

My eyes fell on my mother. *Was that a twinkle in your eye?*

"Christina is very special, and she's been through quite a lot," she stated. Aside from her lips moving, she sat motionless like she was part of the chair and stared him down.

Avery replied, "There is no one more special."

Okay. All right you two. I rolled my eyes. *Am I watching a sappy TV drama?* I cleared my throat. "Avery, I told my mom about Paul raping me. She knows you know too. You two are the only ones who know. Let's not make this any weirder than it already is."

My mom's gaze was directed at me. Her eyes softened. "What are you two up to?" she asked.

Avery turned to me and asked, "Wanna grab something to eat?"

"Yeah, let's go." I glanced in my mom's direction. "I'll be home in time for dinner," I said and walked off with my lunch date.

On the way out, my mom said even-toned, "Enjoy your lunch."

I took note of the song "When I Think of You" as I walked in the diner and pictured the adorable Janet Jackson dancing in her music video. However, my mind drifted to the matter at hand that I couldn't shake since I left my house.

Once seated at a table for two, I dropped my head and focused my attention upward toward Avery. "There's no one more special? Really?" I said sarcastically.

"What?" he asked as he was taking the utensils out of the wrapped napkin.

"Come on." I said in disbelief.

Avery placed the white napkin on his lap. "What did you want me to say?" He had a point.

I shook my head and performed another eye roll. "Well, I guess I asked for it, letting you two go head-to-head with no notice."

His eyebrows furrowed. "Yeah, what was that about?" he asked.

I brought Avery up to speed. "I had a heart-to-heart with my mom. I was curious to see how she would react to you. She always liked you, but you did break my heart, you know."

"You know how sorry I am. If I could do it all over, I would." I heard the sincerity in his voice.

"Yeah, I know," I said. After a second, I decided to share my conclusion based on Avery's most recent interaction with my mom. "My mom must really like you."

"What makes you say that?" He asked with a puzzled expression on his face.

"She doesn't warm up to people, but she does to you."

Avery's eyes grew wide, and he shot back with bewilderment, "You call that warming up? Your mom is kinda terrifying."

I waved off his comment and smirked. "She let you off easy."

"Easy. I would hate to see what hard looks like." Avery's eyes went skyward as he sucked in some air.

I laughed and was about to broach a more serious subject when the waitress came by to take our orders.

After the waitress left, I made a point to say, "By the way, my mom didn't ask any details about us getting back together. She doesn't know why you br—let me go and I don't want her to. It's none of anyone's business."

"Why don't you want anyone to know?" Avery asked.

"Because they will judge you. I think it's better left unsaid," I stated.

"For you or for me?" There was a slight edge in his tone that I didn't comprehend but sensed its relevance.

"What do you mean?" I asked.

"Is it better that I don't tell people for your sake or for mine?" Avery clarified.

"For your sake, of course," I stated as if it was obvious.

He responded with a sarcastic tone, "Of course."

"What is that supposed to mean?" I asked, crossing my arms.

"I think you're embarrassed," Avery surmised.

I tucked my chin in. "Why would I be embarrassed?"

Avery straightened his back. "Because your boyfriend was a porn addict."

"That's your issue, not mine," I remarked as I pointed my finger at him.

Avery leaned in. "Right, but they may judge you for going out with someone like me."

I hadn't thought about it like that. In fact, I hadn't thought about his addiction much at all. *Did I rush into things with Avery?* "The thought never even occurred to me." *Maybe I need to think things through, but I can't break up with him after we just started going out.*

Avery posed the burning question, "So, it doesn't bother you if everyone knows I was addicted to porn?"

Well, now that you put it like that. "Why do people have to know?"

"See, there it is." Avery flung his open hand away from his body.

"There what is?" I started to feel anxious due to all the questioning.

"You're embarrassed. It's understandable. I shouldn't expect you to be okay with it. You haven't had much time to process everything." Avery concluded like he was my therapist giving me a psychological assessment.

I wanted to argue, like I should defend myself, but he was right. I didn't process it. "I honestly don't know what to think about it." I shrugged, unable to come to any conclusions at the moment.

Avery nodded and his eyes softened as if he understood where I was coming from. "That's fair, but just so you know, not many people know. I've been trying to work on behavior modification and substitution…"

What? I shot him a confused look.

He elaborated, "Sorry. My counselor and I felt like I needed to change my habits before I went public, if I went public that is."

I nodded to show him I was paying attention and for him to proceed.

"Basically, I had to find things to do in place of the porn." *This counseling stuff isn't too bad.*

"Like what?" I asked out of curiosity.

"For one I work out a lot." *Like I haven't noticed.* "It's like running for you, I would imagine."

"Yeah, I can get that, but you can't exercise all the time." Even I knew that because I wished I could run all the time.

The familiar and catchy tune "Faith" by George Michael caught my attention that moment as we spoke about our issues.

"Right. I also read." He hesitated. "I actually study the Bible like crazy. Apparently, I have an addictive personality disorder…" He shrugged. "So, I may as well throw myself into something worthwhile."

"Yeah, but do you like it?"

Avery's face lit up. "Studying the Bible? Yeah, I love it!" His face beamed.

His excitement put a smile on my face. Then a warm, fuzzy feeling came over me. Our mutual interest in the Bible felt like a good reason for us to be together. I had the urge to mentally check off boxes for why we should be together to justify my decision for going out with Avery without carefully weighing the pros and cons. I reacted more on impulse, how he made me feel at the time. Feeling validated, I was pleased to say, "So do I. It looks like we have that in common."

Avery replied, "I think we always had that in common, but I got sidetracked."

"What makes you think you won't get sidetracked again?" I winced at my concern. "I don't mean to sound judgmental. I honestly don't understand how you can prevent yourself from going down the wrong path again. You were doing all the right things before…"

"No, it's okay. Actually, I don't know, but if I'm open and honest from now on, I have a chance of staying on the straight and narrow. Trust me. I know there's no guarantee," he spoke as though he had given it a lot of thought and understood my concern.

"Like accountability." Avery told me about accountability when we started going out our freshman year of high school, except that time it was regarding remaining a virgin before marriage.

With a nod, Avery said, "Yes, I have my parents, my counselor, the pastor, the staff at Pennsford Christian Academy. I still keep in touch with a few teachers… and hopefully, you."

"Avery, you will always have my support. No matter what. Even if we break up, I will help you however I can."

His eyes full of hope and resolution bore a hole in my heart when he said, "Breaking up is not in the plan, Christina." He leaned closer. "I'm all in, and I hope you are too."

I didn't want to hurt his feelings, but I wasn't at the same spot as Avery. It felt right to agree to go out with him… but those were only feelings. I didn't think things through.

The waitress dropped our food off, and I took note of Belinda Carlisle singing "Mad About You," a song I could have sung about Avery.

I waited until we were alone at the table to say, "Ave, I'm gonna be honest. I spent the last few years trying to get over you. I didn't dare entertain the notion of going out with you again. I need time to catch up to you."

My gaze shifted downward to the plate the waitress placed in front of me. The flavors of turkey, bacon, lettuce, tomato, and mayonnaise were calling my name, so I wrapped my hands around my turkey club. When I sunk my teeth into the huge stack, I managed to get every bit of the ingredients in one big, delectable bite. *Yum.*

Avery took a sip of his Coke to wash down his chicken sandwich. "Fair enough," he said in response to me needing time to get to the same place as him.

He panned the ceiling, recalling a time when we were no longer together. "I couldn't imagine my life without you. You have to understand that I have been praying for us to get back together since I started therapy. We'll take it slow. I don't want to jeopardize our relationship," he said in earnest.

"When did you start therapy?" *You sound like a therapist.*

As if in a hurry, Avery swallowed a bite of his lunch. "Immediately. When we started back to school our junior year. I couldn't drag you into the mess I created."

"You didn't give me the option," I retorted before taking another bite of my mile high sandwich.

"I was too ashamed to tell you what was going on. I had to sort things out first."

"Why wait so long? Why cut me off? Why cut all your friends off? People break up all the time and don't start a whole new life." It felt good to express my lack of understanding.

Avery let out a big sigh. "It's hard to explain. I felt like I had to start new, start fresh. It was a way of penance for me. I told you that before." There was a note of frustration in his voice.

My eyes squinted as if they would be able to unlock the confusion I felt. "Yeah, I just don't get that. It was rather extreme and sudden. It took me a long time to trust anyone after that." I sought comfort in my turkey club.

He shook his head. "Yeah, I'm sorry about that. Really, I am. I had no idea what you had been through."

I sighed deeply, trying to squelch the hurtful memories as I didn't want to make a public spectacle of myself in the restaurant. It was almost painful trying to suppress my feelings. I had no words, so I bit into my turkey club.

As if reading my mind, Avery said, "How about we take it slow?"

"I can do that," I said with an encouraging smile.

"Then slow it is." He smiled back and took a bite of his chicken sandwich.

Chapter 20

T he once familiar cold air greeted me as I breezed into the lobby of The Manor midday the following day. With my fingers crossed, I asked the front desk clerk if Miss Brenda was working.

"Yes, she's downstairs in the lounge. May I ask who is inquiring?"

"Yes, my name is Christina De Rosa. I used to volunteer here when I was in high school."

The Director, Mrs. Brooks, greeted me upon seeing me across the room. "Christina, so good to see you! What brings you here today?"

"I was hoping to see Miss Brenda."

With a tilt of her head, Mrs. Brooks said, "I'll tell you what. Why don't we make arrangements for you two to have lunch together? My treat. Just give me a few moments."

"Okay, thank you."

Mrs. Brooks returned, "Miss Brenda will meet you in the break room." She looked at the watch on her left wrist. "Her lunch starts in about ten minutes. I hope you don't mind, but I asked her to get you spaghetti and meatballs. It's the special for today."

"Great. Thank you."

"So, Christina, tell me what you've been up to. You're in college, right?" Mrs. Brooks asked.

"Yes, I'll be a junior in the fall at Sylvania Ridge University."

We continued to discuss the usual college particulars for a few moments. After I updated Mrs. Brooks, I headed to the break room.

I saw Miss Brenda immediately when I walked in the break room. The bright smile that lit up her kind-loving, middle-aged face rivaled the pretty red shirt that looked good against her espresso-colored skin. "Well, I'll be! If it ain't my dear friend, Christina! Mrs. Brooks didn't tell me who I was eating with. She just said I had a special guest and to pick up some extra spaghetti. This is quite the surprise! Come here, sugar!" I walked toward her as she held out her arms. She wrapped me in one of her wonderful hugs as I put my arms around her large girth. She pulled away, held onto my arms, and said, "Let me look at you!" She looked me over and smiled. "Uh, uh, uh, look at you! You look fabulous! Life sure does agree with you!"

Miss Brenda always had a way with words that made me feel special. We sat down at a round table. It was just the two of us. "Let's say grace, shall we?" She bowed her head and said, "Father God, thank you for this food and for surprising me with this special guest. Bless this food to our bodies in the name of Jesus. Amen."

"Amen," I said softly.

She took a plate of today's special and placed it in front of me. "Here you go. I got you a side salad too."

"Thank you." My free lunch looked appetizing. Not too bad for an old folks' home.

My old friend leaned in. "So, what do I owe the pleasure? Not that I don't love you stopping by." She twirled her fork in the spaghetti.

I cut the meatballs into tiny pieces and mixed them in with the spaghetti. "You have been on my mind a lot lately. How are you doing?" I took a fork full of the spaghetti and meatballs. *Pretty good. I don't remember eating this here before. Must be a newer menu option.*

Miss Brenda took a sip of her drink and said as she placed the plastic glass down, "Oh, I'm fine. Couldn't be better, now that you are here. So, tell me, honey. What's on your mind?"

I'm sugar and honey. I couldn't resist smiling at her terms of endearment. "I have something to tell you." I hesitated a moment. Miss Brenda had a way of even making dead silence comfortable. "I'm here to tell you what was going on in my life back in high school. You see…I…The reason why I…"

Miss Brenda grabbed hold of my hands. "You can tell me, sugar. It's all right."

Her caring and compassion penetrated my heart. *I can't believe I didn't tell her sooner. Okay, Christina. You got this. Just tell her. It's Miss Brenda for heaven sakes.* "I was raped the summer before my freshman year in high school." *There I said it.* I let out a huge exhale.

Miss Brenda nodded, her eyes welled up and she said, "Sweet baby Jesus. I cannot tell you how sorry I am to hear that. Breaks my heart. Sweet baby Jesus."

Still holding my hands, she tightened her grip and closed her eyes. "God the Father, I lift up my sister, Christina. Lord, You know all she has suffered better than anyone. Please, Heavenly Father, take this pain and suffering away from this sweet sister of mine. I know she still feels the pain. I can feel it, Lord. Oh, I know it's there."

As hard as I tried to hold back the tears, they came streaming down my face. She knew. Miss Brenda knew I was still hurting.

Miss Brenda's voice was my main focus. "Only You can take that pain away from her. You are the Master Healer, our Sovereign God, our Mighty God. You have the power to rid Christina of this torment once and for all. I ask You this in Your holy name. Amen. Praise Jesus!" She squeezed my hands and released them from her loving grasp.

I wasn't expecting her to go into prayer right away, but I was glad she did. She was right. *I'm still suffering. Thank you, God, for putting Miss Brenda in my path.* I wiped my tears away and felt a great sense of relief. I hooked some noodles around my fork and took a bite of the mini mound. It was still warm.

We talked a little more while we ate, and Miss Brenda thanked me for the letter I wrote her back in high school. I got busy with sports and could no longer fit The Manor in my schedule. After that I was out of the habit of going but felt compelled to let Miss Brenda know how much she meant to me, so I sent a letter addressed to her at Pennsford Manor. "It touched my heart that you spent the time to write me. I think of you often and wonder how you're doing," she said.

"I think of you a lot too. I knew I had to tell you in person what happened to me. You're the third person I've told."

She placed her right hand over her heart and said, "I'm honored, especially after all these years."

The passing years didn't put distance between us as I still felt connected to Miss Brenda on a deep level. "Being here with you and the residents got me through a difficult time in my life. I needed a safe place without all the reminders of what happened. You were a big part of how I became a Christian, and you will always have a special place in my heart."

Miss Brenda took hold of my hands and said, "You are a big part of who I am today. I liked sharing the gospel with you and telling you about Bible verses so much that I decided to lead my own Bible study. We meet at my house, and I serve your favorite." She chortled. "Sweet tea." She laughed again and said, "I don't make it as sweet as I like it. Turns out folks around here don't like their tea very sweet." She looked at the clock on the wall. "Well, I best be going. Time for me to return to work. It was great seeing you, Christina."

"It was great seeing you too, Miss Brenda." My visit was long overdue.

"Now, don't be a stranger. My door is always open." She jotted down something on a wrinkled piece of paper. "Here's my address and phone number. Let me know if you need anything, ya hear?"

She handed me the paper. "I will. Thank you." We ended our time together with a hug. *How I miss your hugs. Best. Hugs. Ever.*

I will never forget how Miss Brenda handled the death of her teenage son with amazing grace only a few weeks after I experienced the first major sinister act against me. She remained steadfast in her walk with Christ and exuded a peace that planted the seed of my faith. Later that day I thought of her when I read, "Thou wilt keep him in perfect peace, whose mind is stayed on thee: because he trusteth in thee" (Isaiah 26:3).

Chapter 21

*A*very's parents invited me to dinner. I hadn't seen his mom since that horrible day after school after he broke up with me, the day I failed to win him back. It feels different this time around, especially since I'm driving now. I parked my Honda in front of Avery's house, walked up the driveway and rapped on the door. His mom answered the door with a grandiose smile spread across her face, making me feel welcomed. Mrs. Evans hadn't changed a bit. She still had ash blonde hair that fell to her shoulders, most likely styled by thick rollers. "Hello, Christina, please come in. How are you?"

"Hi, Mrs. Evans. I'm fine. How are you?" I didn't realize how much I missed Avery's mom until I saw her.

"Couldn't be better. I'm so glad you're joining us for dinner later," she said, drying her hands on a towel.

Avery walked in the kitchen. "Hi, Christina. Hey, Mom."

"Hi, Ave." I may have sounded nonchalant, but in actuality I was excited to see him. He always took my breath away.

"Let's go in the family room. Mom, are you joining us?" Avery motioned to us to follow him.

She turned to me as if to seek approval. "Oh, I don't want to intrude."

"You should join us. I came early to catch up," I assured her.

"Okay, then." Mrs. Evans began the conversation once we took our seats, "So, Avery tells me you've been attending Sylvania Ridge University. How do you like it there?"

"I like it. The university has been flexible with my course selection where I'm able to get credit and be paid to speak, so I'm grateful for that." *At least something good came out of that terrifying assault.*

"Oh, that's right. You spoke at church. I'm so sorry I missed that," she said with regret.

I waved her off because I didn't expect people to show up just because they knew me. "It's fine. You go if you feel compelled. Most of the time I don't know anyone in the group I'm talking to."

Avery's mom asked, "Is it hard to talk in front of strangers?"

"It's probably easier when I don't know anyone, since the nature of my topic is very personal and can make them feel uncomfortable." I was able to answer with ease because I wrote about my observations as part of my course credit.

Mrs. Evans clamped her hands together. "We don't have to talk about it if you don't want to."

"It's okay. It helps to talk about it, but I'm fine now either way," I said in a carefree manner.

With compassion in her voice, Mrs. Evans said, "You're very brave, Christina."

The edges of my mouth moved up and widened. "God gives me the strength." *Lord knows I would be a complete mess otherwise.*

Avery interjected without sounding condescending, "She is brave, Mom. I'm so proud of her."

I looked down, at a loss for words. For a while I was merely surviving. I finally felt like I was on the verge of thriving again.

A verse from the Old Testament jumped from the page while sitting on my bed later that evening, "O God, thou art terrible out of thy holy places: the God of Israel is he that giveth strength and power unto his people. Blessed be God" (Psalm 68:35). We discussed this verse in my cell group in college. As a group, we translated it to mean that God is awesome from His sanctuary, and He gives strength and power to those who believe. That night, I had hope that God would restore me, although I didn't know how or when.

Chapter 22

Saturday arrived, and I was gearing up for my next talk at a local church. I noticed how much better I felt after telling Avery, my mom, and Miss Brenda that Paul raped me. The change was dramatic. I felt so much freer, like I could breathe with ease and not feel like I was walking on eggshells.

After the head of the women's ministry introduced me, I walked behind the podium and looked at all the faces before me in the classroom setting. As I scanned the room, I noticed my mom sitting at a table in the back. She must have snuck in a couple minutes ago. I preferred giving my talk in a more casual setting like in a classroom as opposed to speaking at the pulpit in the sanctuary. It felt more intimate, and I didn't feel as much pressure to be this amazing preacher. I inhaled, closed my eyes to anchor myself, and began…

"I went through a traumatic event. Some of you have heard about how I was raped and had a knife held to me in college, but that's not the only reason I'm here today." I paused to let my statement sink in.

"I'm here to tell you how I was also raped the summer before my freshman year in high school. This is the first time I'm going public with my first rape. In fact, I just told three people, and when I did, I felt like I was freed of it." I looked at my mother who nodded. That was a huge acknowledgement from her, giving me the assurance to continue.

"I had tried all kinds of things to help me cope with my rape, like listening to music, meditating on scripture which helped, but there was nothing like speaking about it. Once I told someone, I felt like I was on the path to healing like it didn't have a hold on me any longer. Don't get me wrong. Those other techniques were helpful and got me through the toughest times, but it wasn't until I unleashed what I held so closely that I could finally feel like a survivor and not a victim."

With steadfast conviction, I raised my voice and said, "I'm no longer a victim of rape. I'm a survivor. I'm here to tell my story and to make sure you share yours, so your chains will be broken like mine were. There is power in the spoken word. I'm proof of that. If you are holding onto a secret, you need to release it. "And ye shall know the truth, and the truth shall make you free" (John 8:32). I know this from experience." All eyes were on me, and no one stirred.

"For years I carried this huge burden with me like there was a heavy backpack permanently strapped on my back. It weighed me down. I was afraid to tell anyone, because initially I was threatened that if I did, my perpetrator, okay, the guy who raped me, would kill me and my boyfriend. I believed he would kill us, especially after his heinous crime against me." I scanned the room and inhaled deeply before continuing.

"He also told me that his mother was friends with all kinds of influential people, people of authority like judges… So, I kept the rape a secret. I bottled it up. I had nightmares, sweats, anxiety attacks, and I even started cutting myself." There was a gasp. "Yes, I engaged in self-mutilation. I'm not proud of it. This is the first time I'm going public about the cutting. No one knew. I'm telling you, because if I can stop the self-harm, then you can too. You can do what seems impossible. Get help. Tell someone. Keeping it inside doesn't help you. It only keeps you down." A couple people nodded their heads in agreement.

"If you want to start healing, you need to open your mouth and start that conversation. Confide in someone you trust. If you have no one you trust, you can tell me. I am here for you. I want you to start healing. I want you to experience the weight that will be lifted by telling someone the same way I did. I don't want you suffering any longer. You suffered long enough." A woman seated in the front to my right wiped a tear away.

"If you haven't accepted Jesus as your Lord and Savior, that is the best gift you can ever receive. Once I did that there was a peace that fell over me that I still don't comprehend, but I know that by the grace of God I am a child of God. I will have everlasting life. Some days that's all I can cling to. Every day I wake up and give it to God. I pray for the Holy Spirit to give me strength, to guide and direct my path. It hasn't been easy, but there has been comfort in the midst of horror. Sometimes you may feel like God is this far away being that doesn't care about you, but that's not true. He is there for us at all times, especially when we are suffering or feeling overwhelmed. Psalm

34:18 reassures us that, "The Lord is nigh unto them that are of a broken heart; and saveth such as be of a contrite spirit." I let them take in the verse before proceeding.

"I can't imagine going through all I've endured without Christ. Well, actually, I can because I did. It was excruciating. For months I suffered totally alone. I hadn't knowingly experienced the love of Jesus. I was totally in the dark, in deep despair. Once I became saved, I started to heal." A few women smiled after seeing the grin on my face.

"The Lord showed me ways to help ease the pain. I started to read scripture and commit certain verses to memory. That alone helped me tremendously. I prayed and prayed and studied His word. I started going to church, I attended Sunday school, and absorbed as much as I could about God's word. Luke tells us in chapter 11 verse 28, "But he said, Yea rather, blessed are they that hear the word of God, and keep it." *Please let these words penetrate my mother's heart.*

"Music became a solace. First classical, then Christian. I started running, which helps clear my head and releases much of the tension. Maybe God will reveal ways for you to heal. There isn't a one size fits all. God cares about you. He numbered every hair on your head. I'm still finding my way. God is good, and He is faithful. He is still telling me ways to reconcile the past, so I can move on and live a productive life. 2 Thessalonians 3:3 states, "But the Lord is faithful, who shall stablish you, and keep you from evil." *Amen.* I scanned the room to let them know that this message was for them.

"That's why I'm here today. For me, I realized it helped me dramatically by revealing my deep dark dirty secret. My college suggested I give talks like this and write about my experience for course credit. I saw the difference when I accepted the course program as a way for me to not only earn credits but to heal in the process. Writing about my feelings gave me clarity." I licked my lips before proceeding.

"Telling people that I was raped released the hold it had on me. I didn't realize at first why I was able to feel differently about my most recent rape that was even more traumatic, because he was on the verge of killing me with a knife right before I was rescued." I lifted my hand as if I held a knife ready to stab someone. My voice cracked, "I was bound with a scarf, unable to speak or scream." Taking a deep breath helped to propel my words.

"The big difference was that I spoke about that rape, and I wrote about it as well. Now I know why they say you should go to counseling. The spoken word is powerful. I know first-hand how hard it is to talk about a tragic event, especially after being threatened that if you do, you will be killed. I believed that my first rapist would kill me if I told anyone. Of course I did. Why wouldn't I after what he did to me? If he was capable of one despicable act, then he would be capable of another. Let me be blunt…" I took the time to annunciate each word, "If he was capable of raping me, he was capable of killing me."

"Why didn't I go to the authorities back in high school? My rapist told me that it would be his word against mine. He said his mother was connected to judges, the police, the media… He would claim it was consensual. After all, I had been seen in public kissing a boy two nights prior. That was the first time I ever kissed a boy. I felt guilty, ashamed, dirty. Who would believe me? I couldn't take the chance." My voice quivered, "He threatened to kill my boyfriend and me. I couldn't let that happen." I shook my head for emphasis.

"Now, you know why I was silent. Now, I'm telling you why not to be silent. You will die inside by keeping it all bottled up. It's a different kind of death, but a death, nonetheless." I paused momentarily while I surveyed the room. All eyes were glued on me and not one person moved.

"Not only was I silent about being raped, but I lied to cover up what happened and to explain my peculiar behavior. I never lied before I was raped, and the lies ate away at me. Proverbs 12:22 states, "Lying lips are an abomination to the LORD: but they that deal truly are his delight." In other words, God doesn't like it when you lie. Even though it didn't feel right to lie, I justified my lies." I shifted from one leg to the other. "Finally, that conviction has made me come clean, and it feels so much better to come out with the truth. I was riddled with guilt from lying. No more secrets. No more lying. Withholding the truth is a lie. It's a lie of omission. My friend told me that, but I dismissed it and resented her for saying that." A picture of Faith, my friend from school came to mind. Our friendship ended after she moved before our sophomore year.

"If you are here but never experienced anything like what I mentioned, I hope you were able to gain something from your time here. If you're not a believer, talk to someone like me about becoming a Christian. We'll be happy to answer any of your questions." I gestured toward the ministry director.

"I know we're in a church, but that doesn't have any guarantees. You could be a guest. Perhaps someone brought you here," I said as I tilted my head.

"If you are a believer, then what can you do to grow in the Lord? How can you serve? Maybe you can be a sounding board for others, an empathetic ear, an encourager," I said, knowing that not everyone present was assaulted or was hiding something.

"Perhaps you need to take care of your needs first. Maybe you can take up running or start a craft like knitting to reduce your stress. We all have stress on some level. We all need God." *Please, God, don't let this fall on deaf ears.*

"We need each other too. Reach out to someone. Be a friend. Be a good listener. Volunteer at a soup kitchen. Read to children at the library. Do something that will help others, and it may end up being a gift to yourself as well." My words began to speak to me too.

"Thank you for having me and for coming today. I'll be available for a few minutes afterward should you want to talk."

One of the women in charge approached me. "Lovely speech."

"Thank you," I replied.

Another woman peeked out from behind the ministry leader. "May I have a word in private?"

"I'll leave you to it," the women's ministry leader said with a nod and walked away.

A brunette woman of average frame introduced herself, "Hello, I'm Rebecca Stanford."

I smiled. "Hi. It's nice to meet you."

"I have a story to tell." She wrangled her hands. "I was raped when I was ten."

I closed my eyes at the sting of her comment. "I'm so sorry," I replied, shaking my head.

Her gaze lowered as she pressed her lips together. "Yes, well. It was my uncle. My mother's older brother. I told her what happened. Well, I tried to at least. I didn't know what he did was called rape. I was only ten years old, but I knew it was wrong. He threatened to kill me if I said anything. I did anyway." Ms. Stanford took a breath, pursed her lips, and continued, "My mother slapped me across the face. She said she would wash my mouth out with soap if I continued to tell lies.

I couldn't lie about something like that. I was too young to make it up. Anyway, from that moment on I couldn't trust my mother with anything. My uncle continued to rape me until I was fourteen. I knew by then what he was doing was rape, and I knew it was vile and heinous." I cringed with empathy as she spoke but wanted to shed a tear for her horror.

She gestured with her right hand. "There was a special health class we were required to take in high school that talked about what to do if you were ever raped, so I told my teacher. She contacted the authorities, and an investigation ensued. My uncle was convicted and thrown in prison for only five years. He got out on good behavior. I was twenty when he got out of prison and came looking for me. I was terrified. I thought he was going to kill me. Turns out I was right. His cell mate got a message to my mother stating what my uncle had planned. He was going to shoot me." I hung on her every word.

I noticed the room got quieter and discovered that most of the attendees had left. Ms. Stanford's lips formed a straight line across her face and picked up where she left off. "I moved out of my home as soon as I turned 18. I found a tiny apartment and was living on my own. Even after the trial, I couldn't trust my mother. I didn't turn 18 fast enough. Long story short, he found me, even though I was unlisted. My mother was there trying to convince me to flee the state. That's when I found out he raped her too. There was a scuffle between my uncle and my mom. The gun went off. My mother looked horrified. My uncle collapsed and died from the gunshot. My mother was declared not guilty after the DA brought charges against her. My testimony basically saved her life. She saved mine." There was a slight glimmer in her eye.

"Our relationship has been strained since I was 10, but it's on the mend. I wish I had told someone else sooner. That's my biggest regret. He went on to rape me for four years. Four years of living in hell and all the years up to now. I don't think rape is something you ever get over. It's something you manage." She stopped talking, and I didn't know what to say at first.

"How do you manage?" I asked.

"I go to the gun range. I know that might sound counter intuitive, like I'm exchanging one type of violence for another, but it's not like that… I have a sense of being in control, of having the power. I needed to take back my power."

For a lack of anything else to say, I said, "I'm glad you have a way to manage it."

She responded with a head nod. "Me too. You were right in that survivors of rape need to find something to help them heal, to give them that power back. Thank you for sharing with us."

"You're welcome," I replied with a smile.

"I'm considering hiking now as a hobby. I know you mentioned running, but I think I might enjoy hiking better." The lights flickered. I noticed that the room was almost empty.

"Let me know how that works out." I handed her my business card with my phone number written in pen on the back.

"Okay, I will. Thank you," she said as she turned to leave.

"Take care." I waved goodbye.

"You, too." She waved back as she was heading toward the door.

Avery and I made plans to meet up after my talk. For a change, we decided to hit the new salad place that was across the street from the church. Otherwise, I would be too tempted to have a cheeseburger and shake at the diner. Lucky for me and my waistline, Avery was amenable.

The restaurant had giant photos of salad hung on its walls, making salads look scrumptious. The music added to the atmosphere by playing soft rock hits like "Hands to Heaven" sung by the English band, Breathe.

Avery approached me with a smile and leaned in to kiss me on the cheek.

"Is that the best you got?" I teased.

Avery shook his head. "Here we go again. More mixed messages."

I laughed as I knew what he meant. Back in high school I gave him mixed signals. "Well, we are official now, aren't we?"

"We are finally," he said, as his eyes glimmered a bright blue in the light. This time he firmly planted a kiss on my lips.

My knees gave out. "Much better. You've always been a fast learner," I jested.

Once seated inside, Avery asked, "So, how did your sermon go?"

"My sermon?" I asked. I didn't consider my talks to be a sermon.

"Or whatever you call it. How did it go?"

"My talk went fine. I went public with what happened in high school," I stated in a casual manner.

"Wow, That's a big step. Do you feel any different having gone public?"

I nodded. "Actually, I do, like a huge burden was lifted."

"That's great!" Avery's face showed his excitement for me. It was apparent that he understood the magnitude of my reveal.

In a nonchalant manner, I said, "My mom was there."

"Yeah, I saw her leave. She said you did great." He grinned.

"Oh, she did? I didn't get a chance to talk to her—"

"Let me guess, you were talking to someone," he assumed.

"Yeah, my mom told you?"

He smiled. "Yeah, she said you were captivating."

Captivating. Hearing that made me smile. "I'm glad I told her before going public." I knew that what I said was probably hard for her to hear, but it would have been shocking if I didn't already share my story with her.

Avery raised his eyebrows. "No more secrets then?"

"Hey, look who's talking!" I said, not letting him off the hook since he also kept a huge secret from me.

He held up his hands, "Myself included. So, no more secrets?" Avery reached out for me to shake his hand.

We shook hands, and I said with certitude, "No more secrets."

"So, what's good here?"

"I hear the salads are good." I smirked.

Avery threw his hand up in the air. "I would have never guessed, especially since this is a salad place."

"Well then, you're not too swift, huh?" I teased.

"I got the girl, didn't I?" He quipped, as he raised his eyebrows up and down.

"Yup," I said, smacking my lips together. "You got the girl," I acknowledged.

"Then that's all that matters." He said with a wide grin.

Chapter 23

I met up with Sherrie to see how she was doing. We went for a walk around our neighborhood. This was a good sign because she refused to go anywhere after Paul raped her.

As we approached the woods at the apex of the hill, she said, "I go to church now with my friend, Tracey. I really like it, and I'm learning a lot about God and Jesus. We go to Sunday school too. It's like getting an extra dose of Jesus."

I was delighted to hear that Sherrie was doing well and growing in her faith and hoped she would continue to do so. As a result, I couldn't hide my excitement for her. "That's great! Maybe you could join a youth group." Mentioning youth group made me think of Avery and how he got into porn. *Maybe that's not such a good idea after all.*

"What's a youth group?" Sherrie asked, her face contorted.

"It's when teens get together supervised by adults and learn about Jesus. There's usually games and food involved," I shared, not speaking from personal experience.

"That sounds awesome! Did you do that?" Sherrie sounded interested. *Maybe if I had, Avery wouldn't have turned into a porn addict.*

"No, I didn't, but I know people who did," I answered, trying to sound encouraging.

"Why didn't you?" she asked.

I thought for a second before responding. "I didn't think my parents would let me since they weren't into the church thing at all. I guess I didn't want to push my luck, because I was going to church with my boyfriend as it was."

"Oh, wow," she said as if she cared and understood.

I hesitated to say something, but the internal nudging persisted. "Sherrie, I have something to tell you…"

"Yeah," she said as a cue for me to continue.

"I was raped in high school."

"I thought it happened in college," she said, sounding confused.

"It did, but I was also raped in high school."

"Oh my gosh. I'm so sorry." I could hear the sincerity in her voice as we continued to walk.

"That's not all. You aren't going to believe who did it."

There was a chilling moment of silence when Sherrie stopped abruptly. A look of discovery pained her face. She exclaimed, "Oh my G—, it wasn't—?" Sherrie couldn't say Paul's name the same way I couldn't until recently.

"Yes, it was Paul," I confirmed.

Her voice was loud, her tone accusatory. "And you never told anyone? Why not?"

In an attempt to explain, I answered, "He threatened to kill me and my boyfriend."

Sherrie didn't break her stance. "He threatened me too, but I said something—eventually," she ribbed.

Ouch. "I'm really sorry," I said. *I feel sick about this.*

Her face was boiling red. "I can't believe this. If you said something, he probably wouldn't have—Oh, my G—!" Her eyes bulged, and her face writhed with revulsion. "I can't believe this! I can't believe you! You should have told someone!" She yelled from the top of her lungs, her hands flailing.

I cuffed my mouth, and the tears began to gush. "You're right. I should have told someone. I wish I did. I'm so sorry!" My hands rubbed against my cheeks and came together at my mouth. "Please forgive me!"

"Get away from me! Don't come near me again," she screamed and ran away.

I knew I could easily catch up with Sherrie, but she was too upset to console, especially by me. She needed time to sort things out. After all, I dropped a huge bomb on her.

It was my fault. If I had told someone that Paul raped me, he probably wouldn't have raped Sherrie. I was to blame. Instead, he got away with not only one, but two rapes, and maybe even more. *Was I the first? Or did he rape someone else before me?* All along I never considered he raped other girls.

I distanced myself from Sherrie with each step. The trees surrounded me as I followed the familiar dirt path. I spun around at the sound of leaves crackling within close range. The flutter of a bird flapping its wings was heard nearby. I wanted to fly away, to experience the freedom to soar in the sky, to escape.

The river trail, miles away, was calling my name. With a sudden burst, I darted out of the woods and ran toward the river. Remembering the long distance to reach my goal, I began to slow down, knowing I had to pace myself if I wanted to run the entire way. The river was on my mind. Reaching it became my quest. *Why am I so drawn to the river?*

The river was like a magnet pulling me toward it. One step after another, I drew closer to my destination. Pit-a-pat, pit-a-pat, pit-a-pat. My arms moved to the same rhythm of my legs. A light wind refreshed my spirit. *Keep running. Just keep running. You're almost there.* Sweat was pouring down my face and stinging my eyes. The sun, high in the cloudless sky, was mocking me as it beat down on my defenseless body. My arms pumped faster as I climbed the crest of a hill. Pump, pump, pump. *I will not be defeated. I shall overcome.* The wood bridge straddling over the river was a welcoming sight. *Only a few steps away.*

I slowed down my pace before coming to a complete stop. With my hand on my hips, I slowed my pace along the perimeter of the bridge. While wiping the sweat away, I took a deep breath and released the lingering tension. I shook my arms out as if to dislodge them from my body and bent forward only to gasp on the fresh air. The railing of the bridge offered support to me as I peered toward the horizon of the stagnant river and soaked in the framework of the expansive trees.

For a few precious moments I was able to be free—free of the rapes, free of my guilt, free of blame.

As I felt the sun's rays penetrate my body, my soul, scripture came to mind, "And ye shall know the truth, and the truth shall make you free" (Malachi 4:2). *Lord, I cry out to you. Let your healing rays restore Sherrie and me. Help us to enjoy life to its fullest.*

Chapter 24

T ime for a girls' night out. Social Director, Morgan, had been taking a summer class consuming all her spare time. She called Katie, Amy, and me to go out to dinner after a long week of schoolwork. We met at a quaint café and managed to be seated outside on a deck despite it being a busy Friday night.

Morgan started the conversation, "It's so great to see you all. I'm glad we could all meet here for dinner."

Amy jumped in, "Me too. I'm dying to know how everyone is doing." She swallowed her words when she looked in my direction. "I'm sorry, Christina. I know things were rough for you over Christmas break. How are you doing now?"

Trying to sound as normal as possible, I replied, "I'm okay." I didn't want to talk about my situation in public let alone bring down the crowd.

"Well, you look really good," Amy said as an attempt to smooth over her previous comment.

"Yeah, you do," Katie agreed.

Morgan turned to me and asked, "Are you still running?"

"Yup, just went for a run today as a matter of fact. Katie, are you still working at the clothes store?" I deflected the conversation to Katie as I didn't want the focus to be on me.

Katie gratuitously responded, "I am, and Amy is one of my best customers."

"A girl's gotta do something to stay busy," Amy quipped.

Katie volleyed, "Amy, you should get a job. You have way too much time on your hands."

"What I would give to have a moment to myself. I'm so sick of school," Morgan said as if it physically weighed her down.

Amy leaned across the table and said, "But, you're so good at it, Morgan."

"It can't be over soon enough. I want to be able to enjoy my summer," Morgan said, slurping her Coke.

"Are you still seeing Derek?" Amy asked.

"Yeah, but he's in Virginia and I'm here." She sighed. "What about you guys? Anyone dating?" Morgan took a turn looking at each of us.

Amy threw up her hands, "Nope, not me. Always flying solo. Only way I know."

"Me neither," Katie shook her head.

All eyes were on me. "What?" I asked in an attempt to look innocent, but my acting skills lacked at the moment.

Amy asked, "You're going out with someone, aren't you?" I squirmed in my seat.

Morgan launched. "I know that look. You *are* going out with someone. Spill. Who is it? I could use some good news."

I held up my hands, "All right. All right. Guilty as charged."

Amy reproved, "You have been holding out on us this whole time?"

"Well, tell us about him. What's his name? What's he like? Where did you meet him?" Katie fired questions at me.

I waited for her to finish her barrage of questioning before answering. "Well, it turns out you already know him."

"Who is it?" Amy asked. It was obvious she was dying to know.

"Christina, tell us already," Morgan said.

Since they already guessed I was dating someone, I felt like it wasn't right to hold out any longer. I wasn't in the mood to play games, so I answered without hesitation, "Avery. It's Avery."

Katie's eyes widened. "As in Evans?"

I nodded in confirmation.

Amy was at the edge of her seat, clapped her hands a couple times and pleaded, "Tell us everything." Her reaction felt like déjà vu when Avery and I had our first public kiss the night of the pageant, but so much has happened since then.

Morgan's forehead creased. "Are you okay? You don't seem too happy about it," she said. Astute as ever, my best friend perceived something was wrong.

I answered lightheartedly to keep them from prying, "Oh yeah, it's not Avery. I have a lot going on."

"Like what?" Katie asked. I walked right into that one.

Think fast, Christina. "You know how I give talks at churches… Well, it's hard to explain, but it's been kinda stressful lately."

"How so?" asked Amy, sounding concerned as well as curious.

"Uh, people tell me very personal things, heart-wrenching stuff really, and I try to help them. They're not my stories to tell," I answered. *I'm a master crafter of lies. Old habits die hard.*

"How did you and Avery get back together?" Morgan asked.

After taking a sip of water, I licked my lips, and replied, "Avery heard that I was speaking at his church and approached me afterwards. We went to lunch so he could tell me why he broke up with me—"

Amy interrupted me by asking, "Why did he break up with you?" *Oh, no! I did it again. I walked right into it. What is the matter with me?*

I shrugged, hoping to stave off the inquisition. "Again, it's not my story to tell."

"So, he told you why and just like that," Katie snapped her fingers, "you're back together?"

Katie made me getting back with Avery sound so absurd. *How can I make it sound better?* "No, it's not that simple. We ran into each other the next day. It turns out that neither of us got over the other one."

Amy said, "You two were so great together." Chills ran through my body as I was in complete agreement.

"Why did he leave Pennsford?" Katie asked.

"Let me guess, it's not your story to tell," Morgan jumped in. "But you're sure you're okay?" Morgan's cat-like eyes were penetrating.

"Yeah, I'm fine." I changed the subject to avoid a probable meltdown. We ended the evening discussing the possibility of getting together with the old gang from high school from when I dated Avery. I kept quiet knowing Avery ditched all his friends, not just me. A reunion would have been awkward to say the least.

Chapter 25

organ called and said she needed to talk privately. Her family was out of state visiting a sick relative. She didn't go because she had too much homework to be gone for an entire day.

I pulled in her driveway and walked around the back entrance. She opened the door and said, "Hey, thanks for coming. Can I get you something to drink?" Morgan learned how to be hospitable from her mom.

"No, I'm good. Thanks." I followed her to the living room.

She gestured toward the brown couch and plopped down on the adjacent matching chair. "Have a seat." I waited for her to speak again, not having a clue why she wanted to talk. "I know you're wondering why I needed to talk to you."

I turned my body to face her. "Yeah, what's going on?"

Morgan leaned forward and placed her hands on her lap. "Well, here's the thing. You seemed off last night like something was wrong. For some reason, I didn't think it was the right place to discuss it. Don't worry, I didn't mention my concerns to Katie or Amy just in case. So, am I right? Is something wrong? I won't repeat it. I promise. I just had this sense you needed to talk in private."

How did you know? Was I that obvious?

I took a deep breath and closed my eyes for a second. "I don't even know where to start."

"How about the beginning?" Morgan suggested.

Feeling like I was in a safe space, I blurted, "Okay…" I wasn't prepared for this, but Morgan was my best friend, and my deep, dark secret was no longer dead and buried. *Here goes…* "I wasn't just raped in college. I was raped in high school too." *There's nothing like dropping a bomb.*

Morgan's eyes shot wide open as I watched her mouth drop to the floor. "Oh, man! I wasn't expecting that. I'm so sorry. I have so many questions, but I'll let you tell the story. Go on." She stopped for a second then continued abruptly, waving her hands, "Unless this is too hard for you to talk about. I don't want to pry or push you. I can only imagine how hard this is for you."

"Uh, no, it's okay. It helps to talk about it, but not in a place like a restaurant." I assured her. *At least not to initially tell a group of friends.*

"Of course. You sure you don't need a glass of water or something?"

"No, no. I'm fine. Thanks. Okay. So, where was I?" I panned upward to capture where I left off. "Right. Yeah, so, Paul Martin raped me the summer before our freshman year, two days after the beauty pageant."

I paused to collect my thoughts when Morgan exclaimed, "Paul Martin! That lousy low life scum!" She realized the intensity of her outburst and said, "I'm sorry. This is hard to process."

"Yeah, try living it." I said, in a tongue in cheek kind of way.

Morgan threw her hand over her face. "Oh my gosh, I'm so sorry. I didn't mean…"

I didn't want Morgan to beat herself up, so to placate her I said, "I know. It's okay. It's a lot to take in. I've been dealing with it for six years now, and I only recently told someone for the first time. In fact, I told Avery. He came over to my house one day. Ah, this is such a disaster." Taking a physical reaction out of Morgan's playbook, I rubbed my face out of frustration. Spending time with Morgan lately caused her face rubbing to rub off on me.

She blinked and nodded with encouragement. "It's okay. Take your time."

I panned the ceiling to snatch the next part of my story. "Avery wanted to get back together. He told me that a couple times before. I agreed to go back out with him. This was after he told me why he broke up with me."

"Why did he break up with you?" Morgan asked the question of the weekend.

"That's a whole other story. One I can't get into."

"Okay. I understand."

You do? Because I don't. "Okay, so I was jogging the day after we met, trying to release all the stress and tension from finding out Paul raped another girl several years younger than us. I felt so guilty that I went for a run and ended up running near Avery's house which was weird, because I never ran in that direction before on my own. Joey and I used to run around his neighborhood." I paused for a second as I had a realization. "Maybe that's why I ran in that direction. Huh." I shook my head. "It's been years since I ran with Joey of course. Anyway, Avery saw me running while he was mowing his lawn and chased after me without me knowing, and we literally bumped into each other. We had a moment and we kissed and—"

"You kissed Avery in the middle of the street on a jog?" she said, bewildered.

"Pretty much." Morgan leaned forward and I continued. "Then Avery said something about the kiss reminding him of our first kiss at the Martin's house, and I lost it. I ran away. He called after me, but I took off. Later that same day, he came to my house while I was reading outside. We talked some more, and I broke down and told him that Paul raped me. That was the first time I told anyone."

I started to get choked up. "He consoled me, and we decided at that point to start dating. It was all so fast and confusing. In the meantime, I was in touch with the other girl who was raped by Paul too. She apparently went public with it, but I don't know the details. He moved away." I waved my hand. "Anyway, the girl was still having a tough time. She's anorexic, possibly bulimic. I don't know. Long story short, I led her to Christ."

Morgan gestured with her hand. "So that girl is now a Christian?"

I nodded and started to tear up, "Yeah, but we went for a walk yesterday and I told her how Paul raped me too. You see, she didn't know that before. At that point, I had only told Avery, my mom and a woman from The Manor who knew all along back that summer that something was wrong. I had to tell her. I knew I would eventually tell you when the time was right, and here I am telling you."

"I'm glad you're finally telling me. Again, I'm so sorry you went through all that by yourself," Morgan said, then handed me a tissue box.

"Yeah, well." I shrugged and tears began to bubble over my eyelids. I blew my nose and wiped my tears with a tissue from the box Morgan gave me. "Oh, so back to the girl…" Visions of Sherrie appeared in my memory. I recalled how upset she was when I told her Paul was also my assailant. Tears fell on my cheeks, and I wiped them with a tissue. After attempting to pull myself together, I said, "She flipped out when I told her that Paul raped me too. She said—" I tried my best to compose myself again. "She s-said it was m-my fault Paul raped her, because I n-never told anyone." I sniffled, and it was difficult to continue. Filling my lungs up with air, I exclaimed, "It's my fault, Morgan. It's all my fault that she was raped." No longer able to contain my regret, I sobbed with complete abandonment.

Morgan sprang up from her seat and wrapped her arms around me and repeated, "It's not your fault. It's not your fault. You can't blame yourself. That wasn't your fault." I let it all out. I didn't hold back, and it felt good to cry hard.

After a few moments, I was able to settle down. I dabbed my eyes with a tissue and said, "There's more to it, but that's the gist of it."

Morgan took hold of my hands and began praying, "Dear Heavenly Father, wrap Your loving arms around Christina. Heal her of this pain, guilt, and torment she is feeling. Let it be clear to her that she is not responsible for Paul's actions. I ask that You heal this other girl too, and allow her to understand that this is not Christina's fault. In Jesus' precious name, we pray. Amen." Morgan rubbed the sides of my arms and said, "Now, can I get you something to drink? How about we make milkshakes?"

I laughed at her suggestion. "I'll just have some water. Thanks."

Morgan persisted, "You sure? I can whip us up some shakes." She grinned at me sideways and gave me the thumbs up.

She's really pushing the shakes. "Oh, what the heck. Sure, why not?" I was such a sucker for a chocolate shake.

A little later, Morgan took a sip of her extra thick, extra chocolatey shake and said, "Man, you have been through quite the ordeal, and I had no idea this entire time. Is there anything else I should know?"

"My talks now focus on making sure victims of sexual assault share their stories, since talking about it has been a huge part of my healing process." That proverbial backpack I've been carrying around all these years is getting lighter and lighter. *It's a good thing I consume milkshakes, or I might float away.* I justified to myself for indulging yet again.

Morgan nodded and said, "I can see that. Why didn't you tell anyone before?"

"Oh right. I forgot that part. I never said anything because Paul threatened to kill Avery and me," I responded without any drama, and I noticed it was getting easier to tell my story.

Morgan shook her head. "Oh man. That makes sense. So, you lived in fear this entire time? Why say anything now?"

I answered, "The girl I told you about—her mom told me Paul raped her, so I knew I had nothing to lose—and I realized how much it helped me to talk about how I was raped in college. I had more of a peace about that rape, even though it was much more violent."

"Tell me how I can help. Is there anything I can do to help you through this?" Morgan asked with an eagerness to help in her voice.

"You helped me all along without even knowing. I'm so sorry for lying to you. That was one of the hardest parts. I thought I was protecting Avery and me. I was stupid and scared," I said, shaking my head as I second guessed the severity of the situation I endured.

Morgan threw out her arms and leaned forward. With certitude, she said, "No, don't say that. You're not stupid. Don't *ever* say you're stupid. You're not stupid at all."

"Please forgive me for lying to you…"

Morgan was swift in her response, "You don't have to apologize at all. I understand. You were terrified and rightfully so. There's nothing to forgive. You're very strong to go through all that by yourself." Morgan shook her head. "I couldn't go it alone. I'm sorry you didn't feel like you could say anything to me or anyone else." Drawing a deep breath, Morgan continued, "What I want to know is how you and

Avery are doing now? How is he? What's going on between you two?"

Hearing Avery's name brought a smile to my face. "We're good. He was very persistent in getting us back together. He's been great. Very understanding, but he doesn't know what happened yesterday with the other girl."

"Why didn't you tell him?" Morgan asked as she smoothed hair behind her ear.

"I didn't want to get upset on the phone and then have to meet you guys later at the restaurant. I knew I would start crying, and I didn't want him to worry. I expend a lot of energy trying not to fall apart. It's exhausting, and I decided not to tell any more lies," I declared as I shook my head. "Lying is equally exhausting. I want this all to end. I'm so sick of living like this with all the lies, living in fear. Now that you know, and Avery knows and my mom knows that Paul raped me, I can get on with my life. Oh, and now that girl knows too, and she hates me for not telling anyone." I grimaced when I pictured the horrified look on Sherrie's face when she drew the conclusion that I was the reason for all her pain and anguish. The terrorized look on her face said it all. I caused all her crying fits as well as her eating disorder. I was the wolf dressed in sheep's clothing.

Morgan lifted her head in confidence, "I'm sure she doesn't hate you."

I came back with force, "Yes, she does. She screamed at me and basically told me to stay away from her. I hope she doesn't lose her faith. I witnessed to her, and she became saved. She started doing so much better too… and now this… I know she feels betrayed."

Morgan rubbed my arm and gave me a sympathetic look. "It never occurred to me that Paul would rape someone else. I feel horrible for not saying anything. I would have said something if I even thought there was a chance he could do that to someone else. Instead, I only thought about myself."

"You thought about keeping Avery safe too. Don't forget that," Morgan pointed out.

I nodded. I shuddered thinking how I thought Paul could kill my mom too.

"Just pray that the girl—" I indicated with a head bob and went on, "Continues with her faith. That's my biggest concern right now."

"Okay. Let's pray about that right now," Morgan suggested.

I didn't mean literally right then and there, but that worked for me.

Morgan grabbed hold of my hands and began praying. "Dear Heavenly Father, we lift up Christina's new friend, the one she witnessed to, and ask that her faith in Your Son grows stronger and deeper. I also ask that she forgives Christina even though she didn't do anything wrong. God the Father, please protect Christina from any more harm as she has been through more than anyone I know. Lord, You are our healer, our protector, our redeemer, and our Savior. I lift up all these requests as your humble servant. Amen."

"Amen." I opened my eyes and was extremely grateful for the person in front of me.

"Are you going to my church tomorrow?" Morgan asked hopefully.

I shifted my neck to the right, suddenly having more options of where to go to church. "I'm not sure. Avery wanted me to go to his church since we're back together. His parents even asked me to join them."

"You should go with him then," Morgan suggested with a definitive nod.

"Why do you say that?"

Morgan shared her wisdom with me, "It just makes sense since you're a couple now. You should do things couples do, and it's great that he wants you to join him."

I let out a chuckle. "If it were up to Avery, we would be spending every waking moment together."

"That's understandable and normal, but it doesn't sound like that's what you want," Morgan said.

I pouted, thinking about all the recent changes in my life that I didn't see coming. "I don't know what I want. It's not like I don't enjoy spending time with him. I do, but…"

"You don't want to be tied down?" Morgan speculated.

Knowing that wasn't quite right, I shrugged in response and replied, "Something like that."

"What is it then?" Morgan's tone was more than curiosity. It was comforting knowing I had a friend who wanted the best for me and was willing to help me figure that out.

I crossed my legs and sat back. "I want to take things slow. Ease into things. I have been through so much already that all this change is overwhelming, even though some of it is a good kind of change."

Morgan pointed her index finger in my direction. "You have to decide what's best for you. Do you think Avery's the one?"

"There is something about Avery that…" I closed my eyes and pictured his handsome face and how he made me feel. "That draws me to him. He makes me feel safe, always has." The warm fuzzies filled me up and oozed out when I said, "We have this unbelievable connection that is undeniable. I'm not sure that kind of connection could exist with anyone else. It's quite powerful." I laughed and continued, "I know that sounds crazy, but it's true. It's hard to explain." I imagined that I sounded like a crazed, lovesick teenager. Maybe because I was a crazed, lovesick teenager. I better snap out of this before I turn twenty. *Christina's tumultuous teens.* I laughed silently to myself.

"He must have had a *really* good reason to break up with you," Morgan said in between bits of laughter.

Thinking of Avery's porn addiction, I scrunched up my face before responding, "It's not like I accepted his apology and jumped into his arms. It took me years of trying to get over him and in the end, I guess I never did."

A twinkle appeared in Morgan's eyes. "Well, I hope it works out between you two. I have never seen two people more suited for each other."

Wanting desperately to get the focus off of me, I changed the subject. "So how are you and Derek doing?"

"Oh, we're fine. Just doing the long-distance thing for the summer. After this class is over we'll visit each other."

Turning the tables on Morgan, I asked, "Do you think he's the one?"

She puckered her lips as she contemplated her answer. "Could be. I'm really not sure yet."

Remembering my embarrassing episode the day I met him I said, "I know I didn't give him the best first impression over Christmas break."

With a flick of her wrist like she was shoeing away a fly, Morgan assured me, "Oh, don't worry about that. You were fine under the circumstances. Great actually. You'll get to see him again this summer."

"Good. I'll have a chance to redeem myself." I looked at my watch. "Well, I better get going. I know you have homework and studying to do."

My sweet friend rolled her eyes and frowned. "Yeah. I can't wait to get back to it."

Chapter 26

I drove over to Avery's for dinner with his parents. It felt like old times. I always enjoyed hanging out with his parents. We got close the last year we were together, because we made a point to be in public as much as possible to avoid the temptations from being alone. *How ironic.*

After dinner Avery asked, "I started learning how to play a new song on my guitar. Wanna hear it?"

I helped his mom clear the table and load the dishwasher. It's what I was used to doing when I ate there years ago. Doing the dishes made me feel more like part of the family. His mother resisted at first, but I ate there frequently and didn't want to become a burden like my mother warned.

I heard the guitar as I was putting a plate in the dishwasher and Mrs. Evans said, "Go ahead, I'll finish up in here."

"Okay. Thanks."

I walked into the family room where Avery was doing warm-ups on his guitar. Mr. Evans was seated on a chair with his legs crossed, across from Avery. Avery looked up as I walked in the room, and I sat down beside him.

He put his head down and fingered the guitar. "This is the song I started playing a few days ago." Avery used to be shy about playing his music in front of people. That all changed when we decided not to be alone as much back in high school. He taught me some songs, and we started playing the guitar together. After a while, I wasn't even self-conscious about learning in front of his parents.

He strummed the guitar and played "Every Breath You Take" by The Police.

His mother beamed, "That was wonderful, Avery."

"Thanks, Mom," Avery replied with a smile.

Mr. Evans complimented him too, "Yes, Avery, you're quite the accomplished guitar player now."

The guitarist acknowledged his father. "Yeah, thanks, Dad." He glanced my way then motioned to the guitar next to him and said, "Hey, Christina, grab the other guitar so we can play together."

As I picked up the guitar laying on the other side of Avery, I frowned. "I'm super rusty."

Avery hung his head in my direction and said, "Let's do some warm-ups first. Why don't we strum first? I remember how you liked doing that."

"All right," I said, happy to oblige.

Avery instructed, "Let's strum down first."

After strumming both up and down, I played through the A minor scale to acclimate my hands to the guitar. I laughed when I goofed up. "It feels like I'm starting over."

"Nah, you're doing great!" Avery said with an encouraging smile.

Then I played through the open chords, G, C, D to get the blood circulating. "Ah, I keep messing up!" I said in frustration.

Avery was quick to respond, "You're fine. Remember, it's been years since you played. Give yourself a break."

"Yeah, you're right," I conceded.

Mr. and Mrs. Evans left the room in the middle of our warm-up. After about a half-hour of re-acclimating myself to the guitar, we played the first song I learned, "Teach Your Children Well" by Crosby, Stills, Nash and Young.

Avery placed his right hand on the string of the guitar to stop the reverberating upon finishing our mini jam session. "Wow, that was great! You haven't lost your touch, Christina."

I smiled back, feeling like a pleased pupil. "Thanks. It was fun. I forgot how much I enjoyed playing the guitar."

"Do you mind if we take a break?" Avery asked as he pulled the guitar strap up and over his head.

"No, that's fine," I said, feeling satisfied with our session but taxed nonetheless.

His eyebrows knitted together. "You didn't have one of your talks today, did you?"

"No, I went to Morgan's."

"I thought you saw her last night," he said with a quizzical expression.

"I did," I replied in a casual tone.

"How was your night out with the girls?"

"Good," I replied.

He leaned his head forward. "Do they know we're dating?"

"Yeah, I told them," I replied.

He continued with his questioning, "Do they know why I let you go?"

I shook my head in response. "No, I didn't tell them," I said without giving it a second thought.

"Why not?" he asked with a sideways glance.

"I didn't think it was my place to tell them," I said without reservation.

In an accusatory tone, he said, "You mean you didn't want them to know the real reason."

"No, not really. It's your story to tell, not mine," I answered, careful not to sound defensive.

"So, if I told them I was addicted to porn, and I didn't want to bring you down, you would be okay with that?" He probed.

"I don't think it's their business," I answered.

Avery raised his eyebrows. "What if I wanted them to know?"

I smirked while I shrugged my shoulders. "Well, I guess that's up to you then, but it's still none of their business."

Avery faced me head on and asked, "Are you embarrassed by what I've done?"

In an even tone, I replied, "No, I just don't think people need to know."

At first Avery lowered his eyes as if he was dejected. Then after a brief moment of contemplation, his face revealed a certain fortitude and he stated, "Christina, I intend on going public with my porn addiction at some point. It's not something I want to hide if I want to be a pastor someday."

"I don't understand why people will need to know that," I said, expressing my confusion.

"Because I want them to see that if I can change my ways, then so can they. I want it to be part of my ministry. I want to be an open book and have others trust me to help them work out their sin. That would mean me coming clean with my porn addiction."

My stomach began to tighten as I tried processing what Avery was saying.

He looked at me expectantly and asked, "What do you think?"

"What do I think about what?" I returned. *Did I miss something?*

Avery turned his hands palm up and heightened his shoulders. "Everything. Me telling people about my porn addiction. Everyone will know eventually. How do you feel about that?"

My stomach churned when I said, "Uh, I don't know. This is all so new to me."

He nodded as if he understood my perspective. "I get that it's a lot to take in. Will you be able to support me?" he asked with a hopeful gaze.

"I'm not sure what you mean," I stated.

Avery was quick to explain his intentions, "Will you be okay with everyone knowing about my porn addiction? I plan on telling people sooner than later. I know this won't be easy, but I need to know if I can count on your support?"

"Oh, uh. I guess so," I replied, not quite understanding the magnitude of my commitment.

With an edginess in his voice, he said, "Christina, that doesn't sound too convincing. Are you embarrassed by my past?"

"Avery, to be honest, I haven't thought about it," I answered, regretful that I haven't considered his issues. I was more concerned about Sherrie. Too much was happening at once. I couldn't focus on everything at the same time.

With a disappointing look on his face, Avery said, "I get the impression that you're ashamed of me, since you haven't even told your friends why I let you go."

In my defense, I replied, "I already told you. I didn't think it was for me to say. It's *your* story to tell, not mine."

Avery was sending a vibe that was both hopeful and fearful. "It's your story too now. That is if you want to continue to go out with me, or are you too ashamed of my past?"

Whoa! This is all too much. Why are you badgering me? "Avery, you had years to come clean about your addiction. I need time to process this."

Avery looked how I felt, confused. "What are you saying?" he asked.

"Just that I haven't thought about your addiction much or how it relates to me." I crossed my legs and folded my arms. "I had no idea you wanted to go completely public about it."

Avery persisted with his questioning, "Do you think you will be able to stand by my side when your friends or even your parents find out?"

I DON'T KNOW! Exasperated, I threw my hands up. "You keep asking me that, and the answer is I don't know. Where is this coming from? You said you would take it slow, and you're coming at me with this. You're the one who wanted to get back together. Avery, I can't take this kind of pressure. I've been through a lot." I started to get up.

Avery held up his hands. "Wait. Don't go. I'm sorry. You're right. You have been through a lot."

I settled in my seat despite the urge to run. Avery's face softened, he took a deep breath and explained his line of questioning, "I'm just anxious to move on to the next part of my life, to put the addiction behind me. You said yourself that telling people was freeing. I felt the same way when I told you about the porn. Like a weight has been lifted. You were so great about it that I assumed you were okay with it. I guess I panicked when I thought you were ashamed of me. Will you forgive me?"

I felt my eyebrows crease and I asked, "What am I forgiving you for exactly?"

Avery let out a huge sigh and answered, "For being impetuous. I should have explained my dream to help others by revealing my porn addiction. I've been praying about it for some time now. Although it's not new to me, the idea is brand new to you. I'm sorry for dumping this on you. Please forgive me." Avery's magnificent blue eyes pleaded for forgiveness.

His apologetic words refreshed my lungs, allowing me to breathe easily again. I didn't even realize I was holding my breath, in a manner of speaking. "Yes, I forgive you, but please don't come at me like that again." *Or it might be the last conversation we ever have.*

"I won't. I'm sorry," he said in earnest.

I gave him a nod with a reassuring smile. "Ave, I've had a long draining day. I better get going."

"Right. Sorry." I shot him a look that he read correctly as his next words were, "I mean, okay. Will I see you at church tomorrow?"

"Yeah. I'll see you then."

"How about I pick you up? We can go out to eat afterward. Just the two of us," he suggested, raising his eyebrows in hopes of a positive response.

As much as I liked joining his parents for lunch, I felt like Avery and I needed more time to ourselves. "Sure, pick me up."

Later that night as I lay in bed, I knew I needed to think about what Avery said about me supporting him. After thinking about it, I had to admit to myself that I didn't like the idea of everyone knowing that Avery was a porn addict. People sinned all the time, and their sin never became public knowledge. *What would my parents think? What would my friends think? Would they disapprove of me going out with him?* Did their opinion matter to me? *Does he really have to tell everyone for the sake of his ministry?* Was it really necessary? *I don't know Pastor's former transgressions. I'm not sure if I want to know.* It seemed to discomfit me at first for everyone to know that Avery struggled with pornography, but the more I thought about it, the less it seemed to matter. He was only 16 years old, and he immediately began to turn his life around and found his calling as a pastor. *If people can't accept that he was once addicted to porn, then shame on them. They're being judgmental. I know Avery will feel better once it's out in the open, but I also know he will get push back from putting it out there that he was addicted to porn. Am I ready to stand by Avery's side as he unveils his deepest transgression to the world?*

I decided to skim through the book of Psalms and came across the following verse, "In God I will praise his word, in God I have put my trust; I will not fear what flesh can do unto me" (Psalm 56:4).

Chapter 27

W e were seated at the diner after church when I said, "Avery, I thought about what you said last night, about me supporting you."

"Yeah… And?" He gave me a hopeful look.

"I'd like to hear more about your dreams of becoming a pastor."

Avery's face lit up, "Sure. What do you want to know?"

"Tell me how you came to realize you wanted to become a pastor."

He smiled brightly and said, "All right. Well, I felt horrible about my addiction. It made me feel, well, yucky for a lack of a better term. I started to go to Christian counseling, and my counselor said that I should consider Replacement Therapy. Basically, he said I needed to find something worthwhile to replace my addiction."

Avery went on to quote Ephesians 4:22-24, "That ye put off concerning the former conversation the old man, which is corrupt according to the deceitful lusts; And be renewed in the spirit of your mind; And that ye put on the new man, which after God is created in righteousness and true holiness."

The waitress came by and took our order. Neither of us looked at the menu, but we had our orders ready.

After the waitress took off, Avery bobbed his head toward me. "You know how I transferred to the Christian Academy?" I nodded. "Well, I was taking a Bible class as part of their educational requirements, and there was a lot of research for this one class. It's nothing I had ever done before, and I was fascinated by what I discovered. It was like I uncovered this hidden treasure. Only it's meant for us to discover. It's all there in the Bible."

I watched as Avery's visage glowed before me. "The more I dug deeper, the more fascinated I had become. I mentioned this to my counselor, and he suggested I pursue the work of a Bible scholar, one who provides a synopsis of the written word based on extensive research. He said it's the kind of job that you immerse yourself in, and it's ongoing. I thought he was on to something, but I later came to realize that wasn't something that would fulfill me.

"The following semester I took another class that required we preach a sermon to the class. Kids hated this class. It wasn't a requirement, but students took it because it was the only class that could fit into their schedule. I was one of those students, because I had to fit other classes in my schedule as a new student.

"Anyway, I loved it! I loved preaching. I loved preparing for my sermon. I loved doing the research, finding the background that was happening at the time the verses were written." The more Avery spoke, the brighter his face became.

He smiled, recalling a pleasant memory. "After my speech, the class gave me a standing ovation. My teacher told me it was my calling. I haven't looked back. I took every class I could on teaching, preaching, research and loved every bit of it."

He shook his head and said, "Don't get me wrong. Some of those classes were killer. They challenged me, and I learned so much. I learned a lot about myself too. It's like every moment spent is a moment worthwhile. I always get something out of it." I couldn't help but notice Avery's eyes sparkling as he sat in front of me in the diner. I almost forgot where we were, having been caught up in his passionate speech.

There was a break in his sharing, so I took the opportunity to ask, "Is it normal for the class to give a standing ovation?"

"No, not at all. Kids hate that class. Most of the kids in the school are there because their parents force them to go. Okay, maybe not most, but a lot of them. They thought I was crazy for begging to go there. No one there knew why I was attending Christian Academy. My parents weren't even on board at first. It took a lot of convincing. They made up their minds at the last minute. I figured it was just as well in order to get a clean break from everyone."

"From me," I stated, acknowledging my place in his story.

"Yeah, you, Joey, the gang, everyone." He took hold of my hands and said, "Christina, it killed me not to see you anymore. But..." He paused to choose his words and said, "But ultimately it was for the best. I don't think I would have approached my classes with such vigor if I had you in my life. I felt like if I could find my way back, you know, redeem myself, then I would be deserving of you. Until then, I had to work on my relationship with Jesus and ground myself in God's word."

"You feel like you're grounded now?" I asked.

"Yes, I do. It took years to get to this point, but I feel like I finally have a firm foundation," Avery replied.

"I'm happy for you, Ave."

"But..." he fished.

I shook my head. "No buts. Hearing that confirms that I made the right decision in starting over with you. I support you in your decision to become a pastor and... I support your decision to go public with your addiction."

"You do?" Avery asked with an element of surprise in his voice.

"Yes, I do. But—"

Avery cut me off when he said, "Oh here comes the but."

I waved my hand and projected, "No, it's not what you think. It's just that, don't kid yourself. You will get pulverized when you go public. Some people will wish you dead..."

"Is that what you experienced?" Avery asked with concern in his eyes.

"Oh, yeah. One guy had to be restrained from coming after me. It was horrible. I got to have nightmares about that too. Like it wasn't bad enough that I had nightmares about someone trying to kill me with a knife after being raped. That's after it took years to stop having nightmares from my first rape. People are cruel, Ave. Your friends may no longer be friends with you," I warned.

Avery shifted in his seat and asked, "Is that what happened to you?"

"No, my situation is different. People look at me with sympathy now. As much as I hate it, I understand. Most people have been compassionate. At least the people I was already friends with. The ones who have been cruel were Ryan's friends. I didn't even know them. Actually, his roommates were great. They knew what happened and came to my rescue. They were very protective of me afterwards. At least three of them were. The other two I rarely saw."

"Man, you really are brave. I'm so proud of you. Wait. That didn't come out right." I watched Avery squirm to find his words. "You are brave for being able to talk about what happened. It must be like reliving it," he stated as if it were a question.

"Yes, in some ways it is like reliving it. However, in other ways, I get the victory of survival, of being able to forge ahead with my life and have the opportunity to make a positive impact on others. Empowering women to live their lives in spite of doubt and trepidation."

"You see, this is why you would make a great pastor's wife," Avery said with a wink.

I placed my hand on his. "Let's not get ahead of ourselves. One step at a time."

"At least you didn't bolt," Avery joked.

I chuckled, "Next time I might."

"Would it be that bad being married to a pastor?" Avery challenged with a grin.

"I would like to graduate college first. With two years to go, I have plenty of time before I would consider being lawfully wedded. I'm in no rush."

Taking what I said into account, Avery puckered his lips and said, "I'm not suggesting we get hitched right away. Simply entertaining the possibility that we will someday."

"All right. Let's leave it at that for now," I said, satisfied with his response.

Later, I went to speak at a church that was a 25-minute drive in the country. On my way to my speaking engagement, I passed corn fields and farms with cows and horses, before I pulled into the parking lot of a plain white church with a tall steeple.

After the head of the women's ministry introduced me with a short yet thorough biography, I prayed to receive the strength and courage I needed to bare my soul in order to help others.

At the Holy Spirit's urging, I launched into what was plaguing me. "I have something to confess. Please bear with me as I share my story. I was raped not once but twice. It wasn't until after my second rape that anyone knew about the first rape. I kept the first rape a secret, because I feared for my life and that of my boyfriend. My rapist threatened to kill us both if I told anyone. He also said he would deny it and claim it would be a 'he said she said' situation. As a result, I kept the rape a secret until recently."

I shifted my balance from one leg to the other as I scanned the room. "You see, I found out a few weeks ago that someone I know was raped after I was, by the same person. Because I was terrified to tell anyone about my first rape, someone else was raped. It never occurred to me that he would rape anyone else. I was devastated when I found out that this young teenager was raped. You cannot imagine the guilt I feel. I know logically that since I wasn't the rapist, I am not technically responsible for her rape. However, I have to live with the fact that the rape may have been prevented if I had said something. If I told someone that he raped me, then she may not be going through the living nightmare one goes through after being raped."

As I made eye contact with my audience, I tucked my hair behind my ear and continued with my story. "Why am I telling you this? I mention this, because I don't want you to make the same mistake I did by keeping something like a rape to yourself. There is a good chance that your perpetrator has committed the same or a similar act of violence to someone else.

"We victims, no—," I shook my head and corrected myself, "we survivors should not feel guilty or ashamed of what happened to us. We should not live in fear, but we do. I know I did for a long time and part of me still does. You don't just get over something like rape. Another survivor told me recently that we learn how to manage it."

I licked my lips as if it fueled my talk. "Well, I don't want to only manage rape. I want to conquer it. I want to move forward in my life with my head held high, with the help from Jesus, my Lord and Savior, and live a life with grace and dignity."

I read the Bible verse I set aside, "In the old testament, Lamentations 3:22-24 states, 'It is of the Lord's mercies that we are not consumed, because his compassions fail not. They are new every morning: great is thy faithfulness. The Lord is my portion, saith my soul; therefore will I hope in him.'"

I went on to explain practical ways to live a productive, fulfilling life the way I had many times before. I wrapped it up with the following verse, "Remember ye not the former things, neither consider the things of old. Behold, I will do a new thing; now it shall spring forth; shall ye not know it? I will even make a way in the wilderness, and rivers in the desert" (Isaiah 43:18-19).

Content that I was on the right path in life, coupled with the running around I did earlier in the day, made for quick prayers of thanksgiving while I lay in bed later that evening. *Thank you Jesus for dying on the cross for me. Thank you for giving me eternal life. Thank you for giving me a wonderful family and friends. Thank you for my speaking engagements...* Not long after my head hit my pillow, I was sound asleep.

Chapter 28

The following day Avery and I were alone in his house for the first time since we started dating again. His dad was at work and his mom went out to lunch with a friend.

We finished a jam session with the guitars in the family room. "That was so much fun! I'm starting to get the hang of this again!" I said, feeling confident with my newly acquired guitar skills.

"You're doing great! Pretty soon you'll catch up to me." Avery winked.

"No, I don't ever see that happening. You're such a natural. I could never play as well as you." I nudged him.

"Let's take a break," Avery suggested.

We put the guitars down and the quiet took over.

Avery tucked a ringlet behind my ear. The touch of his hand smoothing my hair back seemed innocent enough, but I knew well enough what it would lead to. He leaned in... Even though we had been dating for a couple weeks, we barely kissed. I closed my eyes and felt his lips on mine. A titillating sensation skittered through my veins. As he leaned into me, he kissed me with more fervor leaving me wanting more. I responded with equal intensity. All the tension and stress from the past few days was released like an avalanche. I could feel the emotions getting away from me with uncontrolled abandonment. *Oh, Avery.* His sweet lips tasted so good on mine. The more we kissed, the more I craved his sweetness. I wanted more, but was this acceptable behavior for a recovering porn addict? Was this forbidden fruit? My attempt to search for answers was futile while I remained entwined with the tempter.

"Christina," he panted. Upon hearing my name, I awoke out of my revelry, and I pulled back gasping for air.

"I...," Unable to put my feelings into words, I sat there waiting for clarity.

"You what? What's the matter?" Avery questioned with a look of bewilderment.

I took a deep breath and prayed the correct words would follow. "Ave, is this okay for you? I mean... I don't want to cause you to stumble."

"Oh, uh, yeah. That was pretty intense. Are you okay?"

"Me? Yeah, I'm fine." I was more than fine, but I was worried that Avery might be going down a slippery slope with his addiction. "I'm concerned about you, Ave. Are you okay?"

"Never better." He grinned.

I wasn't an expert on porn addiction, but it seemed like the kind of behavior we displayed could lead to him falling back into old habits.

My face must have reflected my thoughts because Avery asked, "What's the matter?"

"Ave, be honest with me... What we just did...?" I shifted uncomfortably on the couch. "Will that cause you to backslide?"

"Oh." He pursed his lips together and scratched his head. "Honestly, I don't know. This is new territory for me."

"Well, I don't want to be the cause for you going down the wrong path. What do we do now?" I asked, rubbing my hands together.

Avery smirked as he wiggled next to me. "My gut tells me that it's okay to kiss."

I shot him a knowing look. "Oh, really? You sure it's your gut that's telling you that?"

"My gut and a few other parts." Avery's laughter released the tension enabling me to laugh along with him.

"Yeah, I thought so." I interjected in a playful manner.

It looked like someone turned on the light in Avery's brain, when he suggested, "I'll tell you what. I will talk to my counselor about it and see what he says."

"When's your next appointment?"

"I have to make one." I gave him a jarring look. "What? I've been doing so well that I don't feel the need to see him as often."

"Okay, but things are different now that we're dating," I volleyed.

"You're right. I'll schedule an appointment as soon as possible. Are we cool now?" Avery sought my approval.

"Yeah, we're good," I affirmed.

The following verse came to mind, "Let us not therefore judge one another any more: but judge this rather, that no man put a stumbling block or an occasion to fall in his brother's way" (Romans 14:13).

Chapter 29

A couple days later, Avery picked me up for lunch. As I was putting my seat belt on, he said, "Good news! My counselor says it's no problem to kiss."

I can see what's on his mind.

"Well, hello to you too!" I said in a vivacious sarcastic tone.

"Oh, sorry. I just couldn't wait to tell you, since you were so concerned and all," he said as he backed out of my driveway.

I eyed him up. "Yes, I was concerned. This is good news."

"So, I thought we could get started right away." He wiggled his eyebrows.

"All right then. Pull over," I joked.

"Funny," he replied, keeping his eyes on the road.

"Two can play that game."

Once we got out of the car, we came together like magnets and almost banged into each other. We stopped as we approached the door, and we leaned toward each other for a kiss. "And my day just got better." He grinned. We walked into the diner holding hands and were seated immediately.

"I was thinking more about getting the gang together." My stomach turned to knots upon hearing Avery's suggestion. "What do you think?"

I sighed at his suggestion. "I don't know, Ave. I haven't seen the guys since…" I flashed back to senior week when Joey broke up with me. It felt too awkward bringing it up.

"I figured as much," he said, but wouldn't let that deter him. "I can get in touch with the guys. Can you contact your friends?"

Guess we're hosting a party like the good old days. "Yeah, not a problem. Are you planning on telling everyone why you left Pennsford at the party?"

Avery rubbed his chin with his thumb and index finger. "I don't know. I need to talk to some people face-to-face. Maybe I should talk to everyone in person."

"Including my friends?" I gulped.

He shook his head and said, "Uh, no. That's not a good idea. Would you mind telling them?"

This is not a conversation I want to have. "Uh, yeah, but let me meet with them first. It might take some time before I can get in touch with everyone."

"Okay. Good idea," He affirmed with a nod.

Avery looked up, and I followed his eyes. A couple guys from high school walked in, and they started to walk toward us. I squeezed my eyes shut like I was a genie hoping my action would make them disappear. I opened my eyes and the next thing I know, they're standing at our table. *Darn! It didn't work, and now I look stupid.*

"Yo, Avery, what's up? How ya been, man?" Larry asked, giving Avery a buddy shake as they clenched and twisted each other's hands.

Steve followed Larry's lead by saying, "Hey, Avery, long time no see. How ya doing?" He motioned toward me. "Hey, Christina."

"Hi," I replied, struggling to get the word out. Steve was not high on my approval list ever since he cheated on Morgan. Both guys looked broader since the last time I saw them two summers ago. Their hair was shorter too.

"Larry, Steve, good to see ya. Hey, have a seat." Avery looked to me for approval, so I nodded.

"You sure?" Steve asked, although he clearly wanted to sit with us.

Avery insisted, "Yeah. Yeah. Take a seat."

What is happening? The guys sat down at our table, and the waitress came right over.

"What can I getcha?" The waitress said as she chewed gum.

After placing our orders, Larry asked, "So are you two an item again?"

Avery plastered a huge grin on his face. "Yes, as of recently we are."

"Good. Good," Steve said, nodding excessively.

Larry added, "Yeah, that's great. You two always made a great couple."

Both Avery and I thanked them.

We talked about college, jobs, summer, among other things when our food came out.

Avery took a sip of his soda prior to saying, "Hey, I hope you guys don't mind, but I've been meaning to talk to you about something."

My eyes grew wide with dread in fear that Avery was going to drop the porn bomb. His focus was on our former classmates. I cleared my throat hoping Avery would get the hint, but he ignored me. I bit into my Buffalo chicken wrap and watched anxiously to see where this conversation was headed.

"What's up?" Larry asked before digging into his burger.

"I wanted to explain why I left Pennsford so suddenly without any contact."

Oh. My. G—. Is he kidding? Not here, Avery. To keep from interjecting, I took another bite of my wrap as I winced inwardly. *He's going to spill the beans in public while we're eating.*

The band, Cutting Crew started singing "(I Just) Died in Your Arms" and I felt like I was about to die of embarrassment in the diner. *Why can't you do this in private, Ave?*

"I was wondering about that," Larry said in response to Avery as he grabbed his drink.

Steve concurred, "Yeah, me too."

Brace yourselves. I swallowed a bite of my wrap in haste. "Ave, I'm not so sure this is the time…"

Avery chimed in, "I know this isn't the ideal time to say this, but it's been on my mind for some time to tell you…"

"Spill it already, Avery," Larry said, holding his burger.

Steve added while he wiped his mouth, "Yeah, how bad could it be?"

Spoken like the cheater you are, Steve.

"All right. I left for a fresh start. I became addicted to porn." Avery paused to let it sink in I assumed.

"Like Playboy, Hustler?" asked Steve.

"That, and on TV," Avery elaborated.

Shaking his head and raising his voice, Steve remarked, "You ditched us because of that?"

Avery attempted to explain, "No, I was ashamed and needed to distance myself from my old life to be able to create a new one without porn."

Larry responded while chewing his burger. "That's dope, dude. Talk about drastic measures."

Lunch and a show. How lovely.

"That's just it. I felt like I had to take drastic measures to kick my addiction. It was taking over my life," my boyfriend justified.

"Man, sounds rough, but I feel like we could have helped you. Like you didn't need to shut us out," Larry mumbled after he bit into his burger.

I understood how they felt.

"I prayed about it, and it was the solution I came up with. It's a sacrifice I felt like I had to make," said the wannabe pastor.

"Why couldn't you just tell us?" Steve asked.

After Avery swallowed a bite of his burger, he said, "I needed a clean break. I had to work it out, and plus I wasn't ready to come clean."

"I hear ya but…" Steve shook his head. "Man, all that because of a little porn."

Avery nodded to show he understood what Steve meant. "I know. It's crazy, but I hope you'll forgive me."

The cheater answered, "I don't know." Again, Steve's head shifted from right to left and back again. "It's a lot to ask." I held my breath as I watched the display before me. "Nah, I'm just messing with you." He laughed and said with a grin, "It's all good. You're okay now, right?"

Avery was quick to answer. "Yup. No more addiction. Thanks for understanding. Are we cool?"

Steve and Larry looked at each other and then back to Avery and replied at the same time, "We're cool."

I noticed one of my favorite songs was playing, "Lean On Me" by Club Nouveau. *This song has the best beat. Best remake ever!* I found myself moving to the beat. The song alone put a smile on my face.

"Awesome. You have no idea how relieved I am," Avery stated with a look like he could walk on sunshine.

"Hey, I'm glad you told me," Steve said.

Larry imparted, "Yeah, next time don't be such a stranger."

"Hopefully, there will be no next time," Avery said.

"I guess you're cool with all this too, Christina? Is that why you two broke up back then?" Larry asked.

I answered with a shrug, "I'm okay with it."

Avery spoke over me, "Yeah, I left Christina in the dark too."

"You're lucky, dude, that she's so understanding. I mean you left her high and dry, you know," Larry stated.

"Yeah, it was a matter of time before someone snatched her up," Steve said.

Avery bobbed his head up and down. "Trust me. I know. That was the hardest part of all, but I couldn't drag her into the mess I created."

With a wave of my right hand, I said, "Um, I'm right here, guys."

Steve blurted, "Yo, does Joey know?"

Bringing up Joey took longer than I thought it would. *As if this conversation wasn't awkward enough. Thanks, Ave.*

Larry gave Steve the evil eye.

"Yeah, I already talked to Joey."

That's news to me.

Steve's head dropped. "Sorry, man. I wasn't thinking." *Do you ever think, Steve? You broke Morgan's heart and to think I thought you were one of the good guys.*

"It's okay," Avery responded.

Once again Steve opened his big mouth, but at least it didn't have food in it. "This is like something out of the movies." Larry shot Steve another glaring look.

I couldn't agree more with Steve. Except it's worse as we rehash a crappy time in our lives.

The waitress stopped by our table. "Can I get you anything else?" She asked in between chomping on gum.

After we told the waitress we were finished eating, she left the check at the edge of the table. The guys threw money on the table. After Avery counted the money and confirmed we had enough to cover the tip too, he said, "Hey, you guys interested in getting together sometime soon? I thought it would be good to get the gang back together."

"Who you thinking of?" Asked Larry.

Avery rattled off names, "Peter, Doug, Tom, John, Adam, you know, the guys and Christina's friends—like old times."

Steve laughed, "That's going back a few years, but yeah, I'm game."

"Me too," Larry said with a nod.

"All right then. I'll be in touch and uh, thanks for being so understanding about everything," Avery called out before they left.

"It's all water under the bridge," Larry said, waving his hand like it was no big deal.

With a content smile, Avery said, "I'm glad you see it that way."

"It's all good. See ya later. Bye, Christina," Steve said.

Did he just wink at me? Feeling like I had to shake out the icky feeling Steve threw my way, I replied with great finality, "Bye."

We waited for them to exit before getting up to leave when Avery said, "Well, that wasn't so bad."

Not for you. Steve didn't cheat on your best friend. In order not to deflate Avery, I responded, "No, it wasn't." *It could have been much worse. We could have had bad music with our lunch.*

"Where to now?" Avery asked.

"Let's go for a walk," I suggested, wanting some alone time with my man.

We strolled hand-in-hand at a nearby park. Kids were running around the playground, sliding down the slides, climbing the monkey bars, swinging on the swings...

We decided to go back to Avery's house where a handwritten note was left on the kitchen counter.

Gone shopping. I'll be back at 4pm. Love, Mom.

With a glint in his eyes, Avery said, "Looks like we have the place to ourselves."

"It appears that way."

Avery inched closer to me and pulled me against his chest as his arms wrapped around my waist. The heat between us rose as I lifted my chin upward. Avery lowered his body to match my height. I felt his breath on my face as our lips grazed. Warmth filled my heart when our lips pressed against each other. My mouth rolled over Avery's and back over again. He tasted like heaven. We lost ourselves in each other as we savored each moment we were entwined. Our lips broke loose from one another, yet the tingling sensation lingered. Avery's eyes smiled at me. In a breathy voice, he said, "I can't get enough of you."

"Ave," I uttered, and I swallowed air before pouring my soul into his being. Our lips collided with the urgency to be connected. We fed on each other's desires to keep the momentum going, knowing at some point it must come to an end, yet we fought for perpetual bliss. My nails clawed into his back practically ripping through this shirt, yet there was more than a shirt between us. The kisses were wet and wild and spiraling out of control. I turned my head away and Avery chased after it. "No," I gasped and wiped my mouth.

"I know," he whispered. "I know." My head settled under his chin as we held each other in an attempt to catch our breath. I rested my hand on his chest and swirled my finger in circles. I couldn't get enough of him. I didn't want to let go. Ever. I felt a kiss on my head and looked up. Our lips found each other again. My hand explored the nape of his neck as my fingers danced in his hair. I felt like I was on fire but enjoyed the feeling of being ablaze. My hands moved to cup his face. The roughness of his sideburns caught me a little unawares.

I pulled back creating the slightest distance between us, tilted my head forward, and said breathlessly, "I love you, Avery. I never stopped loving you."

Avery's hands framed my face and he replied, "I will always love you, Christina." He swooped in and pressed his lips against mine. Our kisses became fast and furious.

I wet my lips and cried, "Oh, Ave!"

He returned by calling out to me, "Christina!"

Hearing my name jolted me back to earth and caused me to choke on air. I shook my head, and exclaimed, "No, Ave. Stop."

"Christina," he repeated.

"Ave." I had no more words.

He drew me into his chest and held me. The pounding of his heart cut through my heavy breathing. *This is what happens when we're alone in private for one minute. There's no denying our passion for one another.*

Avery's words interrupted my thoughts, "Do you want something to drink? How about some water?"

"Yeah. Water would be great. Thanks." *Just throw it on me. I could use a cold shower.*

I watched Avery fill the glass with water, and I felt like I needed a lifeline. He handed me the clear beverage. "Ave—"

Avery gave me a knowing look and said, "I know. That was intense." We both gulped the water down. "Let's sit down in the family room."

Careful not to sit too close, we left some space between us as if that would make a difference. My concern got the best of me. "Ave, what are we going to do? We obviously can't be alone together."

"We're alone now, aren't we?" he laughed nervously.

"Seriously, this is a problem. We had this problem before, remember?"

"Yeah, how can I forget? Were we always that intense?" His eyes widened. "Never mind. I remember how hard it was for me to keep my hands off you."

Feeling embarrassed, I blushed. "I remember how conflicted I felt, like I feel now."

"Yeah, no, I remember that too. I wish it weren't so hard. You're just so, so darn irresistible."

A smile gave way. "Irresistible, huh? I can live with that." My smile grew larger.

"In the sexiest way," he continued.

"Sexy, huh?" I leaned forward and licked my lips.

Avery met my gaze. The force bringing us together was too great to resist as Avery stretched his upper body until we bonded. The energy grew within each of us, decreasing the space between us. We moved in sync. As he moved toward me, I fell with my back parallel to the seat cushions lost in desire never once disengaging. The ignited passion drowned out the words of caution that attempted to break through. I loved Avery, and nothing else mattered at that moment. The flames were burning red hot and after everything I suffered over the years, I felt like I was deserving of unbridled pleasure.

The voices in my head, however, began to grow in volume and were relentless. *You can't go through with this. This is wrong. You will never forgive yourself if you give in. You know better.* I fought the voices until I was reminded of God's will for me. *What am I doing?*

Without warning, I stopped and moved out of Avery's reach and put my hands in front of my face. As I rolled away from Avery, I sat up and said, "Ave, no. We can't keep doing this!" I bent over and cried in my hands.

"I know. I know. You're right. I'm sorry. I'm so sorry, Christina. Please forgive me! It won't happen again. I promise!"

Hearing those words again gave me even more doubt. *Will we recover from this?* "I can't keep doing this," I said in desperation. "It's too dangerous for us to be alone. That hasn't changed. I need to go." I got up and started walking away.

"Wait, don't go." Avery reached out to me in an attempt to keep me from leaving.

I did my best to control the tears from falling down my cheeks. Wiping them away, I turned back without looking at Avery and said, "You don't get it, do you? I have to go. We can't go on like this. It's not fair to either of us. It's killing us both."

Avery's voice was desperate, "What are you saying?"

"I'm saying either we make sure we're not alone or we break up," I solemnly answered.

Avery urged, "Let's talk about this." I shook my head. "At least let me drive you home."

"No, I need to walk this off," I said, leaving my lips to flatline.

Avery cupped my chin and lifted it up gently. He whispered, "I'm not letting you go. You do know that, right?"

I swallowed back my tears. "Yeah, I know."

"We'll start fresh tomorrow. I think we need time apart to cool down," he said like he was pitching an ad campaign he wasn't sure of.

"Yeah, I'll see you tomorrow," I said with a hint of sorrow in my voice.

I managed a nod and sucked in a deep breath to keep my resolve before walking away.

I had to get out of there before... I don't even want to go there. We're back to where we were when we were freshman. Eh. Jeez, I was so young then too. It was uncomfortable thinking about how we were all those years ago. We were able to have a great relationship that wasn't so physical before, so I figured we should be able to do it again. I just had to get out of there. *Sometimes you need space to put things into perspective. It's crazy how much passion is between us. Still. Even after all this time. I don't know what came over me.* The magnetic pull was intense. *I can still feel him on my lips. My entire body is inflamed. I need to go for a run.*

Before I knew it, I started running. Running always helped clear my head, and it was a great stress releaser. Something about running in nature was like therapy for me. I loved listening to the birds sing their songs. It was better than listening to the top ten tunes on the radio. Letting my mind wander helped me gain great insight to my problems. Pit-a-pat. Pit-a-pat. Pit-a-pat.

Avery.

I wasn't upset with Avery. Okay, maybe I was. But if I'm honest, I was angry with myself for not being able to control my desires. Pit-a-pat. Pit-a-pat. Pit-a-pat.

I watched a bright red cardinal fly on a tree branch. *Cardinal sin. Lust.* Feeling ashamed, I picked up the pace. I cringed as I pictured myself a few minutes ago in Avery's house. Pit-a-pat. Pit-a-pat. Pit-a-pat.

I stopped to wait for a car to drive by before crossing the street. That's one of the many reasons I preferred the jogging paths. Then again this wasn't supposed to be a run. Pit-a-pat. Pit-a-pat. Pit-a-pat.

Avery.

I needed to create some distance between the two of us. Time to cool down like he said. A time to reflect. *Is Avery reflecting? I wonder if he's upset with himself. Does he think I will break up with him? Is that the answer? That would be the easy way out. Somehow, I don't feel that's right. Breaking up isn't the answer.* Pit-a-pat. Pit-a-pat. Pit-a-pat.

Confronting this… whatever this is, is what I'm supposed to do. What is going on? We were fine. Then, all of a sudden, we can't keep our hands off of each other. What changed? We were alone. That's what changed. Does this mean we can't be alone… ever? That's ridiculous. Maybe it's not so crazy. Pit-a-pat. Pit-a-pat. Pit-a-pat.

The more the sun beat down on me, the more I felt alive. I wiped the sweat off my face to prevent it from stinging my eyes. Pit-a-pat. Pit-a-pat. Pit-a-pat.

Do other people have this problem or do they just cave? I laughed out loud. *I think most people give in to their desires, but I can't do that. Neither can Avery. I'm willing to bet that most people don't have as much passion between them.* Pit-a-pat. Pit-a-pat. Pit-a-pat.

As much as I loved Joey, we didn't have the same kind of electricity between us. My stomach fluttered. *Oh, Joey was so sweet, but he never did compare, did he? He never had a chance against Avery.* Pit-a-pat. Pit-a-pat. Pit-a-pat.

Maybe I got this all wrong. Maybe Avery and I are toxic. Pit-a-pat. Pit-a-pat. Pit-a-pat.

A sickening feeling arose in the pit of my stomach. I needed to make sense of all this. I had to figure out what was going on. *Lord, what do you want me to do? Should I break it off with Avery? That doesn't feel right though. Should we cool it and not spend time alone in private? Yeah. That's it. We're back to our freshman year in high school. I feel incredibly juvenile. Eventually, we have to learn how to manage on our own.* Pit-a-pat. Pit-a-pat. Pit-a-pat.

Later that evening before bed, I turned to a passage in my Bible, "Trust in the LORD with all thine heart; and lean not unto thine own understanding. In all thy ways acknowledge him, and he shall direct thy paths" (Proverbs 3:5-6).

Chapter 30

The phone startled me as I was getting dressed the following day. I leaped to answer it thinking it would be Avery. "Hello."

"Hi, it's me." I was right. It was Avery.

"Hello, me," I joked.

"You're funnier than I thought you would be first thing in the morning." He sounded like he was in a good mood.

"Oh, I like to start my day with a good dose of humor," I replied.

Avery asked, "Did you eat yet?"

"Uh, no. I just got up. Why?"

"I'm picking you up for breakfast."

"Oh, you are, are you?" I said with lighthearted intrigue.

"Yeah, be there in a few minutes."

Looks like I got me a breakfast date. I made a conscious effort to put on my sneakers. *Just in case I need to go for a run.*

I waited outside for Avery. It wasn't too long before he pulled in my driveway.

Avery greeted me with a wide smile, "Good morning!" He started to back out of my driveway.

"Good morning!" I said matching his energy. He had "Making My Life Brand New" by David Meece playing on his CD player, a perfect choice for what we were both going through.

He turned toward me for a quick second before looking at the road and said, "I hope you don't mind me springing breakfast on you last minute."

"Oh, no. I haven't eaten yet, so the timing is good."

With continued enthusiasm, he said, "Honestly, I couldn't wait to see you."

Awe. "I missed you too." *I hope that's what he meant.*

"I thought we could talk about how things ended yesterday," he said, keeping his eyes on the road.

That didn't take long. We didn't even make it out of my development. "Can it wait until we at least get to the diner?" I didn't want to have a serious conversation while he was driving.

"Yeah. Sure. It can wait."

We were seated right away upon arriving at Pennsford Diner. My mouth watered when I saw the giant Belgian waffle on the breakfast menu. I loved Belgian waffles but rarely ate them. "I know what I'm having," I declared as I closed the menu.

"Let me guess…a Belgian waffle," Avery said.

"Am I that predictable?" I asked.

"You used to order them when we went out to eat with my parents after church."

"Oh right. I forgot about that." *But we didn't come here.*

After Avery told the waitress he wanted eggs over easy with bacon and toast, there was complete silence between us. A minute went by before Avery said, "Thanks for agreeing to have breakfast with me on such short notice."

"No problem," I replied as I loved going out to eat.

Avery fidgeted in his seat. "I have to admit. I'm pretty hungry. I got up early and worked out."

That explains his energy.

"I was going to ask you if you wanted to workout later," I said, a little disappointed.

Avery's eyes grew wide, and a hopeful grin appeared. "You were?" he asked.

"Yeah, I thought it could be something we could do together like we used to." I felt like we needed to do something besides eating out. All these meals out were adding up. I knew Avery had a job, but it didn't pay that much, and he always insisted on paying.

With a look of relief, he asked, "So, we're still together?"

Laying it on thick, I puckered my lips, and batted my eyelashes toward Avery, while responding in a playful tone, "You didn't think you could get rid of me that easy, did you?"

Avery shook his head like he was trying to shake his doubts and confusion and shared, "I didn't know what to think. You had me worried."

"Aw, Ave, I'm sorry. I needed to think things through," I said, wishing I had spared him all that grief since we parted yesterday.

"Yeah, no. I get it." Avery said as he rolled his head around in order to get up to speed with our current situation.

I put my hand on Avery's and said, "I really want us to work. I just don't think we can be alone together—like alone, alone, by ourselves with no one around." I think he got the picture.

"You sure about this?" he said with furrowed brows.

"Yeah, I'm sure." I squeezed his hand.

"If that's what it takes, then okay. I can't lose you again." His eyes flashed a sorrowful look.

While locking eyes, I said with determination, "We'll make this work."

"Whatever it takes," he said with equal fervor. We rested on those words as we waited for our meal to arrive.

As the waitress set our breakfast on the table, I asked, "Maybe we could go hiking sometime?"

Avery mulled the suggestion over for a second as he took a sip of his drink and said, "Hiking? Yeah, we could do that."

"Yeah?" I asked, pleased with his response, and began cutting my waffle into small bite-sized portions.

Avery swallowed some of his egg. *He must have been hungry not to say grace. Maybe he said it privately.* I took a second to bow my head to give thanks for my meal.

"Yeah, when do you want to do that?" he asked and then took a bite of his bacon.

I poured syrup over my waffle while saying, "I don't know. I just thought of it. It's not like I've gone hiking before. I guess I figure we can walk and talk on the trails."

Avery dipped his toast in the egg yolk and said, "I'm game."

"Great. It's a start. We need to come up with more things to do besides going out to eat," I said, excited to start a new activity with him. Then I took a bite of my waffle drenched in syrup. *Yum! This is so good!*

"About that…," Avery said as he chewed. He took the time to finish chewing and said, "Let's get the gang back together."

Not this again. "Ave, really? You sure you want to do that?" I said, on the verge of whining while I swirled a forkful of waffle in syrup.

Avery picked up his glass of orange juice and said, "I have to give it a go. It's worth a shot. Don't ya think?"

"I don't know," I said, anxious to eat the rest of what was once a thick giant waffle.

Avery tilted his head forward without breaking eye contact and said, "I want to make amends. At least try anyway."

I held up my finger to buy me time to comment while chewing. After taking a drink to wash down the waffle, I said with conviction, "All right. I'll support you." I'm not sure who I was trying to convince, Avery or me, or perhaps both of us.

Resolved that we would be hosting a party for our old crowd—the same people Avery ditched without explanation—I looked down at my plate and was disappointed to find only soggy crumbs.

Avery and I decided that it was best for me to talk to the girls first before having a big bash. I asked Morgan if she could host the reveal at her house. But, before we had the girls over, I needed to give Morgan the heads up. We met up at Morgan's and began discussing why Avery let me go.

We were sitting in her rec room by ourselves. Morgan was all ears when she said, "You piqued my curiosity. I mean to go through all this to explain why your now boyfriend dumped you back in high school."

I cringed when I heard Morgan say "boyfriend dumped you." Avery's choice of words rubbed off on me to the point that it bothered me too now. "Okay, for the record, Avery hates it when people say he dumped me. He doesn't look at it like that at all. He prefers to say why he let me go. It may not seem like a big deal to you, but it is to Avery, and I'm starting to understand why."

"Oh, come on. Dumped or let go. What difference does it make? That sounds like semantics. Just tell me why," she said.

Already on edge that I had to share Avery's story, I barked, "Morgan, look, this hasn't been easy for me either. My entire life turned upside down and flipped again once I started going out with Avery this time around. You have to be patient with me here."

A look of both empathy and regret formed on Morgan's face. "You're right. I'm sorry. I should have realized that this affects you too. You are the one telling me. Why is that anyway?"

Ah, this is harder than I thought it would be. Why am I the one telling this story? You know why. Just tell her. I sucked in air to give myself the guts to explain Avery's choice and said, "I'm telling you because of the nature of the topic. You see, Avery let me go because he was addicted to pornography." *There I said it. Was that so hard? Yes! I hate how I'm the one telling her.*

Morgan threw her arms up. "That's your big secret, or rather his big secret?! He was addicted to porn!"

"Yes, well, it's more than just flipping the pages of porn magazines. He watched porn on cable, and he was obsessed. Avery's grades dropped, and he became engrossed in porn every spare moment. He lied to me about doing youth group activities when he was checking out porn," I added, hoping she would now have a better understanding.

Morgan shook her head and said, "All this time I thought it was because he cheated on you with Mindy or something like that."

I scrunched my nose in disgust and replied, "Ew. Thanks for the mental picture. Now I can't get it out of my head."

Morgan laughed, "Oh, sorry. I guess that's not funny, but I still don't see what the big deal is."

"You know. That's what I said. In fact, that's what Larry and Steve said."

"Steve? When did you see Steve?" Morgan asked with intensity.

"The other day at the diner. Avery and I just sat down when they walked in. Avery decided to tell them right then and there that he was a porn addict. I almost died of embarrassment... like right in the middle of the restaurant." I made a face and shook off the unpleasant feeling.

Morgan had a puzzled look on her face. "I'm sorry, but I don't get you. You suffered through two incredible ordeals... I mean things I can't even fathom experiencing, and you were embarrassed by what Avery did? After what you've been through, I don't understand why that matters to you."

When you say it like that I feel kind of stupid now, like it shouldn't matter. "Well, I guess that's it. What Avery did didn't happen to me. I mean it affected our relationship, and he feels horrible for the whole porn thing, but he felt like he had to let me go to pay restitution for his sins."

"Well, that's just stupid," Morgan declared.

"What?" I was shocked by her boldness and confused by her statement.

Morgan explained, "I mean really. We all make mistakes. He went to extremes. I think that was totally unnecessary to break it off with you and all his friends. I'm kind of angry at him for breaking it off with you. He should have told you and let you decide what to do, whether or not you wanted to continue going out with him."

I listened to Morgan's diatribe before saying anything. "Huh. That's how I felt about it. I guess I still do, but Avery explains it differently. I think that's why it was hard for me to tell you. It's not my story. I don't quite understand this whole porn thing. You know I wanted to tell your parents about what happened. I know that may seem weird, but I don't feel their judgment on me. Maybe they could put some perspective on this."

"You want to tell my parents?! Are you crazy?" Morgan exclaimed. She turned it down a notch and asked, "Why do you feel the need to tell anyone?"

"I don't feel the need to. Avery does. He wants it to be out in the open now because he wants to become a pastor and wants his sins to be transparent. He doesn't want people to find out later. He wants them to know upfront."

Morgan shook her head. "Wow! I don't think his past sins need to go public."

"That's what I said, but Avery is adamant that people know. He wants people to come to him because they will think that he will understand where they are coming from… like he can relate to them."

Morgan's mouth flattened and her eyes squinted. "Oh. Okay. I guess that makes sense, like how recovering alcoholics help each other."

"Yeah, something like that," I shrugged.

"I'm not so sure his line of thinking is right. I mean, my problems are not about addiction, so I couldn't relate to him on that level. Actually, it might put me off to have a pastor who was involved in porn." Morgan rubbed her hands up and down her face.

"That's kinda what I was thinking too. I don't mean to be judgmental, but I'm not sure if it can be helped," I admitted.

"And you're okay with Avery's past?"

I replied, "Well, yeah. I mean it was a short blip in his life, and he has since repented and has grown closer to the Lord."

"But he took such drastic measures and cut off everyone in his life, like he was running away."

"I suppose you could look at it like that, but according to Avery, he needed to have full focus to turn his life around. I mean it is an addiction after all. If it were so easy to stop, it wouldn't be called an addiction." Explaining it to Morgan helped me understand Avery's plight.

Morgan nodded, "Yeah, good point. Speaking of addictions, you wanna milkshake?"

"You joke, but I think milkshakes are our addiction."

She gave me a dismissive wave, "Nah, milkshakes don't control our lives, and we're not hurting anyone by drinking them."

"True, but we are hurting our bodies," I argued, even though I wasn't about to stop my milkshake habit.

"Maybe, but I feel like we make good choices to balance things out. I mean, it's not like we just eat junk food."

"It's all about balance I suppose," I agreed.

"Yup. Now let's go make those shakes," Morgan said with excitement.

Mrs. Ricci entered the kitchen as we were pouring the heavenly mixture into milkshake glasses. "Hello, Christina. How are you doing?"

"Fine, thanks. How are you?"

"Glad to be inside in the air conditioning instead of enduring the heat," Mrs. Ricci replied.

I returned with a smile and said, "Yes, it is hot outside today, but there's nothing like milkshakes to battle the heat." Morgan laughed and continued with the concoction by adding whipped cream.

Morgan's mom nodded, "Ah, to be young again. Well, enjoy your shakes." She turned on her heel, ready to walk out of the kitchen.

"Mrs. Ricci, can I talk to you about something?" I asked before she left the room.

"Sure. What is it?" She turned around and asked.

I took a deep breath and heard a shakiness in my voice when I said, "It's an awkward topic to discuss, but I need some understanding."

Mrs. Ricci sounded a little wary upon replying, "Okay, I'm listening. Why don't we sit down and talk?" She gestured toward the kitchen table, and we both sat down. Morgan cringed but handed me a glass filled with the anticipated chocolatey goodness and sat next to me.

I began, "I recently started seeing my boyfriend Avery again. We went out in high school but suddenly broke up back then. He didn't give me a reason at the time, and he broke all ties with everyone." I paused for a second and continued, "A few weeks ago, Avery told me that he broke up with me because he was addicted to porn. Now, he wants to come clean with all his old friends from high school because his desire is to be a pastor, and he wants to be upfront about his past. I don't really know anything about porn addiction, but I feel like he went to extremes when he broke ties with everybody, and I don't feel like it's anyone's business what he did in the past. I mean, he repented and doesn't watch porn anymore, so what difference does it make that he tells anyone?"

Across from me, Mrs. Ricci pursed her lips and said, "That's a lot to take on with everything else you have experienced. I'm not exactly sure I can help you. I can tell you that I admire your boyfriend's willingness to be open about his addiction. I think that's a positive step in the right direction."

Morgan's mom shifted in the kitchen chair without breaking eye contact with me. With empathy in her eyes, she said, "I can see why you wouldn't want people to know, since it can be embarrassing for you as his girlfriend."

She leaned in toward me and offered some advice, "However, if you want to continue to go out with him, you need to support him. You need to consider what he needs in this case, not what you need. If that is too much for you, you may consider putting your relationship on hold. He should respect that, especially after what you've been through this year at school. Your healing is just as important as his, maybe even more so in your case, since it was so violent."

"You think it makes sense to go public with his addiction?" I took a sip of my milkshake.

With a tiny sigh, Mrs. Ricci replied, "Well, that's up to him. There is no right or wrong answer. If his heart is in the right place, and he wants people to know and forgive him for breaking ties with them, then I think he's doing what's right for him. Why did he break up with you? Did he tell you?"

"Yes, he said that he had to let me go to protect me, like it wasn't fair to me to be mixed up in that, and he was too ashamed to tell me he was addicted to porn. He said he also needed to focus on kicking his addiction, and it was his way of punishing himself by breaking it off with me." I noticed it was getting easier to discuss Avery's porn addiction, even with a friend's parent.

The redheaded woman, whom my best friend resembled, nodded and said, "I see." After a brief pause, she continued, "Well, he did what he felt was right at the time, which didn't make it any easier on you I'm sure." She gave a knowing frown and stated, "Break ups can be hard, even high school break ups. But it sounds like he knew he needed to devote his attention to getting well, and in the meantime feels led to become a pastor— or did he always want to be a pastor?" Morgan's mom asked.

"No, he transferred to Pennsford Christian Academy. That's where he discovered he wanted to become a pastor. He likes reading scripture and preaching," I replied.

A smile drew across Morgan's mother's face. "He sounds like a nice young man, and he's on a good path. One of the things about conquering addiction is having a support group. If everyone knows his weakness, he may be less likely to engage in it. We all have our demons. Some more than others. What do your parents think about all this?"

Feeling uneasy, I faltered, "I, eh, my parents don't know any of this. I haven't told them."

"Why haven't you?" asked Mrs. Ricci.

"I didn't want to worry them. They are already concerned about me as it is," I replied, pleased with my answer.

Mrs. Ricci's lips pressed together, and her eyes glassed over. "Naturally, they're concerned about you. You have been through an ordeal. You're their baby, and they love you very much and want only the best for you."

In an attempt to explain my reasoning, I said, "I don't feel like they would understand Avery's perspective... Him wanting to be a pastor, his need to repent and ask for forgiveness. My parents don't go to church."

As she squinted her eyes, Mrs. Ricci said, "Are you ashamed of Avery's past addiction?"

I shifted in my seat, took another sip of my milkshake for fortitude, and said, "Not really. I'm afraid people will judge him harshly."

"So, what if they do?" she asked nonchalantly.

"I just don't want him to feel discouraged or ashamed," I replied.

Morgan sat quietly drinking her milkshake and watching as her mother and I discussed the awkward topic of porn addiction. Mrs. Ricci continued to gaze at me and said with wisdom, "You can't control how Avery feels about himself. If anything, this could make him stronger."

I hadn't thought about it like that. "But what about how he handled his addiction...? How he isolated himself. Is porn really that big a deal?" I asked.

Mrs. Ricci pierced her lips and with a thoughtful expression on her face, she said, "Any addiction is a big deal because it interferes with daily life, relationships. Your relationship was affected. He felt ashamed and couldn't tell you about it, so he broke it off. He felt the need to take drastic measures, and he sought the will of God, or so it seems. You have to respect him for that. He could have continued with the addiction, but he chose to face it head on. He wasn't ready to admit his addiction in high school, but he's ready now."

Morgan's mom stopped to consider her next statement before continuing, "The thing about pornography though, is that it's one of those things that is inherently evil even without being addicted. It seeps into one's soul and is not at all pleasing to God. However, it sounds like he is facing his addiction head on, and he's not engaging in pornography anymore."

Mrs. Ricci put her hand on mine and said, "You need to figure out if you can support him, if you want to support him. If a relationship with him is worth it. I can't help you with that. That's your decision. You need to ask God what he wants you to do."

I got chills upon hearing about asking God, and I replied softly, "I did ask God."

"And?" Morgan's mom prompted.

"I feel like He wants me to be in a relationship with Avery, even though it won't be easy at times."

Mrs. Ricci relaxed her body and stated, "Well, then, there's your answer. Relationships aren't easy, but if it's God's will, then your relationship will be blessed. You need to keep Christ at the center of your relationship at all times. It's not easy, but it will be worthwhile."

"Honestly, I felt like it would have been easier to break it off with him than to face all this addiction with him," I admitted.

I watched Mrs. Ricci's mouth curve upward as she said with tenderness, "It sounds like you know what to do."

"Thanks, Mrs. Ricci."

She waved her hand as she got up from the table, "No need to thank me. I'm here if you need someone to help you work things out."

I couldn't resist smiling as I felt incredibly grateful and at peace when I said, "Thanks again."

I turned to Morgan and said, "Looks like we're planning a gathering."

"Heh?" Morgan said, puzzled.

"Avery wants to have a bash at his house to get the gang all together again. We thought it might be best to get the girls together first so I can tell them why Avery left school and broke it off with me."

The confusion left her countenance, so Morgan replied, "Oh, okay. I'll check with my parents, but I think it will be all right."

Later that evening, I found the most amazing passages of scripture that helped me understand the Lord's forgiveness. I wanted to feel armed before revealing Avery's biggest transgression to my friends. Colossians 1:13-14 painted a clear picture that God is the great redeemer, "Who hath delivered us from the power of darkness, and hath translated us into the kingdom of his dear Son: In whom we have redemption through his blood, even the forgiveness of sin:"

Chapter 31

The following evening I arrived early at Morgan's before everyone arrived. My stomach felt a little queasy confirming my nervousness to talk to my friends about Avery's deep dark secret. Morgan answered the door. "Hey, come on in. Are you nervous for the big reveal?"

"Yeah, I am actually."

Morgan sang with a sappy grin, "I have Oreos. Your favorite."

My stomach lurched but not in a good way. "Maybe later," I said as I frowned, hoping the butterflies would go away.

"You must be nervous," Morgan observed.

One by one my friends came. Now that we all had our licenses, we didn't come in droves. We picked a time that Katie didn't have to work, since Morgan and I felt she would be the most supportive. Everyone was chatting in the basement playing catch up with each other.

I approached Valerie and asked, "How is your summer going?"

"I'm babysitting three kids who live in my neighborhood. They're really good kids. I like watching them," she said like it was rehearsed. As cute as ever, it looked like Val was growing out her strawberry blonde hair. Until recently she wore it short.

I overheard that Cheryl was working at a jewelry counter in the mall. Based on her nose ring, I guessed she was a customer too. She had come a long way from the girl who wore glasses and braces. Her high volume shoulder length hair had streaks of blonde and her teeth were gleaming white.

Seated next to Cheryl was Jackie. Her short hair lacked the luster it once had, making her hair more of a light brown now compared to the dirty blond she had. Apparently, Jackie got a job working at her mom's office. She was too shy to go on interviews to get a job anywhere else.

Choosing not to work, Amy felt the need to be a free spirit after the constraints of being a college student and was the envy of everyone.

Before the conversations got any deeper, I thought it best to announce the purpose of our get together. "Hey, everyone, thanks for coming. You're probably wondering what this is all about." I scanned each person. "Well, you all know by now that Avery and I are back together."

"Oh my gosh! You're engaged! But I don't see a ring," Valerie burst out.

The absurdity of her statement caused me to laugh, which eased the tension a touch. "No, no. Nothing like that. We're not engaged. Avery wanted me to explain to you all why he left Pennsford and why he broke up with me, since it was all so sudden and mysterious. Believe me, it was sudden and mysterious for me too. I just found out the reason."

"We're all ears," said Valerie.

Amy echoed Val's sentiment. "Do tell."

"First, let me just say that it is awkward for me to talk about, because it's Avery's issue, but in light of the subject, he wanted me to tell you."

"All right already, what is it?" Val asked with intense curiosity.

"Yeah, out with it!" Cheryl demanded.

In order to placate my impatient audience, I held up my hands and began, "Okay, okay. You see, Avery became addicted to pornography." *There I said it.* "Porn consumed his every waking moment. I knew none of this until recently. We were in tenth grade at the time when it started. Our relationship wasn't at all physical at the time which was intentional on both our parts. The porn came after Avery and I decided to put the brakes on the physical part of our relationship. To be clear, we never had sex. We were waiting until we were married for that. He didn't know— actually, no one knew I was raped in high school. That all came out recently."

With both concern and confusion in her voice, Abby said, "Wait, what? You were raped in high school? I didn't know that. I thought it happened in college."

"It did happen in college and also in high school. I guess I figured everyone knew by now," I said surprised the news didn't reach Abby.

The tan color of Abby's face turned white, "No, I had no idea. Did everyone else here know? Christina, I'm so sorry you had to go through that and twice no less. Are you okay?"

Touched by her concern, I replied, "I'm dealing with it. It's hard, but I manage. Some days are better than others. I'm not going to lie."

Abby shook her head in disbelief, "This is a lot to take in. You are incredibly strong. I can imagine what you're going through. Whatever you need, let me know. We should all be here for you."

Tears welled up in my eyes, for her concern for me was apparent in the tone of Abby's voice. This wasn't supposed to be about me but about Avery. "Uh, thanks. I appreciate that."

Eager to also offer support, Cheryl said, "Yeah, whatever we can do. We will support you any way we can." A chorus of agreement among the girls in front of me warmed my heart. It never occurred to me that they would respond that way. My focus had been on Avery, not me. It didn't feel right to let the topic of Avery's porn addiction go to the wayside, yet I wanted to acknowledge their support.

"I don't know what to say. I'm touched by your support. Really, I am, but I don't want to make this all about me. Avery wanted everyone to understand why he left school so abruptly, without any explanation or good-byes. He thought that given the subject of pornography it would be better for it to come from me rather than him, considering the mixed company."

Abby took the lead again by saying, "Okay. We're listening, but understand that we want to help you in any way we can." She turned to each person in the room, and said, "Am I right? Christina can count on us for anything?"

The uproar of responses was unanimous. Once again, I started to get teary-eyed. With a heartfelt smile in an effort to keep my tears from fully forming, I responded, "That means a lot to me. To know you are here for me means the world to me. I can't thank you enough, but you might regret it when I call you in hysterics at two o'clock in the morning."

Quick to respond, Abby stated, "No, no. I mean it. Whatever you need."

"Thanks. I appreciate that. Don't worry. I can't see myself calling anyone like that," I said with gratitude.

Without hesitation, Abby assured, "It's okay if you did. I think everyone will understand." Again, I witnessed nods of affirmation by each individual.

"Okay then. That goes for me too. I'm here to help anyone anyway I can." I meant it too.

Jackie poked her hand up and said, "I have a question. Why did Avery go to another school? Why did he just leave without telling anyone why?"

Ready to answer any and all questions relating to my boyfriend's past porn addiction, I stated on his behalf, "Avery was ashamed and embarrassed. That's why he didn't tell anyone. He decided it was best for him to go to a Christian school to start fresh. He broke it off with me as a way to punish himself, and he didn't want to drag me into the predicament he created. Breaking it off with me was hard for him. He had no idea that I had been raped or realized how hard the breakup was for me. We never stopped loving each other."

"Awe, that's so sweet," Val gushed.

Cheryl commented, "You two were perfect together. I never saw a couple more meant for each other."

I smiled, and before I had a chance to respond, Amy asked, "How is Avery doing now with his porn addiction?"

"He hasn't engaged in any porn in years," I answered as I sat up straighter.

"Wow. That's great!" Katie exclaimed.

"Good for him," Cheryl said.

"I don't get it. Why all the secrecy?" asked Amy.

"Like I said, he was mortified and ashamed. He couldn't face anyone. He felt that he needed a clean break to start a new life, to start new healthy habits and to punish himself as a way of retribution. Trust me. I don't get it either. Not entirely."

"So, you forgave him? Just like that," Amy said with the snap of her fingers.

"No, it wasn't that simple. I didn't even want to talk to Avery when he first approached me."

"When was that?" Val asked.

I told them the story about Avery and I eating at the diner and then later how we bumped into each other.

Humored by what I said, Amy interrupted, "You literally bumped into him. That's kinda funny."

"Yeah, and then I ran away after we kissed because he brought up the first time we kissed which was at Paul's house. I got triggered and ran because that's where Paul raped me."

Shocked by my statement, Abby blurted, "Paul? Paul who?"

Without hesitation, I replied, "Paul Martin."

"Oh my G—! I can't believe he did that!" Val exclaimed as she threw her arms in the air. "What a…!" Val shook her head in shock.

"Didn't he move or something?" Jackie asked.

"Yeah, he did. A couple years ago I think. I remember that he didn't graduate with us," Cheryl said.

"I'm glad he moved away. What a piece of garbage!" Val's face was contorted and red.

"Well, Val, I couldn't agree with you more. Paul is a piece of garbage to say the least, but if you don't mind I want to get back to the story."

"Oh right. Sorry, but I still say he's a piece of garbage!" Val spat.

I nodded at Val's vehemence and continued with my story. "After Avery kissed me, I took off running, because Avery triggered me by mentioning the piece of garbage's house." I smiled warmly at Val and continued, "Avery stopped by my house after that, and I told him why I ran away. That's how it all began. He was the first person I told that Paul raped me. I was dealing with some other stuff, and I couldn't hold it in any longer. Avery was so insistent that we go out again and with it being such an emotional, intimate moment we shared, I agreed. I didn't even think about the consequences of his porn addiction. Too many other things were going through my mind at the time, but it felt right saying yes. I considered breaking it off because I didn't think it through, but my heart always belonged to him. I don't know why I'm telling you all this..."

No one spoke. The silence scared me. *Why isn't anyone responding? Do they think I'm crazy or something?*

After a few seconds passed that seemed like a lifetime, Amy said, "So you kissed him in the middle of the street when you were all hot and sweaty from running?" *That's what you got from this?*

Katie hit Amy in the arm and admonished her with a look.

Morgan spoke up and laughed, "That's what I said."

"You guys are missing the point. Avery and Christina are finally back together after all this time, after all they've been through. They are a solace to each other," Jackie summed up. That's the most I heard Jackie speak at once. *Even the meek ones are interjecting. Didn't see that coming.*

"Since when are you such a romantic?" Cheryl asked Jackie.

"Oh, come on! As if you don't see it too!" Jackie replied.

"I see it," Val concurred.

Amy said, "So do I."

"See?" Jackie said to Cheryl.

"I was just kidding," Cheryl said in her defense.

"Well, that about sums it up. Avery wants to have a party like old times, you know, like when we all got together with his friends, but he wanted you all to know about the porn addiction first."

Val was quick to respond with, "That would be awesome! Would Joey be there?" Immediately, Val realized what she said, and she looked like she swallowed a tomato. The entire room filled with tension. "Oh, gosh. I'm so sorry. I didn't mean..."

Looks like Val still has a crush on Joey. I wonder if anyone else has a crush on my ex-boyfriend. I wonder if anyone has a crush on Avery for that matter.

In my most gentle tone I said, "Oh, no it's okay. I don't know if Joey will be there or not. I do know that Joey now knows what happened to Avery back in high school."

"How are things between you and Joey?" Amy asked. Katie shot Amy a look of disapproval.

I released a dismissive hand wave in their direction to indicate that I was fine with Amy's question and answered, "We haven't spoken since a short time after we broke up. We ended on decent terms though. No hard feelings—at least not on my part. Joey's a great guy. I was fortunate to date two great guys in high school that happened to be best friends at one point."

"We always knew Joey had a thing for you even when you were with Avery," Katie said.

Val added, "Yeah, he used to stare at you during Algebra." She gasped, "Oh my gosh!" Her hands covered her face on impulse.

"What?" I asked Val.

"Nothing," Val answered. Her eyes darted side to side.

I shot back, "That wasn't nothing." Val shook her head while her hands remained glued to her face. "Tell me," I insisted.

Val's intense eyes gave her away. She released her hands from her face. "I remember someone else staring at you too."

Chills covered my body, and I could feel the blood drain from my face. "Now you know why," I replied.

Val nodded. "I'm so sorry. I wish I knew. I had no idea."

I whispered, "It's okay. No one knew." A hush came over the room. Sad faces were either staring at me or completely avoiding eye contact with me. *It will take time before they will look at me and not see me as the girl who was raped not once but twice, and whose boyfriend was a porn addict. Maybe they will always look at me and see all that. How depressing.*

Morgan held up a plate of Oreos and said, "Oreos anyone?"

"Yeah, I'll take one," Amy said.

"Me too," Abby followed. *There's nothing like chocolate to perk people up.* A few more hands grabbed the cookies, including mine.

With a cookie in my grasp, I stretched out my arm as if to toast and said, "Here's to not keeping secrets that can destroy us."

"No more secrets!" they chanted back. Abby glanced downward as she shielded her face with an Oreo.

Amy couldn't wait long enough to swallow her Oreo before she began talking to Morgan, "Got any milk?"

We ended our time discussing college, work, family, summer, and dreading going back to college at the end of our warm weather hiatus.

Chapter 32

The much-anticipated night arrived. The gang was gathered downstairs in Avery's basement. Our friends were mingling, eating, laughing when I saw Macey walk down the stairs. *What is Macey doing here?* Avery followed my gaze, wondering why my jaw fell to the floor.

Morgan ran up to me and asked, "Who invited Macey?"

"I don't know," I answered Morgan. Then I turned to the host and asked, "Ave, did you invite Macey?"

Avery exclaimed, "Are you kidding? She's one of the last people I would invite, especially after the spin the bottle fiasco."

"We've got bigger problems than that, Ave." I forgot to tell him when I had the chance about how his buddy Steve cheated on Morgan with Macey. It was bad enough for Morgan that Steve was there, but she insisted she was okay with it.

Macey sauntered up to Steve and drawled as if she were in a red-light district, "Hey, Steve."

Puke.

With a look of shock, Steve managed to respond, "Uh, hey, Macey."

Valerie walked over and grabbed Macey by the arm. "Macey, what are you doing here?"

"I couldn't miss the party of the century and let you have all the fun," Macey responded at an uncomfortable volume.

I turned to Morgan, "Guess we know who told Macey about the party."

Based on the body language between Val and Macey, they were arguing through their whispers.

Morgan with her arms folded said, "Yeah, but she didn't get the picture that she wasn't invited."

Avery walked to the middle of the room and threw his arms up in the air. "Hey, everybody! Thanks for coming. It's been a while since we all got together. Let's have a good time."

Macey yelled across the room, "Can we watch porn?"

Avery replied with an authoritative yet calm demeanor, "Macey, I don't watch porn anymore. I haven't in years. You can leave to watch it on your own, but I don't recommend it. To be clear, I suggest you do leave but not watch porn."

"Are you kicking me out? Some pastor you will make. Aren't you supposed to love your neighbor as thyself?" Macey slurred as she recited from her Catholic upbringing.

Avery stood his ground. "Macey, you were never invited to begin with. I think someone should drive you home."

Valerie leaped toward Macey and was quick to volunteer her services, "I'll drive her home."

Macey yelled as she attempted to push Val away, "I can drive myself." Losing her balance, she nearly fell when Larry grabbed hold of her and escorted her toward the staircase with Val trailing closely behind.

"Well, that was fun." I heard someone say.

"If anyone feels the same way as Macey, you're welcome to leave. I prefer you stay to give me a chance to explain my actions from high school, you know, to clear up anything."

"Yeah, I have a question," a familiar voice said behind me. I turned around to see Joey standing there looking as handsome as ever. Perhaps even more so from what I remembered the last time I saw him, the day I tried to win him back at the park two summers ago. Joey's dark chocolate brown hair was clipped shorter from the last time I saw him. There was no doubt he made an effort to stay in shape based on his bulging biceps. He appeared taller too.

By the look on Avery's face, he was surprised to see his long-time childhood friend. "Hey, man, you made it!"

"This oughta be good," I recognized as the same voice who bellowed the last crack. It belonged to John. In addition to sporting the massive soccer thighs that were intimidating to an opponent, John emanated a negative intensity about him that was off-putting.

"Yeah, what's going on? I saw an inebriated Macey stumbling out with Larry and Valerie. You can't be serving alcohol," Joey said befuddled.

"Na, man, she came like that, uninvited too."

Joey said, "I didn't know this was by special invite."

Avery offered an explanation, "Yes and no. I don't want people here who wreak havoc wherever they go, not caring who they hurt. You're definitely welcome—that is if you're not here to cause a scene. I want this to be civil. I get that everyone here has been ticked at me, and I don't blame them."

Joey threw up his hands and declared, "I come in peace."

I noticed the song "A Bizarre Love Triangle" by New Order came on, and the urge to crawl under a table was fierce.

Avery said to Joey, "That's great. Glad you're here. Can I get you something to drink?"

"No, it's okay. I'll help myself." Joey paused and looked my way. "It's good to see you, Christina."

The words managed to come out of my mouth, "Good seeing you too, Joey." It was awkward, but it seemed like a step in the right direction regarding the relationship between the three of us.

A look of concern crept in his eyes when he asked, "How are you doing?"

Not knowing for sure what he meant, I answered with the assured head bob, "I'm doing pretty good. How are you?"

"Good. Good," he said with the same head bob. "I think I'll get that drink now."

After Joey walked away, Avery whispered, "I hope you don't mind that I invited Joey. I should have checked with you first to see if it was okay with you."

"It's fine. I hope you two can repair your friendship. I don't want to come between that," I replied.

"It's going to take some time, and I'm not sure we'll ever be close again, but that's on me, not you."

As John strode over to us, images of him yelling at Avery when we were playing spin the bottle flashed before me. I was brought back to present day when I heard him say, "Hey, I gotta hand it to you, Evans.

There's few people who can pull off what you did and come out smelling like a rose. I mean, you got your girl back, and your best bud forgave you. You did good, my man."

Avery's eyes grew to the size of saucers in a split second. "I'm very fortunate that Christina and Joey forgave me. I prayed for years that they would."

"Ave, I'm not into the Christian scene at all, man. It's great they forgave you and all. I'm not so sure I would if I were in their shoes. I mean, you left them in the dark with no warning. That's harsh. I forgive you and all, but we weren't as close, know what I mean?"

"Yeah, I do know what you mean. I'm thankful to both of them and you for forgiving me, and I don't take it for granted."

John looked at me with softness in his eyes that I'd never seen before. "Was it easy? To forgive Avery, I mean."

Was it easy to forgive Avery? "Yes and no. It was both the easiest and hardest thing I ever had to do."

"How's that?" John asked me as he tilted his head slightly.

I did my best to explain, "Well, it was hard because I felt betrayed in a way. I wasn't given an explanation, and it came out of the blue. I was also distraught, and it took me months before I could move on or trust anyone. On the other hand, it was easy because I could tell Avery was sincere and that he thought he had my best interest at heart by letting me go. Since I never stopped loving him, it was both easy and hard at the same time."

"Yo, that's epic. I get it now. Ave, don't mess this up, man. She's a real keeper," John said with a wink my way.

Avery returned with a smile that flickered to both John and me and attested, "Don't I know it! I can't imagine my life without Christina."

A vision of an older version of Avery and me sitting together on a bench overlooking a lake in a park transferred a feeling of sheer contentment that filled my body from head to toe. We reached for the other's hand at the same time. Avery gave me a loving squeeze that affirmed his feelings for me.

John nodded in approval, slapped Avery on the shoulder and remarked, "Happy it's all working out for you, man."

"Hey, thanks, man," Avery replied with a grin.

When Val and Larry entered the room after dropping Macey off, they both noticed Joey. Judging from the look on their faces, they were surprised he was here. Catching me by myself as I was snatching a few chips, Val couldn't wait to ask, "Is it awkward that Joey's here?"

"Well, hello to you too!" I returned.

A guilty grimace appeared on Val's face. "Oh, sorry. Hey, hi!" she said, to make up for her haste. "I couldn't help but think how you and Joey dated after you and Avery broke up. You three are like a love triangle."

With my arms crossed, I asseverated, "We are not a love triangle. Joey and I broke it off on decent terms. He's here for Avery."

"Does that mean they're friends again?" Val asked.

"They're working on it," I answered.

"Is Joey seeing anyone?" Val asked with bated breath. *That didn't take long.*

I stifled an eye roll. "I have no idea. What happened with Macey?"

"We took her home. She's safe and sound. We left her car here." She laughed. "She'll have to pick it up tomorrow. What did I miss?"

"Nothing. All quiet on the home front," I replied.

"In that case I'm going to catch up with Cheryl and Jackie."

As Val was leaving, Abby approached me. Her silky dark hair looked gorgeous against her crisp white shirt. "Hi, Abby. You look so pretty tonight." I couldn't resist throwing a compliment her way.

"Oh, thanks," she said, kind of off guard, then asked, "How are you?" There was a touch of concern in her voice.

"Good. I'm good," I said, trying to sound convincing.

With a motherly look of concern, Abby said, "Christina, I realize this party is about Avery making amends, but how are you doing with everything?"

"What do you mean?" I asked.

Abby elaborated, "I mean you've been through a lot. I think it's great you're supporting Avery, but this can't be easy for you on top of everything you experienced this year. How are you holding up?"

I was surprised Abby asked me that as we were never that close. *How am I holding up?* "Honestly, it's been kind of a distraction. I haven't been focusing on me as much, and it's a refreshing change."

"That's good, but be careful not to neglect your needs. That's all," Abby advised.

Abby sounded like she knew from experience. *What are you not telling me, Abby?* "Thanks, I appreciate your concern, but I'm fine. Really."

What's going on with you? "Abby, is there something going on with you that you'd like to share? I talk to people all the time about very personal things. You can talk to me. It stays between us. You have my word," I encouraged.

"I, uh, no, no, I'm fine. Nothing for you to be concerned about," she said with too much protest in her voice.

Something is definitely going on with her.

"Okay, but I'm available if you need to talk. I found that talking about my rapes has diminished the power they have over me."

"Uh, yeah. Sure, but I'm fine," Abby struggled to convince me.

That's three fines. Something's up. I can sense that now is not the time to pursue this. "All right then," I said with finality.

The silence was awkward between us, so I munched on a handful of chips. *Say something to end this uncomfortable chasm.*

I was enjoying the song, "What's on Your Mind (Pure Energy)" by Information Society, when Abby rekindled the conversation between us. She leaned forward, "You mentioned that you give talks. Where do you speak?"

I happily answered, "I go mainly to churches now. Word has gotten out that my talks are inspiring and provide scripture. I have a gig next Sunday morning about an hour from here at The Lord's Blessings. It's a nondenominational church. I'm speaking to a woman's group after their church service at noon."

"Can anyone attend?" she asked.

"Yes, as a matter of fact, they encourage visitors to come and listen and to attend the services beforehand," I replied before popping more chips in my mouth.

"Sounds very welcoming," she remarked.

"Every speaking engagement I've been to has been incredibly welcoming regardless of whether or not it was a church," I stated.

Abby continued to question me, "Besides churches, where have you spoken?"

"One time I spoke at a woman's shelter for battered women. I wasn't allowed to divulge the address to anyone in order to maintain the safety of the women. That kinda freaked me out, but I felt at ease once I got there," I recalled.

With a glint in her eye, Abby stated, "It sounds like you're doing good work helping women."

"Thanks. I find it rewarding. It's a reminder for me to put things in perspective. That things could be much worse for me. A reminder that by God's grace, I'm able to get through anything," I shared.

Abby sent a hopeful smile my way. "Your faith amazes me. I wish I had your kind of faith. You seem so grounded. I remember you talking with such conviction when we were in Morgan's Bible study."

An idea came to me that I was excited to share, "Why don't you…"

I was cut off when I heard Avery's voice, "Hey, everyone! Thanks again for coming. I appreciate your friendship and support. Most of all, I wouldn't be here if it weren't for Christina." The room was silent. All eyes were on Avery. "She inspired me to be a better person. I wasn't sure if she could ever forgive me, but she did, and I couldn't be happier."

With a smile as wide as the Grand Canyon, Avery stood looking in my direction from across the room. He raised his red plastic cup and said, "Christina, thank you for giving me a second chance."

Avery turned to his childhood best friend who was standing next to him, and toasted him as well. "I also want to say thanks to Joey for forgiving me too. I know I don't deserve his forgiveness or anyone's for that matter, but I'm grateful, nonetheless. Here's to forgiveness and second chances."

A prickling feeling ran through me as everyone raised their cups and said, "To forgiveness and second chances." Too stunned to get all the words out, I could only manage to raise my cup.

"Cheers to Avery! May he live the life of a pastor and always have the support of his friends," Joey said as he raised his cup.

My cheeks began to burn hearing my former boyfriend toast his former best friend, my current boyfriend. *When did life get so complicated?* A vision of me struggling in Paul's living room flashed before me.

Suddenly, I lost my balance followed by Abby saying, "Christina, are you okay? You look like you're about to faint." She grabbed hold of me and suggested, "Let's sit down. You're trembling." We sat on two chairs next to each other. "What happened? Are you okay?" Abby asked.

Feeling dizzy, I raised my right index finger to give myself a moment for the room to stop spinning. *Inhale. One. Two. Three. Four. Five. Exhale. One. Two. Three. Four. Five.* "I'm okay now. Thanks for catching me."

Avery swooped by my side. "Christina, are you alright? Abby, what happened to her?"

With panic in her voice, Abby answered, "I don't know. She got pale, then lost her balance."

Hearing Avery's voice, I knew I had to put his mind at ease, so I answered as quickly as I could without lifting my head. "I'm fine. Really. I had a flashback. I get them sometimes, but I'm okay now." *But not okay to move.*

Morgan rushed over. "Why don't you give her some space?"

Avery stayed by my side.

Morgan asked as she crouched down by my side, "Christina, do you need some water?" I nodded, my head low.

Avery motioned to Joey who swiftly left and returned with a cup of water. My stomach felt like someone kicked it. I took the cup from him, and everything felt like it was going in slow motion. *Why me? Why now in front of everyone? This is Avery's night.* I wanted to disappear.

There was concern in Avery's voice when he said, "Are you feeling better now?"

I swallowed a mouthful of water and said faintly, "I'm okay. I just needed a minute." The comfort of Avery holding my hand flowed through my body.

Do I explain what happened? Or do I let it go and pretend like nothing happened? I don't want this night to be about me. Why do I keep having these flashbacks? I was doing better. At least I thought I was.

"Do you want to talk about it?" My worried boyfriend asked.

"Not now. Maybe later," I said, nearly breathless. I wasn't in the mood to socialize any more. I felt like I had the wind knocked out of me. *Lord, help me shake this off, so I can enjoy myself and not make this about me.*

The rest of the night was tolerable. Despite feeling drained from my episode, I managed to socialize and avoided answering why I almost passed out. I feared another onset if I talked about what happened. It didn't seem like the right time or place regardless.

The party had come to an end, and everyone left except... Joey. I was surprised that Joey stayed. Actually, I was surprised that Joey came to the party.

"Nice party. Thanks for inviting me," my former boyfriend said to my boyfriend. *Don't you guys think this is weird? Why am I the only one here who finds this awkward? Maybe it's because Avery wasn't around when I dated Joey. If they can be big about this, then so can I.*

"Hey, man, thanks for coming," Avery responded to Joey by patting him on the arm.

With puppy dog eyes, Joey turned to me and said, "I hope you don't mind me staying. I feel kinda responsible for what happened to you, Christina. I mean, you nearly fainted when I was toasting Avery. I was hoping we could talk about it, but I don't want to make things worse."

He still cares about me. I felt happy and sad and confused all at the same time. *Do you still like me? Yes. That's the vibe I'm getting, and that he's very concerned.*

I replied to Joey, "I guess I should explain what's been going on. I didn't want to say anything before, because the night was about Avery, not me."

Fatigue took over, so I sat down on the closest chair. Avery took hold of my hand as he sat beside me. Hunched over in my direction, he said, "All that matters is that you're okay. You had us worried..."

Joey spoke, "If me being here is too difficult for you, Christina, I can go."

I shook my head and replied to Joey, "It's not what you think. Well, I don't know what you're thinking…"

Why can't I have a normal life? Sitting before me were the two guys I cared about the most in a romantic way. They were best friends until… until Avery's porn addiction caused him to cut ties with us. Joey was a reminder of what I went through after Avery let me go. Then Joey broke up with me. Even though I knew it was the right thing to do at the time, it was nonetheless hard to endure another break up. We both knew I wasn't over Avery. *How can I explain what happened earlier tonight when I'm not quite sure why it happened?*

Avery's voice interrupted my thoughts. "It's okay. You don't need to say anything. If you feel like talking, I'm here."

After breathing wisdom into my lungs, I felt compelled to talk it out. "Bear with me, as I try to explain what happened, or at least why I think it happened."

I paused to collect my thoughts. "It's best if I get straight to the heart of the issue. I was forever changed when Paul raped me. I've gone through some healing, yes, but I still relive it. I think things are worse in some regards because of having been raped a second time with a knife to my throat."

I started to choke up. Visions of the light reflecting off the knife stirred that fear in me once again. In an attempt to comfort me, Avery cupped our hands together.

Avery spoke in a soothing tone, "I know this is hard for you. I just want to understand."

"You're never going to completely understand what I went through. It was horrific, and I had to go through it again, only worse. I want to move on with my life, but I can't. I'm reminded of…" A second passed as I recalled the beginning of my nightmare. I picked up right where I left off, "of how messed up my life was… still is… How it's not normal."

I drew a breath to fuel the energy needed to go on. "I have a boyfriend who is a recovering porn addict which I didn't even know was such a thing. My former boyfriend walks back into my life, and for some reason I'm surprised by that. Shouldn't I be?"

With a sarcastic tone, I said, "I mean it's perfectly normal that my current boyfriend and my ex-boyfriend are becoming friends again without any thought or consideration of how I might feel."

I sensed they were about to say something, so I held up my hand. "You wanted to know why I nearly fainted. Well, I'll tell you why…"

I turned to Avery and said, "Joey was toasting you, and I'm thinking, when did my life get so weird, so messed up? That's when I had a flashback to the day Paul raped me. No, it's not pretty. It's ugly and horrible, and it's still like I'm living that nightmare all over again. I was silent for too long."

I continued to lay my sights on Avery. "Well, I will be silent no longer, and if you can't handle it, then we need to end things, because I obviously have a lot to sort through. I understand if you can't handle it since you're going through your own stuff, but I'm done hiding it. I'm done with feeling ashamed, with trying to convince myself that everything is okay when it's not okay."

I didn't care that I sounded harsh, because what I experienced twice in my life was beyond harsh, and they both needed to hear how it affected me.

Joey began to speak, "I should go…"

Instantly, I threw my hand up at Joey. "No, you need to hear this too. I kept all this from you as well. I wasn't just dealing with Avery breaking up with me back in high school. I was dealing with being raped. Even though it didn't just happen, the rape was always there hovering in the background at the very least. I was too afraid, too ashamed to tell anyone. I hate Paul for what he did to me. He ruined my life. Now I'm afraid of being triggered. What people will think."

Out of nowhere, I got a boost of clarity and raised my voice, "You know what? I don't care anymore what people think. I didn't do anything wrong. I'm no longer a victim but a survivor. God will get me through this next phase. That much I'm certain of."

I turned to Joey who sat there looking both uncomfortable and concerned. "Joey, I'm glad you could forgive Avery. You two were the best of friends, and I truly hope your friendship can be fully restored."

The fatigue got the better of me when I said, "Avery, I'm not so sure you realize how blessed you are. Your friends rallied around you. Sure, Macey did her thing, but as far as I'm concerned, you got off easy." *What did I just say? I can't believe I said all that.*

Joey said, "I feel like I'm intruding…"

I interrupted Joey since I was on a roll, "We," I pointed to each of us. "Need to work this out. You two don't get to patch things up and leave me hanging out to dry. The three of us need to work through this. If God got us this far, He'll see us through."

My attention turned to Avery. "Avery, you're on track to be a pastor after overcoming your porn addiction. What you overcame is incredible, and you have a bright future ahead of you."

I closed my eyes briefly to give myself strength to say the next part. "I survived not one but two rapes. Joey, you made amends with someone who you were once best friends with after they walked away from a lifelong friendship. Whether we like it or not, the three of us are connected. It's weird, and it's awkward, and it will stay that way until we break through those barriers. I think we need to face this head on… so we can move on with our lives."

"How do you propose we do that? Work it out between the three of us I mean?" Avery asked.

Joey shook his head and said, "Hey, I don't want to get between the two of you. I said my piece two summers ago."

I quickly volleyed, "No, uh-uh, I'm not buying it. There's no way there isn't any animosity between the two of you regarding me. I'm not that naïve."

"Do you want me to be jealous?" Avery asked, his eyes narrowed.

Ow. That stung. "No, of course not. I don't want you to be in denial like this is all okay." I motioned to each one of us.

Avery spoke louder as he held his gaze on me, "All right, I admit it. It about killed me seeing you go out with Joey."

His eyes darted back and forth to Joey and me as I squirmed in my seat. He raked his fingers through his hair as he shared a painful memory, "I knew you two were dating. I saw you together."

Avery turned his attention to me, "It hurt, but I had no right to stop it, to claim you, Christina. No matter what I did though, I couldn't shake the thought of you. I still loved you, and you were off with my best friend."

Avery's eyes filled with devastation. My heart went out to him, but my attention was diverted when Joey jumped in, his tone accusatory and all his focus directed to Avery. "After what you did, we were no longer best friends. You were long out of the picture before Christina and I even started dating. You had no claim on her, but it didn't matter because you were always there."

Joey hung his head low matching his volume, "But I couldn't help myself. I still loved her despite the fact that she couldn't let you go."

All the frustration and anxiety I built up was released in the form of tears rolling down my cheeks. "I'm so sorry. I didn't mean to put you both through that. Please forgive me. I didn't mean for any of this to happen." I realized I hurt the two people that meant the most to me during times of struggle.

Avery put his arm around me, "It's not your fault, Christina. I let it happen by letting you go. It was the biggest mistake of my life," his voice heavy with regret.

He turned to look at Joey. "Letting our friendship end like that was a huge mistake too, Joey. I really screwed up. I'm sorry."

"Yo, man, let's not cry over spilled milk. I forgave you," Joey replied.

"But do you forgive me, Joey?" I asked with a quiver in my voice.

Joey's eyes became glassy, he closed his eyes for a brief moment and said, "It never occurred to me that I needed to forgive you."

I knew right then we finally came to the crux of it all. Joey never truly forgave me for breaking his heart.

"You're still in love with her, aren't you?" Avery dared to ask.

"No," Joey answered, shaking his head in protest. "No," he repeated, "but I do still care about her."

Avery pressed, "Admit it, Joey, you still love her."

What did I get us into? My thoughts get dark at night, especially when I'm tired, and I'm past being tired. God forgive me for opening this can of worms.

"It's clear you two belong together," Joey stated as if he was admitting defeat.

Avery threw up his hands, "I knew it! He still loves you. Of course, he does."

"Look, Avery, it's not like I'm going to get between you two," Joey assured.

Avery asked, "Did you forgive me out of guilt because you're still in love with Christina?"

Where did that come from?

Joey stated, "No, man. I knew you were sincere in your apology about how things went down between us. We had a bond. We were like brothers."

Oh, thank God.

I watched for Avery's reaction, "Yeah, we did. I miss that. I missed you, bro."

"Me too. Can we still be friends even though, you know?" Joey tilted his head slightly my way.

I can't tell if this is better or worse from when we started this crazy conversation.

"Yeah, man, why not? Stranger things have happened."

Like what? I wanna know.

"Cool," said Joey with a smile and they hugged it out. *That only took about four years.*

The Lord pressed a verse on my heart upon witnessing something I never thought I would see, all around forgiveness for three individuals who shared a unique bond.

"In whom we have redemption through his blood, the forgiveness of sins, according to the riches of his grace; Wherein he hath abounded toward us in all wisdom and prudence;" (Ephesians 1:7-8).

Chapter 33

Streaming through the bottom of my bedroom window underneath the opaque white shade, the morning light disturbed my much-needed slumber. Remaining in the comfort of my bed, I ignored the morning call for hours. Thoughts and images of the moment my life took a turn for the worse plagued me throughout the night and stayed with me through daybreak. Intermittently, scenes of the night before also wreaked havoc on my psyche. The combination of both troublesome matters caused me to toss and turn all night long.

I woke up exhausted and with a heavy heart knowing Joey was still in love with me. I believed him when he said he wouldn't come between Avery and me, but I didn't want him walking around with that burden of knowing his heart's desire is unattainable. *Lord, please have Joey get over me. I know the feeling, and it's awful. He's a great guy, and I want him to move on.*

Something else was clawing at my heart, ripping it to shreds, and it was huge. I decided to talk to my mom about it, which was a feat of its own since we rarely spoke beyond idle chatter.

Like most days, I found my mother sitting at the kitchen table with a cup of tea. I thought it best to eat something knowing my conversation would be a hard one.

In typical Mom form, she greeted me through pursed lips. "Good morning, Christina."

"Morning, Mom." I sat down at my usual spot and poured Rice Krispies in the bowl set out before me. Looks like I was starting my morning with the company of Snap, Crackle and Pop, old friends of mine.

I finished the last explosion in my mouth when I said, "Mom, I need to talk to you about something." I assumed her silence indicated she was listening.

"I want to bring charges against Paul Martin for raping me." I let that sink in before continuing.

Silence.

More silence.

Exasperated from feeling ignored, I said, "Mom, did you hear me? I want to…"

"Yes, I heard you, Christina." Her voice was calm with a slight edge. She looked at the clock on the wall. "That's a lot to take in at nine-thirty in the morning."

And to think I slept in.

Feeling the need to explain myself, I replied, "Well, I need closure and assurance he won't do this to anyone else. He raped Sherrie too, and I can't forgive myself for that. He shouldn't be allowed to roam free after what he did to us. We're not free, not completely. We never will be."

My mother sat across from me seemingly unraveled after I poured my heart out. She pressed her lips together and said in an even tone, "You do realize that you will be opening yourself up to criticism. Your life may be under a microscope if it goes to trial."

My reply was quick and to the point, having given it much thought. "I have nothing to hide. I did nothing wrong. People already know I was raped by him."

"You may lose speaking engagements," my mother informed me like she was my financial advisor.

I fired back, "I may also gain them. Whatever. That doesn't matter. He needs to reap the consequences of what he's done."

"What does Avery think about this?" she asked flatly.

"I haven't told him."

"You should at least discuss this with him since you two are in a serious relationship," my mom suggested, jutting her chin ever so slightly.

"What makes you think it's serious?" I asked, not understanding the relevance of her statement.

With a trace of a wince, she responded, "Christina, you can't fool me. You're the type that gets serious and the way you two look at each other…" My mom stopped briefly and nodded, "You're in a serious relationship."

"Okay, so I'm in a serious relationship. It doesn't change the fact that Paul is still out there and could be raping other girls. This has to end," I exclaimed.

"All right. It sounds like your mind is made up," she said with resignation.

Knowing I needed guidance, I asked, "What do I need to do?"

Her eyes were piercing as she considered the options. "I'm not sure. I suppose you need to speak to the district attorney."

"All right then. I can do that," I said, determined.

"Christina, has anything else happened to you that makes you want to prosecute?" My mother said, her eyes remained intense.

"No, other than I can't let him rape someone else and ruin another life," I answered with conviction.

"I see. Is that all?" She said with the same intensity as our most recent exchanges.

"Isn't that enough?" I answered, feeling impatient.

"Yes, that's more than enough," my mom said, apparently satisfied with my response.

"So how do I find a district attorney?" I asked, wanting to get a move on my latest quest. An idea came to mind, "The yellow pages?"

"Yes. I can help you with that," my mom offered.

Are my ears deceiving me?

"Really?" I questioned my mom for clarity.

"Don't be so surprised. I am your mother after all." She sounded like Morticia Addams, the matriarch of the *Addams Family*.

"Yes, but you usually don't get involved," I reminded her. Essentially, I experienced the trauma of two rapes and the devastation of two break-ups without any interference from my mother.

She drew her teacup to her mouth, took a sip of her favorite beverage, and set it down. Then my mother sat back and crossed her legs. With a sideways gaze for my benefit, she said, "That's because I wanted you to become strong and independent. And you are already strong and independent. I think you've been through too much at such a young age. It's time you let others help you. I think it's about time I help you where I can."

Who are you, and what did you do to my mother?

"Thanks, Mom."

She nodded. At least it was some form of acknowledgement. I didn't want to press my luck after she bore her soul after boring a hole in me with her penetrating looks. "I'll call and make an appointment for you, but in the meantime tell Avery what you're planning on doing and if you change your mind, let me know. Come to me immediately. Don't worry that you changed your mind, okay?"

"Got it. Thanks." I told her I was going on a hike with Avery, but I'd be back soon since he had to go to work afterward.

Shortly after my morning conversation with my mom, Avery picked me up to go hiking on a nearby trail. I climbed in the passenger seat to Steven Curtis Chapman singing "Dying to Live" and Avery saying, "Hey, beautiful!" The greeting took me back to our high school days when we started dating. For some reason it caught me off guard this time too.

"Howdy, handsome!" I replied with equal vigor to Avery's jovial greeting. *Two can play this game.*

It was great hearing Avery's laugh first thing in the morning. "Howdy, handsome?"

"Yeah, I like alliteration," I said playfully.

"Hey, I'm not complaining," he said with a grin.

"Good. I reserve the right to use it."

"I can live with that." He looked away from the road for a moment, directing his attention toward me. "You seem to be doing pretty good this morning."

"You put me in a good mood," I stated in a cheerful voice.

"Glad I could be of service. Something on your mind?" he said, detecting something was up with me.

"Actually, yes. There's something I wanted to talk to you about, but don't worry. We're good. This has to do with me." I didn't want to cause Avery any undue worry.

He turned to me and said, "Okay. You have my attention."

"Not now. We'll discuss it on the trail, okay?" Again, I didn't want to discuss a serious matter while Avery was driving.

"You have me curious," Avery admitted.

"You should be curious," I said in a teasing manner, despite the severity of the topic to come.

Once we got into a rhythm of hiking in the woods, I said, "My episode last night got me thinking."

"Yeah, what's that?" Avery asked, his eyebrows arched.

"I want to bring charges against Paul for raping me." *I'm getting good at dropping bombs.*

"Oh, wow. Can you do that? I mean, it's been like six years since it happened," he said, not making a misstep along the trail.

"I don't know for sure, but I think so since it's a serious and violent crime," I ducked under a tree branch that was hanging overhead on the path. "I talked to my mom about it this morning, and she's making calls to get more information and make an appointment."

"What made you decide to do this?"

After zigzagging through the trail in the woods, we came to a straight path which made it easier to talk. The sun peaked through the imposing trees providing additional warmth. I took that as a sign to clue Avery in on the reason for my latest mission. "I keep having these episodes of reliving what he did. I used to get them before all the time in the form of nightmares when it first happened. After a few years, I would only get them when I was really stressed... Until recently after I got raped again, the haunting images won't let up in my sleep or when I'm awake."

"Yeah, that's understandable I guess. I'm sorry you have to go through that. Is there anything I can do?" Avery offered as he pushed away a hanging branch.

"Just be in my corner, and let me work out this mess. It helps if I talk about it, but I don't want to discuss it all the time with just anybody."

Gripped by fatigue from a restless night, I was grateful Avery stopped upon being greeted by a babbling brook. Facing each other, Avery grabbed ahold of my hands and said, "I'm honored you feel comfortable discussing it with me."

I looked up at him, recalling how my mom said we were in a serious relationship and silently acknowledged she was correct. "Ave, you know you were the first person I told that Paul raped me. That was a turning point for me," I shared, grateful he gave me the space to be me in a moment of need.

Avery rubbed my arms and said with transparency, "You have been so brave this whole time dealing with everything by yourself. Now I know why you were okay with me punching him in the face, and to think I struggled with that back then."

"You did?" I asked, not aware that it was even an issue.

"Yeah, I'm not a violent kind of person, and I wasn't in the habit of harming anyone, but there was this strange energy in the air and now I know why." He turned to face the brook.

I kept my gaze on Avery. "Did you feel guilty for punching him?" I asked.

Avery turned his body to face me and answered, "I did, but I brushed it off. It seemed like things got better for you after that. Did they?"

I blinked at the thought of how one simple violent act helped to dissipate the terrible turmoil I had been experiencing. I wanted Avery to know what he did was not in vain and answered him, "They did. He backed off after that. I guess he was scared of getting beat up."

"That'll do it. Most guys fear getting beat up, even bullies," Avery stated and began walking away from the brook.

I followed Avery's lead by trailing right behind him and said, "I was at a loss for what to do back then. I guess I justified you punching him as partial payback for what he did to me. I know violence isn't the answer, but somehow it brought me some peace because he stopped tormenting me after that. Well, at least he did in person."

Avery slowed down his pace but remained quiet while I shared my trials, past and present. "I still had nightmares after that, and now I have episodes that I relive in public. You know, like the one I had last night. I just want them to end, and I keep thinking that maybe they will end if I have some closure with it."

Avery placed his hand in mine and continued our hike. I took that to mean we were on this journey together.

Without stalling, I proceeded to share my struggles with my boyfriend, "Perhaps if I take matters in my own hands, I can right the wrongs he started. If I even thought for a second that he would rape someone else, I would have said something, but the thought never entered my mind."

Seeing an opening, Avery said, "Christina, you can't blame yourself for what that jerk did. He's a monster. I even thought about hunting him down, but I keep coming back to my senses. God doesn't want the violence to perpetuate. Two wrongs don't make a right. God blessed us by having Paul leave you alone after that, but I can't even condone me punching him. What's done is done at this point. We need to work on getting you restored, and that's focusing on what God's will is surrounding this."

With what sounded almost like a desperate plea, I said, "Ave, I pray for the Lord's will in my life all the time. Sometimes it's not that clear of a path. Like right now, bringing up charges against him seems to be where He's leading me, but I'm not one hundred percent certain that's what I should do."

"Why don't we pray about it now? If that's alright with you," my wannabe pastor suggested.

"Yeah, okay," I agreed.

The tranquil woods beckoned us to a complete stop along the path. Avery reached for my other hand and as we closed our eyes, he prayed, "Heavenly Father, we ask for guidance and direction for Christina. She is plagued by the haunting memory of her rapes and wishes it to end. Please provide her with definitive answers for a plan of action to help her rid this unrest she continues to experience. Please give Christina the peace, joy, and comfort of knowing You are in charge of her life and only have her best interest at heart. Thank You for sending Your Son to the cross, and for sending the Holy Spirit to dwell within us. We humbly ask these things. In Jesus' name we pray. Amen."

I echoed the sentiment, "Amen."

Avery dropped me off at home instead of us hanging out longer, since he had to go to work at the church. When I walked in the kitchen, my mom was still seated at the kitchen table, as if nothing had changed since I left earlier, and asked, "How was your hike?"

"Good. I told Avery I wanted to press charges."

"What did he say?" she asked.

"He asked what brought it on, and I told him about the episodes I've been having."

I could hear the concern in her voice when my mom asked, "What episodes?"

"I keep having these flashbacks of my rapes in front of people," I answered.

My mother raised her eyebrows. "Why didn't you tell me this before?"

I shrugged and told my mom the truth, "I didn't think of it. It's not like I'm trying to hide it. I just want them to go away."

"You should tell me these things, Christina. Do you want to go to counseling again?" I could tell she asked out of concern for me.

A sigh escaped me. "I don't know. It's not like I don't talk about it already. I mean, I share my experiences with you, Avery, my friends, and I speak at churches. I'm open about it now, so I'm not sure if counseling will make a difference."

My mother shared her wisdom, "I'm no expert, but a counselor may make suggestions. It's not just about sharing your feelings or experiences with them."

I shrugged again, suddenly feeling fatigued. "Yeah, I guess so."

"You're going through a lot, Christina. Why don't you consider scheduling an appointment?"

"I'll think about it," I said, hoping that would end the conversation.

"That's all I ask." The air in the kitchen seemed to get lighter, when my mom said, "Oh, I have good news for you. I was able to talk to the assistant district attorney to prosecute your case. Her name is Allison

Bouchard. Give her a call to set up a meeting with her. Her office is by the courthouse, not too far from here. Here's her number." She handed me a piece of paper.

"Thanks, Mom." *This is getting real. I may face my rapist on my day in court. Maybe then these episodes will disappear.*

Once I got in my bedroom, I sat on my bed and prayed. *Lord, help me decide what to do. Should I call this lawyer? Should I drop it altogether?*

I picked up my phone and began dialing the number in my mother's handwriting.

"Allison Bouchard's office. This is Samantha speaking. How may I help you?"

"Hi, I'm calling to make an appointment to meet with Ms. Bouchard."

"May I ask who is calling?"

"Christina De Rosa. My mother called earlier. She may be expecting my call."

"Yes, Christina. I can make that appointment for you... Due to a last-minute cancellation, I scheduled an appointment for this afternoon at two o'clock." *This is moving fast. What does someone wear to meet with an assistant district attorney?*

After showering, I changed into a decent pair of black pleated shorts and a floral short-sleeved shirt. It was too hot for make-up. I threw on small gold hoop earrings to complete the outfit.

As soon as I stepped in the office, a woman with short walnut brown hair seated behind a desk, wearing a lovely cream-colored blouse and charcoal slacks, greeted me warmly, "Hi, you must be Christina. I'm Samantha. We spoke on the phone. Ms. Bouchard is expecting you. Please go on in." She waved her hand in the direction of her boss's office.

"Okay. Thank you," I returned with a smile.

I opened the door to the Assistant District Attorney's office. A tall, thin sophisticated woman who wore her champagne-colored hair in a neat bun sprang out of her chair to greet me. Once she stood up, I could see that she was wearing a beautiful navy-blue skirt suit that matched her blue eyes. She held out her hand, and greeted me, "Hello, Christina. It's so nice to meet you."

I reached out to shake her hand. "Hi, nice to meet you, Ms. Bouchard."

"Please call me Allison. Have a seat, and we'll get started." She motioned for me to sit on the couch, and I did as I was told. "Can I get you something to drink, water, coffee?" she offered.

I don't suppose you serve milkshakes here. "Oh, no. Thank you."

Allison sat across from me in a high winged back chair. She crossed her legs and leaned back in her chair. "Normally, the police will take your statement, and if they think they have a case, they contact my office and I review the case. Your mother must know some powerful people to have you speak to me directly without going through the police."

I shook my head out of utter ignorance to my mother's connections. "I had no idea. She didn't say anything." *Way to go, Mom!*

Allison waved me off. "It's fine. I wanted to give you a heads up that this is not normal protocol, but I'll make sure you receive the best prosecution available if it comes to that."

"Thank you." *I'm glad I don't have to talk to the police.*

She indicated with a head nod. "Okay. I'm going to ask you some basic background questions to start." She held a pen in her hand and balanced a notebook pad on her lap.

After an onslaught of answering questions about my personal history, Allison said, "All right. I need to know what happened that brought you here today. Okay?"

"Okay," I said, starting to get nervous.

"In your own words, tell me what happened. I will need certain points of references. Let's start off with when this occurred."

I told Allison what happened, how Paul lured me there under false pretenses pretending his mom had a gift for me. I never talked about that before, but it felt good to release those details. Hearing my own words describe what happened gave me more peace about pressing charges, because I didn't sound absurd.

My thoughts were validated when she said, "This is good information. We should be able to establish that this was premeditated." I nodded and felt a twinge in my stomach.

Allison stopped taking notes, and unfolded her legs. She leaned forward and said, "I need you to tell me in detail exactly how he sexually assaulted you. Before we get started, do you need anything to drink, a bottle of water perhaps?"

Upon thinking how I reacted to flashbacks of what happened that summer afternoon, I decided to accept the water. From there, I told my story in all its graphic glory.

"... He was on top of me..." I said my voice aquiver. Despite mentally preparing myself for this as much as I could on such short notice, I managed to tear up.

"It's okay. This is a safe space. Take your time. You're doing great." Allison sounded more like a therapist than a lawyer, and she put me at ease with her encouraging words and soothing voice. I proceeded without too much faltering.

"Tell me what is motivating you to press charges after..." She quickly performed a mental calculation. "After 6 years since the assault."

I told Allison about Sherrie, and the water works made their presence known. The guilt of not telling anyone gripped me and squeezed the life out me like a little kid squeezing a tube of toothpaste having the toothpaste gush out of its holding cell.

Allison clicked her pen and held onto her pad of paper. "Do you think Sherrie would testify as to what happened to her?" She asked.

"I don't know. Sherrie was in bad shape, completely withdrawn. She even has an eating disorder that landed her near death in the hospital," I said, feeling guilty all over again for what Sherrie went through.

With her lips pursed, Allison asked, "I may need to speak to Sherrie. Is she still in the hospital?"

"No, she's home now last I heard..." My head hung low as I thought about my last encounter with Sherrie. She was so angry with me when she found out Paul raped me too, and I failed to tell anyone.

"What are you not telling me, Christina? Any detail you can think of can be relevant to your case."

"I don't think… It's just that…" *Was this really relevant?*

"Go on," Allison encouraged, tipping her head forward.

"Sherrie and I haven't spoken since I told her that Paul raped me. She ran away furious with me and she…" My breathing became erratic, and I choked on my words.

"It's okay. You can tell me anything," Allison assured me.

"Sherrie blamed me for Paul raping her." I waited for a response that never came. "He wouldn't have raped her if I had told someone he raped me."

Amanda's voice softened, "Did she say that?"

"Yes. Yes, she did because it is my fault, and I can't let him rape anyone else. I have to put an end to this." I pulled a tissue out of the box that Allison handed me and wiped my tears away.

"Did Paul rape anyone else that you know of?" She questioned.

"Not that I'm aware of," I replied.

It was about a half hour from that point before we finished our initial consultation. Allison handed me her business card and encouraged me to call if I had any more details to share, and that she would otherwise be in touch.

Chapter 34

The following morning Avery picked me up to go out to breakfast at the diner. After ordering, Avery said, "You seem different."

"How?" I asked as I leaned my head toward him.

Avery answered with a gentle smile, "More relaxed."

I raised my chin and cupped the back of my head with my hands, "I feel like I'm finally ending a horrible chapter in my life. It's the beginning of the end of this nightmare."

Avery cocked his head. "You got all that after one visit with your lawyer?"

"She's the assistant district attorney, and yes," I closed my eyes and tilted my head back, "I'm taking control of that part of my life, and it feels great, like I can breathe better now."

"That's incredible. I'm happy for you," he said, displaying crow's feet at the corners of his eyes.

"Thanks. How are you doing?" I stuck my chin out. "You sounded upbeat last night on the phone. What's going on?"

Avery's gleaming eyes gave away his excitement before he even said anything, "Nothing big. Just that my internship at the church is going very well. Pastor said he sees real promise in me being a pastor."

"That is big. It sounds like you're on your way." I held up my glass of water to celebrate our lives together, "Here's to our bright futures!"

"Cheers!" We toasted while listening to Survivor sing "Is This Love" in the background.

After breakfast we walked over to the nearby trail. We were in a fabulous rhythm of being active outdoors by walking, hiking, and jogging. Not only did I feel a greater connection with nature, but I felt more connected to Avery and grateful that he enjoyed the outdoor activities as much as I did. It was a great way to start our day before the sweltering sun made its appearance known. This path was more open and flatter than the hiking trails we took. Nonetheless, we were surrounded by trees and various waterways along the path. As we approached one of the larger streams, Avery said, "You're quiet today."

I stopped and smiled as I gazed out in the direction of the glistening stream. I took pleasure in observing the reflection of the landscape on the water. "I'm just enjoying the scenery and company." I was relishing in the peace I felt from taking control of my life.

"It is peaceful out here," Avery remarked. How comforting it was to be in sync with Avery. He came from behind me and wrapped his arms around my waist. "I can't tell you how much I enjoy spending time with you."

"It is nice, isn't it?" I smiled as I turned around to face him. I took a moment to drink in Avery. His hair was blonder from that first day earlier this summer when he convinced me to grab a milkshake with him, the day that laid the groundwork for us to be together. His gaze back at me told me that he was taking me in as well. *I wonder what he sees.*

The sun was to my back providing an extra layer of warmth. The pull between the two of us was too strong to resist any longer. Avery's lips were soft and supple and carried me away to a place of bliss.

We broke apart and there was this undeniable bond between us that was greater than any kiss, deeper than anything we could grasp at that moment. We stood there staring into each other's souls while being swallowed up in the delicious confirmation that we were meant to do life as one.

Avery cut the silence by declaring, "I would walk through fire for you."

No words could express the mutual devotion we felt for each other. An intense burning flame filled my lungs as we shared another intimate interlude. The energy to sustain our passionate moment came to an end where I found myself nuzzled on Avery's chest listening to the thumps of his heartbeat as his arms remained around me.

Treasuring that kind of closeness was something of a privilege I hoped to never forget. Although my eyes were closed to capture those heart-warming emotions, I was aware of the pounding of the pavement as joggers ran past us. Pit-a-pat. Pit-a-pat. Pit-a-pat.

I craned my neck and said, "Let's not ever forget these moments."

"Never," he whispered.

I returned to my nestled position and thanked God for His graciousness.

Before long, we walked hand-in-hand along a tributary. The sun, high in the cloudless sky, caused beads to trickle down off my forehead.

"How about we get out of the sun and go to my place for lunch?" Avery suggested.

"Lunch already?" As if on cue, my stomach growled.

"Yeah, time flies even when you're enjoying a stroll in the park."

We drove to Avery's with the air-conditioning blasting in the car and Rick Astley singing "Together Forever" on the radio.

Mrs. Evans was in the kitchen doing the dishes when we walked in. "I made your favorite, Avery, homemade chicken salad, and we have crescent rolls."

"That's perfect, Mom. Thanks."

"Hi, Christina, I hope you'll join us for lunch," Mrs. Evans said, her voice welcoming.

"I wouldn't miss your chicken salad sandwiches for anything, Mrs. Evans," I said with a willing smile.

Avery opened the fridge and said, "Mom, do we have any pickles?"

"In the fridge on the left side in the pickle bag. I went to the deli and picked out a couple of plump ones."

"Found them. Thanks, Mom." Avery put the bag on the counter, looked up at me and said, "Would you like to do the honors and cut them? I know how much you love pickles."

"Sure. Why not?" I said and moved in front of the pickles.

As I was careful not to cut my fingers off with the super sharp knife Avery handed to me, he was pouring potato chips in a bowl.

Avery's mom turned to me and said, "What would you like to drink? We have milk, soda, iced tea, and of course, water."

"Milk, please," I answered.

"I'll have the same, Mom."

"Two milks coming right up," Mrs. Evans said with delight. I loved the ease of being with Avery's mom. She even made beverages fun. We took our seats at the table and began eating. The chicken salad was delicious as always.

Mrs. Evans waited to finish chewing before asking, "What have you two been up to?"

"We went for a walk after breakfast," I answered, since Avery was munching on his sandwich.

"How lovely. Where did you go?" Avery's mom asked.

"The trail by the diner," Avery answered, having finished chewing.

"Let me guess. You ate at the diner." Mrs. Evans presumed.

"Affirmative," Avery responded like he was in the Army.

Mrs. Evans faced me and asked, "Christina, do you cook?"

"No. My mom does most of the cooking," I responded.

"Avery isn't much of a cook either, but you two are more than welcome to make meals here if you like. You could save a little money that way," she said, throwing a cute little smirk our way.

Avery wrinkled his nose and remarked, "Yeah, but we have to do the dishes then."

"A little housework won't kill you," his mom said with a lilt in her voice.

"Don't be so sure, Mom," Avery returned with a playful grin.

"Well, my offer to use the kitchen still stands. It might be fun for you to cook something together or for each other." She winked.

We wouldn't have any problem heating up the kitchen. Just thinking about it made my temperature rise. *Can she see my burning red cheeks from imagining cooking with Avery?* I reached for the glass of milk to cool me down.

Avery and I decided to play the guitars after eating lunch. We progressed through our normal warm-ups and began working on a new song, "I Love Rock and Roll" by Joan Jett.

"You're doing great!" Avery's praise was displayed from ear to ear as well as in his elated voice.

"Maybe it helps that I like this song," I said, trying not to allow the compliment go to my head.

"That makes sense," he said as he leaned inward.

After a moment, Avery clapped his hands with excitement, "We could start a band. We can call it, The Evans Band."

"Oh, are your parents in the band?" I asked, quizzically.

"No, you and me," Avery stated.

"Why don't I get a mention?" I asked.

Avery squared his shoulders and said, "Well, I figure it will take a couple years to get pretty decent, and by then we'll be married."

With a simpering smirk, I rubbed my forehead and replied, "There are so many things wrong with that statement. I don't even know where to begin."

Slumping forward, Avery asked, "What? Why?"

"Ave, I'm living day by day here. The only things I have planned are my speaking engagements," I said flatly.

There was an empty stare when Avery looked at me. "You don't want to get married?"

I scraped my bottom lip and swallowed hard before answering, "Someday, but I don't want to plan that far in advance. I want to enjoy what we have now. I don't see what the rush is."

Avery's eyes glazed over. With a tight-lipped smile, he said, "Don't you get it? I can't see my life without you ever again. I can't wait for you to be my wife."

My lips were pushed down by the weightiness of the subject. "Well, you're going to have to wait. We can still be in each other's lives." I threaded back a clump of hair behind my ear. "I'm not ready for all that responsibility. Neither of us have jobs that we can live off of. Who's to say we will once we graduate college? There are no certainties." A lopsided grimace found its way to my face.

Avery spoke with a certitude that exceeded any and all professions of love in romance novels, "I'm certain I love you, and I have faith that it will all work out."

I have these episodes, and I don't want to carry that baggage into a marriage. "We both have a lot to work through, Ave. I can't think that far ahead. I need to get through this stage first before I can even consider anything else." *I'm already dealing with too much.*

While pressing his index finger on his cheek, Avery asked, "Let me ask you this, and I'll drop it. Can you picture us being married someday?"

I couldn't help but think of Joey when he brought up marriage that day during senior week. I reacted badly which led to our breakup. I was devastated that day but knew deep down breaking up was the right thing to do as I wasn't over Avery.

"Christina, you seem like you're a million miles away. Are you okay?" Avery's voice brought me back to present time.

"Uh, yeah," I answered, rubbing my jaw.

Avery leaned in, "I need to know, can you picture us married someday?"

Without even thinking, I answered, "I can't imagine my life with anyone else but you."

Avery placed his hand over his chest. "You scared me for a second."

"Don't rush things, please. I need to land on my own two feet first before I get married. I owe that to myself and the person I marry, which I can't imagine being anyone but you. Okay?"

"Yeah, I get it. I didn't mean for you to feel rushed into marriage. I can wait as long as I have to," he stated with understanding eyes.

That warranted a warm smile from me without the display of teeth. The topic of marriage was far too premature to be discussing. I didn't want to have a discussion like that for a long while. We were only going into our junior year in college after all.

We rocked our session of "I Love Rock and Roll" after we had the M word talk. I think Joan would have been impressed with our practice session, although I doubt she would be booking The Evans Band to open for her any time soon.

We walked upstairs, and I saw rain pouring down through the kitchen window. "Hey, Ave, can you give me a ride home? I don't want to walk home in the rain."

He grabbed his keys and before long we pulled up in my driveway.

My mom came outside when I got out of the car and said with panic in her voice, "Christina, I have to leave with Uncle Joe. You should ask Avery to stay with you if he can."

"Why, Mom, what's wrong?" I turned to Avery and put my hand up for him to wait.

"Your brother is in jail a couple hours away. We are going to bail him out."

Every muscle in my face tensed up. "Why is Jared in jail?"

"Because he beat up Paul Martin," My mom answered, her brows knitted.

I squinted through the rain, "Why is Uncle Joe going with you?"

"Because someone needs to drive the car back just in case. I can't explain everything now." She gestured toward the car that pulled up behind Avery, "There he is. I have to go. There's no time to waste. Your father will be home soon. We couldn't wait for him to get here." My mother's eyes darted all around, "Why don't you all order pizza? I have to go."

I watched my mom dodge the raindrops, hop in the car with my uncle and drive off to get my brother out of jail.

I motioned for Avery to pull up and park.

Avery got out of his car and approached me with a puckered forehead, "What's going on?"

"Let's get inside first." I wanted to get out of the rain.

I told him what my mom said once we were in the house.

Avery's eyes became narrow slits, "Did you have any idea Jared would do that?"

In an attempt to make sense of the current situation, I ran my hand through my hair, "No, I didn't even know he knew that Paul raped me. Maybe this is about something else. I don't want to draw conclusions."

Avery shut his eyes while he rubbed his eyebrow, "I think it's pretty safe to say Jared found out."

Avery called his mom to let her know he'd be staying here for dinner. We waited for my father to arrive before ordering the pepperoni pizza. It would be an hour or so before he came home traveling from Center City, Philadelphia.

Avery suggested we pray for Jared. Knowing the power of prayer, I had already shot up a few of my own prayers. Reaching for my hands as we sat side by side on the couch in the family room, we postured ourselves for some quality time with our Lord.

Avery led us in prayer, "Dear Heavenly Father, we don't know what is going on, but we ask for safe travels for Mr. and Mrs. De Rosa and Christina's uncle in this rain. We put this situation with Jared in Your hands and ask for Your favor and blessings surrounding it. Please be with Jared and his family, Mr. and Mrs. De Rosa, Christina, and Uncle Joe. Give them the wisdom and clarity to know how to handle the situation whatever it may be. Help me to be a calming presence during this time while we wait to find out what transpired. Lord, You are the almighty God, maker of the universe. Your ways are just and good, and we put our faith in Your hands. In Your Son's name we pray. Amen."

"Amen," I said with a tight-lipped smile.

Shortly after we prayed, my dad came home. "Hi, Dad."

"Hi, Pooch. Hello, Avery. How about you order pizza, Christina? You're welcome to stay for dinner, Avery."

"Thanks, Mr. De Rosa," Avery said.

Per usual, my dad went upstairs to change out of his suit. I couldn't help but send up another prayer. *Lord, please grant Your mercy on Jared. He must be so scared if he's in jail.*

Avery's voice interrupted my random thoughts. "I know this is hard on you, waiting to find out what is going on. No matter what, I'm here for you."

Worry squashed my ability to smile. "Thanks for staying here with me."

"No problem," he said as his brows pulled together.

My dad sat in the chair adjacent to the couch Avery and I were sitting on. We were discussing our day when the doorbell rang. Avery grabbed the pizza box, so I could pay with the money my dad handed me. The pizza smelled so good that I couldn't wait to dig in. The gooey cheese and crispy pepperoni hit the spot as I waited anxiously for an update. With a mouthful of the savory goodness, I said, "This pizza is so good!"

Avery concurred, "It is good. First time I'm eating pizza from Donato's. We usually order from Vito's Pizza. I would definitely order from here next time."

My dad chimed in, "We Italians know our pizza, right Pooch?"

"Yeah, Dad," I said with a smile peeking through.

"But South Philly has the best pizza in the world. No contest. It's too bad they don't deliver this far," my dad smiled Italian style.

I added jokingly, "The sacrifices we must endure."

"You joke, but there's something to be said for good food," my dad said.

The phone rang, and I jumped up to answer it. "Hello."

"Hi, Christina, it's Mom. I have seen Jared, and he is physically fine, a bit rattled but that's normal under the circumstances."

"What circumstances?" I asked.

"He was arrested and put in a holding cell for assault. He can be released with charges dropped, but that depends on you."

"Me? Why?" I asked, baffled.

"Paul Martin said he would drop the charges, if you drop the lawsuit against him. Please understand that the charge of assault can land Jared up to ten years in prison. It's your call if you decide not to testify. I need you to tell me how to proceed. I know it's a lot to absorb, but we need a decision right away."

My heart was beating out of my chest, and my head was spinning out of control. I didn't even bother controlling my emotions. I cried, "You have to release Jared. I can't let him go to prison."

With relief in her voice, my mom replied, "Okay. The three of us will be home in a few hours if all goes well. Bye, Christina."

"Bye, Mom." I hung up and wiped my tears.

"Is Jared coming home?" My father asked with moist eyes.

"If all goes well. Mom said that if I drop the assault charges against Paul Martin, he will drop the charges against Jared. Otherwise, Jared could risk being sent to prison for ten years." My stomach felt like it had taken a ride on a roller coaster. "That jerk is getting away with it again!" I yelled.

"Christina, you can't risk Jared going to jail. You did the right thing," Avery said, his voice steady.

My hands were flailing, my body shook, my voice shrilled. "I know, but I want him to pay for what he did to me and to Sherrie! He can't keep getting away with it!"

My dad interjected, "I know this must be hard for you, Christina. You were brave enough to go through with charging him, and he robbed you of being able to seek justice for his…." My father shook his head, "…his heinous crime against you. I wish there were something I could do to help you."

"I'm kinda glad I punched him when I had the chance," Avery blurted.

"When did you punch Paul?" my father asked Avery.

I shot Avery a look that when he looked at me, he realized he revealed a secret I wished was buried.

Without hesitation I answered, figuring it was about time to unveil all my secrets. "Paul was bothering me when Avery and I started dating. It was after he raped me, and he kept threatening me."

My father stood up, his eyes filled with tears as he approached me. He shook his head and ran his fingers through what was left of his thinning hair. "My Go-. He's going to wish he were dead."

My stomach dropped, and I pleaded in desperation, "No, Dad. Not you too. Two wrongs don't make a right. Enough damage has been done. This has to end now." We embraced as my father and I shed tears over a violent crime that took my youth, my innocence and turned it into lies and more violence.

My dad pulled away, held firmly onto my arms, cleared his throat and said, "I knew you were strong and brave, but I had no idea the magnitude of your strength and bravery. I'm so proud of you."

"Lately, I haven't felt strong and brave," I said with a shaky smile as I squeezed my eyes shut.

My dad cocked his head, "Why?"

"I've been having these episodes," I frowned.

"What kind of episodes?" My dad asked with a look of concern.

"The kind where I relive the nightmare in public." I felt my eyebrows raise and pull together.

My dad stated, "That sounds like PTSD. Post-"

I interrupted my dad, "I know what it is. My counselor told me. I just want it to stop." *Lord, please make it stop.*

"Is that why you brought charges against him?" My dad asked.

"Yeah. I wanted to take control. I thought that might help but now..." I scratched my forehead.

"Jared," my dad said, filling in the blank.

Although I did my best to hide my frustration, I couldn't help but give a half-hearted smile.

Avery broke his silence when he said with determination in his voice, "We'll find a way to stop the episodes."

"There you go. You'll have Avery's help too. We're all here for you. You made it this far," my dad cited the biggest pep talk of his life.

Is there a way to stop the episodes? I'm doing everything I can, and they keep coming. I'm even doing more now than ever, and I still end up reliving both rapes. Will it ever end?

The day's events were taking a toll on my body. I was feeling fatigued and couldn't shake the uneasiness I felt. *Please God, let Jared be okay. Keep him safe. Don't let him go to jail. This is all my fault.* My body shook like a bolt of lightning ran through it. *No, Christina, stop it. It's not your fault. You can't think like that.*

In the middle of talking myself down, I heard a door slam. *Jared's home.* "That's them," I said, anxious to hear what happened.

We turned to watch Jared walk into the family room. My father, already standing up, held out his arms and Jared folded into them. My mother followed in silence. My baby brother cut the quiet with tears in his eyes. "I'm so sorry, Christina. I ruined everything for you."

"As long as you're not in jail, that's all that matters. I'm glad you're home safe." Jared walked a few steps in my direction, and he drew his arms around me.

"Please forgive me," he pleaded as tears broke through his tough exterior.

"Nothing to forgive." I stood back and scanned him from head to toe to determine if he were physically okay. "Are you okay? Are you hurt?" As I said that, I saw bruises on his face, and my stomach flinched. *Paul hurt him too. Will this ever end?*

"I'm okay. You should see the other guy," he laughed nervously. "He landed in the hospital."

My eyes grew wide, "What?"

"Hey, Avery, how's it going?" Jared asked as if this were a party.

"Good, man," Avery answered.

After I rolled my eyes at their exchange, I kept my attention on Jared, "Wait a second. Back up, Jared. Tell me what happened."

Jared told us what happened like he was grocery shopping, "I went to find that slime ball to beat him up. Someone called the cops. I got arrested, and slimeball went to the hospital." *Slime ball. Yeah, that works.*

Mom cut in, "Jared and I had a little talk on the way over, but apparently, he forgot." She shot him a look, and if looks could kill...

"Okay, Mom. I promise to do better," he smirked.

My mom piped in with an admonishing tone, "Jared, this is no laughing matter, you can go to prison for discussing what happened, especially making light of it."

"What?" I kept playing the guessing game.

"He's under a gag order. The details must remain confidential or the agreement that we made to keep Jared out of prison is null and void."

"But they're family." Jared said.

"Not everyone present is family." She turned to Avery. "Please understand for legal reasons we cannot discuss today's events with anyone outside of Jared's immediate family. I hope you understand."

Avery said warmly, "Not a problem. I understand. I better get going then."

We said our good-byes and agreed to meet up for a jog the next day.

Chapter 35

The next day Avery and I went for a run together. We stopped when we reached the bridge overlooking the river. I was hunched over when Avery suggested we take a break.

"Yeah, sure. No problem," I said, out of breath.

He gasped, "Good, because I'm not sure I can run much more." After he caught his breath, he said, "I think we broke a world record."

"Running felt great. I needed that." I stood erect and started jogging in place.

Avery keeled over with his hands on his side and looked up, "Next time give me a heads up that you want to run full tilt."

"I never know until I start running. What's the matter? Too much to keep up with a girl?" I winked.

Still panting, Avery replied, "I can keep up with a regular girl, but you're like superhuman."

My eyes narrowed, "Are you serious?"

"Christina, put it this way. I think I left a kidney back there."

"What?" I squinted.

Gasping for air, he said, "I'm done running for the day. I hope you are too."

"Fine," I said, disappointed as I had some more left in my tank. "We can walk back."

"Great. I hope I can get a kidney replacement."

What is he talking about?

"Christina, where are you?" Avery asked.

"Huh?" I replied.

"You were a million miles away. Are you thinking about what happened yesterday?" Avery surmised.

Ding, ding, ding. You're the winner of guessing what is preoccupying Christina today.

I stopped jogging in place and answered, "Yeah."

Avery twisted his lips, "I know you can't talk about it with me."

"I trust you. My mom had to be tough on Jared to make sure he doesn't discuss what happened and why with anyone else or he can go to prison."

Avery's brow furrowed, "You're allowed to discuss it with me?"

I scraped my lower lip, "I have to be discerning. She knows I can keep my mouth shut. If I told someone back then, none of this would have happened."

"Hey, don't blame yourself for what happened. You know that's not your fault."

"I know that, but then I forget. It's hard not to blame myself for everything that's happened. My silence had a snowball effect on people's lives, not just my own but Jared's, Sherrie's..." My body slumped over feeling the weight of destruction on me.

"Yes, but you're not responsible for anyone's actions but your own. You need to work through it. It takes time, but you're off to a good start by running me into the ground," he ended with a slight laugh, still sounding breathless.

"Well, the good news is that I won't have to endure a trial," I said with a half-smile.

"Yeah. I know you said you wanted to take control of the episodes. I didn't say anything last night, but I can't stop thinking about that. I know it's hard, but you need to let God be in control. I know from experience. It seemed like every time I tried to take matters in my own hands, it would blow up in my face," Avery's head dropped.

He looked up at me, took a deep breath and said, "I think you bringing up charges against that jerk took courage. I'm proud of you for doing that. You have my support every step of the way, whatever that may look like."

"Thanks." A jogger ran past us, and I felt envious that they were running.

"Ave?"

"Yeah?" he answered.

"Never mind," I shrugged it off.

"What? You can tell me," Avery pressed.

"Do you mind if I go for a run? I need to let off some steam."

"How long are you going to be?" he asked.

"As long as it takes," I said, throwing out my hands.

"Take as much time as you need. I'll meet you by the picnic tables," he said, walking like he was constipated.

"Okay. Thanks," I replied, and darted in the opposite direction of Avery and ran with the wind in my face. The light breeze was all it took to refresh and rejuvenate me. I thought about how Jared spent time in jail. I thought about Sherrie being raped. I thought about Avery waiting for me while I ran. I thought about trusting God.

Lord, help me get through this. Take away the episodes. Help me live a normal life. Show me what my next step is. Help me to be strong and courageous. Show me what your will is for me.

I let my mind go adrift. My thoughts were random, scattered, jumbled, and free. As my thoughts blew by, so did I. I picked up my pace and passed people in a blur. The freedom of running created a feeling of flying in the air, soaring among the clouds, and weaving through the trees. My mind could fly all day, but my body knew its limitations.

One last sprint implored my spirit. I dug in deep, pumped my arms and dashed as if I was representing the United States in the Olympic games. An explosion of cheers greeted me at the finish line. My efforts, my determination, won me the gold. Sweat poured down my face as I consumed the salty taste of victory. To cool my body down, I lapped the loop at the edge of the archway hearing the roar of the crowd with each wave of the American flag.

The verse in Hebrews 12:1 came to mind, "Wherefore seeing we also are compassed about with so great a cloud of witnesses, let us lay aside every weight, and the sin which doth so easily beset us, and let us run with patience the race that is set before us."

I made my way over to the picnic area to find Avery talking to a young mother and her toddler son. By the time I reached the picnic table, the couple had left to explore the playground.

"Did you have a good run?" Avery asked me.

"Yeah, it was great," I said as I stretched out my calves. Little did he know I won the gold medal for the United States.

"How 'bout we go to the diner for some breakfast?" he suggested, and my stomach growled in agreement.

Food sounded incredible, especially after only consuming wet salty droplets as evidence of a successful run. "That sounds perfect."

When Avery dropped me off at my house, I noticed my mom's car wasn't there. My stomach dropped as I feared Jared was out causing trouble. My mom wasn't sitting at the kitchen table which gave me hope that she took the car. I climbed the stairs to take a much-needed shower when I heard a door shut. I passed the hallway bathroom and heard water running. *Good. Jared is home. Lord, please keep Jared from doing something stupid again.* I couldn't bear the thought of Jared in prison.

After my shower, I descended downstairs to find Jared in front of the TV playing a Mario Brothers game. "I'm surprised you're home. You're rarely home," I said.

"Shawn's busy. He got a job as a busboy. Maybe I should get a job," he said as he shifted on the floor to move his animated character.

"Mom doesn't expect you to get a job because you play sports. You're lucky because she hounded me every day until I got a job," I said, rolling my eyes, recalling how my mom was relentless.

"She did? I don't remember that." Jared said, while his hands and body made jerky movements.

"That's because you were never home," I reminded him.

He turned around to look at me, putting the game on hold, "Hey, I am sorry I messed things up for you. You know, with Martin."

"Just don't do anything stupid like that again. You had us all worried," I replied with my arms crossed.

"Yeah, including Avery. What's going on with you two?" Jared pushed his chin out.

"We're back together," I answered like I was ordering lunch.

"It looks serious between you two."

"I guess," I said without any inflection.

Jared examined me, his eyes squinty, "You don't seem too thrilled."

"Oh, no. I didn't mean it like that," I said to assure Jared that I'm happy to be in a relationship with Avery.

"How did you mean it then?"

"I just have a lot on my mind, but Avery is one of the best things in my life right now," I answered, thinking about how supportive he's been.

Jared's eyes lowered, "I guess I'm to blame for that."

"I just thought if I could seek justice I would stop having episodes," I shared.

With a tilt of his head, Jared asked, "What kind of episodes?"

"The ones where I relive the rapes. For some reason I picture Paul with the knife at my throat as well as what he did to me," I answered like I was giving a bad weather report.

Jared's eyebrows knitted together, "You don't see the guy from college?"

"Not usually," I grimaced.

Jared's mouth twitched to one side, That's weird."

"Yeah. I know," I agreed, my eyes blinking uncontrollably.

"Now I feel even worse," he said, hanging his head low.

"Oh, no. It's not your fault. Who's to say the episodes would disappear if he was convicted. It could have ended up even worse, so maybe I was spared," I offered a possible scenario.

Jared's mouth curled up a tad, "I feel better with that theory."

"As long as you feel better," I said with sarcasm.

He shot back, "Hey, look I said I was sorry, and I mean it."

I volleyed, my eyes narrow as I zeroed in on Jared, "I know, but you didn't think. You landed yourself in jail. I don't understand how you could do that."

"How I could beat him up, you mean?" he asked.

"Yeah."

"When you came home from college after, you know," he bobbed his head, "I wanted to kill that guy. Then I heard that he died, and I felt like he got what he deserved. But when I heard Mom talking on the phone trying to get you a lawyer, I figured I had my chance to get justice."

I fired back, "Yeah, but it wasn't your place to seek justice. What you did was vengeful on my behalf, and I don't condone that sort of thing."

With his chin jutted out, Jared exclaimed, "He hurt you in such a despicable way that I couldn't think straight. He was my friend. We hung out and played sports together. I couldn't sit by and let him get away with what he did."

"He got away with it for years," I stated nonplussed.

Jared clenched his fist, "My point exactly. He needed to be taken down."

I whipped my finger at Jared, "Not by you putting your future at risk. Not to mention that violence is not the answer. Two wrongs don't make a right."

"Yeah, yeah," he smirked.

With my hands on my hips, I berated Jared, "I mean it Jared. It wasn't worth you going to jail. Do you have any idea how worried we were? How worried I was? I wouldn't have been able to forgive myself if you went to prison. You could have been charged with ten years for aggravated assault!"

"I know. I know! Don't remind me." Jared yelled.

Realizing the conversation took a turn for the worse, I controlled my anger and frustration, "Mom and Dad are worried enough about me. I see it in their eyes, the sadness, the pity, the anger. I don't want them to worry about you too."

"You're right. I get it. I will be the perfect son and brother from now on," he said, rolling his eyes.

"No one expects perfection, Jared. Just think before you act. Think of the repercussions," I advised.

"Think about what Jesus would do?" he sneered.

"I know you're mocking me, but yes, that's always a good rule of thumb," I stated.

With a slight head bob, Jared said, "You know Mom asked me if I wanted to go to church."

Upon hearing his comment, my eyes became wider with curiosity, "She did? When?"

"Last week sometime."

My mouth managed to smile part way, "I didn't know that. Did she end up going?"

"Yeah, she did. Are you trying to turn Mom into a Jesus freak?" Jared asked with a scrunched-up nose.

I felt my forehead crease. "What? No, but I do want her to go to church and being a Jesus freak is better than being a jailbird."

"Well, I'm neither," he pouted.

I gave Jared a sideways glance, "And what do you have to show for it?"

"To show for what?" he curled his upper lip.

"What good in this world have you done? How do you show you care for people?" I asked.

"I beat up a guy for my sister."

"No, Jared, you beat up a guy for yourself, and where did it land you?" I asked. Instead of waiting for a response, I yelled, "In jail!"

"I didn't beat him up for me. I did it for you!" he yelled back.

Knowing this discussion was getting too heated, I consciously slowed my breathing down and said calmly, "No, Jared, you were seeking your own sort of justice on a friend that you feel betrayed you. The only justice to be done is by God." *I need to let it go too.*

"Then why did you bring charges against him?"

Jared's question disarmed me because he didn't ask me in an accusatory tone. He seemed to be asking out of curiosity. What Avery said earlier about letting God be in control suddenly resonated with me. "Maybe because I didn't put all my faith in Jesus. I wanted the episodes to go away, and I convinced myself that it was my only recourse."

"Did you just figure that out now?"

I lowered my voice by an octave and said, "Yeah, I did."

"Then I did you a favor," he said smugly.

I smirked at the arrogance of my brother's comment and took the opening to declare God's goodness, "God can make good out of even the worst of situations."

"I guess you would know," he blinked.

I presented Jared with a reassuring smile, "I do know. I'm living proof of that." *Mom is going to church now.*

"Well, don't expect me to get all churchy," he said, sticking his tongue out.

"I don't want you to get churchy. I want you to accept Christ as Savior so you can have eternal life," I said as if his life depended on it, which it did.

Jared rolled his eyes, "Like I have no clue what you're talking about."

I threw my hands over my mouth before saying, "Jared, we talked about this before many times. It's believing that Jesus died on the cross for our sins, yours, mine…"

His eyes became saucers. "That's it?"

"Pretty much." I could almost hear his thoughts. "Jared, you have to ask Jesus for forgiveness of your sins first. Then ask Him to dwell in your heart, and you can have eternal life."

"I am sorry for what I did." Then he added, "And not because I got caught. What I did was wrong. I get that now." His head sagged from the weight of his transgressions.

"Don't tell me. Tell God," I encouraged.

"Can you help me?" Jared asked sheepishly.

"Sure. Repeat after me." I bowed my head and waited for Jared to do the same, "God the Father, I'm sorry for all the sins I've committed, especially beating up Paul."

"God, I'm sorry for beating up Martin and all the other wrong stuff I did."

I swallowed a smile when I heard his paraphrase.

I continued, "Heavenly Father, thank you for sending your Son to die on the cross for my sins."

Jared reworded my statement, "God, thanks for sending Jesus to die on the cross for me."

"Lord, I ask that you live in my heart, and I will look to You to do what's right." I waited to hear Jared's remix.

"Lord, please live in my heart, so I can know what to do," he said with conviction.

"Amen," I said with finality.

"Amen." He looked up and asked, "That's it?"

I gave him a distinct nod. "Yup, the hard part is living it."

"Piece of cake," Jared declared while snapping his fingers.

"Cake? Now I want cake," I said, my eyes dashing.

Jared grinned, "I asked Mom to buy Tastykakes."

"Is that where she is? Food shopping?"

"Wait. I think that's Mom now," he said. Jared stood up. "I'm going to help her."

Talk about a quick transformation.

Jared asked, "Hey, Mom, did you buy the Tastykakes?"

"You'll find out once you put the food away," my mom replied, her lips pressed together.

"I'm on it." Jared turned on his heel to bring in the groceries.

With a confused look, my mom said to Jared, "Who are you, and what did you do with my son?"

"I'm a child of God," Jared responded with a grin.

"What?" my mother asked in disbelief.

"Ask Christina. She'll tell you." He rushed out the door to bring in the groceries.

My mom waited for me to explain. "Your son is now a son of God." She gave me a blank stare. "Really Mom, Jared's a believer now."

"Well, I'll be darned. Wonders never cease," my mom said as she shook her head and smiled.

Chapter 36

Sunday morning, I followed the directions to the church where I was giving a talk. There were so many back roads, it took me about an hour to get there. I thought about asking Avery to come with me but decided against it. My need to be independent overrode my desire for support.

Before each talk, I took a minute to survey the room to see who was in the audience. To my surprise, I saw Abby sitting at one of the tables. *That's right, I told her at Avery's party about my talk today. Should I say something to her?* Looking at my watch, I realized there wasn't enough time to talk to her.

After the Pastor's wife introduced me, I approached the podium. A quick scan of the room grounded me before I began, "Hi, I'm Christina De Rosa and I'm a survivor. I survived, not one but two rapes."

I waited a second to let my statement take effect. "No one knew about my first rape until fairly recently, even though it occurred six years ago before my freshman year in high school."

I took a deep breath to give me the resolve to continue without faltering. "You see, I didn't tell anyone, because the boy who raped me threatened to kill my boyfriend and me. Naturally, I believed he was capable of murder since he was capable of rape. I regret not telling anyone. He raped someone I know after he raped me. I blamed myself for that. I still have to reconcile the guilt each time I think about it. In my mind I know it's not my fault, but Satan has a way of weaving lies that I must frequently work through to live in the truth to have peace. It's like I'm fighting myself.

"I was able to overcome much of the emotional distress of my first rape by the grace of God and doing all kinds of things to help me heal." I settled on each technique for a moment to allow the attendees to take it in before moving on to the next one, "Like meditation, listening to classical music, running, reading, and memorizing scripture."

I rubbed my lips together to give me the momentum to go on. "My friends helped me tremendously without them even knowing I was raped. They practically forced me to be social, and that made a world of difference. I wasn't isolated and living the torment over and over in seclusion the entire time."

Taking the time to make eye contact with a few members of my audience gave me a sense of how I was doing in my talk. Everyone appeared to be listening as all eyes were on me. *Thank God no one is yawning.*

"Fast forward to my sophomore year in college this past fall. I was dragged to the woods and bound and gagged by an upperclassman, my neighbor. After he raped me, he held a knife to me and was ready to kill me when his roommates found us. I wouldn't be here today if his roommate didn't follow his intuition that something was wrong and held a search party with his two other roommates to track me down." The memory of Jake, Tony, and Bob rescuing me caused me to squeeze my eyes shut to hold back the grateful tears.

"When that rape went public, I still didn't tell anyone about the first time I was raped before I started high school. After the second time I was raped, I started to have episodes in public where I was reliving the rapes. This is different from experiencing the nightmares and the sweats I initially experienced. I still have both types of these episodes. They are part of the post-traumatic stress that I experience." I paused and then added with a smirk, "Lucky me."

"I tried to take matters in my own hands, in hopes that the episodes would go away, but something happened beyond my control that I am not at liberty to discuss, and I'm back to square one in dealing with my PTSD," I frowned.

My face painted a huge smile as I thought about what I was going to say next, "However, that's okay because the greatest thing that I could have ever asked for happened. My brother Jared became saved," I said through joyful tears.

My voice was aquiver when I said, "God took the most horrific, awful experience and used it so my younger brother can now live life eternally. That's how God works. That's how powerful God is," I declared.

"If I had to suffer two rapes, and a near-death experience for my brother to be saved, then I have to say that it was worth it. I did not suffer in vain. My Heavenly Father was by my side every step of the way. He sent his Son to die an agonizing death on the cross for my sins, *my sins*!" My voice cracked when I emphasized saying my sins the second time.

When I visualized Jesus on the cross and the thought of how undeserving I am to have eternal life, I said, "I don't deserve His grace or mercy. He also put the girl in my path who was raped by the same boy as me, and she too is now saved."

Thinking about how God worked all these miracles, I declared, "God is good."

"God has a purpose and a plan for every one of us. It's up to us to be in the Word, to grow closer to Him, to find out what that plan is and then live it out no matter how painful or scary it is." I licked my lips before continuing, "I promise you that God will neither leave you nor forsake you. There may be moments that you feel like God abandoned you, but He won't."

I dug deep and spoke louder with inflection, "Reach out to our Lord Almighty and ask him for strength, courage, and wisdom to accomplish His will. Get on your hands and knees as an act of submission, especially if you're at your wits end. Whatever you do, do not close yourself off from everyone. God created us to be social beings, to lift one another up.

"Satan will attack you when you are alone and isolated. I know this firsthand, but I was fortunate enough to have a built-in support group established before I even knew I needed one. I'm telling you that was all God, and I'm incredibly thankful for His provisions."

As I looked around the room seeing all the faces of people I could potentially help, I smiled. "Coming here to speak keeps me accountable. I have to figure out what to say, how it relates to scripture, and get in the right mindset. That takes time with the Lord that I normally wouldn't carve out otherwise. I need to be intentional in my message yet allow the Holy Spirit to speak through me. Fortunately, I don't see my talks as a burden but a blessing. If I can make an impact on just one person, then it's worth it. That impact may be on me too, but I need to be obedient, nonetheless." *Who else have I reached that I don't know about? I have to be reaching someone or God wouldn't keep giving me the opportunity to speak.*

"To be clear, it's not through me that anyone is saved or finds their purpose, it's all through Jesus. Jesus is the way, the truth, and the life. I'm simply the messenger. You can be that messenger too. Perhaps you already are. I'm sure you have been rewarded for your obedience."

I lingered on certain random individuals before continuing. "Take a moment to acknowledge how God has blessed you. Is it through wonderful children, a close-knit family, a loving husband, a nurturing mother, a trusting best friend, a lucrative job, a thriving ministry, your good health, your beautiful home, your amazing talents, the gift of time…? God is good…"

The Holy Spirit took over and spoke for me. I quoted scripture and don't recall what I said exactly. A jolt of electricity coursed through my body, and I knew that God was using me to reach someone. Mid-sentence, Abby darted out of the Sunday school classroom. My time allotted was nearing the end, so I wrapped up with a prayer.

"Heavenly Father, thank You for sending Your only Son to die on the cross so we may have eternal life. Thank You for the many blessings You send us each and every day. We ask that the Holy Spirit guide and direct our paths to do Your will. Allow us to feel Your Son's presence in our lives every second of every day. Give us the strength, courage, and conviction to make a difference in this world. Help us to help others in the capacity that makes us unique and special. Let us always remember that we are Your children, part of Your glorious kingdom, and that we are loved. In Jesus' name and in accordance with Your will, we pray. Amen."

Abby. Why did you run out of here? What's going on?

While I was talking with some women afterward, I saw Abby walk in the Sunday school room. Many women were milling about chatting with other church members. Abby approached me when she saw an opportunity to talk to me one on one. "Great speech," she said with a tone that indicated she had more to say.

"Thank you. Why don't we grab something to eat nearby? I noticed a restaurant on the way over called Our House. What do you say?" I asked.

"Sure. That would be great," she said without much enthusiasm.

Abby and I were seated after a few minutes of waiting in the breezeway. At least we didn't have to wait outside because I broke a sweat going to and from my Honda.

"It was nice to see a familiar face at my talk today," I began. "Even better that I get to eat with someone before heading home."

"You're probably wondering why I ran out."

"The thought crossed my mind," I said in a breezy manner.

Abby winced, "This is hard for me to say…"

"Take your time," I said softly.

Abby's mouth twitched upward, "I wish I was as brave as you."

"You are. You just don't know it yet," I said smiling with my eyes.

Her eyes became glassy and her lip quivered, "I… uh…" She swallowed hard and continued, "My stepfather, he uh… he's been—"

Chills covered the span of my body, and it wasn't from the air-conditioning. For clarification, I asked, "Did he rape you, Abby?" I was hoping Abby had another reason for showing up to my talk, but my intuition proved correct when I watched her nod. I reached out to her by placing my hands on hers and said, "I'm so sorry." I didn't want to say too much or bombard her with questions. I removed my hands from hers and waited for Abby to speak.

She was playing with her ring on her left index finger when she looked up and said, "He's been doing it since middle school. Since I was in seventh grade. I haven't told anyone but you."

I had to fight the urge to shed a tear for my friend's suffering in silence, a state of being I knew too well. I had so many questions, but my intuition told me to let Abby tell her story at her own pace.

Abby continued to twist her ring, and she couldn't keep a steady gaze in my direction. "He stopped last year right before I went to college. I almost didn't come home because I was afraid he would continue. I feel stupid for saying anything now, since he stopped..." Abby choked on her words as the tears welled up in both our eyes.

All this time Abby had been raped repeatedly by her stepfather and no one was the wiser. She looked up and her gaze fell back down again. She was focused on her ring when she said, "I gained weight because I ate my feelings of shame and fear."

Abby swallowed her tears. "I rationalized that if I were fat, he wouldn't be interested in me anymore and would leave me alone." She shook her head like it was a physically painful task. "Unfortunately, I was wrong, but I had developed bad eating habits and couldn't stop eating my feelings." *So that explains her sudden weight gain before high school.*

With tears streaming down her face, Abby sniffled, "I experienced a double whammy. I was fat and a victim of—" Abby couldn't even say the word, and it took her all these years to tell someone. I've been there on both accounts. All because of shame and fear. *My God is stronger than that.*

Without thinking, I blurted, "You know what you have to do, right?" I regretted the words as soon as I said them.

"I can't. I just can't," she bawled, covering her face. Abby took a moment to compose herself.

"That's why I ran out. I can't tell anyone else. I'm not brave like you, Christina." Abby had a look of defeat written on her face.

"Abby, what are you afraid of?" I asked.

"He said he'd kill my mom and me if I said anything."
Sounds about right.

"Abby, he can't get away with this. He could be raping other people," I stated.

"I know, but I'm too afraid to say anything. What if...?" She paused. Abby's eyes bulged and the brown color intensified into pools of black. Her face contorted as if she stumbled onto a dead body.

"What if what?" I asked in response to her terrified look.

"What if he comes after us?" She froze deadpan, staring into space.

"We need to come up with a plan. I have an idea. Maybe we can call someone to see if she can help us."

Abby adjusted her position in her seat and asked me from a different angle, "Like who?"

"I know an assistant district attorney, so it would be confidential," I said with confidence.

With a meekness in her voice, she said, "Okay."

I dug into my wallet and pulled out Allison's business card. "Here," I said and handed it to her. "Keep this. Call her tomorrow first thing to make an appointment with her in person."

"I guess it couldn't hurt to see what she says."

Chapter 37

The following day Avery picked me up for our morning run and post workout brunch. After we slid into our booth adjacent to a window at the restaurant and ordered, Avery said, "I'm helping to plan the youth group summer retreat, and Pastor asked me to attend. My compensation will be room and board."

"Wow! That's great, Avery. I'm happy for you. Your internship is working out for you." I said, delighted to hear good news.

"I'm excited to go. Wish you could come with us," his eyes crinkled at the sides.

My hands covered Avery's and squeezed them, "You should be excited. This is exactly what you signed up for, but I don't think it's a good idea for me to go. You need to focus on the kids. I don't want to be a distraction."

"Yeah, I guess you're right. How did your talk go yesterday?" he asked.

We didn't see each other after my talk yesterday, and I didn't want to bring it up. "It went well. At one point the Holy Spirit took over. I don't even remember what I said," I answered and rested with a twisted mouth.

Avery's eyes became wide and full of light, "I wish I could hear your talks. Let me know when you speak to a mixed crowd."

The waitress came by to drop off our silverware that she forgot to give us when we first sat down. Avery took the napkin off, and the sunlight hit the knife causing a reflection. "Ahhh!" I screamed in a panic and bumped the table causing even more of a stir.

The waitress came running over. "Oh, my goodness! Are you okay? What happened?"

At the same time, Avery was saying, "It's all right, Christina. You're here with me now."

I looked at Avery, then turned to the waitress with my hand on my heart. I covered my face with embarrassment, while I heard Avery say, "Everything's fine. Thank you."

Everything's fine? I screamed in the middle of a restaurant for no apparent reason, and that's his response? I'm not fine.

"Miss, are you sure you're okay?" The waitress asked with concern in her voice as her eyes darted back and forth from me to Avery and back again.

I did the best I could to reassure her, "Yes, I'm fine. Thank you." *Everything is fine. I'm fine.*

I watched the waitress scurry away. "Fine is such a knee jerk response," I concluded, rolling my eyes.

"What?" Avery asked, not understanding what I was talking about.

"We both said fine when the waitress asked if we were okay," I recapped as if he should be able to figure it out.

"So?" Avery said, still not comprehending.

I shut my eyes for a moment, rubbed my forehead, and said, "Everything isn't fine, Avery. I jumped out of my skin from seeing the light reflect off a knife. That's not normal. That's not fine." I released a heavy sigh.

"What I meant was that we were in no immediate danger," Avery explained.

I shook my head out of frustration, "I get that, Ave, but I thought I was in danger at that moment." I exhaled loud enough to make a statement while my lips were pursed.

Avery's eyes were wide with empathy, "I know you did, and I'm sorry, but you're okay now."

"Am I?" I asked, biting on my thumb.

"Yes, you're safe with me at this moment in this restaurant," he said with empathy in his eyes.

"But am I really fine? People who are fine don't go screaming in restaurants," I whispered in disgust with myself.

With a slight tilt of his head and concern in his voice, Avery suggested, "Maybe you should start seeing your therapist again?"

"Maybe I should." I said with a quiver, after feeling myself unravel right there in a public restaurant.

When I got home from breakfast, I made an appointment to see my therapist. She was able to get me in that afternoon since I told her I was having more PTSD episodes.

My therapist's hair was slicked back in a polished ponytail, pulled together by a dark golden-brown scrunchie that blended in with the color of her hair. She gave me a warm greeting. "Hello, Christina."

"Hello, Dr. Frazer." I almost resented having to see her.

She motioned to the brown leather loveseat. "Please have a seat." I made myself comfortable by resting my arm on the arm of the two-seater.

My therapist sat back in her matching brown leather chair and stuck her chin out, "Can you tell me about the most recent episodes or nightmares you've experienced?"

After I told her what happened at the restaurant and then at Avery's party, she said, "What's going on in your life right now? I need to know all the details. No detail is too small."

I proceeded to tell her about Jared going to jail after beating up Paul, and Avery's attempt to make amends with his friends from high school, but I purposely didn't mention Joey's involvement. She would have had a field day with that alone. *Ex-boyfriend, former best friend of current boyfriend, professes his love for me. I'll leave that for another day.* I mentioned how Abby confided in me about being raped by her stepfather. That reminded me about Sherrie, so I told her how Sherrie blames me for her rape.

Dr. Frazer jotted down some notes as I provided her with the highlights of the past few weeks. She sat back, crossed her legs and asked through probing eyes, "How does all this make you feel? How do you feel right now?"

"I feel lots of emotions. I feel like I want to get on with my life without having episodes, especially the public ones."

"Why the public ones?" She asked as if that was the key to my setback.

"Because it's embarrassing to scream in front of people."

"What if you only had private episodes? Would you be here?" She delved deeper.

"I don't know. Maybe not. I used to get nightmares all the time. Now I relive the rapes when I'm awake. I'm afraid that I will scream in public again, and something bad will happen."

"Like what?" she asked without any movement or reflection in her voice.

"I don't know," I shook my head as all kinds of crazy thoughts entered my mind but were too absurd to say aloud. The questions were making me more anxious.

Dr. Frazer unfolded her legs and leaned forward, "Christina, you do realize that you've been through a lot this past year. The past few weeks are fallouts of your rapes, except maybe your boyfriend's issues. Your life circles around rape. Your friend just confided in you that she was raped. A girl you started a closer friendship with is based on the fact that you were both raped by the same person. Your brother sought revenge on the guy who raped you. You brought charges against your rapist and can't go through with the prosecution due to your brother's assault. You're dealing with a lot of stuff here and most of it corresponds to rape. You *are* reliving the trauma. Then you have your boyfriend's pornography addiction. That's enough to make anyone scream."

"Are you suggesting that this isn't PTSD?"

Dr. Frazer's head moved slightly from side to side. "No, not at all. I only meant that you're dealing with multiple major issues all at once, and you haven't dealt with the trauma of your rapes. You never truly dealt with the first one, and it's presenting itself all over again, because the most recent one is triggering the horrid memories of the first one. We need to get you involved in Exposure Therapy, so you can overcome the rapes here in a safe environment."

I bit my lip, "I like the part about overcoming, but is the exposure part what I think it is?"

Dr. Frazer leaned back and crossed her legs. Her voice was steady when she began explaining the treatment, "We will have you recreate the rapes in your mind, but you will ultimately conquer them and put them behind you. The process will take about ten to twelve sessions and I believe that you are a great candidate for Exposure Therapy."

She uncrossed her legs and with a glimmer of hope in her eyes, she stated, "It's extremely effective with victims of sexual assaults, and you are very strong. There's no question that you are a powerful young woman, and you will be able to be even a stronger force once you tackle these fears. The first few sessions are usually distressing to say the least, but the results are well worth it in the end."

Since the therapy sounded promising, I agreed to do it.

Abby called me later to let me know that the police met with her instead of Allison. They discussed Abby's situation at length and came up with a plan of action. Abby would inform her mom what has been going on under her own roof as orchestrated by her husband. The next step would depend on her reaction. Abby said she would move out if her stepfather remained in the house, putting Abby's mom in danger, but that would be her choice. We prayed that Abby's mom would kick him to the curb after she got everything in order, including her finances. Abby agreed to keep me posted on any updates. She knew I was concerned about the safety and security for her and her mother.

Morgan swung by to pick me up for a girl's night out. She was making up for lost time from when she was taking that summer course. We were meeting Katie and Amy at an American bistro near the mall.

As we pulled into a parking spot, Morgan pointed and said, "Oh, look, there they are." I followed her finger to see Katie and Amy approaching the restaurant on foot.

Once we sat down at our table, Amy said, "How's everyone's summer going?"

Katie responded as if she were brushing it off, "You know, working, not much else but of course dinner with you guys."

Morgan replied, "I'm finally finished with my class. It was short but intense." She took a breath and said, "This means I get to see Derek. I plan on having a get together, so don't make any plans." She turned to me and said, "Christina, you have to bring Avery! By the way, how is Avery doing?"

I answered, "Avery's fine. He's planning a youth group retreat down the shore, and he gets to go for a few days, so it depends on when you're having your party as to if he can attend. Otherwise, I'm sure he wouldn't miss it."

"When is the retreat?" Morgan asked.

I squinted, "Come to think of it, I don't know, but I can find out for you."

"Good. That way I can work around it," Morgan replied.

Amy directed her attention toward me, "Christina, Abby told me she went to hear you speak at a church the other day. She said you were great and suggested we all go sometime to hear one of your talks."

With a half-smile, I replied, "Yeah, I was kind of surprised to see her there. We had brunch together afterwards." *Did Abby say anything else?*

"Unfortunately, she couldn't make it tonight. She's doing something with her mom," Amy reported.

It doesn't seem like Amy knows what's going on. I noticed George Harrison's voice singing "Got My Mind Set on You" in the background.

"My mom surprised me one time at one of my talks. She started to go to church too." I got even more excited when I told Katie and Amy that Jared was saved. I called Morgan right away to give her the great news minus the part where Jared was in jail.

"That's great, Christina!" Katie said.

Amy followed suit, "Yeah, congrats to Jared!"

I shared, "It would be wild if my entire family went to church together."

"I can't imagine my family not going to church together," Katie said.

"Getting my brother to go was always a feat. My parents eventually gave up on him," Amy stated.

I added, rolling my eyes, "I'm the one wanting my family to go together. It's a strange role reversal."

"At least something positive came from…" Amy didn't know how to finish her sentence, but we all knew what she meant.

I jumped in to save Amy, "Yes, God is good, and it's good to recognize those blessings."

Morgan turned to me and said, "God is working in your life, Christina. He's definitely using you to further His kingdom."

I blurted, "Yeah, but it hasn't been easy. I keep getting PTSD episodes, so I decided to start seeing my therapist again. I start a treatment called Exposure Therapy where I face my fears head on. It's supposed to be very effective for survivors like me."

"Sounds scary," Amy said.

"It is. I have to relive the most traumatic moments of my life to overcome my fears, so I don't flip out in public. Lucky me." I said trying to sound flippant to lighten the severity of the therapy.

Katie said in a comforting tone, "We'll be here if you need us."

"I might take you up on that." Just thinking about it scared me, but I wanted the outbursts to stop. I thought about Abby. "It's not easy being a rape victim… uh survivor. I know it's a difficult conversation, but sometimes it has to be spoken about. Remember that in case you come across someone who was raped. We survivors need all the help we can get. Sometimes just being there is all that's required. We need to know that people are in our corner since we've been violated in the most unimaginable way. I know it's not comfortable or easy to talk about, but there are times when support is paramount to our healing."

Amy said with an impressed inflection in her voice, "Wow, you sound like a counselor, Christina."

"Have you thought about counseling as a career?" asked Katie.

"Uh, no, not really. I haven't figured out yet what I want to do."

"I think you'd be good at it," Morgan stated.

"Thanks. I know what survivors go through. Even though you didn't know what I was going through in high school, each of you helped me by being a friend."

I made eye contact with Amy, Katie, and Morgan separately, and began to tear up as I continued with my soliloquy. "You didn't let me isolate myself. I know I would have been worse off if I was left alone to my own devices, so thanks for being there for me." I was grateful for each one of them, and they had to understand how much of an impact their friendship made in my life. I was hoping they would be there for Abby if the need arose.

The four of us wiped our tears away.

Katie reached out her hand and placed it on mine, "Whatever you need. We're here for you."

Tears pricked behind my eyes and I nodded, "Thanks. That means a lot." *Please be there for Abby.*

The tears continued to fall down our cheeks, and we couldn't wipe them away fast enough to hide the embarrassment from our initial blubbering. The soppy wet stuff was a much-needed release of the sad and happy emotions I had been keeping bottled up.

Chapter 38

The next day I showed up to my appointment for Exposure Therapy. I walked into my therapist's office ready to take on my demons of fear. Seated on a big brown chair with notebook and recorder in hand, Dr. Frazer greeted me, "Good morning, Christina. Shall we get started?" She pointed to the chaise lounge across from her.

My head bobbed up and down as I followed her finger to the fancy tufted brown leather couch and lay down. I told Dr. Frazer what triggered my episodes, like hearing someone say the word kill, a shiny knife, or a train of thought that led me to the Martin's house that summer day. *How am I supposed to fight against a random memory that triggers episodes?*

Dr. Frazer set the stage for the new therapy. She explained that we would start out small and work our way up. I listened carefully as Dr. Frazer gave me instructions. Again, I followed her lead, only this time they were all verbal. With my eyes closed, I concentrated on her soothing voice which transported me to a different place and time. This place was dark, eerie, and all too familiar.

I lay pinned down on the cold hard ground with my mouth sealed shut from the ink-tasting bandana. As I tried to break free from my fiercely strong oppressor, I looked directly into his feral eyes and saw a thirteen-year-old Paul Martin holding a shiny knife threatening to slice open my throat.

Gripped by fear with a sense of being immobilized, I screamed at the top of my lungs, shaken to the core. My reaction to the horror woke me out of the therapy-induced nightmare and in the comforting arms of my therapist. "I can't do this anymore. It's too hard," I sobbed uncontrollably.

"It's okay. You're safe, Christina. You're safe. No one can hurt you," she repeated over and over. Hanging on her every word for reassurance, I squeezed Dr. Frazer tighter, willing my demons to stay away. Still trembling with fear with a heart rate that rivaled that of an Indie racecar, Dr. Frazer's words of instruction slowed down my speedometer. Later that evening, those same words lulled me to sleep after praying I wouldn't have any more nightmares or episodes.

"Fear thou not; for I am with thee: be not dismayed; for I am thy God: I will strengthen thee; yea, I will help thee; yea, I will uphold thee with the right hand of my righteousness" (Isaiah 41:10).

Chapter 39

The light of daybreak awoke my spirit. I hopped out of bed and decided to go for a run before it got too hot. In a matter of minutes, I was climbing the hill to the woods. I loved the peacefulness of the early morning because unlike the evening, the light brought a sense of safety and hope. I toyed with the idea of stopping my therapy. The thought of repeating the nightmares and episodes caused my eyes to well up and my stomach to ache. The dread of the counseling sessions was like carrying a lead weight as I trudged up the hill.

However, the thought of never experiencing the episodes again drew a smile on my face and made me feel lighter and more determined than ever. *I can't give up now. I have nothing to lose. If I stick it out, the episodes may not return. I have to give this new therapy a try. Exposure Therapy. I feel exposed when I have my episodes. Not just exposed. Vulnerable too. I hate feeling so vulnerable. I never know when or where the episodes will strike. I feel like I'm walking on glass. Even though it's all in my mind, it's almost like experiencing physical pain. It's all in my mind yet I can't shake the feeling that I'm going to be stabbed to death.*

A picture of a knife dripping with blood after cutting my throat flashed before me. I shuddered. *NO!* The need to shake my arms, my head, my torso all at once helped me to rid the intrusive mind attacks.

I can't keep replaying a scene that never happened. I'm safe now. The terror, although real and debilitating, has got to stop. I want to be able to live my life and not feel like a freak. Lord, help me to get rid of the episodes, the nightmares once and for all. Help me to focus on You, on healing as You are the almighty healer. Help me to help others with their struggles. How can I help people if my life is such a mess? People have witnessed my episodes up close. My friends have seen full blown episodes, strangers have had front row seats to them.

Please God, make them disappear. No more nightmares. God, give me the strength to continue therapy, to end the episodes. Please Lord, I can't do this on my own.

The sound of my running shoes striking the payment created a rhythmical pattern… Pit-a-pat, Pit-a-pat.

A vision of God scooping me up and carrying me on the beach as the waves crashed to the shore replaced the bloody images. An overwhelming feeling of being loved, protected, and comforted replaced the feelings of violation, dread, and terror. I saw the rays of sunshine streaming through the clouds. I felt the cool breeze on my face, tasted sea salt on my tongue, heard the squawking of seagulls flying above me, and I inhaled the clean fresh air while my every movement was propelled by my beloved Father as He held me in His loving arms.

After I finished stretching from my run, I took a shower. I stepped out of the bathtub and a few strokes of my hand wiped the steam off the mirror. The message God sent me was as clear as looking at my reflection in the mirror. I knew what I had to do and went to my early morning therapy appointment.

Feeling confident about the therapy session I just had, I smiled on my way to Avery's. His mom greeted me warmly per usual. "Hello, Christina. How are you today?"

"Great, thanks. How are you?"

"Fine. Thank you. Avery's in the basement."

The door opened and Avery walked into the kitchen.

Mrs. Evans laughed and said, "I spoke too soon. Well, I'm off to finish the laundry. You two have a nice day."

"You too Mrs. Evans," I said with a tiny wave.

Avery stopped his mother before she walked out, "Mom, I need to get some gear for the retreat."

"All right. I'll see you for dinner then?" Mrs. Evans asked.

"Yeah. I should be home for dinner. I'm working from twelve-thirty to four-thirty today," he said.

It was my turn to decipher Avery's plan, "Let me guess. We're going to the mall before you have to work."

"If that's okay with you," he said with a hopeful smile.

"I'm fine with that. Why are you in such a hurry to get what you need today? The retreat isn't for a few weeks."

Avery shrugged, "I don't know, but I have this compulsion to go today before I have to go to work."

"We better get going then. We don't have much time."

It wasn't difficult finding a parking space at the mall. Since the temperature was already 87 degrees, I was glad we parked close to the main entrance. Avery wanted to buy a new pair of sporty sunglasses, suntan lotion, and flip-flops. The drugstore as an obvious choice became our first stop. We cruised down the aisle with the skin care and found an entire selection of sunblock. He grabbed a brown bottle of Coppertone with an SPF of 15. We headed to the back where we found a carousel of sunglasses. When I noticed his sunglasses tucked in the front of his shirt, I asked, "Why are you buying sunglasses? You already have a pair."

He pointed to his sunglasses and said, "I don't want to wear these on the beach. I want a cheap pair that I don't care if they break."

I took that to mean his aviator sunglasses were pricey.

Avery tried on several different frames and turned to me to model them. I grimaced when he put on ugly sunglasses. One pair was neon green, and I gave him two thumbs down. "How about these?" He asked after putting on a tight-fitting black pair that wrapped around his head.

I scrunched up my nose. "Are they comfortable?"

"Yeah, they are. What do you think? Do they look okay?" He asked.

They started growing on me the longer I stared at him. "Yeah, they look pretty good."

He placed them back in their slots and picked up another pair. "How about these?"

"Wow! I think we have a winner." The tortoise color enhanced his blonde hair, and he looked good, maybe too good.

"Cool. Now on to finding some flip-flops," he said.

"I think we passed some in a bin at the front of the store."

Sure enough, there was a huge selection of flip-flops. I don't think I'll be doing much walking, so any of these will do. I need a size eleven."

We rummaged through the bin, and I pulled out a size eleven. "What about these?" They were bright green. *What's with all the green?*

Avery struggled a bit to try them on with the price-tagged string tied at each thong that held both the right and left flip-flops together. They fit perfectly once he was able to slip them on. "I'd rather wear a different color," he frowned.

We went back to bin diving and kept digging through the flimsy footwear. "I found a black pair, size eleven," I said like I won the lottery.

After sliding them on as best as he could, he declared with a grin, "I'll take 'em."

On our way out, I spotted Sherrie with two girls that looked to be her age. She turned away from me, but I was certain she saw me.

I whispered to Avery, "That was Sherrie, the girl who uh…" I paused as I wasn't sure how to describe her. "You know," I said, willing Avery to read my mind.

Avery's eyes bulged as he cracked my code, "Oh, right." He hesitated and with a sympathetic tone said, "I'm so sorry… for both of you." I shrugged at the comment not knowing how to respond.

"You know I should thank her." I shot Avery a confused look. He presented his case, "Think about it… If it wasn't for her, we probably wouldn't be together."

What?

Avery elaborated, "You cried on my shoulder that day on your patio, because you were upset about Sherrie, the day we got back together."

"Right," I said at the realization that Sherrie was, in fact, a catalyst that brought us together in a way. If I weren't so upset about her being raped by Paul, I wouldn't have been so vulnerable, which led me to reveal my deepest, darkest secret. "I wish she wasn't still mad at me."

With compassion in his eyes, Avery said, "Give her time. She has to work it out herself. Just pray that she continues to grow in her faith."

"I do," I informed him with an edge of frustration in my voice.

Avery responded with a hard nod, "Good. That's all you can do for now."

"I guess," I said, resigned that there was nothing left for me to do where Sherrie was concerned. Then it dawned on me that Sherrie was with her friends, and I got excited, "Avery, she was with her friends!"

"Yeah, so?" Avery asked with a quizzical look on his face.

"That's huge! She wasn't socializing much before, but she did start going to church with a friend."

"She's making progress then," he said, understanding the strides Sherrie made.

"Exactly my point. This just made my day," I beamed.

With a light-hearted tone, Avery asked, "Shopping with me wasn't a highlight?"

"Oh, yeah, my day wouldn't be complete without dumpster diving for flip-flops." We both chuckled at our silly banter.

I drove home after Avery dropped me off at his house after shopping at the mall since he had to go to work. When I walked into the kitchen, my mom said, "Abby called."

I ran upstairs and dialed Abby's phone number.

"Hello," the person on the other end answered.

"Is Abby there?" I asked.

"This is Abby."

"Abby, it's Christina. My mom said you called."

"Christina, you aren't going to believe what happened." My stomach sank for a second until Abby continued, "The police arrested my stepfather. My mom didn't want to take any chances, so they were there last night when he came home from work."

"Oh my gosh, Abby! Are you okay?" I asked.

"Yeah, I'm fine. My mom is too. We both filed restraining orders to keep him away from us."

"What do you mean?" I questioned.

Abby went on to explain, "In case he gets released, he can't come within 300 feet of us, or he can be fined and go to jail. My mom packed up all his belongings. He'll have to make arrangements to get his stuff out of the house. I was told someone will be there to supervise to make sure he doesn't cause any destruction or steal anything that doesn't belong to him."

"But he's in jail now?"

"Yes, he's in jail. He has to go before a judge today to see if he can get out on bail," she said.

"Are you going?"

"No, I don't want to see him ever again."

I don't blame you.

"What's the likelihood he'll get out on bail?" I asked.

I could hear the disgust in her voice, "Very likely because he has no prior convictions. I don't plan on being home when he picks up his stuff. I can't stand the sight of him."

I questioned her, "Won't you have to testify if it goes to trial?"

"Yes, but I'm hoping he will plead guilty."

"Do you think he will?" I asked.

"No, unfortunately, I think he'll fight it, but I have to hope."

"Oh, Abby, I'm so sorry you have to go through all this." *Did she detect the guilt in my voice?*

She responded, "I felt like this was the best solution. I had to do something. I can't let him get away scot-free."

"You're so courageous," I said, afraid for her.

"Thanks, but I am scared," she admitted.

"That's what makes you so brave."

"I plan on telling Katie, Morgan, Amy and Erin what's going on."

"I think that's a great idea. Morgan, Katie and Amy have been very supportive of me," I told her.

"Not Erin?" she asked with a note of wonder in her inflection.

"Erin and I are not that close. I haven't even seen her recently," I said, stating the facts like I was reading from a history book.

"Oh, right. She wasn't at Avery's, was she?"

"No, she wasn't," I said.

"Well, in her defense, I think she had to work," Abby stated like she was Erin's defense attorney.

"It doesn't matter to me one way or another. The get together was for Avery, not me."

"You don't like her, do you?" Abby probed.

I crinkled my nose. "Let's just say I don't know her that well," I said, trying to be diplomatic.

She laughed at my comment. "And you're not in any hurry to get to know her, are you?"

"Not especially, but that doesn't mean you can't confide in her. The more support you get the better," I encouraged.

"Would you mind being there when I tell them, even though you're not a fan of Erin's?"

"Whatever you need, Abby, I'm there for you," I assured her.

"Thanks," she said.

"Sure. No problem."

I decided to read after hanging up with Abby, so I grabbed the book *Christy* by Catherine Marshall about a woman who travels to Tennessee to teach in an impoverished area in the Appalachian Mountains during the early 1900s. The story was well-written and so far held my attention.

I was halfway through the book, when the urge to get some fresh air caused me to go for a walk. When I opened the door to go outside, the heat and humidity engulfed me, almost changing my mind to pursue the bout of exercise.

Determined, I strolled down my driveway and turned to climb the hill. Normally, I would walk towards the woods, but this time I took a different route and found myself walking toward Sherrie's house. A sadness consumed me as I looked at her house, followed by joy when I remembered her accepting Jesus as her Savior in her bedroom. *She's saved. That's all that matters.*

My eyes were fixated on her bedroom window when a car drove past me and turned into the driveway. Feeling like a peeping Tom, I quickly looked away and hoped no one saw me gazing in that direction. *Why do I feel like this? It's not like I can see anything.*

Lost in my thoughts of justifying that I'm not a voyeur, I heard a noise that became increasingly louder. "Christina! Wait!"

I turned around to find Sherrie approaching me. She panted a little as she caught her breath. "Hey, I have something to tell you."

I stopped and waited for her to continue. "The ADA called me. I'm testifying against, ah, you know..." She indicated with a head bob.

My wide eyes gave away my shock, followed by my exclamation, "Oh my gosh, I had no idea! You're okay with that?"

For being willing to take on such a brave act, she answered rather timidly at first, "Yeah, I wasn't at first. She said that you wanted to but couldn't for some reason. Initially, I told her 'no way'."

Sherrie looked up to capture her thoughts. As she progressed with her story, I could hear the determination in her voice become more and more evident, "Then I thought about it and decided to 'cause it was eating away at me. I don't want him to get away with it again. Who knows how many others there are or will be? I knew I had to do something, and I thought you should know."

"Thanks for telling me. What's going on with all that?" I asked.

Sherrie pressed her lips together, "He was let out on bail since it was his first offense. Apparently, that's normal if they can make bail. The trial is set for the beginning of September."

"You'll be in school then?" I stated.

Sherrie blinked her eyes and grimaced, "Yeah, that's okay, even though my parents are afraid it may do more harm than good, they support my decision. I can't help feeling like this is something I have to do. Once I made the decision, it felt like a weight had been lifted off of me, although different from the weight I felt when I became saved. Know what I mean?" She held her gaze at me with her big pretty russet-brown eyes.

I held her gaze and nodded. "Yeah, I know exactly what you mean. I felt the same way."

Sherrie pursed her lips, "So why can't you testify against him?"

"I'm not at liberty to say. I would if I could, and I would tell you why I can't if I could."

Her shoulders shrugged like she expected me to say that. "Yeah, she said the same thing." She swung her hand like she was swatting a fly and said, "It doesn't matter. No matter what happens I know I did what was right for me."

"I'll be away at college, but you can call me if you want to," I encouraged, not breaking eye contact.

"Oh right, you go away to school. I keep forgetting that. Is that why you can't sue him? Because of school?" she fished.

"I can't say. I would if I could. Trust me," I said, my lips pierced.

"That's okay. I understand."

You do? Because I don't. I wish we could trade places since I feel responsible. This is all my fault. All of it.

In a shaky voice, I said, "I'm really sorry."

With a tenderness in her tone, she replied, "Hey, don't worry about it. This may be what I need to move on from what happened. My therapist says I would be facing my fears and said it might empower me."

"That's why I wanted to testify against him. That and I feel responsible for what happened to you," I shared.

"Yeah, about that," she said as if she was leading up to something big. With resolve in her voice, Sherrie said, "It's not your fault. I had to work through all that, and it took some time, but I now know that you were a victim too."

"Sherrie, we're survivors." I corrected her with my head held high, refusing to live in that victim mindset.

"Right," she said with conviction. "We're survivors." There was a brief moment of silence.

"I saw you at the mall earlier today. Was that your boyfriend?" Sherrie stated, breaking the quietude.

"Yes, that was Avery."

"Wow! He's super cute." With more emphasis, she said, "Super cute. You two make a cute couple."

Something tells me she thinks Avery and I are cute. I suppose there are worse things to be called than cute.

I felt my mouth forming an upward curve and swallowed a silent laugh. "Thanks."

"Well, I better get going before I sweat to death. It's so hot out here. I just wanted to let you know about, you know," she said, tilting her eyes and head back and forth in conjunction with each other.

"Thanks for letting me know. Good luck with everything if I don't see you," I said.

"Okay. I will. Bye." She waved and dashed away.

"Bye," I returned with a wave.

Sherrie was right. It was hot, and I couldn't wait to enjoy the air-conditioning in my house. Once I got home, I picked up my book and continued reading it from where I left off before my walk.

Brrring. I answered the phone. "Hello."

"Christina, it's Abby." Abby sounded upset.

"Hey, you okay?"

"My stepfather came home after his bail hearing. Christina, he came after me, but my mom, my mom," Abby paused and then cried, "she jumped in front of me to protect me. He whacked her in the face. The police barged in and arrested him. They arrived just in time. He could have killed us!"

"How's your mom? Where is she?" I asked.

"She's okay. She's home now. The doctor said her face was only bruised. It's swollen, but nothing was broken."

"I'm so sorry, Abby. How are you doing with all this?" I said as my body shook. I did my best to hold it together while I was talking on the phone.

"I'm upset. He was so angry that he was going to kill us. It was terrifying," she cried.

"Do you want me to come over?"

"Let me check with my mom first. Hang on. I'll be right back," she said and put me on hold.

Lord, lift up Abby and her mom. Keep them safe and give Abby courage to go through with keeping her stepdad behind bars. I waited a couple minutes before Abby returned. "Christina, you still there?"

"I'm here," I responded.

"My mom said you can spend the night too if you want to."

"I'll be right over."

Chapter 40

T he next morning after spending the night at Abby's, I went home to change for a run. Jared was sitting on the couch watching TV when I walked in.

"What's up?" I asked casually.

"Where were you last night?" he asked in an accusatory tone.

"I stayed over at a friend's house."

"Avery's?" he speculated.

"Yeah, right," I said dripping with sarcasm.

"You two seem to be… close," he said after carefully choosing his words.

"Not that close," I winced.

"You mean you guys haven't?" he flinched.

I imitated his expression, "No, we haven't… Not that it's any of your business."

"Oh, come on! Is that a Christian thing? Because if it is, I'm not sure I'm down with that," he exclaimed.

"Yes, but it's not just a Christian thing," I replied.

"I'm not so sure I'm cut out to be a Christian," he said as he shifted his head in several small back and forth movements.

"Why do you say that?" I asked.

"None of my friends are Christian," Jared stated, as if it were fact and not supposition.

"How do you know that?" I asked.

"I know," he said like he was God.

"Maybe you'll be surprised," I said with a lilt in my voice.

"Doubt it," Jared frowned.

"Make new friends then," I suggested.

"Yeah, right!" he said sarcastically.

I offered a viable solution. "You don't necessarily have to dump your friends. Just meet people who are Christian."

"What am I supposed to do? Hang out at church all the time?" he said, defeated.

"Cute. No, join a youth group," I suggested.

"A what?" Jared shot me a puzzled look.

"A youth group. That's when kids your age hang out, eat, play games, learn about Jesus."

Jared's face lit up. "That doesn't sound half bad. "Where do I do this?"

"Avery's church hosted events. You could call the church office for info."

Jared turned his head and asked, "Did Avery go to the youth group?" *Unfortunately, that's how he got involved with porn.* "Uh, yeah. He did." *Maybe this isn't such a good idea although I suggested the same thing to Sherrie, and it seemed to work out.*

"Why didn't you go?" Jared inquired.

I answered, "I didn't want to push my luck with Mom and Dad. I was already spending a lot of time with Avery as it was."

Jared shrugged. "Guess that makes sense."

"Give youth group a shot. You have nothing to lose," I said, hoping I didn't regret it later.

"I'll think about it," Jared said in a noncommittal way.

When I returned home from my run, I panicked upon hearing my mom and Jared arguing. *What did Jared get into now?*

I walked into the kitchen when Jared said, "Hey, Christina, I called Avery's church like you said. They have a retreat in a few weeks, and they said I could go, but Mom won't let me."

"Why won't you let him go?" I asked my mom.

"I don't know any of these people, and it's not cheap," she answered in a huff.

"Well, he gets room and board for a few days. He will have a lot of fun and learn about Jesus. Avery will be there too to watch over him. It's a win-win," I said delighted with my assessment.

Jared chimed in, not helping the situation, "I don't need anyone watching over me. I can take care of myself."

"Said the boy who was thrown in jail for fighting," I stated, not helping his cause.

"Yeah, yeah. Those days are over. I really want to go, and Avery will be there! Mom, you gotta let me go!" Jared implored.

My mom asked, "Why is Avery going? Isn't he too old for a high school retreat?"

"He's going in a leadership capacity as part of his internship because he wants to be a pastor someday," I answered.

"Oh, I see," my mom said, and I could see the wheels turning in her head.

Jared persisted, "Mom, can I go? It beats sitting around here since all my friends are working."

"Christina, do you honestly think this is a good idea?" My mom asked.

"Yeah, Mom, I do. I heard kids have a blast, and they grow in the Lord. This is a great opportunity for Jared to meet some believers, open up his circle of friends."

Jared pleaded again, "See, Mom? It will be good for me, so can I please go?"

"Jared, I'm sorry to tell you, but it costs too much money," my mom replied.

"What if I get a job?" Jared asked.

"All right. You can go, but only if you get a job, and you'll have to work out the scheduling to go on the retreat," my mom said reluctantly.

"Thanks, Mom! You're the best! I'm going to see if I can find a job." Jared ran upstairs. *Did I see a slight smile on my mom's face?*

"I hope you're right about this," my mom shared once Jared was out of the room.

Me too. "It will be fine. He'll have a great time. You'll see," I said. *I hope I'm right. Please Lord, let Jared get a job so he can go on the retreat. I pray he has a good time and grows closer to you during the retreat.*

Chapter 41

The next day, Jared secured a job at the Pennsford Country Club at the snack bar, but his hours conflicted with the youth group meetings, so he didn't meet anyone from youth group.

The following Wednesday, Morgan decided to have her party. Avery picked me up, and I was excited for him to meet Morgan's boyfriend Derek. We entered through the front of the house this time and were greeted by an enthusiastic Morgan and a more reserved Derek at the front door.

Morgan gestured toward us, "Avery, this is my boyfriend, Derek. Derek, this is Avery, and you already know Christina."

We exchanged greetings, and the guys shook hands. Avery and I were ushered to the rec room. Avery and Derek played foosball while I chatted with my friends. I wanted to touch base with Abby, but she looked deep in conversation with Erin whom I hadn't seen in forever, not that it mattered. I was surprised to see Jackie there too.

Abby told Morgan, Katie, and Amy what happened with her stepfather the week before when Erin couldn't make it again due to work. Everyone was super supportive and compassionate toward Abby as they had a lot of practice with Avery and me.

Morgan walked up to me and remarked as she looked in the direction of the foosball table, "Looks like they're getting along."

"Yeah, I'm not surprised though," I said, looking on.

"Me neither. I'm so glad Avery could come."

I was about to respond when Val bounded down the stairs and ran over to us.

"Guess who I ran into today?" She held out her arm as we followed its direction and watched Joey walk down the stairs.

I blurted, "You have got to be kidding me!"

Morgan whispered, "Val, are you nuts?"

Val said in her defense, "What? Oh, come on. He's so nice, and we need another guy here tonight." *You mean you want another guy here tonight.*

Morgan held her arm out in front of me and said, "I'll be right back." I watched as Avery introduced Joey and Derek to each other. Morgan graciously welcomed her unexpected guest to the party. "Joey, I'm glad you could come."

I heard Derek say, "Hey, we need a fourth player. Morgan, you wanna play?"

Morgan looked at Avery and Joey when she replied, "Sure, Derek and me against you two."

"All right. Game on," Joey declared.

Val laughed, "They don't know what they're in for. Morgan is a champ at foosball."

As I watched a fierce game of foosball played by my best friend, her boyfriend, my boyfriend, and my former boyfriend, I didn't know what team to root for. *This is weird on so many levels. Why didn't Val invite Sam while she was at it? I'm sure Katie would love to see her ex-boyfriend. Then it would be like old times with us double dating.*

Before long, it was like watching an actual football game in South America with spectators cheering and shouts of "GOAL!" from the announcer reverberating throughout the stadium. I never saw Jackie have so much fun yelling "GOAL!" when someone scored. *She seems to have come out of her shell.*

While Morgan was clearly the best player, Avery and Joey had a better team dynamic. This made for a very entertaining foosball match that attracted everyone at the party, including Erin and Abby. After a while of playing, Avery excused himself to go to the bathroom.

"I'll play!" Erin said as she jumped into the spot Avery left vacant. A reluctant Joey agreed. I could tell that Joey didn't want to team up with Erin, but he played alongside her. *He is not liking this.*

Val grumbled under her breath, "I can't believe the nerve of her!"

Engrossed by the game, I didn't notice Abby approach me. "Christina—" I jumped. "Oh, sorry. I didn't mean to startle you."

"It's okay. What's up?" I asked.

"Mind if we talk?" she asked.

I answered in a willing tone, "No, not at all." We sat on the tan couch and were able to have a private conversation while the foosball match ensued with loud cheering and banging.

"I wanted to let you know that I'm in counseling now. I know how you said it was helping you, so I decided to give it a try," Abby said.

"How's it going?" I asked.

Abby's head teetered back and forth, "Good so far. My counselor said she was amazed at my ability to forgive my stepdad."

Impressed, I said with a smile, "Wow. That's great. I struggle with that myself. It's definitely something I need to work on. I know I need to forgive, but..." *What Abby went through was worse than what I went through, yet she can forgive her rapist and I can't.* "How do you do that? Forgive someone who violated you repeatedly?"

"It wasn't easy, especially after he tried to kill us, but I don't know," she shook her head. "I just let it go and forgave him. I was tired of holding on to it."

God, help me to forgive. I need to forgive.

Abby leaned in and tapped my arm. "Anyway, I wanted to thank you for inspiring me to take action. If it weren't for you, my stepdad wouldn't be behind bars where he belongs."

I gave Abby an encouraging smile, "You did the hard part by taking action against him. We survivors need to stick together."

Erin sat down next to Abby. I noticed how perfectly coiffed she was. Her makeup was immaculate. Erin turned to me and said, "So, you and Avery, huh? I can't believe you two are back together after all this time."

"Yeah, we're back together," I said in a sing-song kind of way while I listened to George Harrison sing, "Got My Mind Set on You."

Erin added, "And he's recovering from his porn addiction. Wow. That must be hard."

"He's doing well. He hasn't had any issues with it in years," I replied.

"I meant for you. It must be hard for you," Erin explained.

"At first it was hard to understand it all, but I'm okay with it now," I said.

"Well, good for you," Erin said in a condescending way.

Abby glanced at me with a puzzled face. She turned to Erin and said, "Avery acknowledged Christina's support at his party. She's been there for him since they got back together."

"Yeah, I heard about that. Too bad I couldn't make it to the party. Sounds like it was fun. Didn't you faint or something, Christina?" Erin said, thrusting out her chin.

"I had a flashback, Erin. I didn't faint," I pointedly corrected her.

Erin cocked an eyebrow, "Right. That must have been scary. What was it from?"

With a tightness in my voice, I replied, "It's rather involved and would take a while to explain."

Erin settled in, her lips pursed. "I'm not going anywhere. We're all friends here."

I pressed my lips together and through narrow eyes, I responded to Erin, "I'd rather not discuss it at the moment."

I got up to leave and turned to Abby, "Abby, I'm glad you're doing so well."

"Thanks, Christina. I owe it all to you," Abby said, smiling.

I gave Abby a dismissive wave, "I didn't do anything. You did the hard part." I turned around to see Avery, Joey, and Derek talking together, so I walked over to the foosball table and watched Cheryl and Jackie take on Amy and Katie. Morgan and Val were cheering the teams on.

Just as the song "Don't Be Cruel" by Cheap Trick started playing, Val whispered in a snippy manner, "So what did Miss Priss have to say?"

"Who, Erin?" I asked.

"Who else would I be talking about?"

"Right," I nodded.

"Well?" Val persisted.

I shrugged, "Oh, nothing." I didn't want to add fuel to the fire.

"I like it better when she has to work," Val whispered.

"Well, she's friends with Morgan, Amy, Katie, and Abby," I stated.

Val's brows furrowed, "And not you?"

"I never considered her a close friend, but that doesn't mean she's not a good friend to others," I stated with my mouth pinched.

"You're so diplomatic, Christina."

I decided to take it as a compliment and said, "I'm not without my faults, Val, but thanks."

"Do you think I have a shot at Joey or not?" I shot Val a look. "What? It's not like you're going out with him," her gaze focused on me.

"True. However, if Joey wants to go out with someone, he's sure to let them know. Trust me on this one," I nodded to the point that my neck hurt.

She snapped her fingers out of disappointment and exclaimed, "Darn!"

"Someday, Val, you'll find someone who appreciates you for you. Never settle for anything less," I said to encourage her and meant every word.

"That's easy for you to say. You're going out with a Rob Lowe lookalike," Val said, her lips twisted.

I shook my head and laughed, "You're too much, Val."

As soon as the Bangles started singing, "Walk Like an Egyptian" Cheryl, MTV's biggest fan yelled, "Stop! Time out!" and broke out into the famous dance moves putting the foosball game on hold. It didn't take long before everyone joined in, including the guys which had us rolling with laughter. Morgan, the guys, and I danced to the beat using funky arm and hand gestures. Not before long we created a huge dance circle reminiscent of our high school dance days.

This reminded me of the time when Joey impressed us with his dance moves at Junior Prom. Smiling at the fond memory, no one was the wiser that I was thinking of Joey busting a move dancing to "Just a Gigolo" without causing me to have a panic attack. *I'm making progress.*

After the party, while I was in bed, I thought about how Morgan's party was a huge success. Everyone was very welcoming to Derek.

I thanked God that Derek and Avery hit it off like they were old friends, while Avery and Joey had an opportunity to rebuild their friendship. I also got a chance to talk to Abby.

My mind wandered to forgiveness. *Lord, help me to forgive Paul Martin for raping me. I forgive you, Paul. I don't condone what you did to me, but I forgive you, nonetheless. You have no hold on me. I am forever free of your hold on me. I am no longer in bondage to you or Satan.* I envisioned a chain being broken and fell into a tranquil slumber.

Chapter 42

T he following Monday was the fourth of July. Avery came to pick me up before the crack of dawn so we could spend the day down the shore and watch the fireworks. Still clearing away the cobwebs from getting up before the sun during summer vacation, I grabbed my bags and fumbled out the door. The temperature was cool at that hour of the morning, but I knew it would heat up in no time. Avery got out of the Escort to greet me with one of his grand smiles, "Good morning, beautiful!" He gave me a quick kiss on the lips and opened the back door of his car. It already started to heat up.

"Morning," I said with a scratchy throat. That was all I could manage at the moment but delighted in the kiss, nonetheless.

"Put your stuff in the back seat. I brought a small cooler for hoagies and water."

"You think of everything," I said, my voice still rough.

"My mom gave me suggestions but cautioned me not to bring too much stuff, because we have to carry it to the beach."

We made a hoagie run to Wawa, and we were in and out in record time. *Gotta love convenience stores.* "That's everything! We're shore bound!" Avery exclaimed with a cup of coffee in hand.

We decided to go to Wildwood since the beach is free and we could walk on the boardwalk after a day on the beach. There were no crazies on the road at that hour, except for us.

Avery played his Christian rock music. "I burned these songs on CDs. I hope you like them," he said with his chest puffed out.

"Cool," I nodded, unable to form another sentence before the roosters crowed.

Avery drove in silence with the understanding that I needed time to wake up. I got out some grapes that I packed hoping that some nourishment would help.

The praise song "Step By Step" sung by Rich Mullins came on and I said, "Oh, I like this song!"

"And she speaks," Avery remarked with a big ol' grin.

"Sorry, I just needed time to wake up," I winced.

"No problem. Are you good now?"

"Yeah, but I have to warn you. I'm not that talkative in the car or on the beach," I stated, my smile tight-lipped.

Avery nodded. "Duly noted."

I found that "Great is the Lord" by Michael W. Smith lifted my spirits but the song, "Victory Chant" lifted me up even more. The first line grabbed me with "Hail, Jesus, You're my King," and I began singing the rest with full verve. Avery turned to me with a smile of approval when I burst into song, matching my zeal for the chant and its meaning.

When Keith Green's "Keep All That Junk to Yourself" came on I thought of Jared. "I think Jared would like this song."

"How is Jared? He hasn't come to any of the youth group meetings," Avery asked.

"He can't because of work," I explained.

"Oh, that's too bad."

"Yeah, but he wants to go on the retreat. He plans on giving my parents his entire check. At least that's what he said." I looked out the window and watched the landscape repeat.

"I think youth group will be good for him. I can watch out for him too. Make sure he's hanging out with decent guys," Avery offered.

"How can you do that? No one knew what you were up to." I didn't mean that in a judgmental way.

"I think people did but didn't care enough to say anything. Maybe they didn't think it was serious enough. I don't know." Avery shook his head, then continued, "Walt looked like a total prep on the outside, clean cut, and everything, but he was bad news. Joey knew something was up with him, but I shrugged him off."

I turned to Avery. "That's what I mean. What if you approach Jared and he shrugs you off?"

He glanced over at me for a second, "I won't let it go if I think it's at all serious. I'll have people be on the lookout too just in case. Whatever it takes."

"You better." *I can't let anything happen to Jared. Lord, please protect him.*

"You have my word," he quickly turned my way.

The drive to the beach was surrounded by trees, not much else to look at. It was exactly the same scenery for miles. It was as if we were in a loop that started back to the beginning. We had been driving for well over two hours, and I was encouraged after seeing signs for the beaches. Finally, I saw a sign for The Wildwoods! *We're almost there!*

Even though our windows were rolled up to keep the highway noise down and we were miles away from our destination, the unique smell of the salty sea air engulfed me. We got more excited as the wheels of Avery's Ford Escort drove us closer to our get-away.

After circling for a parking spot, we decided to use one of the paid parking lots near the boardwalk. I looked at the cost to park for the day and cringed. I resisted the urge to kiss the ground once we pulled in and staked our claim to the expensive little spot on the lot. We made it to our destination! *We're at the beach!*

We grabbed all our gear out of the car and headed to the beach. In a matter of minutes, the fresh sea air filled my lungs and my feet welcomed the warm sand. The long trek toward the ocean was brutal carrying a chair and a few bags, but at least there was a light pleasant breeze that somehow seemed to lighten the load. Avery lugged the cooler, a chair, and a bag. His mom was right about not taking too much stuff, but we parked as close to the ocean as possible.

Beach goers were already setting up on the beach even though it was early in the morning. I think it had more to do with the holiday than anything else, because I don't remember people being on the beach at such an early hour on previous vacations. It was a gorgeous day to be on the beach. The sun was shining amid the light blue sky and not one storm cloud dared to make a presence on Independence Day, 1988.

We set up close enough to the vast body of water to relish the ocean breeze but not too close to get splashed by the waves rolling in. I plopped down in my chair with a sigh of relief, dug my feet into the sand and said, "We couldn't have planned for better weather."

Avery grinned, "I know. This is great! We really lucked out!" He brought music to listen to except this time he had popular songs from the last few years.

The music started off with "Vacation" by the Go-Go's which set the tone for the rest of the day. Despite having a base tan, I slathered suntan lotion over every exposed part of my body I could reach knowing how easy it was to get burnt from the sun, especially on the beach. I wasn't taking any chances. "Ave, can you get my back?" I asked as I held out the suntan lotion.

"At your service," he replied with a keenness in his voice.

I was wearing a floral two-piece, as opposed to a skimpy bikini, so I said, "Make sure you cover every inch and get under the straps."

Avery's touch sent shivers down my spine. "All done. Now my turn," he said as he handed me the brown bottle.

I suppressed a grin as I lathered the lotion over Avery's broad shoulders and slim waistline, his muscles bulging at all the right places. My man was ripped! He had a V shaped body like the models on the covers of romance novels. *Yowza!* It was getting hotter by the second.

Avery could have any girl he wanted, yet he pursued me. Me! The song "Keep Your Hands to Yourself" by The Georgia Satellites came on, and my smile within transformed into a laugh.

"What's so funny?" Avery asked, partially turning around. *It's probably not a good thing to laugh when you're putting lotion on someone. It could give them a complex.*

"Nothing," I replied breezily as I patted him on the back to signify that I was finished with the application.

Soaking up the sun, breathing in the fresh air and feeling the light breeze on my face was all it took to release much of the tension I had been carrying. The soothing tunes of U2's "With or Without You" aided in my almost stress-free induced coma.

"Earth to Christina," Avery said as he tapped me on my arm.

"Huh?" I responded, lost in thought.

"I'm going in the ocean. Wanna come?" he asked.

As I contemplated joining Avery, I felt the sweat forming on my forehead as well as other unmentionables. "Yeah. Let's go."

After a few long strides, we were in the Atlantic Ocean. A big chill ran through me when I stepped into the icy water. "It's cold!" I yelled, shaking my body.

"It feels great! See!" Avery affirmed as he splashed me.

I fired back, and the splashing war ensued. I laughed so hard that I fell crashing down into the pool of water. Avery came over to lend a hand to pull me up, but I surprised him by yanking him toward me. He stumbled but didn't fall.

"That's so not fair!" I pouted. He laughed at my pathetic attempt to bring him down with me.

At this point I was drenched, so I lunged forward and ran further into the ocean. Avery chased after me while I ran through the oncoming waves, my every move creating splashes. Once he caught up to me, he grabbed onto my waist. I craned my neck and kissed him as he wrapped himself around me. We stood there enraptured by the beauty of the ocean, and the playful sounds of the sea goers.

The ocean called us further out to jump the waves. Then each of us waited for the big waves to ride in. After we had our fill of ocean antics, we headed back to our little oasis.

"I'm going to grab a hoagie. You want one?"

"Yeah, thanks!" I peeled away the paper layer first, then the inner protective layer so I could sink my teeth into the deli delight. I loved eating chips with sandwiches. "Hey, can you pass me the potato chips please?" I popped a chip in my mouth, and life couldn't get any better.

"That was fun," Avery said as he leaned back in his chair.

"It was. I'm glad you had the idea to come down here."

"I had to think of something to catch you in a bikini," he peered over at me, wiggling his eyebrows.

I smacked him on the arm. "It's a two-piece. You won't see me in a bikini."

Avery's brow furrowed, "What's the difference?"

"Coverage."

Avery shook his head in acknowledgement. "Well, even still. It was worth it," he said with a lopsided grin.

"You better be kidding me," I said before taking another bite of my hoagie.

His eyes narrowed, "About what?"

I put my hand over my mouth as I swallowed a portion of hoagie. "That's not the reason why you wanted to come down here?"

"No, I really didn't give that a thought until you took off your shirt and then—" His eyebrows danced.

"Stop," I giggled. "You're making me feel self-conscious now."

"Don't be. You look great! And I'm not just saying that because you're my girlfriend," he said with a dimpled grin.

I blushed, "Thanks." I took another bite of my delicious hoagie when I witnessed seagulls swooping in overhead. "Seagulls are like Chihuahuas in how they're both so annoying," I said as I turned my head toward Avery with hoagie in hand when a seagull swooped in and swiped it right out of my grasp. "Darn bird flew off with my hoagie!"

Avery laughed, "Serves you right for insulting it."

"Whose side are you on anyway?"

"Here, you can have the rest of mine," Avery said, holding his hoagie out for me to take it.

"No, it's okay. You finish it," I sighed.

"You sure?" He held out his hoagie in my direction again.

"Yeah. At least he didn't poop on me," I laughed.

"It's good luck if they do."

"Tell that to the person they poop on," I smirked.

Paranoia got the better of me as I ducked for cover in response to seeing the seagulls hover above me. "Those seagulls have it out for me," I said as I put my hands over my head out of impulse and jerked away from them.

"Be careful or they will fly off with your chips too," Avery warned.

Guarding the bag of chips with my life, one by one I munched on the rest of them, crunching my frustration away with each bite. The hunger pangs coupled with gurgling sounds gave way to me hunting for more food. Finding a bag of blueberries gave me the feeling of victory as I listened to the next song on Avery's playlist, "Nothing's Gonna Stop Us Now" by Starship.

Remembering it was time to reapply the lotion, I asked Avery to assist me, "Can you get my back again, please?"

"Your wish is my command," he said, and I took him at his word.

"All right then. Let's go for a walk."

After we finished with our sun protection, we strolled hand-in-hand where the waves disappeared into the wet sand. Toddlers scurried from the baby waves with adorable smiles on their faces while their proud parents looked on and stored the memories. Bigger kids were showing their parents their great finds of sand crabs and seashells.

Recalling fond memories, I remarked as I sloshed through the water, "I remember digging for sand crabs not that long ago. I always found them fascinating and liked how they tickled in my hand."

"I was in the water every chance I got," Avery said as he looked toward the ocean.

"You want to go in again, don't you?" I asked as I watched Avery's eyes twinkle upon gazing at the vast ocean.

As we strode along together, he said, "We can keep walking."

"But you do want to go in the ocean, right?" I pressed.

"I'm perfectly content walking with you right now."

"All right." I shrugged. "I used to take walks with my dad. He played games like paddle ball with Jared and me on the beach. He was always such a good sport."

"My dad and I threw a Nerf football on the beach." Avery grinned. "I was going to bring one but decided against it with all the stuff we had to carry."

"Maybe next time," I said.

"Yeah?" Avery smiled with delight.

"Sure, why not? We used to play catch. Remember?" I decided to walk down memory lane.

"Yeah, we did, didn't we? Remember that first time we played baseball with the guys? I batted after you, and we both scored," he reminisced.

"Yeah, you were on my heels. I thought you were going to pass me." My mouth curled upward thinking of the fond days.

"You run too fast for me to pass you now," Avery said.

I scrunched up my nose and asked, "Ya think?"

Avery gave me a distinct nod, "Definitely."

A loud whistle blew as we passed a lifeguard stand that startled me, causing me to bump into Avery.

"I always thought it would be neat to be a lifeguard," Avery said.

"So why didn't you become one?"

"I would have, if we had a shore house here. No way was I going to live in one of the dives where lifeguards live together. I would throw all my money away on rent."

I tilted my head, "Instead, you throw it away on eating out."

"Yeah, but it's cool. Maybe we should cut back," he glanced my way.

"You say this when we're on a day trip?"

"I mean after today," Avery suggested.

"I'm okay with that," I agreed without hesitation.

We walked along the beach weaving in and out of people's way, listening to the joyous laughter and screams, seeing all the smiling faces…

Avery sounded excited when he said, "We can take my mom up on her offer to use the kitchen."

"Sounds good to me. You are doing all the cooking and cleaning, right?" I winked.

"I thought you would be by my side sharing in the cooking and cleaning," Avery said, feigning disappointment.

"I might be persuaded," I teased.

"And to think I would walk on hot coals for you," he volleyed.

"I'm kidding!" My grin was as wide as the ocean was deep.

"I'm not kidding. I would walk on hot coals for you," he said, as we walked on the wet sand through shallow waters.

I leaned into Avery. "What did I do to deserve you?"

"Christina, don't even joke about that. I waited years to get my life back on track so I could be worthy of your love again." Avery sounded like he received a punch in the gut as he walked with his head down.

"Ave, look at me," I said firmly. He lifted his head in my direction. "Where is this coming from? Neither of us is perfect. I'm no better than you. You had one major mishap and made restitution for it. I know it's an ongoing process, but think about the strides you made so far."

Avery's eyes sparkled in the sunlight. "See, it's when you say things like that that I fall deeper in love with you. You must give good talks."

Where do I go with that? "I'm sure you're equally talented with your preaching, but I'm confused. What brought this on?"

Avery shook his head around, "I don't know. You don't mess up. Terrible things have happened to you, and you pour your heart into other people."

"You do the same thing, Ave. You're one of the reasons I get by each day. You might not see my internal struggles all the time, but they're there. I brace myself for my next panic attack. But I still don't get it. What triggered your response? It's like something flipped a switch on you."

"You're not going to like what I have to say," he warned.

"Try me."

Avery combed his fingers through his golden highlights. "All right, all right. I've been watching guys gawk at you since we've been walking."

"What?" I noticed no such thing.

"Yeah, you think I'm kidding. Trust me. They have been."

"Ave, have you seen you?" I asked with my jaw hanging.

"It's different for guys," he said dismissively.

"How so?" I arched an eyebrow.

"Guys are much more visual."

"I get that, but what are you going to do? Get all insecure every time a guy looks in my direction? I only have eyes for you. You get that? It took me months before I would even consider going out with Joey, and even then we broke up because I still loved you."

Avery's brief smile disappeared when he said, "I hated myself when you two went out, but then I thought at least you were with a decent guy. I figured he would treat you right."

"That's just it, Ave. He did. Joey treated me like a princess, but you were always my prince, and he knew that. He always knew that deep down. I guess he thought I would get over you eventually, but I couldn't. As God is my witness, I tried to stop loving you. I never stopped loving you, Ave. You were always the one."

"Say you'll never leave me," Avery requested.

I seriously considered what he said, and for all intents and purposes I had no intention of leaving Avery. He held my heart in his hands. Always and forever. The idea of giving such a declaration seemed almost silly considering how couples break up all the time. However, I couldn't deny how I felt about him and declared, "I will never leave you."

Upon hearing that, Avery reacted like he won the Olympic gold. He spun me around, and I couldn't help but beam. After he put me down, he said, "That's what I'm talking about! You are my world, Christina De Rosa!"

Acutely aware of my surroundings standing in the middle of a packed beach on the most popular beach day of the year, I replied, "You are my world, Avery Evans!"

In a burst of excitement, Avery took off in the ocean to celebrate his victory, and I followed him willingly, to share in our glory together knowing how it feels to win the gold.

The Lord put a verse on my heart, "I have fought a good fight, I have finished my course, I have kept the faith: Henceforth there is laid up for me a crown of righteousness, which the Lord, the righteous judge, shall give me at that day: and not to me only, but unto all them also that love his appearing" (2 Timothy 4:7).

We splashed around and rode the waves with even more vigor than before. Avery really was my world as much as any human could possibly be. *Lord, thank you for this day and bringing Avery back in my life.*

On our way back to our beach spot, a purple hue caught my eye, so I bent down to pick it up. Before me was a beautiful purple rock. "Look how pretty this is," I remarked, holding it up to show Avery.

Avery's focus was on the pretty purple pebble. "You should keep it as a special memento of our trip."

"I think I will." I smiled at Avery knowing how fortunate I was to have him in my life.

Then I heard the all familiar call. "Ice cream! Fudgy Wudgy! Get your ice cream here!" shouted the traveling salesman. The Fudgy Wudgy Man pushed his loaded cart in the sand in between customers.

Avery asked, "You want some ice cream?"

"Nah, I'm saving up for later on the boardwalk." I wanted soft serve.

Avery smirked, "We can get some now and later."

"You go ahead. I'll wait." *Annoying seagulls might snatch the ice cream from me anyway. Stupid flying Chihuahuas!*

"We'll get some together on the boardwalk."

Avery put his music on and "What I Like About You" by the Romantics had me dancing in my beach chair. I was impressed with Avery's choice of music.

While listening to Bon Jovi sing "Livin' On a Prayer" Avery said, "This holds a special meaning for me. I prayed every day since I let you go, that we would be able to get back together again. I was living on a prayer, and now I thank God every day that you are in my life."

I returned with a smile and said, "God is good."

Around four o'clock, families started to pack up. I wanted to enjoy the surf and sand as long as possible, so we stayed to enjoy the serenity of a desolate beach. At five-thirty, the lifeguards abandoned their stands, even the seagulls gave us quietude. Tiffany sang, "I Think We're Alone Now" on Avery's special soundtrack. After an hour or so, we packed up and stored the bags, cooler, and chairs in the trunk of the car. We grabbed our sweatshirts and headed to where all the action was.

As we meandered to the boardwalk, Avery asked, "What do you want for dinner?"

Knowing that I was going to indulge in boardwalk treats after dinner, I said, "Hum, how about pizza?"

"You're on."

We each took a slice of pepperoni pizza and sat by the benches facing the boardwalk. I bit into my hot, spicy pepperoni pizza and watched as hordes of people walked past us. One guy wore a gray T-shirt of the TV series Cheers logo that said, "Est. 1895 Where everybody knows your name."

It didn't take long before we heard the familiar sound, "Watch the tramcar, please. Watch the tramcar, please." *Once you've been on the boardwalk in Wildwood, you will never forget that annoying sound announcing the tramcar. It's forever embedded in your brain.*

While I chewed on my last bite of the cheesy tomato goodness, Avery asked, "Where to now?"

"Let's walk for a bit," I suggested.

Linking arms, we passed tons of stores selling T-shirts, flip-flops, jewelry, sunglasses, sweatshirts, jackets and so on. Store after store of basically the same poor-quality merchandise. We approached Morey's Pier, the pier famous for its rides and games. The pier, illuminated with stagnant and dancing multi-colored lights, created a festive atmosphere. I pulled on Avery's arm, "Let's go on the Ferris wheel."

"Okay," Avery said, once again amenable to my suggestion.

We climbed on the Ferris wheel seat and strapped ourselves in. Little by little we ascended as the next passengers got on. Our legs dangled as we watched the sun begin to descend. The yellow sun encircled by orange blended into the cobalt blue backdrop as it mingled with puffy swirls of white.

"Ave, check out the sunset."

He turned to me and said, "Beautiful."

Frustrated that he was looking at me instead of God's breathtaking handiwork, I repeated, "Look at the sunset. You can't miss it. It's stunning."

"I see lots of beauty before me."

His words made me melt in the hovering seat. It wasn't just what he said, but the way he said it and how he peered into my soul declaring his love for me without saying the words, "I love you."

Our lips gradually drew closer to each other until they were connected, sending signals to other parts of the body, confirming that love does conquer all. The seat rocked, startling me, causing my stomach to drop, and we soared to the apex of the Ferris wheel. When the sunset was out of sight, we resumed the activity we were doing before we were rudely interrupted by the moving cart.

Once the ride began, I took in the beauty of my surroundings. The dazzling lights, the sounds of merrymaking, and the incredible ocean view created a magical moment. The song "Sittin' On The Dock Of The Bay" slowly guided us to the end of the ride.

Ice cream called my name after we vacated the Ferris wheel.

"Chocolate ice cream dipped in chocolate and chocolate jimmies, please," I stated as I gave my triple chocolate order.

"Jimmies?" The clerk asked in a Russian accent.

"Sprinkles," answered Avery on my behalf. "They don't call them jimmies here," he reminded me.

"Right," I recalled, thankful for his correction.

"Let's sit down and eat," Avery gestured to an open bench.

The sky was getting darker with each lick of the ice cream. This time the sun glowed blood red painted on a dark blue sky surrounded by red streaks of light. It was magnificent! I witnessed God in His glory, His manifest presence.

I leaned into my boyfriend. "Ave, let's go on the beach."

"Why?" he asked.

"Because. I just wanna go."

A desperate need to be alone with Avery overtook me. We started walking on the beach and without warning darkness took hold of me. I latched onto Avery as we continued to stumble in the blackness.

My body ceased to move after fumbling in the tenebrosity of the night. I gingerly put my arms around Avery's neck to secure our position together. We drew closer, and I could smell the garlic and pepperoni on Avery's breath. Our mouths grazed each other, then rolled over one another and back over again. We moved in sync, careful not to separate. His lips were tender yet confident, the perfect balance to ignite a fire within that took a mighty force to extinguish it.

The night air was cool, but I was burning hot. I inched Avery's sweatshirt upwards while kissing him feverishly, and he completed the act by tossing it on the sand.

I raised my arms in the air as Avery lifted up my sweatshirt in one fell swoop. My hands found Avery's bare back and caressed it while he caressed mine, my shirt providing a layer between us.

The crisp air felt amazing on our warm bodies. Our kisses grew with more intensity, more passion, more heat. We fell on the sand without breaking our hold on each other, our moans drowning out the various sounds of the boardwalk.

My body was screaming for something more, something forbidden when I felt tiny pinches all over my frame from head to toe. I broke away, lunging forward, careful not to crash into Avery. "Ave, I'm getting eaten alive," I said, swatting and scratching body parts.

"Ouch! Me too. Let's get outta here," Avery said, scrambling to get up.

We blindly searched for our sweatshirts, not finding them fast enough, and ran off the beach laughing hysterically. After washing up in our respective restrooms, we stood in line to indulge in a caramel apple funnel cake. We found a bench near where we were told we would have a good view of the fireworks. "This funnel cake is delicious!" I said, licking my lips.

"Yeah, I would never have thought of getting an apple topping," Avery stated with a look of approval.

I nudged him with my elbow, "It's good, isn't it?"

"You know your junk food," he said, impressed with my suggestion of the culinary combination.

I'm my father's daughter.

"I wouldn't steer you wrong." I shot him a knowing grin.

There was anticipation in the air awaiting the fireworks. Crackling and popping sounds, along with Bruce Springsteen singing "Born in the U.S.A." captured our attention.

We looked toward the sky where an assortment of colors dotted the midnight blue canopy. A loud squealing followed by a big boom produced a gigantic spread of red crackling for our pleasure. This was quickly repeated by displaying white, then blue, representative of our national colors in honor of our great independence from Great Britain and its king.

The fireworks continued for a half hour. Avery insisted we stayed for the grand finale which was absolutely spectacular. A fury of fireworks one right after the other in quick succession dazzled us with each snap, crackle, pop, sizzle, squeal, and boom.

My face lit up like the fireworks, "Best fireworks ever!"

"Definitely worth waiting for." He replied and I suspected it was with double implication based on the wide grin he sent my way.

"You really know how to pick 'em," I said, testing my theory.

"You're proof of that. You were worth the wait," Avery commented, holding his gaze on me.

Ding, ding, ding. We have a winner. I was right.

"Took you long enough," I chided.

"You're saying I wasn't worth the wait," Avery teased.

"I wasn't waiting… but I must say I'm liking the finished product," I returned with a grin.

"I'm a work in progress," Avery noted.

"We all are, Ave. We all are." *I'm more than content with the work in progress sitting next to me.*

On our drive home I watched the sky light up in an array of colors; red, white, blue, green, yellow, orange, purple… Each color and shape as beautiful as the one before.

Music from the radio entertained us by playing a variety of songs like "Something So Strong" by Crowded House. The song made me think that my relationship with Avery was strong, solid.

Avery had to stop for coffee to keep himself awake for the drive home. I bought hot chocolate to stay awake to keep Avery company. When we returned from our beverage break, Billy Ocean was in the middle of singing "Get Outta My Dreams." I had to laugh at the lyrics that followed since we just got in the car. After that the beautiful and fun song, "(I've Had) The Time of My Life" from the Dirty Dancing soundtrack filled the car.

"Ave, isn't this song perfect for the day we had?"

"Yeah, I had the time of my life today. Cheers to a perfect day!" Avery said as he held out his coffee in my direction.

"Cheers," I replied as I tapped my hot chocolate to his coffee.

With all the traffic, we didn't get home until almost two in the morning. I was exhausted. Avery dropped me off, and we said a quick good-bye. As soon as my head hit the pillow, I was asleep after thanking God for a glorious day with my always and forever.

Chapter 43

Two weeks after the fourth of July, Avery picked up Jared to go to the retreat together, because the church van wasn't big enough to fit everyone going on the trip. Jared slid in the front passenger seat while I said my good-byes to Avery.

My arms were hung loosely around Avery's neck when I said, "Have a good time and keep an eye out for Jared, okay?"

"I will. I'm going to miss you."

I puckered my lips. "I'm sure I'll miss you more. You will have so much fun." I jumped away from Avery upon hearing a loud beep from Avery's Ford.

"Hey, let's go!" shouted Jared as he leaned over to the driver side of the car.

"Bye, Christina." Avery kissed me.

"Bye, Ave." Avery turned around and climbed into his car. "Bye, Jared!" I waved. "Have fun!"

Chapter 44

Sunday, I walked downstairs after showering from an afternoon run and found my mother sitting at her spot at the kitchen table. I took a seat across from her.

She asked, "How was your jog?"

"It's a run, Mom, not a jog and it went well. Is Jared home yet from the retreat?" *Someone is testy. And that would be me.*

"No, not yet," she answered, stoically. *That means Avery isn't home yet.*

"Where's Dad?" I asked.

"Playing racquetball with Uncle Joe," she said, putting her teacup down.

"When is he coming home?" I asked.

"I don't know. Why?" She asked.

I shrugged, anxious to see Avery and find out if Jared had a good time. "No reason." I sighed as it had been a long few days without my favorite person keeping me company.

I heard the back door slam, and soon after Jared walked in with a big grin on his face followed by Avery.

"I had the best time!" Jared exclaimed with his arms raised like he was celebrating a victorious fete.

"I'm glad you had fun," I said, unable to suppress a smile.

Jared's voice grew louder, "I can't wait to go next year! It was epic!" *He's already looking forward to next year. That's a good sign.*

"Avery was like the coolest. Christina, you should see him play beach volleyball. He has sick moves." *I'm sure he does.* Jared turned to Avery, "Thanks, man. I had a great time!"

"Yeah, I'm glad you got to go. It was a lot of fun," Avery replied.

"Did you learn anything spiritually?" I had to ask Jared.

Jared nodded and smiled, "Yeah, I learned lots, especially since I didn't know squat going in. That was a drag at first, but it turns out that a lot of kids didn't know much either."

Avery jumped in, "Jared was like a sponge. He soaked up all the lessons." He turned to Jared and slapped him on the back, "You did great, man."

"Yo, thanks. I can't wait to go back," Jared grinned.

"You can join our youth group," Avery suggested to Jared.

"Yeah, definitely," Jared looked at my mom as if he spoke too soon. "I can go to youth group, right, Mom?"

Her eyes twinkled when she answered, "Of course, you can go."

Of course, you can go!? Did I hear that correctly? He does know that he has to work out his work schedule to be able to attend.

"Cool. Thanks, Mom. You're the best." Jared went upstairs after he kissed her on the cheek.

A kiss on the cheek too! Well, that's a first!

I heard him sing the lyrics to "Keep All That Junk to Yourself" by Keith Green, and I about fell over. *He does like that song.*

Before me sat a blushing mom who rarely showed any kind of emotion in all my 19 years of being her daughter, and my brother, the jailbird, was singing praise music. *God really does work wonders.*

The blushing mother nodded toward Avery and said, "Thank you for taking care of Jared for us."

"Oh, no problem. He was great to have around. Everyone loved him," Avery stated.

Everyone? It seemed like something else happened that Jared didn't let on. *A girl maybe?* I wanted to find out, but not in front of the blusher, so I asked, "Ave, I know you had a long ride, but would you mind if we went for a walk now?"

Avery answered, "Yeah, I could stretch my legs. It was nice seeing you again, Mrs. De Rosa."

"You too, Avery," my mom answered.

It was a beautiful sunny late Sunday afternoon. I knew I missed Avery but didn't realize how much until I laid eyes on his tanned buff body. I couldn't help but notice how good he looked. He reached for my hand and clasped it. I took my free one and rubbed his arm and turned facing him. "I really missed you."

"You have no idea how much I missed you. Your brother is no substitute. Don't get me wrong. I like your brother, and we had a great time, but there's no comparison," he shook his head as he rolled his eyes.

I playfully hit him on his shoulder. "Better not be!" We walked up the street towards the woods. "I'm glad you both had a good time. I prayed Jared would have a positive experience."

Avery turned to me, "He did. I'm sure of it. It was amazing watching him grow. You could see it in his eyes when he understood what he was learning. It was like a lightbulb went off. He got into it too. I was kind of surprised. I had him pegged for playing it cool and sitting back and observing, but he jumped in and asked questions. It was neat to watch him take it all in."

I raised my eyebrows, "So, my prayers paid off."

"Without a doubt," Avery confirmed.

"Jared's great experience wouldn't have anything to do with a girl, would it?"

"Well, there was a girl from Pennsford Academy. I knew of her when I attended the school because it's so small."

"And?" I asked, expectantly.

"She definitely caught Jared's eye. You'll have to let him tell you the rest." Avery's comment earned him another slap on the shoulder. "What was that for?"

"What good is having a boyfriend if he won't spy for me?" I pouted.

"It's not my place to say anything. Besides, I think Jared will open up. He's been real chatty with me."

"Is that so?" I said, arching an eyebrow.

"Yup. We bonded." Avery's smirk made me even more curious.

"Care to share?" I asked, wanting more details.

Avery held his head high and assured me, "I'm sure he'll tell you. It's nothing to be concerned about."

"I'm not concerned. I'm curious."

Upon remembering, Avery added, "Oh, by the way, your friend Sherrie was at the retreat too."

"Really? Sherrie was there? How did she seem?" I asked, hoping for a positive response.

"Great! She hung out with a couple girls from Pennsford High, and she seemed to be enjoying herself."

"Wow! That's great. I'm happy for her. She's getting her life back. Did she and Jared talk?"

"Not that I noticed. Are you worried he might say something to her about beating up Martin?"

"Yeah, I don't want him messing things up again." *Jared needs to stay out of jail, and Sherrie is our chance to getting Paul thrown in jail where he belongs.*

By that time, we were deep in the woods. The birds were chirping away, and the trees provided much needed shade. Avery stopped and put his hands on my upper arms as he gazed into my eyes. "I know you want to find out more about your brother and Sherrie, but let's concentrate on us. I promise you that Jared is fine. He's more than fine. Trust me, and Sherrie seemed to be doing well too."

How can I argue with that? Yet still feeling unsettled about Jared possibly spilling the beans, I said, "But—"

Avery placed his finger over my opened mouth, looked deeply into my eyes and leaned in to kiss me. If I didn't know any better, I would have sworn I was floating in mid-air. "Gosh, I missed you," I said breathlessly.

"As much as I enjoyed the retreat, I was aching to see you."

"Aching?" I repeated.

"Yes, aching," Avery confirmed.

"Well, let me put you out of your misery." Our lips reunited once again, and I was lost in our embrace. Our lips parted from each other, and I laid my head under his chin. Both our hands found their partners down by our sides. Tilting my head to face my soul mate, I wondered how we would get through college without being together.

"Something on your mind?" Avery asked.

I inched away, still holding his hands and said, "We haven't even gone back to school, and I already miss you."

"We can still see each other. We're only 45 minutes apart," he informed me.

My eyes in their surprise widened with delight, "Really? That's all?"

"Yup. I plan on seeing you in the fall if that's okay with you."

"Yeah, that would be great." I looked away.

"But—?" Avery asked, sensing my concern.

"I may have my talks on the weekends, and I might start tutoring again," I replied.

Avery smiled as if he didn't have a care in the world. "We'll work around it." He kissed my forehead, and we turned around to go back home.

A peace came over me as we walked toward my house that everything would work out. I had to trust the Lord that all would be well.

Later that evening I read the passage, "Blessed is the man that trusteth in the Lord, and whose hope the Lord is. For he shall be as a tree planted by the waters, and that spreadeth out her roots by the river, and shall not see when heat cometh, but her leaf shall be green; and shall not be careful in the year of drought, neither shall cease from yielding fruit" (Jeremiah 17:7-8).

Chapter 45

uring my last session of therapy before going back to Sylvania Ridge, a memory from that dark, chilly day in December in the woods at school came charging back. The ground was cold, hard, and lumpy. Somehow my mind reverted back to my high school years kissing Avery under our tree. A warm sensation covered my body, and I felt as if I were drifting upwards toward heaven. Peace and passion filled my spirit.

Next, a vision of Avery in a black tuxedo and me in a white wedding gown standing before our pastor with our friends and family behind us in the pews suddenly appeared. The colorful array of light shone through the stained-glass windows of the church cascaded before us momentarily blinding me, causing me to wince. Out of nowhere flew a white dove breaking through the stream of light. The beauty and majestic movement of the dove flying overhead stunned me, propelling my eyes to spring open.

Before me sat Dr. Frazer with a smile on her face. "Well, that was interesting. Tell me how you feel."

With the feelings of passion, peace, love, joy, and hope coursing through my veins, I beamed with delight, "Like I was about to experience the best day of my life. It even topped the fourth of July."

"That's what it looked like from this end. What did you experience?"

"At first I was pinned down on the patch where I was raped the second time. Only this time, I was transported back to the ground under the tree where Avery and I used to sit in high school. Then, I jumped to the future where I saw us standing in front of a church about to wed."

Dr. Frazer's jaw fell to the floor. "That's remarkable, Christina. I couldn't have planned this any better. Your experience surpassed even my high expectations of how this therapy would go for you."

A hopeful smile covered my face. "Does this mean my Exposure Therapy is complete?"

"Absolutely. Congratulations, Christina. You did remarkably well. There's a very good chance that you may not have any more episodes. Should you feel the need to continue with any kind of therapy, please contact me."

Elated, I walked out of Dr. Frazer's office with the greatest sense of peace, comfort, and joy as well as the desire to celebrate. I drove to Avery's house. His mother answered the door. "Hello, Christina! Please come in. Avery's in the rec room."

"Okay, thank you," I replied with my usual courtesy.

Mrs. Evans looked me over and remarked, "You are positively radiant. What has you aglow?"

Is it that obvious? "I finished my last session of therapy today. I came by to celebrate with Avery."

"Congratulations! It appears to have been a huge success," she said, noting again the change she observed in me.

"Yes, it was. I'm so happy to have that all behind me," I replied, feeling like my smile would become permanent.

With hand gestures that mimicked a tiny cheer, she stated, "In that case, you must celebrate. Why don't you head downstairs and tell Avery all about it?"

As I descended the stairs, I heard a faint strumming of the guitar. Avery's back was to me. I decided to wait for him to finish the segment as the unfamiliar tune was too beautiful to interrupt. Avery paused, giving me the opportunity to approach him. "That was beautiful," I said.

He turned around in his seat. "Hey, how long have you been standing there?"

"Just a minute." I sat down beside him, and he pulled the guitar strap over his head and placed the guitar down on the floor.

"I wrote it for you," he said in a low tone.

"I love it. It's incredible," I gushed.

"Thanks." His eyes gazed downward. "It was supposed to be a surprise."

Placing my hand over my heart, I replied, "I'm sorry."

Avery shrugged, "It's okay. I'll play it for you again when it's finished."

"I can't wait," I said as my eyelashes fluttered.

Avery looked at me like he was drinking a refreshing beverage. "You look... ravishing."

My cheeks warmed up as I couldn't hide my reaction, nor did I want to. "Ravishing?"

Avery looked at me like he was completely enraptured. "Yeah. Beautiful as always but there's something different about you," he said.

"I just finished my last therapy session," I stated.

"By the looks of it, it went great. Is that the change I'm seeing?" he asked, not releasing his gaze upon me.

"Must be. Your mom said the same thing."

Avery snapped out his wonderment, and exclaimed, "Well then, that's cause for celebration! What do you want to do?"

"Let's go out to eat. Nothing fancy," I suggested.

"You got it!" he responded, eager to please.

When Avery and I came back from our day trip on the fourth of July, we took Mrs. Evans' suggestion and began making our meals at his house instead of spending money to dine out. Not only was it fun and we developed new cooking skills, but it drew us closer.

With tearful joy in my eyes, I announced, "Ave, I think I'm finally done with the episodes."

"That's great! I'm glad the treatment was a success. Your bravery paid off," he praised.

"Yeah, considering I almost gave up," I reminded him.

"Most people probably would have."

I thought it best not to tell him the details of my session. I didn't want to give Avery the wrong impression that I wanted to get married soon. As far as I was concerned, the vision of us getting married was in the distant future, not around the corner.

Epilogue

*A*very and I continued to see each other while attending our junior year of college. He visited me on most weekends and stayed with one of his friends from Pennsford Academy.

At the start of the semester we went to the movies and watched *The Last Temptation of Christ*. One of the weekends in late October we saw *Mystic Pizza* with Julia Roberts. The first week in April we watched Kevin Kostner's new flick, *Field of Dreams*. Going to the movies was a nice change of pace for both of us.

We also made a point to keep Christ at the center of our relationship by doing devotions together. I was fortunate enough to have some speaking engagements near college, and I was able to continue with tutoring to help with the cost of tuition.

Morgan and Derek were still going strong, and we were all rooting for them. At the end of summer Morgan stayed with Derek's family. It went so well that she visited him again on Christmas break.

Jared's 'like' interest didn't go anywhere, but he thrived in youth group and made a bunch of new Christian friends. He mentioned seeing Sherrie there and promised he wouldn't say anything to her or anyone else that would land him in jail or jeopardize her case.

Jared and my parents started attending Avery's church together. Sometimes Shawn tagged along. "Pray for Shawn to become saved, Christina," Jared said. It was great seeing Jared not only talk the talk, but walk the walk as well.

Abby called me long distance while we were both away at school in the fall of our junior year. Her stepdad was found guilty of rape and attempted murder in addition to lesser charges and was sentenced to 30 years in jail with possible parole after serving 24 years in prison.

Abby stated to me while on the phone, "I hope he doesn't get out early on parole. There's no telling what he'd do once he got out, even though he would be seventy-nine if he got out early. The longer he stays in the better as far as I'm concerned."

I replied, "I hope for your sake he stays in prison and leaves you alone." I recalled what Rebecca Stanford said about how her uncle came after her as soon as he was released on parole for good behavior. I couldn't bear the thought of that happening to Abby and her mom and kept it to myself.

With excitement in her voice, Abby relayed, "Oh, I almost forgot to tell you that I lost 20 pounds. My mom has been super encouraging. I come home on the weekends sometimes. She and I prepare healthy meals now, and we do aerobics together."

I was so happy for Abby, especially since I knew she struggled with her weight. Matching her volume and enthusiasm, I said, "Congratulations! That's amazing!" Then I thought about her mother's challenges in losing a husband to prison for all his dastardly deeds. Concerned for her mom's well being, I asked, "How's your mom doing?"

Abby sighed at my inquiry. "She's doing okay under the circumstances. Relieved that he's in prison and I'm safe now."

Sherrie wasn't so lucky with Paul's verdict in criminal court. Paul was found not guilty of rape, but she sued him in civil court in the spring of my junior year and was awarded one-hundred thousand dollars for her pain and suffering, although she sued him for one million dollars.

On a long-distance phone call one day during my spring semester, Sherrie said in frustration, "He got off easy if you ask me. It's a mere slap on the wrist, and his parents won't even feel a pinch from the hundred thousand dollars. Apparently, they're loaded but stayed low key. Who knows? Maybe they anticipated that they would have to bail out their poor excuse of a son, so they saved up."

"Sherrie, I'm so proud of you for taking the stand, not once but twice. Do you feel like you can put him behind you now?" I asked, praying for a positive response.

She sighed loud enough for me to hear it over the phone. "No, not really. I'm glad I brought charges against him, but I'm still anxious."

"Have you tried doing a new type of therapy?" I asked, hoping it would push her on the path to healing her anxiety.

"No, I haven't. I think I will though, since your therapy worked so well for you," she said, her voice filled with hope.

"Give it a try. It might help to explore other therapies to target your anxiety and help you with your eating disorders. Ask your therapist to try something new. I haven't had any nightmares or public episodes since the summer."

"That's great!" Sherrie exclaimed, happy for my recovery.

"Thanks." I had an opening and decided to go for it, "Sherrie, have you tried forgiving Paul for what he did to you?" Although I didn't share the verse, Matthew 6:14-15 came to mind, "For if ye forgive men their trespasses, your heavenly Father will also forgive you: But if ye forgive not men their trespasses, neither will your Father forgive your trespasses."

"How can I forgive him?" She sounded angry and resentful.

"I know it's hard. It took me years to forgive him, but once I did I felt free of him, and my therapy sessions went better. Avery noticed the difference in me right after my last session," I shared.

"How are you and Avery? He's so cute!"

I laughed at her remark that Avery was cute yet her segue to avoid the topic of forgiveness didn't go unnoticed. "We're doing great. In fact…" I told her about his most recent visit with me at college…

Avery planned a romantic dinner out at a local restaurant. He told me he picked a place that was on the fancier side. "We'll get dressed up and have a real date. I don't want to think about school or anything else. Just us," he said to me.

I agreed to the fancy dinner, and he picked me up at my house off campus wearing a charcoal suit complimented by a charcoal and burgundy striped tie.

My roommates, Linda and Cassie, were all abuzz since I got dressed up. I borrowed Cassie's dress that was royal blue with a full skirt that flared out and had a sweetheart neckline adorned with sequins. Linda did my hair in an updo with ringlets framing my face. Being from New Jersey, Cassie joked that she only knew how to style big hair. They loved Avery and thought we made a great couple, so they were more than happy to contribute anyway they could. "Have fun!" they yelled as we headed out the door.

It was still light out and the fresh spring air added to the spring in my step. Avery held out his arm for me to hook onto and said, "You look stunning!"

Unable to resist beaming from ear to ear, I replied, "Thank you. So do you." Warm fuzzies took temporary residence in my body.

We were greeted by a maître d' dressed in a tuxedo who escorted us to our table. The ambient lighting and the crackling fire in the stone framed fireplace set the tone for a romantic dinner. Upon entering the main dining area, the delicious aroma of garlic made my mouth water. Hearing Frank Sinatra singing "The Way You Look Tonight" reminded me of how my parents listened to the old classics. We were shown to a small round table with a white tablecloth and a single red rose and a lit candle as its centerpiece.

As I took my seat, I said, "Wow! This is so elegant. I heard it was nice, but I've never been here before."

"Your roommates recommended it," he said as he pushed in my chair.

"They did good. I'm impressed." I couldn't stop smiling. The atmosphere was exquisite, and being able to see Avery was always a highlight of my week.

We had a lovely evening, enjoying our chef-prepared cuisine. After our salads, I relished the spicy shrimp pasta dish as Avery devoured his main course, a well-done ribeye with a loaded baked potato and asparagus.

While we were waiting for our triple chocolate torte for dessert, Avery cupped his hands over mine and leaned in closer. "I love being with you, and I want to spend the rest of my life with you." He got down on bended knee, opened up a little black velvet box and asked, "Will you marry me?"

Sherrie blurted on the phone and said, "No way! Oh my gosh! Are you engaged?"

I responded to Sherrie, "You have to hang tight to find out what happened with the cute one."

I continued telling my story to Sherrie...

I threw my hand over my mouth, mesmerized by the gorgeous ring, a beautiful marquise flanked by two round diamonds. Overjoyed by Avery's proposal of marriage, I started to form the happiest tears ever to salt the earth, "Yes, yes! I will marry you!"

Avery and I sealed our engagement with a kiss and the room exploded in applause. Our faces were plastered with smiles a mile wide. Avery lifted me off the floor, I kicked up my heels, and proceeded with my happy cry.

The End!

A Note From Maria

Dear Reader,

Thank you for reading a piece of my heart. I truly hope you enjoyed reading *Not Again The Fallout* and would be grateful if you would write a review on Amazon, Goodreads, and BookBub. A simple sentence is all it takes. If you haven't read *Not Again,* book one, you can get it on Amazon.

I love interacting with my readers and would consider it an honor if you tagged me on social media.

FOLLOW ME, MARIA T. HENRIKSEN, ON SOCIAL MEDIA:

www.facebook.com/PurpleNchocolate/
www.facebook.com/groups/292254218386413
www.Twitter.com/MariatHenriksen
www.instagram.com/maria_t_henriksen
www.tiktok.com/@mariathenriksen

Visit my website for the most current information on my writings, and subscribe to my newsletter for the most up-to-date announcements and events. New subscribers will receive a relaxation audio download created by yours truly.
www.mariathenriksen.com

Contact me directly via email:
authormariathenriksen@gmail.com
Here are all my links in one spot:
linktr.ee/AuthorMaria

Acknowledgements

To begin with, I would like to thank my family for their support. I know there were times that they didn't understand my commitment to my craft. My hope is that they will see how this book series made an impact on countless lives.

I would like to thank my beta readers as well as the *Not Again The Fallout* Squad. You know who you are! I appreciate your valuable feedback and ongoing support.

My greatest desire is that this novel will transform the lives of many in profound and meaningful ways! Most of all, I hope that my readers are able to develop a deeper and more intimate relationship with our Heavenly Father and Christ Jesus through reading the Not Again series.

Much love,

Maria

Author Bio

Maria T. Henriksen is a lover of reading, writing, and the arts. She considers it a privilege to be able to pursue her dreams of being a multi-published author.

Helping others in any capacity is what drives Maria. This novel was created to demonstrate that by sharing our burdens, as well as asking for and receiving help, anything can be accomplished. Maria believes that it's also important to dig deep and to look upward and outward to help those in need. She feels that giving of yourself may lead to your own restoration, in addition to being a blessing to others.

This born-and-raised Philadelphia suburbanite resides with her husband, Dave, of over two decades, along with their amazing adult twins, Brandon and Kathryn. Maria feels extremely blessed to have such a close family and continues to find each of them as a source of daily inspiration.

Resources for Help & Support

NATIONAL SEXUAL ASSAULT HOTLINE/RAINN
For support, information, advice, or a referral, trained support specialists are ready to help.
1-800-656-HOPE (4673) Free. Confidential & 24/7 RAINN
https://www.rain.org or online.rainn.org
https://hotline.rainn.org

NATIONAL SUICIDE PREVENTION LIFELINE
Support for people in distress, prevention and crisis resources for you or your loved ones, and best practices for professionals in the United States.
1-800-273-8255. Free. Confidential & 24/7
988 has been designated as the new three-digit dialing code that will route callers to the National Suicide Prevention Lifeline beginning July 16, 2022.
https://www.suicidepreventionlifeline.org

CRISIS TEXT LINE
Hurting? Get free help for self-harm and self-injury.
Self-Harm Text Hotline | Crisis Text Line
Text CONNECT to 741741 for 24/7 support
https://www.crisistextline.org/selfharm

THERAVIVE
Theravive is a network of licensed and professional clinical counselors, therapists, and psychologists who uphold clear, compassionate values in therapy for effective and lasting change.
https://www.theravive.com/

SIOS: Self-injury Outreach & Support

SIOS is a non-profit outreach initiative providing information and resources about self-injury to those who self-injure, those who have recovered, and those who want to help.

http://sioutreach.org/learnself-injury/

MHA: Mental Health America

MHA is the country's leading nonprofit dedicated to helping ALL people to live mentally healthier lives.

http://www.mentalhealthamerica.net/

800-273-TALK

NAMI: National Alliance on Mental Illness

NAMI is the nation's largest grassroots mental health organization dedicated to improving the lives of persons living with serious mental illness, and their families.

http://www.nami.org/

S.A.F.E. ALTERNATIVES

S.A.F.E. Provides a list of sites – Safe Alternatives

https://selfinjury.com/referrals/sites/

Made in the USA
Middletown, DE
22 October 2022

13306234R00186